WAY
OF
THE LAMB

WAY
OF
THE LAMB

Lamb of God
Series
Novel One

K. S. MCFARLAND

Paperback

COPYRIGHT

DEDICATION

May the name of Jesus Christ be glorified through this novel.
Praying for every unction of the Holy Spirit.

PREFACE

This is an imaginative work, a novel about the historical and living person of Jesus Christ, whose Hebrew name is Yeshua. While I have tried to be true to our Lord's character, spirit, and words, this storytelling is fictionally rendered. Within the Gospel testimonies we find scant information about the men and women who walked with Jesus during his life. Rather than focusing on the disciples, the Gospels focus primarily on the life and work of Christ.

Therefore, in this novel I have created fictional characters from the bare bones of scripturally mentioned persons. Their character, actions, voices, and backgrounds are purely imagined and created. Since there are numerous Marys, Johns, James, and Simons named within the testimonies, I have modified their names, giving them nicknames to more easily differentiate these characters. See the character name reference on previous page.

I pray your heart will be strangely warmed through this novel. Be blessed in your reading and in your sacred journey with the Lamb of God.

K. S. McFarland

CHARACTER REFERENCE

Novel	Scripture
Yeshua	Jesus
Miriam	Mary the Mother of Jesus
Yosef	Human Father of Jesus
James	Brother of Jesus
Simeon (Si)	Brother of Jesus (Simon)
José's	Brother of Jesus
Jude	Brother of Jesus
Hannah	Sister of Jesus
Yohannan	John the Baptizer, Jesus' cousin
Yohan	John, a Disciple of Jesus
James	Disciple of Jesus
Simon (Rock)	Disciple of Jesus called 'Peter'
Andrew	Disciple Philip
Nathaniel	Disciple also Bartholomew
Thomas	Disciple
Thaddeus	Disciple
Simon (Zel)	Disciple called 'The Zealot'
Matthew	Disciple Also called Levi
James (Alfie)	Disciple Son of Alphaeus
Judas Iscariot	Disciple
Mariamne (Mari)	Disciple Jesus calls 'Magdalene'
Cleopas	Uncle of Yeshua
Mary	Wife Of Cleopas
Lo-Rahamah	The woman at the well

Deborah	Wife of Simon Peter
Abigail	Mother of Deborah
Decimus	Centurion in Galilee
Jairus	Capernaum Synagogue Leader
Lazarus	Disciple from Bethany
Martha	Sister of Lazarus in Bethany
Simon 'The Leper'	Religious leader in Bethany
Caiaphas	Serving as High Priest
Annas	High Priest (Emeritus)
Herod Antipas	Tetrarch Son of Herod the Great

CONTENTS

EPIGRAPH

Behold, the Lamb of God,
who takes away the sin of the world.

John 1:29

PROLOGUE - CREATIONS SONG

I saw a Lamb, looking as if it had been slain,
standing at the center of the throne.
Revelation 5:6
"Worthy is the Lamb, who was slain,
to receive power and wealth
and wisdom and strength
and honor and glory and praise!"
Revelation 5:1
...the Lamb who was slain from the creation of the world.
Revelation 13:8

An energy was building within the dark cloud of mystery. Within, everything that was 'not yet' was being imagined and foreseen. All that 'would be' was being written down on scrolls and drawn into blueprints in intricate detail. The library of creation was forming within the omniscient mind of God. Space and time were designed and engineered. Beyond the veil of the unknown was a mind of infinite power, filled with universes, stars, systems, elements, and atoms.

Currently, the attention of the Almighty One focused on a place he had named Earth. He was designing cells, strands of DNA, neurons and protons, atmospheres, landscapes, flora, oceans, rivers, creatures and people.

From within the cloud came a resonating and lyrical hum of energy, a voice. The voice was singing a song of longing, calling, purpose, and love. The song grew louder with anticipation, creating a magnetic force that began to pull, order, and hold all things together. Hidden within the swirling flames of this omnipotent mind was the essence of everything. This womb of creation was expanding.

A person of light appeared to walk among the Wind and the Flames. His voice was joined with the deep rumbles and the songs of the wind within the bright flames. He was singing a hauntingly wistful song. The energy was love, the very essence of God. The voice spoke and everything paused coming to attention.

"Yeshua, my Son."

"Here I am Father."

"Look at all we have conceived."

"I see." The man of light peered into dimension after dimension.

"This is so beautiful, so detailed!" His heart swelled with emotion.

"This is the gift we have created for you, my Son. A kingdom of light and love."

Images stood poised while the man of light surveyed it all. He nodded his head in satisfaction.

"This is good. Within this creation, our love will be able to grow and expand forever."

As if on cue, images of various prototypes appeared to demonstrate their perfection.

"So intricate," He studied the array of creatures, "so perfect. Shall we build this?"

"We shall. But, first you must know what you will have to do to receive and keep this gift. It comes at a very high price."

"But isn't everything ours."

"Yes, but not quite everything. The greatest gift of our creation will cost you everything, an outpouring of all that you are. It will not be easy."

"Then, how is this a gift?"

"The gift I have in mind for you is mutual love. It is more precious than any other possession. You see, love must be freely given from the heart. It cannot be forced."

"I do so long to give my love and to receive love in return."

"Yes, love is a beautiful thing, it brings the greatest joy. But should love go wrong, it brings pain and heartbreak. Gone wrong, it has the power to destroy. The joy of receiving this a lasting love comes only through great pain and sacrifice."

"Sacrifice?"

"The shedding of blood."

"Life is in the blood. Losing blood leads to death. So are you saying, I must die to have it?"

"You are right. In this way life, death, and love are tied together. Before we bring our creation to life, we must agree to this shedding of blood, of the giving of life."

The flames held up the image of a lamb.

"What do you see?"

"I see a tethered lamb being led to an altar. Its throat is being cut and the blood is flowing out into a golden vessel. The blood is being offered up." His voice became filled with agitation.

He stared at the dying, then lifeless creature. "But why? The lamb did nothing wrong, and now the lamb is dead."

The image disappeared. The voice spoke softly, "No sooner will we create this world, than our creation will begin to die."

"By what cause?"

"Freedom of will. Human frailty. Temptation. Sin."

"Then, how can we ever obtain the joy of this love?"

"There must be a Redeemer, someone willing to pay the price for humanity's sins and failures, someone who embodies our love for our creation, someone who is willing to give of themselves from the beginning. "

"Then that could only be Us." The man of light reasoned.

"Yes, Us. The redemption of humanity will require a perfect, blameless human life be given to cleanse and restore creation from all human sin."

"But we are of light and spirit, not flesh and blood. So how can this be?"

"You are right, there is no other good, no other God. As such, I am in you and you are in me and the Holy Spirit is ours. We are One." The voice affirmed. "However, you will specifically be sent from me to be born in human flesh like them. Emanating from my Spirit, you are my seed, my essence, that will be spoken, planted, in a woman's womb. In flesh you will be born as a son of man and dwell among them as my Son, my emissary, my human representative, sent from my being. No one else will ever be like you, Yeshua, being both God and man. You are the One and Only. You are God's Salvation.

"So I will be both divine and human?"

"Yes and no. When I send you, your divinity will be laid temporarily aside. You will live solely as the Son of Man, even though you are my Son from my essence. Your divinity will operate solely for the sakes of those you are to save, under my authority, as I direct you. Otherwise, you will be totally human. "

And that is not all, for this mission you will also have to lay aside your human will and freedom as well so you can complete your mission. You must lay down your life, your all, for them. You will be human, but holy. This is how you will redeem our creation, by living a totally selfless life, devoid of sin."

The man of light was silent, pondering this function.

"The choice is yours, will you give your life for them?"

Yeshua thought of all the beautiful faces he had seen.

"You, my Son, are set apart for this work and the fullness of my Spirit will be imparted to strengthen and empower you."

"I will be Your Sacrifice?" Yeshua asked. The image of a lamb reappeared.

"Yes, for hundreds and thousands of years lambs will be offered up to make peace with Us through the shedding of their blood."

The image of the lamb changed. Now, the lamb was stretched out and impaled upon a spit and lifted up to be roasted in the flames. People took and ate the flesh of the lamb in the belief that God would save them from their destruction.

"When time has reached its fullness, I will send you forth as The Lamb of God."

A humble cave appeared. It was a stable. In the center was a manger shaped from stone and filled with straw. Yeshua saw a perfect and unblemished lamb lying at its center.

"That, is you, Yeshua." The image morphed into a new born infant.

"We are the prototype for man. They will be made in our image?"

The images of Adam and Eve flashed before him. His heart swelled with love at the sight of them. The days of their life passed before him on the winds. It was painful to see all that went wrong. The pain did not end. There were generations upon generations of pain filled lives. He saw their blunders and the battles for their souls. His heart ached at their sorrows.

"If we create them to be the object of our love, then we must also save them from a certain death."

"Exactly. Your work of salvation is the only way we can share life with them, the only way we won't lose them forever to the void of darkness."

Now, the image of a man suspended on a spit-like structure appeared. The man's features were so marred that he was unrecognizable; he was so beaten, and bloodied. He was groaning in agony.

"This is the sacrifice that has the power to redeem humanity and creation from death. The Lamb of God."

"Yes, Yeshua, this is you."

He watched the spear being thrust into his side; blood and water poured out as if it might cover the whole world.

"Yeshua, only you can save them. You are their Savior."

"Yes, I see." Yeshua said softly. "This is the way of love. Love requires a sacrifice."

"By this sacrifice, you will redeem them to be yours forever."

"But, if I die..."

"Beloved, though you die—you are life itself! Death cannot overcome Us."

Yeshua peered into the future to see all the mutual love this kingdom would bring him. Desire for this love was already beating in his heart. Without it, there would be only nothingness.

The kingdom before him transfigured, appearing as a beautiful woman. Within her were thousands and thousands of the faces of creations children who would come to belong to him forever.

"These are the people we will create to be yours forever. Having a little piece of eternity hidden in their heart, they will earnestly search for you. You will find them. They will be your eternal counterpart; bone of your bone, flesh of your flesh, and spirit of your spirit."

He thought his heart might burst with yearning.

"Father, I will freely give my all for this creation so it might be the object of my love forever."

"Very well. We are of one mind. You, and you alone will be their only way back to Us. Without your sacrifice, this kingdom and everything in it will collapse back into darkness. You will show them the truth of their existence, even though the world will hate you for it. You will be the light that will lead them out of the darkness. In you, they will live and move and find their being. You are the Alpha and the Omega--the beginning and the end of all creation."

"And you? What about you? Where will you be in our plan?"

"I will be your Father. You will be My Son, My Spoken Word. I will be in you and you will be in me. As my seed, you will not return to me void."

"Amen. May it be as you have said." With the decision made, the One and Only, self-existent God gave a loud and mighty shout of for all the joy that lay before Him.

"Let there be Light!" The Winds and Flames sprinted forward to fill the void with such purpose that a million years passed as if it were only a second. The energy of the light expanded rapidly. His breath carried the words to their designated place. Everything that exists began to come into being.

Anticipating the joy set before them, the Father and Son rode upon the winds of the Spirit.

~ 1 ~

THE APPOINTED TIME

Unless the Lord builds the house,
the builders labor in vain.
Psalm 127:1

"It is finished."

Yeshua shouted over his shoulder, to his Abba Yosef. He took a moment to admire the lines and the design. It was engineered to be durable and sturdy. It would afford shade for this family, allowing many long hours to enjoy their life with their children, their children's children, and their guests. The color of the stones made the portico glow with warmth and invitation.

Yosef came to stand by his side.

"Yeshua, your design is beautiful. Already we are getting request from their neighbors because of your skill." Yosef rested his hand proudly on Yeshua's shoulder with a satisfied smile, appreciating it's beauty.

But Yeshua did not feel the same sense of fulfillment he usually felt at a job well done. Lately, he felt distracted and restless. He could not ignore the impression that he was supposed to be doing something else, something more important. He had already decided what he would do.

He spoke over his shoulder, "Abba, before you agree to take on the other jobs, I am going to get away for a while to take some time for prayer. There are things I need to work out."

Yosef was not surprised. He had notice Yeshua's distant stares. He moved to face him.

"What weighs on you?"

"I feel restless in my spirit. It feels like it is time for me to begin my Father's work. I have been waiting patiently for a long time to know my Father's plan for me. Perhaps the time has come."

A look passed between them.

Yosef understood. Yeshua was a man. It only stood to reason that he would begin the work he had been born to do. He nodded, silently accepting that this was likely the appointed time.

~ 2 ~

THE KINGDOM TO COME

"The kingdom of heaven is like treasure hidden in a
field.
When a man found it, he hid it again,
and then in his joy went and sold all he had and
bought that field.
Matthew 13:44

Yeshua made his ascent swiftly. Anticipation of a time of solitude with his Father made his heart beat faster. Soon, the world was falling away below, giving way to a thin space along a narrowing and difficult path. He carried his few necessities in a bundle on his back. His hands swung free as he clamored up and over the rocky path. He was strong from his labors, a man entering his prime, and his feet were like the feet of a young stag. Quick, strong, and nimble.

As he ascended, he went singing the words of Isaiah, *'You will go out in joy and be led forth in peace; the mountains and hills will burst into song before you, and all the trees of the field will clap their hands. Instead of thornbush will grow the juniper, and instead of briers the myrtle will grow.'*

This song was filled with his desire for a world of beauty and peace, where all of creation would praise his Father just as he did! Reaching the summit, he dropped his neatly tied bundle and walked to the ledge of a vast expanse overlooking the valley below. Joyfully he lifted his face upward toward the sky. Like a son longing for his home, he cupped his hands and shouted, "Father, I am here. Come! Let me hear your voice!"

His invitation echoed back to him from the rocks below. Warming rays of the sun fell upon his face, a gentle breeze danced around him, cooling him, encircling him. He could feel his Father's love; he was not alone. So easily their conversation ensued, while Yeshua quickly set up his camp. Below were the beautiful hills and valleys of Galilee, everything was laid out before him from these heights. He spoke his stream of consciousness while he worked. Praying out loud helped to order his thoughts, and trained his ear to listen for his Father's response.

"Father, why have I become so restless? I am longing for something. Is there something else I should be doing?" His mind searched.

"Something more pressing and important for me to build rather than houses, stables, and porticos." He assembled his simple tent quickly, pounding the pegs into the earth with a rock.

"Men my age are moving on to the next step in their lives; building homes, marrying, starting their families, and plying their trade. Shouldn't I now finally be about your business?" He stopped to stare at the rock gripped in his hand as if searching for the answer. He recalled this same passionate desire he felt long ago in Jerusalem after he had just turned twelve.

"I know there is more for me to do than to pound, cut, and set stones and wood. Rabbi Eli has encouraged me to go to school under some Rabbi in Jerusalem. But that doesn't feel right. What can they teach me? Shouldn't you be my teacher?" He dropped back on his haunches.

"Tell me, what have you purposed for me? What are my steps? What would you have me do to begin?" He stood to retrieve his water supply, his dried foods, and blankets. He placed them in a safe place within his tent.

"I have searched the Torah for what it means to be the Son of God. I have these premonitions when I read it. I feel the words are important, I see bits and pieces, but I can't see the whole plan. It feels like it is veiled. Will you show me your will?"

He closed his eyes getting to the heart of the matter. "David was younger than me when you drew him out of the pasture and into a battle against the Philistines. Joseph was running Potiphar's estate. Jeremiah was beginning to prophesy to Judean leaders."

He opened his eyes again and looked out over the land below. "Look, the whole world is lost from you. What can I do? What is your will for me, that it might be done?" He sat quietly, his ear inclined, listening for his Father's voice. He sensed his presence, but heard not a word. He rose to gather and stack the wood to make a fire.

"As Ima always says, 'Nothing is impossible for you.'"

"Abba said I was conceived by your Spirit to save my people from their sins. How am I to do that?" He prepared a fire. Turning away, he knelt down to continue his queries and supplications. Soon, he was sprawled prostrate on the ground. His arms were cast out before him as if reaching for some unseen answer. His hands were trembling. Was he afraid of what the answers might be?

He sat up to wipe his eyes just in time to catch the last vestige of the day. The tangerine sun was just sinking toward the horizon. The wind danced lightly around him. He watched the colors in the clouds above him change from white, to golden, to pink, to lavender, and then to a soft grayish blue. He wrapped his tightly woven blanket around his body, shivering just a little. The spring evening was growing cool. With his back to the warming fire, he looked up into the growing darkness of the evening sky. He waited.

In time a vast breathtaking ocean of scattered lights mapped across the sky in a wonderous and twinkling display, encompassing an infinite variety faraway universes, stars, and lights too distant for the human eye to see. He lay very still, waiting.

He began to sing a Psalm which ended with the words, 'Be still, and know that I am God.' His eyes wavered and blinked, then closed, succumbing to a warm drowsiness. He fell headlong into a deep sleep. Behind closed lids, his eyes began to move.

"Yeshua!" He heard the clarion voice call to him from the depths within. He wondered, how to answer. "Here I am! Speak, Father, for your servant is listening."

"You have done well to seek my guidance. You have asked for knowledge at the appropriate time. Your answers will be given to you."

Yeshua felt the magnitude of Solomon's words. He said, "I am only a little child. I do not know how to carry out my duties. Show me your will and the way I am to go. Show me who I am, and what I am to do, so I might govern this great people of yours."

"Yes, the time has come for you to recall the dream we dreamed together before time began, for the time is drawing nigh for our plan to be fulfilled in you." Awe and reverence filled Yeshua.

In his dream he bowed low before God his Father, the Almighty One. He began to hear a voice singing in a language so ancient that he knew no other ears had ever heard it, but his. It was a song with which he was intimately familiar. Its power rose up from within him. He was being pulled through a passage of the deepest darkness, surrounded by thunder and lightning, the song grew louder. When he broke through the corridor of darkness, he found himself standing in a room of bright and swirling flames. He felt no fear, rather a oneness with his Father.

Words flew on the winds of blue white flames. The perfection of creation, 'His Father's Gift', appeared before him. The ancient plan began to unfold before his eyes. And he took it in, recognizing at once the themes of his dreams over the years as he had slept. A book was opened and he read of the explosive energy of light, creation, the rebellion, the fall, the first murder, the wandering, the violence, the Nephilim, Noah, the flood, Abrams faith, flaming feet walking through the blood of sacrifice to make a covenant, a promise to Abram for a son and many children. The history of his people swirled before him, hard, heartbreaking, yet beautiful at the same time.

"I know this." He uttered.

After, a passage of time, he saw his own birth, the horrifying slaughter of the innocents, and the years since. Finally, he came to look down upon himself fast asleep on the overlook surrounded by stars, the images paused for effect. But the dream did not end there. It continued on to what was to come. He saw the places he would go, the faces of people he had not yet met. Then he saw himself teaching and healing all kinds of people. It ended at a tree with a cross beam. The scene panned, moving around the cross until he came face to face with his own suffering self.

The voice spoke within him. "On the third day, you will rise from the dead. New life begins with you. Your purpose is to fulfill this very Word, which we spoke before time began. You are my Word made flesh, the very embodiment of my Word. My words already live in you. But now, I will stir up all of my words within your consciousness. It is by these words scribed by the hands of my servants that you will lay the foundation for the coming kingdom of heaven."

"I have come to do your will." Yeshua said. "Show me what you would have me to do."

"Find the ancient scrolls and eat them. They will come to life in you. They will guide you and sustain you in the way."

"The way?"

"The way of salvation. Obey them my Son, for the joy set before you."

"...for the joy set before you." The dark curtain of his lashes fluttered, his lips were still moving with the words. The images faded and the words echoed, as if to define his ultimate goal. Stirring, he looked up into the night sky. How long had he been asleep? The fire he had previously built was now glowing with a low flame. He stacked another log to take hold. He lay back under the covers to stare out into the night sky seeing it now through different eyes.

The plans from within the flames seemed to still be swirling inside him. He was stunned by all he had seen. So many things made sense now.

One star shimmered and danced brightly on the horizon, until the sky began to transform into day. So many thoughts tumbled through his mind. He had always known who he was; he was different from those around him. The realities of his purpose had been veiled. The dream of a kingdom had always been hidden just beyond the curtain of his conscious mind.

Now, having been so graphically revealed to him, his purpose overwhelmed him. In his vision it had all made sense. Laying under his blanket, he felt all too human again. The mantle of his calling pressed heavily upon him. It felt like a suit of armor that was too large for him.

'Am I enough to finish this task I have been purposed to finish?' He asked himself. Recognizing the self-doubt for what it was, he reasoned, 'My Father, wouldn't give this to me to do if I don't have it within me to complete it. I will be enough. Though it will require everything that I am, I will do it. I give myself to the will of my Father.' He remembered his mother's favored words, "With God, all things are possible."

~ 3 ~

A MOTHER'S INTUITION

The first offspring of every womb among the Israelites
belongs to me, whether human or animal.
Exodus 13:2

Yosef and Miriam sat by the outdoor oven, enjoying the warmth radiating from it. Miriam was preparing the evening meal.

"He has been gone too long. This was supposed to be a short trip." She said with impatient concern.

"Miriam, stop worrying. He is a grown and capable man, and he is wiser than any old man that I know. The LORD is with him."

"I can't help it. I don't know how to not worry about him. Ever since that day we left Bethlehem, when we heard the screams of all the mothers in the village we had just left behind." She shuddered remembering the trauma of that day.

She thought again, "No, I guess I have worried for him since the day he was conceived." Unconsciously, her hand went to her stomach.

"Yes, but God provided a way for us all and we have hidden him well. He is safe. No one suspects a thing. He is Yeshua, son of Yosef, as far as anyone knows."

"Things are about to change, I can feel it." Miriam lifted her head as if she could smell it on the wind.

She cast Yosef a challenging look. "How can they not, if the prophecy is true? Have you not noticed how restless he is? He has barraged me with more and more questions concerning his birth in recent months, just like he did after his bar mitsvah in Jerusalem. Back then, we could answer him simply and command him to silence. But now, he wants details."

Yosef furrowed his brow. "Yes, I've had conversations with him too. But what can we do? Are we not in this with the LORD? Haven't we always known that Yeshua will fulfill his destiny, for the LORD has spoken it. We cannot frustrate the will of God. We cannot hide from the truth of who he is. He is God's Son."

"Am I being too selfish, wanting to keep him safe for myself?"

"Am I?" Yosef placed his hand on hers. "But he has known his identity for a long time. He has surpassed me in everything I have ever thought to teach him and the Rabbi as well. He has poured over the scrolls of the synagogue. He has memorized the Torah word for word. It is time that he should begin whatever his life is meant to be."

Miriam knew Yosef was right. "What will you do without him when he goes? You depend on him and you are getting older now."

"I don't know." Yosef considered it. "We have quite a brood. James and José's are working with us now. I can bring Judas on, and Simeon will be able bodied soon enough. The Lord has blessed us with four more sons. We will be okay."

He was quiet for a moment, then mused, "It's not his strength or his engineering mind that I will miss so much. It is his company. He makes our labors feel easy and light."

Miriam nodded, completing his thought. "And James makes it difficult."

"It is hard being compared to Yeshua. I try not to do that, but perhaps I still do."

"It frustrates Yeshua, he tries so hard, but James continues to cling to the unsavory rumors of Yeshua's birth story that are still whispered against him around this village. Those rumors have caused him to harbor harsh feelings towards both Yeshua and me."

Yosef's was irate, "Has he disrespected you?"

"Not outright, but his eyes speak for themselves. Although, I'm not sure why he blames me, when Yeshua looks so much like you." She gave a little laugh.

"Haven't you always wondered about that? Don't you think it odd?" Miriam cut a sideways glance at him.

Yosef smiled to himself, "Not really, wouldn't that be just like the LORD? And, both you and I have grown from the same root."

Then, his expression fell. "After all these years, people just can't let it go, even when Yeshua has become an exemplary young man."

Miriam shook her head. "It is strange, isn't it? It is as if some evil spirit keeps stirring up hateful thoughts against him."

Yosef changed the subject, "Word has it that Herod Antipas has a new building project for his palace in Sepphoris. The work is tempting, but I hesitate to apply for it. Yeshua would be right under his nose. And, we all know Antipas has a tainted eye towards those who follow the way of holiness."

"And, you would constantly be surrounded by Roman soldiers." Miriam added. "There is plenty of work elsewhere."

"Yes, there is that, but it would put plenty of food on the table for all our offspring."

Pulling out the large platter, Miriam said, "And with six hungry men, we can hardly fix enough for everyone."

The food was ready. They called their sons and daughter to the table as stair steps, pre-teen, adolescent, and young adults. They were just sitting down with their large brood, when Yeshua came striding into the small courtyard followed by another familiar face.

"Looks like we are just in time! I hope you have food to spare! Look who I ran into as I was coming up from the valley." Miriam was greatly surprised to see Yohannan son of Zachariah trailing behind.

"Yohannan! But how...?" He swept Miriam up into a familial bear hug, lifting her feet off the ground.

"I was visiting in Capernaum, recruiting young men to come study scripture at Qumran, when I thought of my favorite cousin. It is only a day further to come here. We need Yeshua to come and be a part of our movement! We know the Messiah is here and we are waiting for him to reveal himself. Meanwhile, we work to prepare God's people. I know of no other man more knowledgeable for this work than Yeshua. We could use his insights and his help. When I started up the incline to Nazareth, there he was! It was truly providential!"

Miriam's brow creased with bewilderment. "Did you say movement? In Qumran?"

"Yes, and also the Judean wilderness, and Galilee."

Miriam cut her eyes towards Yeshua. Both Yeshua and Yohannan were so exuberant that they totally missed her pensive stare.

Yeshua picked up the conversation, "Yohannan has been telling me about the extensive library of the ancient scrolls that have been preserved in clay jars. These were the scrolls carried from the temple years ago to be preserved by the Righteous Ones. Qumran has become a scriptorium producing copies of these important scrolls. These writings are being sent out to renew the hope of the Messiah and prepare the people to return to God. Qumran is the keeper of the words of God."

Miriam was about to say something when Yosef laid his hand on hers to gain her attention. He gave her a brief shake of his head.

In frustration, she shook off his hand and began to fill two more bowls. She was not ready to hear of more adventures. Yeshua had just returned. Little did it matter. There was no escaping the obvious delight on Yeshua's face.

Yosef spoke the blessing "Thanks be to the LORD who brings forth bread from the earth and the fruit of the vine." Then all of the men fell into a comfortable silence over their lentil soup and delicious bread.

The savory soup had lost its appeal for Miriam.

Yeshua stayed up talking with Yohannan until late in the evening, giving Miriam no chance to question him. Observing her son under inquisitive brows, Miriam could see his restlessness was gone. In its place was a sense great purpose. She had not expected the change to come so quickly. She loved Yohannan, and normally she would be delighted by his visit. But this time, his arrival heralded an unwelcomed transition. Even his words spoke the portent of change to her. She lay awake pondering his words.

'We know the Messiah is here, and we need Yeshua to be a part of the movement.'

She had observed Yohannan and Yeshua talking. She could feel the strength of Yahweh's Spirit between them. Their spirits had been bound since before birth. And, she remembered a day that didn't seem so long ago, when Zechariah had prophesied over his newly named infant son.

'Praise be to the Lord, the God of Israel, because he has come to his people and redeemed them. He has raised up a horn of salvation for us in the house of his servant David. And you, my child, will be called a prophet of the Most High; you will go on before the Lord to prepare the way for him, to give his people the knowledge of salvation through the forgiveness of their sins, because of the tender mercy of our God.'

Miriam closed her eyes, thinking. 'If a movement of God is beginning, then far be it from me to hold it back.'

~ 4 ~

A FATHER'S PRAYER

An angel of the Lord appeared to him in a dream and said,
"...what is conceived in her is from the Holy Spirit.
She will give birth to a son. Name him Yeshua,
for he will save his people from their sins."
Matthew 1:20-21

Yosef was up early the next morning, unable to sleep. He went into his workshop and lit a lamp waiting for Yeshua to come to him. In the quiet of his workshop, he could think. As a father, he understood it was important that Yeshua find and follow his own path.

Still, it saddened him that it would lead him so far from his family. He loved Yeshua as if he were his own, even from the first moment he had torn his way into their world through the veil guarding the way to his mother's womb. He had landed slick and bloodied in Yosef's trembling hands. Yeshua usually joined him after he finished his time of prayer. The sun started to rise. Yeshua must be lingering in prayer this morning. He was not surprised. He continued to sand the piece of wood he was using to make a storage chest.

Finally, a shadow blocked the morning sun that had just begun to stream through the door. Yosef looked up expectantly to find Yeshua appearing as a mighty angel of light framed by the rising sun. Yosef drew in a sharp breath.

"Oh Yeshua, I was lost in my thoughts, you gave me a fright."

"It is just me, Abba." He chuckled and moved into the room, going to the other end of the work table.

"So, with Yohannan here, I never got the chance to ask you. How was your time away?" Yosef 's hand stilled on the wood, and he searched Yeshua's face.

Yeshua also stilled, his eyes were wide as if he was measuring how much to say. He had always talked freely with Abba.

"Was it all that you hoped for?" Yosef prodded.

"Yes, Abba. It was all I had hoped and more."

"You have discovered your purpose then?" Yosef peered at his son.

"Yes, it has taken me days to process it. I am still processing it. It is so much to take in. I lingered. Sorry, if I caused concern from my delay. Ima has given me an earful."

Yosef smiled knowingly. "Yes, I am sure she did. Better you than me. So, what is your future to be?"

Yeshua found it difficult to speak aloud the bizarrely grandiose words. "There is more than I can say, but yes, I am to bring together a kingdom of believers."

Yosef straightened and offered a wan smile.

"But it is not like the kingdoms of men. The foundation of the kingdom will be laid with the outpouring of my blood."

Yosef waited, his face solemn.

"To build this kingdom I have to offer myself up."

Yosef's face contorted with confusion registering Yeshua's words. "What do you mean 'offer'?"

"This must sound irrational to you."

"I'm listening, please explain this to me."

"It won't happen all at once. It is hard to take in and harder for me speak of, even to you, but I need to say it out loud. You have always been my sounding board."

"All people die." Yosef said. "But yours is to be an eternal kingdom as it was promised to David. So..."

Yeshua lifted his fingers, "My death will be different. It is integral to my mission. It will be a horrible and brutal death. I will be the sacrifice for the sin of all our people, I am to be 'The Atonement', surpassing the lambs of Bethlehem offered every year in Jerusalem at Passover. I will abolish sin once and for all."

Yosef was speechless, never having imagined such a sacrifice. He remembered Yeshua's birth in the stable and the strange things that happened thereafter; the shepherds who gathered by his manger, the words at his dedication, his first Passover at twelve.

"Like a lamb?"

Yeshua nodded solemnly.

Yosef wrinkled his forehead at the consideration, searching for an appropriate response. "That could only happen in Jerusalem. But, Jews do not sacrifice humans. It is forbidden."

"That is right, we do not sacrifice humans. The blood of animals has always been offered to appease the wrath of God. But those offerings only set the sin aside, ultimately remaining for me to destroy. Sacrifice was meant to cause sorrow, understanding, and to become a deterrent to sin. Still, these were only foreshadowing of the once and for all human sacrifice. Only human blood can appease human sin. Our people have grown calloused to the death of the animals."

"When? Where?"

"I will be sacrificed outside the city gate. This has been the plan since before time even began." Yosef stared at him

"How did you come to know this?"

"I had a dream on the mountain, a very vivid dream. I was caught up into my Father's presence. The dream felt familiar, like I have had it or ... been there before. It was so real. It was revealed, everything that will happen. It was like I was in the past and the future all at one time. Then, a voice spoke from within me."

Yosef eyes widened hearing these words. His mouth worked, but he had no words.

"I am sure of this, I am the Lamb of God." Yeshua said.

Yosef could not argue. He was familiar with the awe of God and the mystery of divine dreams.

"Don't say anything to dissuade me, Abba. It is hard enough to comprehend it as it is. I sought answers from my Father. Now I have them. He will help me in all he has planned for me to do. I am putting my feet to the path he has laid before me. Going to Qumran will be my first step before I am sent and consecrated to fulfill this work."

Yosef nodded mutely. Hadn't the people of Nazareth believed him cuckolded and of poor judgment after his own revelation? But, he had taken Miriam as his wife anyway, despite her mysterious pregnancy because of his dream.

"When will this happen? I hope not until after my time. I don't think I could bear it." Yeshua ran his fingertips over the wood on the workbench before him.

"Everything is according to my Father's timing. For now, I go to Qumran. There are writings there which I need to study. It is no accident that Yohannan was sent to me at this time. I must take in all of the inspired words of my Father. He told me that I will know his words to me when I see them. His whole plan is written down. All of his words are to come alive and be fulfilled in me."

Yosef rubbed his hand over his beard, something he did when he pondered things.

"But, you already have most, if not all of the Torah memorized."

"You are right. However up to now, I have not had access to all the writings, neither have I studied them or pieced them together as a road map for my mission. Scripture has always spoken intimately to me, but now, it will speak to me even more clearly. Everything I do will be driven by those words."

Yeshua stared back into the past. "Do you remember the first time you took me into the temple with the Passover lamb of sacrifice when I was twelve?"

Yosef nodded.

"I think I have somehow suspected some part of my purpose since that time." Then he asked, "Does this make any sense to you?"

"I remember you were very upset for the innocent animal to be sacrificed."

"Yes. I remember thinking, can the blood of an innocent lamb make retribution for a sinful man?"

"I remember we talked about that."

"As the human Lamb of God, I am God's atonement for the sins of all people. God's retribution will fall upon me."

Yosef scruffed his beard, as if to erase the thought. "That is a heavy calling. Too much for one man to bear. How do you feel about all of this?"

"Right. I feel right about it." Yeshua said, resolute. "I mean, I am not looking forward to it. But it is what I was born to do to save the people that I love."

"Surely, this is a frightening prospect!"

"It is a terrifying prospect." Yeshua remembered the unrecognizable man on the cross. "Pray that the perfect love of my Father will drive out all my fears. Still, this doesn't change the fact that I am the only way."

Yosef felt a terrible pain of sadness in his chest. He dropped his tool onto the table and walked to the other side to enfold his son, pressing him to him as if he could will this all away. But in his soul, he knew what Yeshua said was right, even if he didn't understand it.

He spoke haltingly. "I remember the angel said, 'Give him the name 'God Saves' for he will save his people from their sins.' He also said, you will be called God with us."

Yosef suddenly felt overwhelmed by that thought. He held on tighter, like he was the child. His tears fell upon his son's neck and tunic, with the same love and wonder he'd felt the first time he'd held Yeshua as an infant.

This is God's son. This is God. And, yet he is still no less my son as well.

Sensing Yosef's thoughts Yeshua lifted his arms to embrace his Abba while they both wept grateful tears.

A little while later, when he was ready to depart for Qumran, Yeshua returned to the workshop and gently laid his hand on Yosef's shoulder.

To Yosef, it felt like a benediction. "So, now you are ready to go? What will I do without you?"

"Abba, you have four other sons, a team of laborers are at your disposal." Yeshua reminded him.

Yosef flicked his hand through the air as if to swat that gnat of a thought away. "Yes, yes, but I won't have you."

"Of course, you will! I am always with you. Besides, you know James has been waiting for years to take my place by your side. This is his chance; it will be good for him and in the end, it will be good for you too."

"Of course!" Yosef nodded, "I know you will always be with me in my heart. No matter where the LORD takes you or what great things you do."

He touched his chest, "May your heavenly Father guide all your steps all along the way. I am trusting He will go with you where I can't. Just don't forget your mother and me as you go!"

Yosef moved towards the doorway with his shoulders hunched, he looked down the road as if he hoped to glimpse the future waiting there for Yeshua. Instead, he found the hustle and bustle of Nazareth and Yohannan waiting impatiently.

"You have said goodbye to your Mother then? How did that go?"

"She is upset with me. She worries, as you know. I haven't told her what I have told you. She would not understand. Why worry her now unnecessarily? For a woman who once took such a huge leap of faith to bring me into the world, now she seems to be filled with so many doubts!"

Yosef nodded, "In the beginning, she felt she had little to lose. Now, it is different for both of us. She loves you. She is a good mother."

"She is. I hate that she is so upset, but I am praying she will come to understand and find her peace in due time. I must do what I was born to do." He became solemn, "Please try to help Ima to understand."

"I will try." Yosef looked into Yeshua's compassionate eyes recognizing once more the strong conviction and unshakable faith that he had first seen in Miriam. Yeshua's faith was pure. He had always trusted the rightness of Yeshua's words.

He put his arm around Yeshua's shoulder to walk with him out to join the others. There were more hugs, and words of caution from Miriam.

Yeshua took up the pack of his belongings and turned to Yohannan. "To Qumran then."

He and Yohannan set off with matched strides, strong and sure. Yosef watched Yeshua's retreating back.

"There he goes." Yosef sighed.

Miriam held her hand over mouth, little sobs escaped and she turned and ran inside.

Turning towards his workshop, Yosef wondered yet again, 'Why did God choose me to father His only son? I can't imagine. I hope I have served him well.'

He paused to looked back for one more glimpse .

At that same moment, Yeshua turned back to smile at Yosef. He paused and touched his fist to his chest with a nod. Then he was gone. Yosef felt as if a piece of himself had departed with his son and the whole universe had shifted. Stepping inside his workshop, he bowed his head as he had done thousands of times. He began to intercede for his son. But soon his words disintegrated into a jumbled sob, as he thought again of everything Yeshua had told him about his future. He shook his head sorrowfully.

"God Most High, I have done my very best for your son, and he has been the son of my heart. Now, it seems my work is done. So today, I do what I must; I give Yeshua over into your care and purposes. Be with him now, as he fully discovers what it means to be the Son of Your own heart."

~ 5 ~

TUMBLING STONES

He will be a stone that causes people to stumble
and a rock that makes them fall.
Isaiah 8:14

Two years had passed since Yeshua journeyed to Qumran to study the scrolls. His days had passed quickly, consumed with his study. The more Yeshua examined the scrolls, the more certain he became of the path before him. He understood his Father's plan, and his role in it. At times, he felt the words had been written for him alone, even though he knew these words had also been written to all the people of God.

He had often wondered why his Father had not simply imparted the words to him within his vision as he had to the prophets. Instead, he had sent him on a journey to discover the ancient words in the same way as every man, scroll by scroll, word by word, thought by thought.

Through the light of Scripture all of humanity could know his Father's plan, but it was a path less taken. In his studies, his Father's words spoke to him exactly as promised.

Qumran was unique and set apart from all the other Essene communities. The men who came to Qumran voluntarily entered into a celibate lifestyle similar to the ancient Nazarite vows. Denouncing their passions, they committed themselves to a devout preparation in purity and holiness so they might serve the long-awaited Messiah. Yeshua shared in their conviction and lifestyle. His life was devoted solely to his Father's plan. He had to complete his mission before he would receive his prize; only then could the joy of a counterpart come to fruition.

Although he quietly studied and scribed the Scriptures along beside the other men, his true identity was not yet revealed to them. He taught what he learned through conversations while he gardened, cooked, and worked on a variety of building projects.

He appreciated the zeal with which these men lived their life toward God. Some were of the lineage of the ordained priesthood. As a sect they had become known as the Essenes, 'the Righteous Ones', because they held to the traditional doctrines of the Jewish faith. Previous generations of Essenes had been forced to flee into the Judean wilderness to escape the deadly persecution of the Hasmonean leaders. But Herod the Great had invited them back and leveraged their convictions against the Hasmoneans to dismantled their dynasty. It had been an uneasy relationship. Herod murdered the last Hasmonean son in line for the throne, never mind he was Herod's brother-in-law. The boy had just come of age when he was found drown in the mitzvah.

No longer needing the Essene support, Herod ruthlessly turned on them, finding their morality oppressive and inconvenient. Falling under the rod of his persecution, they fled into the wilderness and to the northern reaches. Herod was finally free of both the Hasmonean threat and the Essenes. He immediately set about restructuring all of Jerusalem's priestly offices with a more progressive mindset.

The more recently formed sect of the Sadducees secured new positions of power by paying tribute to both Herod and Rome from the temple taxes; which, they increased greatly by crafting the temple sacrificial system into a lucrative business. The high priest took control of everything, including the wealthy Pharisees who kept businesses inside the city. The leaders of Jerusalem gained a widespread reputation for being 'a brood of vipers', willing to eat their own.

Yeshua's relative Zechariah had fallen under the scrutiny of the high priest after he had drawn the lot to offer up the prayers of the people in the Holy of Holies. He had received a vision concerning the coming Messiah. He became politically blackballed for his hope of a Messiah.

Eventually, Zechariah was forced to take his family and seek safety in the Judean wilderness. Other godly men joined him as the danger increased because of their convictions. Zechariah and Elizabeth raised their son Yohannan in a small settlement near the Jordan River. In that barren land, they had learned to survive off the land. Zechariah taught a new generation in the way of holiness according to Scripture.

It was no coincidence that years later, Yeshua would come to join with Yohannan and study the ancient texts protected there. Some writings were only found in Qumran. Despite Yeshua's vast insights, he now studied the library of sacred text and the historical documents brought from Jerusalem as they pertained to him. They became a road map. His reputation for supernatural knowledge and insight of Scripture became well known amongst the brothers.

"What's wrong? You seem troubled." Lazarus asked Yeshua.

"I have received a premonition concerning my Abba.

"I'm sorry to hear this. I hope all is well." Lazarus said, picking up the scrolls that Yeshua had just sealed into clay jars for their keeping.

A few days later, Malachi came into the printing chamber. "Yeshua, your brother is here."

His expression was grave and sympathetic. He lowered his voice. "I am afraid he comes with sad news."

Yeshua lay down his pen and stood slowly, feeling a fresh wave of sorrow. Nodding, he moved around Malachi to scrub his hands before going to meet his brother.

James was standing in the courtyard curiously taking in the place, when Yeshua appeared.

"James." He called to him as he approached. "What is it? What has happened?"

Seeing his older brother, James stumbled over his words. Tears sprang to his eyes. He swiped them roughly away them with his sleeve.

"It is Abba, he had an accident at work. He is gone, Yeshua."

Yeshua stepped forward to comfort his brother, but James held up his hand. Yeshua acknowledged his brothers rejection, taking it in stride.

"What happened?"

"It was terrible. Abba broke his own rule, he walked under the stone workers. Who knows what he had on his mind? A heavy stone tumbled from above, hitting Abba in the head. He dropped with the rock, never to regain consciousness. Bildad is distraught over it. Ima believes that if you had been there you could have healed him."

Yeshua heard an edge of irritation in his brothers words. "How is she handling this?"

"She is in shock, but trying to be strong. She wants you to come set everything right as if you could raise Abba from the dead."

Yeshua stared out over the horizon toward his mother, feeling her grief. James continued. "I told her I could handle everything, but she says you are the eldest, you must come home and make the needed decisions."

Yeshua felt James' resentment.

"When was he buried?"

"We did not delay. Everything was according to the law."

"Of course. Thank you for taking care of it."

Yeshua remembered that he had been in prayer, when Yosef's face appeared to him; and a feeling of heaviness had crushed him with a knowing. The heaviness had settled in his heart while he prayed for his Abba. While praying he had seen Yosef's face turn to one of rejoicing as if he was welcoming Yeshua back to him. It had been unsettling, but Yosef's expression had given him a sense of peace.

Now hearing the news, he felt the pain of Yosef's loss all the more. He thought of his mother. He longed to be near her, knowing the confusion and pain that death brings. He could feel his mother's broken heart crying out. Death is everyone's foe and rarely does one know when it will come knocking at one's door. Yosef had been devoted to Ima and his children, despite their rocky start.

Needing some time alone, Yeshua said, "Let me take you to the mikvah for purification. You can prepare to take your evening meal with us."

After getting his brother settled, Yeshua left the community behind, seeking the privacy of the fortress-like cavern paths. He found his favorite perch, a vantage point overlooking the valley of the dead sea. There he allowed his grief to break open. His heart ached. He had loved his earthly father.

This made his mission all the more important. Through it he would redeem Yosef, along with all the others. That knowledge was his solace. He thought of Abba and generations of other precious servants of God sleeping in the earth waiting for him to come and call them forward like dormant seeds waiting for the glory of new life. Their resurrection depended solely on him.

"Father," he prayed, "help me to be strong enough to destroy death forever. Help me to rescue Abba, and all of those who have died believing in your Word."

He remained for some time praying about his decisions and the conversation he would have with James.

Later that day, James stood on the other side of the small room from him.

"Ima expects you to come home and take Yosef's place since you are the eldest son."

Yeshua still had work to finish amongst the scrolls. Yet, he knew he needed to put her fears to rest and establish a new hierarchy.

"I will return to help set things straight. Do you think you can take the lead in my absence? Then, I can return to finish my work here before moving on to do the work my Heavenly Father has prepared for me to do."

"Why do you say, 'Heavenly Father'? Do you think you are the Son of God?"

Yeshua did not dignify his sarcasm with an answer.

"You've always had a delusional and elevated view of yourself. Ima fed this insanity. I don't understand why Abba allowed it. She has no confidence in me to provide."

"She probably feels it is too heavy a burden for you to bear the business alone now that you have taken your new wife."

"She puts you on a pedestal. Abba believed her fabrications to cover her own sin! Who knows who your real father is? Some say a neighborhood boy. Others believe she was molested by a Roman. Some have guested it was a priest in Jerusalem. Of course, you would rather think Yahweh is your Father!"

His brothers words were vicious. James was striking low blows, but why not? He was angry and now his father wasn't there to take him to task for it. He could say what he had always wanted to say.

"I have heard many theories, but I've never heard anyone wonder if you were the Son of God."

"James, let's not do this. You are just angry that Abba is gone. But if you want to know the truth about me," Yeshua voice was low and emphatic, "ask the people of Bethlehem. The people whose baby boys were cut down with the sword! Obviously, King Herod believed I was the Messiah. Didn't he murdered a whole town of baby boys in his determination to kill me. Why do you think our parents fled to Egypt? As a ruse? They would never do that. And why do you think Zechariah was persecuted, because he believed in a coming Messiah."

James narrowed his eyes. "Herod was maniacal! He killed three of his own sons too, perhaps he killed all those babies on a lark. Our whole village secretly whispers about Ima's deception."

"Do not talk to me about other people's suspicions. What about you? You know me. You know Ima and Abba. They are righteous people who have lived to honor God. What do those people know? Even if you doubt me, do you dare to doubt our parents?" Frustration furrowed Yeshua's brow.

He continued, "As for the doubts of Nazareth, no one understands living under their suspicions better than I do. Do I need you to tell me? Even my own brother doubts me! How is it that you do not know me, James? Or the people of Nazareth for that matter? Who have I wronged?"

"If you are the Messiah, then tell me, how are you going to establish your throne? You are a tradesman and a laborer. You are no better than me." James argued, though he knew that was not true.

"Will you overcome the Roman government? I want to see that. What about the Tetrarchs? The Sanhedrin? I think it will take a man far more forceful than you."

Yeshua sighed in frustration and changed the subject, "We will travel home tomorrow. Together, we will make a plan. You can take simple building jobs to earn a living. You have been Abba's second now for two years. Isn't this what you want?"

Guilty relief washed over James face. "Abba has taught me all I need to know!"

He had dreaded coming under his brother's leadership.

Yeshua sighed, how he longed for his brother to understand him. But his words never broke through. His willingness to believe the town's rumor mill was a bitter pill to Yeshua. James' angst was more about his close relationship with Abba and his devotion to God.

What really concerned Yeshua was James' open disrespect of their Ima. No wonder she wanted Yeshua to return.

"Just one thing." Yeshua told him. "If I place you as the temporary head of the house in my absence, you must honor our mother and treat her with the respect she deserves. This I command you. I am not abdicating my right as the eldest. She needs your care and protection. Can you do that?"

James evaded eye contact. Yeshua pressed him.

"James, will you do that? She deserves that, no matter what lies you wish to believe. If Abba were here, he would demand that of you." Finally, James gave a terse nod.

~ 6 ~

THE MESSIANIC SECRET

He was in the world,
and though the world was made through him,
the world did not recognize him.
John 1:10

That evening, smiling broadly, Malachi motioned for Yeshua and James to take the seats beside him. He called on Lazarus, "Would you offer the blessing?"

Lazarus stood up with the bread lifted and the room grew quiet. He spoke the ancient words.

"Blessed are You, Lord our God, King of the Universe, who brings forth bread from the ground to sustain our lives."

Lifting a cup of water, he said, "Blessed are You, our Lord and God, who waters the earth and sates the thirst of men!"

The moment Lazarus dropped to his seat an explosion of conversation began in the room.

Malachi leaned in close to say, "Yeshua, we are all so sorry to hear the sad news of your Abba Yosef."

Yeshua nodded. "Thank you Malachi, our Abba rests from his labors now. He was a special man. He knew how to love and be kind. My family and I will miss him greatly."

"When will you leave for Nazareth?"

"Tomorrow. I will be away long enough to set things right, then I will return. James will take responsibility for our family until my work is finished here."

Malachi was surprised by his words. In his two years, Yeshua had never expressed any desire to join the brotherhood. Even though, he had certainly been with them long enough to gain their approval.

"We are glad that you will return. And, you know we would be happy to count you as one of our brethren."

Yeshua nodded his appreciation.

"So, tell me," Yeshua said, "what inspirations did you discover in the texts today?"

"I was just working on Psalm Twenty-two." Malachi said. "A Psalm of David, I can't place the complaint among the events of David's life."

"Psalm twenty-two is a provocative Psalm." Yeshua said, looking down at the striped bread sitting before him. He began to quote the Psalm in deep clear tones. The men nodded, listening carefully, enjoying the artful way the words rolled off his tongue.

When Yeshua ended the Psalm, Malachi launched into a stream of questions foremost in his mind.

"Who was David speaking of? Himself? Or, someone else? It is not like the songs of praise, or prayers of intercession."

The other men at the table began to pull apart the details, trying to identify possible narratives. The discussion went on for a good part of the meal.

James found himself captivated by their fascination in this Psalm. He had never even given it a thought.

Lazarus said, "The person in question was clearly hated and badly mistreated."

Yeshua suggested, "Perhaps David is writing inspired and prophetic words given by the LORD for the future son of David. Perhaps this is something that is yet to happen."

Malachi considered this. "This makes sense. David the anointed one writing words to inform the coming Anointed One of what will happen. He declares that all who sleep in the earth, who have returned to dust will bow before this afflicted man. If the dead arise and bow down before this afflicted one, he must certainly be the Messiah."

"This is not the only Psalm that points to the Messiah. So many Psalms and prophecies are tied to the coming Messiah." Lazarus said.

"I find this so interesting. I have heard it mentioned that the Messiah is also the suffering servant named in Isaiah. He suffers to bring us salvation." Malachi said.

"To my knowledge the LORD has never fulfilled this Psalm." Lazarus said looking toward Yeshua for confirmation.

"Why was David given such foreknowledge?" James asked with interest.

Malachi shrugged, "I suppose these prophecies were given to him because of God's promise to him of a son that would become the future Messiah—who would rule an everlasting kingdom."

Yeshua dipped his bread into the bowl and chewed appreciatively, listening to the conversation without comment.

After he had swallowed and taken a sip, he asked, "So, what is the consensus about this Psalm? Another Messianic prophecy?"

Heads nodded in a round of agreements. James ventured, "I still don't understand why the Messiah would undergo such suffering. Wouldn't he be all glorious in power and might? Blessed and exalted by God?"

"Many think that." Philip responded. "But when you study the Scriptures..."

"Perhaps, there is an order to the prophecies? If so then perhaps both are true." Yeshua suggested.

"Psalm twenty-two begins as a personal lament of one undergoing severe persecution. He cries out for help and remembers that only God can help him in his affliction. He is dependent on God's merciful presence, when he suffers at the hands of beasts. He prays, but the affliction continues. He feels forsaken by God, but even so he seeks to glorify God because he knows God does not forsake humanity even in the midst of their suffering."

His listeners were pensive.

"It is as if God shares his peoples suffering, even when they have believed they are abandoned by God. The Psalm reminds me that God does not hide his face from human agony. Instead, he answers their cries for help. He enters their existence, and willingly suffers to save them."

Malachi looked unsure. "It says, the one suffering has become as a worm, that is a far cry from God."

"Yes, think of how many afflicted have been laid so low, so vulnerable, so humbled that they are made to feel as insignificant as a worm? Worms are easily and thoughtlessly stomped on and crushed under human feet, are they not? Isn't this the same with God's people at times?"

"So, it sounds like you believe this "wormy man" is God then? This is indeed hard to understand." Malachi shook his head.

"Ah yes, therein is the mystery my friend." Yeshua drank deeply of his water.

Malachi weighed Yeshua's words, considering him more closely, while others departed. "You interpret the Scriptures differently, yet what you say sounds right. I have heard talk of a suffering servant before, but I had not connected that servant to the Messiah. Do you think our deliverer will suffer like this?"

"Yes, I do." Yeshua said softly.

"You suggest the Messiah, even though he is a man, will actually be God? How can that be? Such thoughts are surely too high above my understanding."

Everyone quietly contemplated this for a moment. Then Malachi asked Yeshua, "So what do you think? Is the Messiah here among God's people now, as Yohannan seems to think?"

Yeshua's encouraged Malachi, "I would tell you to keep looking for the person hidden in the words, Malachi. He will become more clear in time. And yes, I am sure the Messiah is here. For all you know he is closer than you think."

Malachi smiled a lopsided smile and sopped up the oil and hummus. "Well, I only hope I will know him when I see him, and that I will live to see his deliverance and glory."

"May it be so." Yeshua said.

James spoke to Malachi to change the subject. "So, tell me about Qumran and what you are accomplishing here."

"Our community is striving to regain the holiness God demands of us. A reformation if you will. We reject the trappings of false religiosity and all of the man-made laws that those in Jerusalem force on us." Malachi looked curiously at James. "Being related to Yohannan and Yeshua, I would have thought you would know all about this?"

"Yes, well, my brother is a dreamer," James said with a glance toward Yeshua, "and I really don't know Yohannan that well."

Malachi looked surprised and shook his head, "A dreamer, eh? Funny, I don't see Yeshua that way. Actually, he is one of the most purposeful men I know. But to answer your question, we are striving to be in a right relationship with God. Therefore, we study and preserve the original scriptures. We search the Scriptures concerning God's promises and prophecies about the coming Messiah. Yohannan has most recently spearheaded efforts to spiritually purify those who are turning back to God through the ritual of immersion and purification rites. Perhaps you should hear him preach. People come from all around."

James said, "Maybe I should."

Lazarus added, "We believe the Messiah is even now among us. This is the foretold time. We know he will be revealed to us soon enough. Our goal is to support the Messiah when he makes himself known."

James pushed his food bowl away and glanced towards his brother, surprised that Yeshua remained unassuming. His head was lowered, allowing Malachi's and Lazarus' testimonies to speak for them self.

"Do you have anyone in mind?" James probed, again cutting a glance towards his brother.

"No, not really, although some have thought that Yohannan might be the one we were waiting for. But, Yohannan flatly denies this."

"We figure we will know who it is, when Yohannan figures it out." Lazarus indicated.

"So, what kind of person would the Messiah be?" James asked, his curiosity getting the best of him.

"I am not an expert. You might get better answers talking to Yohannan or your brother. I am still a novice here, just learning about the Messianic texts. From what I understand the Anointed One would be holy, perfect, a servant, and he must be revealed by God himself. Wouldn't you say so, Yeshua?" Malachi asked.

Yeshua smiled brightly at his assessment, offering a nod.

"That is quite different from what I would think." James picked up his bowl. "I am exhausted. I should get some sleep. Thanks for the dinner." He made his way to the dish tub, and left toward the sleeping quarters.

But sleep did not come quickly for James that night, forcing him to lie awake in the quiet space considering the thoughts the men had laid before him. Obviously this community was waiting for the Messiah, and they esteemed his brother's thoughts. There was one phrase that niggled him from the nights discussion. *'This is the fore-told time.'*

For a brief moment he considered, 'Could there be any truth of Yeshua's identity?'

But before the seed could take hold, it was plucked away and James fell into the dark void of sleep.

~ 7 ~

PREPARING THE WAY

There will come a voice of one
calling out in the wilderness:
'Prepare the way for the Lord!'
Isaiah 40:3

After Yeshua returned to Qumran from Nazareth, Yohannan came bursting back into camp like a whirl wind. Some ran to greet him. Others moved aside, anxious to get out of his path. Yohannan was an acquired taste. He was strong willed, quirky, outspoken, and honest to a fault.

From childhood, Yeshua had enjoyed a special bond with his mother's young cousin. Growing up he had looked forward to seeing Yohannan during the yearly festivals in Jerusalem. He had a brilliant mind and a quick understanding. As Yohannan became a young man, he took his drive for holiness to a whole other level, while dismissing rote rituals. The Scriptures simply spoke more loudly to Yohannan than anyone else that Yeshua knew. He was Yohannan's biggest cheerleader, and about the only one who could smooth his rough edges.

Whenever Yohannan came to Qumran, they spent companiable time together discussing the Messianic texts found within Isaiah, Jeremiah, Ezekiel, and Zachariah scrolls. Their time together was always richly rewarded. When Yohannan began his purification ministry, he'd gone to the Jordan near his home village. Now, their moments together were rare.

Entering Qumran's common area, Yohannan found Yeshua seated at the long table with his back turned to him. He went directly to him and with an uncharacteristically soft voice he bent down to whisper, "Hey cousin."

He placed his hand on Yeshua's shoulder. It had not been that long since Yohannan had lost his own aged parents. A genuine empathy was evident upon his features. He braced one of his swarthy arms on the table as he leaned down, his tangled locks dangled over his shoulder. Yeshua turned slightly, coming face to face with the rough mantle of camel skin like that of the ancient prophets. It smelled of the great outdoors. He stood to receive his cousins back pounding embrace.

Pulling back, Yohannan said, "So awful! Hearing about your Abba! Yosef was one of my favorite relatives. Such a good-hearted man! I know it is a great loss to the whole family. It is hard to lose a parent. I have lost two, and I miss them every day."

Yeshua took in the disheveled, but welcomed, sight of his cousin. He was a far cry from the pampered and well-groomed priests who occupied the temple. He looked more like a Bedouin wanderer than a Cohen priest. Nevertheless, he was pedigreed with the priestly ancestry of both Zadok and Aaron, Yahweh's anointed and authorized priestly line.

"I know that you do."

Yeshua remembered Elizabeth and Zechariah. They were always so happy to see him, and he could tell by their eyes, they knew who he was. But they had never said one word of it to him, nor anyone.

"How is your Ima Miriam?" Yohannan asked, swinging his muscular calf over the bench to straddle it. They both took a seat. Yohannan had a particular fondness for Miriam because of the special closeness she shared with his much older mother.

"Grieving and more than a little angry at me for leaving her with James. He has taken charge of the family in my absence, but you and I know who will really run the household."

He shook his head as his lips tipped upward at the thought. "Ima Miriam will whip him into shape. She is a strong lady."

"So, what brings you in from the wild?"

Yohannan spread wide his expressive hands as if the answer was obvious.

"A need for more workers."

"Ah! So, how is your ministry of baptism going?"

"Actually, I have some exciting news. Word is spreading of my ministry. People are streaming out to the wilderness to hear my message of repentance. It is quite surprising how eager they are to receive the purification rites. Seems I have a new name, 'the Baptizer'." He chuckled.

Yeshua's breath caught at this bit of news, 'It is happening! The work of preparation has begun. That could only mean the time of my revelation is drawing near.'

"Are you okay?" Yohannan asked him, noticing the look of surprise on Yeshua's face.

"Yes, it is just that you have found success so quickly."

Yohannan coughed a little laugh of agreement. "Yes, well it seems the LORD is on my side and moving among the people. Obviously, he is calling them to me. It is going so well that I need help, that's why I am here to recruit a few more good men. I will head back day after tomorrow. Yeshua, we are nearing the recorded time. We cannot delay. Come with me."

His voice was filled with his sense of urgency. Yohannan paused to give Yeshua a chance to agree.

"It is not yet my time."

Yohannan tried again, "Come and help me prepare the people for the coming Messiah. You, of all people, should be a part of this. Surely, this is your desire."

Yeshua smiled at his cousin's persuasive invitation. No wonder people have a hard time resisting Yohannan.

"You are anointed for that work. I must finish here first. You have things well under control. You are a natural and the people are coming out to hear you!"

"You could really help with the work." Yohannan did not relent.

Yeshua shook his head. "There are a lot of eager followers here that will be delighted to come with you to be discipled. Take them and teach them everything you have learned about the Messiah, your message, and work. At the right time, I promise I will join you."

"You are sure?" Yohannan pressed him. "I need a man like you."

Yeshua leaned his chin on his hand, eyeing Yohannan with mute lips and raised eyebrows, indicating the matter was closed.

"Alright. Alright." Yohannan held up his large hands, rising to retreat. "I don't understand why you delay."

He took three steps as if to go, then circled right back, still not willing to give in. Invading Yeshua's space once more, he reclaimed his seat.

"But Yeshua..."

Yeshua laughed at him, nudging him back a bit to regain an appropriate distance.

"Oh sorry."

Yohannan scooted back a bit. His voice growing louder. "There have been so many coming for preparation! In fact, it has become inconvenient and too dangerous to my home community for me to remain so close. If the Sanhedrin come for me near there, they would likely come to Qumran as well. For that reason, I am moving my ministry out toward Salim further away from Antipas and the Sanhedrin. So that is where you can find me, when you are ready."

"Good thinking."

"I have messengers spreading news of a revival all around the country side. People are coming like they are starving for the words of the LORD. The Sanhedrin has begun to dog my steps. There is plenty of water at Salim and areas to make camp."

He paused to take a breath. "I tell you; everyone is waiting for the coming of the Messiah. I know he is here among us already. I just know it! He will make himself known soon. I watch for his appearing every day. You don't want to miss out on that when it happens, do you?"

"No, no I certainly do not."

He asked. "Why are you grinning like a donkey about this? I am serious!"

"I know you are!" Yeshua said, still unable to hide his smile. "Everything in its timing. The Lord will reveal his servant when he is ready for him to be revealed. You won't have to search long or hard. The day will come when suddenly there he will be, standing at the water's edge to cool his feet. Did not the Lord say: *'Seek me; you will find me when you seek me with all your heart?'* You are doing important kingdom work, preparing God's people. Be patient, the Messiah will come."

Yohannan nodded his agreement, "Yes, but you know my impatience and our need for a deliverer. How much longer must we wait? Often I find myself scanning the crowds, looking at all the brothers within our community, trying to guess who might be the One. Surely, he would be a part of our movement. Certainly, he would not be among the Pharisees nor the Sadducees. I tell you he will not be found in the viper's pit, not the Son of David! But, you are right. He will appear when the time has been fulfilled."

"Exactly!"

"So," Yohannan clapped his hands, "is it still a 'No'?"

"Still, no. Some things can't be hurried along. God's timing is always right. I still have work to finish here. Go with God's speed and answer his calling to you. When the time is right, I promise I will come to you. I can't wait to see what a great work of renewal you will be doing! But be shrewd Yohannan, these are treacherous times. Those in power look for any sign of unrest. Your message won't be welcomed, even though our leaders need to hear it most of all. Old structures are not easily changed, especially when they have become corrupt."

A look of resignation passed between them. As an after-thought, Yohannan added, "It is interesting, I have received news that our movement has been greatly received in Capernaum and northern Galilee. That is close to Nazareth, right? But why tell you? You are remaining in Qumran."

Yeshua ignored the dig.

"Thanks to your recruitment skills, your message has really spread. Don't forget you have several Galileans here among us. Why don't you ask them to go work with you," Yeshua suggested. "They might later serve amongst their own people."

"Good idea, I think I will. Then, perhaps when you come to me, you can wrap up their training." Yeshua inclined his head with nod, "Maybe so. Teach them well for me until I can get there."

"I will. Don't delay too long, I will be watching for you."

They both stood then and the two men embraced and clasped hands. "May the power of God go with you." Yeshua said putting his hands on Yohannan's shoulders with a blessing and prayer.

Then, Yohannan was off, strolling to the other side of the room to talk to someone he had set in his sights. He would not stop until he had done what he had come for.

After he had moved on, a burst of laughter erupted from Yeshua. He shook his head with an affectionate amusement at the irony of their conversation.

After all this time, Yohannan still has no idea!

Even after they had talked endlessly about the Messianic texts, Yohannan had registered no spark of recognition. He had always held his peace concerning his hidden identity, sure that when the time was right his Father would reveal him to Yohannan. Even for all Yohannan's enthusiasm, his identity remained hidden from his searching eyes. When his Father wanted Yohannan to know, he would know. Glancing up, he realized his friends were watching him quizzically. He offered then a muted smile. Yohannan always had a way of leaving him in a particularly good humor.

~ 8 ~

HIDDEN IN PLAIN VIEW

Whatever is hidden is meant to be disclosed,
and whatever is concealed
is meant to be brought out into the open.
Luke 8:17

Malachi watched the exchange from the other side of the table with great interest. At Yeshua's unexpected outburst of laughter, Malachi slanted an inquisitive glance his way. Finally, his curiosity got the best of him.

"What was so funny?"

"Oh, just a private thought." Yeshua said.

"I find Yohannan to be a funny sort of fellow, also. But he doesn't exactly crack me up with his jokes. He is usually too busy talking about sin and repentance, or pushing people to do his bidding. He can be a real kill joy."

Yeshua pursed his lips, at Malachi's quip. "You are right. When one speaks the truth, it stings like salt in the wound."

Malachi saw his appraisal had hit a nerve. He pressed on anyway, clearly curious about Yohannan.

"Our nation has not had a true prophet for many years. Everyone says, Yohannan has been gifted with a prophetic voice. It will be interesting to see where that voice takes him."

"Look at the history of the prophets, the prophetic voice leads to trouble every time. It is a hard calling. It is not for the faint of heart. Yet, if God is calling him, dare he resist? Therefore, Yohannan needs our prayers. He is answering God's call to do hard and dangerous things. Who will deny God's words burn in his very bones?"

"Well, it is true, he certainly knows the Scriptures. In that way, you two are birds of a feather. I study the words, but they do not sit me on fire in that same way. You, however? I am surprised you are not going with him."

"We each have our own work to do. You have your work that has been prepared for you to do too." Yeshua's eye contact and words strangely moved Malachi.

Yeshua went on, "Still, in the end, are we not all to serve a common mission? No doubt, Yohannan and I will share the same mission."

"I may be talking out of turn. If so, please forgive me." Malachi fidgeted with his food. "Being that truthful makes Yohannan comes off as being over the top. He too abrasive. Couldn't he soften things up a bit? His message rubs some people the wrong way."

Malachi waited anxiously for Yeshua's reaction, realizing he may have just been too honest himself. He didn't want Yeshua to take his honesty as an insult.

"Sorry. Maybe, I should not have said that. I just struggle with Yohannan."

"A prophet does not speak of their own accord, but the very words of God."

Yeshua watched Yohannan across the room with a bemused expression. Feeling Yeshua's eyes on him, Yohannan glanced his way and flashed him a big-eyed, "What?!"

Yeshua shook his head, then turned back to Malachi. "Is it him personally, or is it God's message to you that you don't like?"

The question caught Malachi by surprise. "It is just that sometimes he wields the truth like a sword, his words can make you bleed."

Yeshua shrugged. "Perhaps that sword runs in our family. Am I not just as truthful. Our message is one in the same."

"What do you mean? Do you agree with his methods?"

Yeshua straightened to give his earnest assessment. "Yes, it is true, Yohannan is not particularly diplomatic, nor in any way apologetic about his words. He has been given a forehead as hard as flint, a booming voice, and eyes bold enough to search for and receive uncomfortable truths. He sees things from a heavenly perspective. Most people find it more convenient to ignore those truths. Yohannan has the gift of knowing God's reality. He knows the Scriptures and he believes what God is saying to him. This is good, right? Who could change his mind?"

Malachi shrunk in his seat, feeling self-conscious.

"Whenever I look at Yohannan, I see that his Creator has made him exactly as required for the work he has given him to do. Wouldn't it take that kind of man to call Israel's stiff-necked people back to God and to begin a revival out in the wilderness in some of the most dangerous of times? Look at him! He is the kind of man that only the wilderness could contain! Yohannan is wondrously made for what he is purposed to do."

Malachi listened. Finally, watching Yohannan, he chuckled, "Yes, perhaps you are right. I couldn't do what he is doing! I am just a scribe and a so-so musician. I have soft skin and love being indoors. I am a people pleaser. I hate conflict and lack his courage. Yet, in times like these, blowing his trumpet too loudly could end with his head on a platter."

A shiver ran down Yeshua's spine at these words. It was true, what Yohannan was doing was like dancing on the tip of a sword. Rome, Herod, and the Sanhedrin would despise his message.

Yeshua spoke out loud as if to someone unseen. "Yohannan was his parent's greatest pride and joy. If they were still here, I am sure he would be their greatest concern. Luckily, they have been spared that pain. His faith is a far cry from the meaningless rituals and traditions of Jerusalem. He has become 'the one calling out in the wilderness, make straight paths for the LORD'."

Now, it was Malachi's turn to feel the shiver of goosebumps.

Yeshua stared into the future, recognizing his own path would ultimately be far more abrasive and confrontational to those in authority. All the opposition the prophets had faced, he would face as well. His mirth drained from his face, leaving his expression grave.

"It is time to get back to work." Yeshua stood abruptly.

"Are you alright?" Malachi realized his words had dampened Yeshua's spirits. "I didn't mean to ..."

"You only spoke what was on your heart. It was an honest conversation. Not to worry."

Malachi looked chagrined, "Yes, well, thanks for the insights." He watched Yeshua clean his plate and cup, propping them on the sideboard to dry. Then he moved across the room, passing by Yohannan as he went. He paused to squeeze his cousins arm affectionately; then moved on through the door to leave the room.

Malachi leaned back considering Yeshua. He intrigued him. He thought, 'There is something about him. At first glance he seems to be an ordinary fellow; he is self-contained and unassuming. Still, his words do cut right to the heart of the matter. Everyone may be watching Yohannan, but Yeshua is the real one to watch. He will surely become a great Rabbi or reformer. Didn't he even hint that he has a calling?'

A provocative thought came to Malachi's mind.

Could Yeshua be the Messiah? No. Surely Yohannan would know it if he were!

Suddenly, a burst of laughter bubbled up, surprising even him.

Clearly, all of Yohannan's talk about the Messiah has stirred my imagination! Still, how foolish we would all feel after searching and waiting for the Messiah, only to discover he was hidden here among us all this time!

Malachi shook his head.

My imagination must be playing tricks on me. Yohannan would surely know him. Won't we all recognize him when he appears?

~ 9 ~

THE LIVING WORD

"Son of man, eat what is before you, eat this scroll;
then go and speak to the people of Israel."
Ezekiel 3:1

Another year had passed. Day after day Yeshua chewed on the words found within the scrolls; finding himself consumed by them.

Recently, however, a familiar restlessness had returned. He wondered, 'Is the Father stirring my Spirit?' Often his mind wandered from the text before him to thoughts of the ministry yet to begin.

Days later, when Yeshua's eyes snapped open well before sunrise, he quietly arose, stepping outside, going to his favorite place of prayer. He asked his Father to show him what he should do. No word came to him, only a confidence that his answer would come.

Later, he went to his scribers table to begin his work on the second scroll of Isaiah. Some time had passed, when suddenly he stopped to lay down his quill. Astonished, he realized he had been writing the text, but had not opened the scroll. He quickly went back to proof his work against the original. He found that every dot and tiddle was in place. The document was perfect. He laid his hands on the table before him to process this. He tried another scroll, only to find he could write it too, then another. He drew in a deep breath and let it out slowly.

My work here is finished. My Father's words are written on my heart and mind. The embodiment is complete.

For three years he'd been consumed with the details of the words, the stories, the prayers, the songs, the sayings, the instructions, and history. Now it was time to begin to live the life that was written about him in those scrolls.

First, however, he had a promise to keep to his mother and his sister Hannah. Hannah was soon to be married in Cana. He could hardly believe this. Three years before, Hannah was but a child. At his visit only two years earlier, he had seen the beginning of her transformation into adolescent. Abba made a marriage contract with his friend and business associate for Hannah to marry his son. The contract was sealed just before Yosef's death. This had been Hannah's final year of preparation before her new life was to begin.

He had been home when the introduction between Zerah and Hannah was formally made. His sister had been as timid as a deer. Yeshua could only imagine how nervous his sister might be now. He had promised Hannah he would be there to stand in for Abba for her wedding.

He packed his few personal items, realizing how sparse his life at Qumran had actually been. This was a good thing; he would have no room at his childhood home. James had taken a wife of his own, so sleeping space was already awkward for all. By now, there was likely a little one on the way.

The brothers gathered to see him off with a psalm of blessing, bereft to see him go. His conversations and teachings had opened their eyes to many new insights.

"Please visit us as often as you can." Malachi said.

Yeshua caught a vegetable cart heading north along the Jordan River towards the Sea of Galilee, where he hoped to find passage to Magdala or there abouts. Though he longed to visit Yohannan at the Jordan, he did not sidetrack. He promised himself that he would visit Yohannan just as soon as he could.

~ 10 ~

THE DIFFICULT CONVERSATION

"Come now, and let us reason together."
Says the Lord.
Isaiah 1:18

Seeing Yeshua at their gate, Miriam came running out to meet him. He caught her up in his arms and swung her around. Laughing, she drew back to look at him and caressed his cheek.

"Look at you, you look different." She searched his features.

"Could it be that I am three years older than when I left?"

She took hold of his clothing and examining it.

"Are these the same clothes I sent you off in three years ago?"

She curled her nose at how grayed and tattered they seemed.

"If you had come to see your mother more, I would have created new clothes for you!"

"Tell the truth Ima, to you, I look like Solomon in all of his glory!"

"Indeed, you do!" She laughed. "I have missed you so."

Hannah came running next to throw herself at him as if she were still a child. A young woman appeared in the doorway. Her stomach protruding under her tunic. He greeted Sarah, James' wife. She bit her lip a bit shyly.

"Where are all my brothers?"

"Out on a job at the moment, but they should be returning by sunset."

"And Si?"

"Simeon is working with the men now, helping with the simple things." His Uncle Cleopas and his wife Mary appeared from within.

"Uncle! How wonderful to see you!" Yeshua hugged his Aunt and Uncle, glad to see them maintaining the family closeness since Yosef passed. Their family homes were built side by side, separate, but attached as one structure. Cleopas was trying his best to be a father to the other boys.

"Yes, it is time for young Simeon to begin his apprenticeship." Cleopas chuckled proudly. "You won't believe how tall he has grown this past year."

"All of my sister-in-law's chicks are growing up before her eyes." His aunt added, taking her turn to hug Yeshua.

Settled in and refreshed, Yeshua said to Hannah, "In just a few weeks, you will be a bride. I can hardly believe it."

At his words, tears leapt to her eyes.

"What? What is wrong? What has happened?" He looked quickly from Hannah to Ima with alarm.

"It is a just a delay." Miriam said to calm her daughter. "Zerah has been robbed by those Roman tax collectors again and the income he was counting on for the wedding celebration was greatly diminished. He has asked for two months to get the money together for the wedding feast. If Rome doesn't rob him yet again, all will be fine. Even though the budget will be tight for the wedding, it is only delayed. All will be fine."

She patted Hannah's hand. "Actually, we are still working on Hannah's wedding clothes. This gives us more time to complete her wardrobe and yours. We can't let you go looking like that!"

"Why are you so anxious little one?" Yeshua spoke to Hannah. "When the timing is right, you will be married. Zerah could search the whole world and never find a sweeter bride. This only means you get to stay with me for a little longer!"

Hannah accepted his encouragement, and laced her arm through his.

WAY OF THE LAMB ~ 51

"I'm glad you're home, Yeshua."

Miriam prepared the celebratory table with a colorful cloth, several lamps of light, and crowned it with some lovely wild flowers and Yeshua's favorite dishes.

"Ima, what are we celebrating?" Yeshua asked to tease her. She swatted at him happily.

"I wonder."

"The table is beautiful. Everything smells delicious."

The table was full of conversation and everyone was in high spirits, laughing, talking over one another, sharing all the local news, and eating more than they should. They lingered. Yeshua shared a few stories from Qumran and Yohannan.

Miriam reached out taking hold of his arm. "It is so good to have you home Yeshua, we will not have to worry for anything with you leading our family now."

James threw a thunderous look Yeshua's way, as if he had somehow betrayed him. "What? Are you returning home? I thought you had great plans beyond Nazareth."

Yeshua gave James a look meant to calm and quiet him.

Taking his mother's hand, he said apologetically, "About that Ima..."

She looked confused. "You are coming home, aren't you? You've been gone three years."

"Let's talk more about that, after everyone has gone to bed." His eyes pleaded with her, not wanting the evening to come to an uncomfortable end.

He had not meant to build up any false hope for her. He had, however, delayed telling her his plans until it was necessary, if only to keep her from fretting over it. He'd wanted to give her time to grieve Yosef and to see that James could provide care for the family. Tonight, the conversation he had dreaded could no longer be delayed.

After dinner was cleaned away and everyone had gone to bed, Yeshua invited his mother to remain in the court yard for a private conversation. They sat together under the night sky, the stars blinking coolly in the blanket of darkness, night blooming jasmine spread its sweet scent throughout the air. All the surrounding homes had grown quiet. Sighing and leaning forward, he broached the subject he had been dreading.

"Ima, I need to share my plans with you."

"Well yes, please do." Miriam clipped testily, looking down at her hands.

"I had asked Abba to share with you my vision on the mountain some years back. Did he talk with you about it?"

Miriam focused unhappily on her hands clasped before her. "Why should he tell me, you could have told me yourself."

"What did he tell you?" He tested her. "Let us talk openly with one another." She resisted, but eventually decided it was no use; she could not withstand his will. She took a deep breath and began.

"He tried to tell me some ridiculous theory about you being the Lamb of God. It made no sense to me. I just thought, it was some wild imagining, some misplaced sense of responsibility."

"I had hoped you would listen to him, that you would try to understand." She shook her head, and closed her eyes.

"How can I?" After a moment or two of awkward silence, Yeshua tried again.

"Ima, do you remember our story, the story of us, you and me and Abba? How did it all begin?" Yeshua was taking Miriam back to the time of her calling.

"Tell me once again about my beginning with you. Think back and remember." He gave the soft command. "Whatever comes to mind."

Moments of silence yawned before them, still Miriam said nothing, resisting his request like a petulant child. All the same, the memories began to come one after another, as if being resurrected from the past where they had been safely stored.

"What did the angel say to you?" He prodded her, not for himself, but as a way to prepare her to face the truth.

"I know what you are doing." She said.

Even so, her mind rolled back to that day when the angel named Gabriel had appeared to her, speaking words so great that they terrified her. She was reluctant to say the words out loud. Once she did, Yeshua would never allow her to store them back in the place where she had packed them away. She just wanted to hold on to Yeshua as her son a little bit longer, fearing where his real identity would lead him. She had avoided this conversation for years. Finally, she drew a deep breath, then exhaled slowly; breaking her silence, she began in an almost hushed whisper.

"He said, 'Greetings, you who are highly favored. The Lord is with you.'"

Yeshua took his mother's small hand in his, squeezing it encouragingly.

"Do not be afraid." Tears slipped from the corners of her eyes, so she closed them remembering the terror and the awe of that day.

"Do not be afraid." He echoed the words to her now.

"Then he spoke my name. 'Miriam, you have found favor with God.'" Her voice evaporated into a high-strung tremor.

"You will be with child, and give birth to a son, and you will give him the name 'Yeshua'." She paused, trying to contain her emotions. Yeshua waited, allowing the memories to wash over her. It was important that she remember the details. Her voice became stronger, and filled with the awe of his words.

"He will be great. He will be called the Son of the Most High. The Lord God will give him the throne of his father David. He will reign over Jacob's descendants forever; his kingdom will never end."

"Did you believe the angel?" Yeshua asked quietly.

"How could I not? I felt the weight of God's presence emanating from him." Miriam confessed.

"As terrifying as the angel was, it was his words to me that overwhelmed me! A child? I was confused, because I was chaste. I had been with no man. Oh Yeshua, that was so long ago that it seems like a dream now. Did it really happen?"

"Only you know for sure. Did it happen?" Yeshua asked. Miriam took a shaky breath.

"Yes. It happened. I know the tongues have wagged all these years, but you do believe me? Such strange things were happening all at the same time. Miraculous things. Frightening things. Things that no one could possibly believe except those of us to whom it had happened."

"The things of God tend to happen in mysterious ways." He encouraged her.

"The messenger called himself Gabriel. He looked like a man, except all too large and glorious, so I knew he was not human. He told me, *'The Holy Spirit will come upon you, and the power of the Most High will overshadow you. Therefore, the holy one to be born will be called the Son of God.'*"

She blinked her eyes and more large droplets released. "Ima, do you still believe I am the Son of God?"

"Yes, even though it is hard to comprehend it. Out of all the women in the world, I wondered why me? But Elizabeth asked me 'Why not you?' I don't know what I expected, however, when you were born I was surprised. You were a baby, flesh and blood, hungry, and needing changing. You needed me and Yosef. That might have made us wonder, but then a group of shepherds came to us from a nearby field. They told us about the appearance of a multitude of angels who had announced your birth to them. Why the shepherds? I couldn't guess." She paused, lost in her thoughts.

After a moment he called her back with a squeeze of her hand.

She looked up, then continued on. "When you were dedicated at the temple, an elderly priest named Simeon, prophesied over you as 'the long awaited One'. At that time, he was renowned for his righteousness. He testified that you were to be ' salvation for all of the nations and a light unto the Gentiles'. He said, you are 'the glory of your people Israel'."

She murmured to herself, "There is only One who is the glory of Israel."

She glanced up into his face. "He said you would cause the falling and rising of many. You would be a sign that would be spoken against. You would reveal the thoughts of humankind." She gazed at him for some long moments, as if she were trying to decipher these words once again as if for the first time. She bit her lip.

"Then before we left, an aged and devoted woman named Anna came hurrying towards us. She was well known at the temple. She had devoted her long life to temple service amongst the women, and she offered up prayers all throughout the day. She called out to her friends to come gather around. She told everyone you were not just any baby, but you were 'the consolation of Israel'."

Yeshua watched her process her own words.

"Both Simeon and Anna had been filled with praise. They began to rejoice in worship to God." She smiled at him through her tears at the memory.

"Time passed and I might have been tempted to forget, when you clung to me and looked into my face. A baby. It was so easy to forget you were a king because you were so little and we were just ordinary people. But one night, a caravan of foreign kings came searching for us. They had been led by the coordinates of one very bright star. They said the star was a sign to them of your greatness. 'The King of Kings.' They had travel great distances to pay homage to you as the one born as such."

She swallowed thickly, "Unfortunately, they had gone to Jerusalem thinking to find you in the palace. They had gone to Herod." She closed her eyes for a moment. 'The truth of your existence was out of the bag. Herod went crazy as only Herod could.

The devout community in Jerusalem was already stirred up by the testimonies of both Simeon and Anna among the righteous ones. People still talk..." She grimaced.

"Another angel appeared to Yosef in a dream, warning us that Herod was sending his men to kill you. We left in the middle of the night and fled. They killed every son under the age of two in Bethlehem and the surrounding area. After that, there was no more forgetting who you were. Yes, I knew it was true; you were the Messiah. And it was our calling to keep you safe."

"With a little help."

"Yes, with a lot of help, actually." She said.

"What about now? What do you think? Am I the Messiah?"

"Now? I am afraid to know what it means that you are the Son of God. When it first happened, I was so humbled. It was such an honor. Why me? Why Yosef? How had we suddenly been given such a huge responsibility?"

She wiped at her eyes, and added, "But you were not the only miracle. As if to prove his point, the angel told me that Elizabeth was expecting a child. She had hoped for a child all her married life, but there had been no conception. She had surpassed her years of childbirth. Amazingly, she was pregnant with Yohannan."

"Yes."

"The angel Gabriel told me that Elizabeth was in her sixth month. He offered me proof, knowing we would need one another. As soon as Elizabeth saw me, she immediately knew I was expecting the Messiah."

"It strengthened you."

"Yes, the angel told me that no word from God will ever fail."

Yeshua bowed his head at those words, gratified to hear this affirmation from his mother's lips.

"And you believed that, didn't you?" He raised his eyes to hers.

"I did. I believed God. Before the messenger of the LORD left me, I believed him and I said, 'I will be the LORD's servant, may your word to me be fulfilled.' I have often wondered, if that was that the moment of your conception. When he left, I didn't know what was to follow. He was there one minute and gone the next like a midst. Everything was normal again. I wondered, did that really just happen, or was it a vision? Nothing was normal after that. Abruptly, I had this secret that I felt I could not tell anyone. Who would believe me? And if they did, what might they do?"

"Every time I thought about it, panic would overcome me as if to strike me down. I had to keep remembering the angel's words over and over. 'Do not be afraid.' It became my daily mantra and I prayed that God would make me strong enough for whatever would come and that I would find peace. Something told me that I could tell Elizabeth, that she would understood how awed I felt; and she did. She assured me that it would all work out. She was just who I needed at that time, someone to believe this news with me and to help me keep the faith. It was such a help."

She covered Yeshua's hand covering hers, holding on to him like she would never let go.

"I remember, when I arrived, Elizabeth was immediately caught up in the Spirit. You were still just a small seed, growing in me. Yet, she knew you were with me! As soon as she saw me she began to rejoice! Breaking out into worship! Even Yohannan got excited, rejoicing at your presence, leaping around in her womb! I got caught up in the Spirit too and words of praise came flowing out of my mouth. I have never worshipped God so joyfully."

She squeezed Yeshua's hand again, all that love springing up within her at the memory. "I was so happy that God had favored me in such an unfathomable way, to bring forth the savior."

"A savior?"

"Yes. We really needed a savior, there was so much injustice and persecution."

"What about now?"

"We still do...." She looked up sheepishly.

Another memory came to her. "Zechariah had lost his ability to speak while serving in the temple. When Yohannan was born, Zechariah surprised us all when he suddenly began to speak again. He affirmed Yohannan's name, and he began to prophesy over Yohannan that he would serve you. Your births, you see, were tied together...."

She looked up with surprise then as if a piece had just fallen mysteriously into place.

"Because of our shared miracles, we remained close, even though we only saw one another once or twice a year."

"Yes." He said softly, "And, Yohannan and I are still bound together. Do you remember what the angel told Abba?"

"Yes, I thought Yosef would have nothing to do with me. I thought I would have to have you without him. And, that was his initial response, but..."

She remembered his face that day, troubled and disappointed.

"I didn't know what I would do without him. All I could do was pray for him to believe me, but how could he when we had never been together. I was so relieved when the LORD sent his messenger to him in a dream. He told Yosef that you were conceived by the Holy Spirit."

Miriam bowed her head. "He was also told, 'You are to name him Yeshua, because he will save his people from their sins.'"

"Did he say anything else?"

"He said, you would be called... 'Immanuel-God with Us.'"

Yeshua leaned in and lifted her face to his. "So, see, you know who I am, Ima. You have always known. I understand why you suppressed these memories. It was not time. You have instinctively protected me. This is what a good mother does, she protects her child. Now I am no longer a child. You have done your job to keep me safe, until the appointed time. It is time for you to let that responsibility go. I must do what I was sent to do."

She bowed her head and nodded warily.

Yeshua said, "I've always known I was different. I have always belonged to God. And as such, I must keep my promises."

The moment he said this, an indescribable fear and awe overwhelmed Miriam making her feel weak. She slipped to the ground on her knees before him as she had on that day when the angel came to her. She began to weep.

After a moment, Yeshua lifted her up, taking her in his arms to quiet her.

"Don't be afraid Ima. Let us speak plainly now. There can be no more secrets between you and I. This is why I cannot return to Nazareth and take up Abba's trade again."

Miriam tucked her head against his chest. Listening to his steady heartbeat, she struggled to resolve herself.

Yeshua continued. "Over the years, I have sought understanding about my identity. Those days on the mountain clarified my purpose. In Qumran, I have been searching the sacred texts, piecing things together, trying to understand the road that has been mapped out for me hidden there within the Scripture. Salvation for every person who has been appointed will depend on me."

He tilted her chin toward his face. Searching the depth of her eyes, he willed her to understand the purpose of his mission. Miriam closed her eyes, as if she could hide from him.

"Look at me!" He whispered urgent and insistent command.

Looking, she saw his determination.

"This world depends on me. The purposes of God cannot be thwarted. I must obey my Heavenly Father as he directs me. Abba understood this and you must understand this too. What did Abba tell you?"

"He told me of your vision. You are meant to bring forth a kingdom, one not built by human hands."

"What else?"

"He told me you were to offer yourself as a sacrifice for our sins." She choked on these words. A keening, at once primitive and sorrowful rose up from her. Her throat squeezed tight, fighting back the tears.

"He said that you are the promised Lamb of God, the only sacrifice that can truly heal us all!"

"Yes, Abba believed me. I am the Son of The Promise. I will fulfill my Father's promises."

Sobbing she asked, "But how can that be Yeshua? How can that be? God has never demanded a human life! He spared Sarah's son. Can't he spare my son too? I didn't know..."

She broke, no longer able to speak.

"Would it have made any difference if you had? This has to be." Yeshua folded her to him and rocked her back and forth slowly like a child, smoothing her hair, and kissing her forehead. His breath was warm on her wet cheek.

He said. "Ima, just as you were overwhelmed by God's presence, just as you could not say no to the will of God, neither can I. I have poured over the scriptures at long length. I have considered all the possibilities. I know how much this is going to cost me. It will cost me everything. But as God's Son, I am 'ani lo', I belong to my Father, he lives in me. I must fully give myself to him and his will. This is the only way. Every human life hangs in the balance, that includes yours, Abba's, our family, and every person who believes. You must understand, I was born for this purpose. I am the ram caught by the horns in the brambles that spared Isaac. I replace Isaac, and Abba, and you."

"When the angel came to me, I didn't know it would come to this! I didn't know this would be demanded of me!" Miriam whispered fiercely as if she could somehow change the outcome.

"But you did trust God. Even so, trust me now. You must not be afraid. Remember all things are possible with God. The things you give over to God will become your reward in my Father's Kingdom. You will never lose me. Do you trust me?"

Nodding slowly, Miriam clung to Yeshua for a long time, staring out into the night sky, searching for the light that had once shone so brightly, but all she could find there now was a deep darkness.

She cried out from the depths of her soul to the LORD to keep for her this beloved son. Yeshua held her close, rocking her like a child, his chin resting on top of her head.

~ 11 ~

WAY IN THE WILDERNESS

...make straight in the desert a highway for our God.
Isaiah 40:3

With the wedding now two months away, Yeshua found himself non-productive and restless. James didn't really want his help now, he had worked far too hard at becoming the crew leader to slip back into second place. Yeshua had to respect that.

He did a few odd jobs around the house, but quickly his list of repairs ran out. He knew his time was too valuable to waste. He longed to go see how things were going for Yohannan in the wilderness. He decided he would do just that, promising he would return in plenty of time for Hannah's wedding.

Yohannan's cry in the wilderness was the talk on everyones lips. He was drawing people from everywhere to make the pilgrimage to the Jordan river, excited to hear the words of a real prophet. Even Roman soldiers were attending. On duty, but others as curious onlookers. The LORD's admonishing message spoke to everyone.

The Sanhedrin was filled with concern at the power and authority in Yohannan's message amongst the people. They came to understand the peoples' response. They wondered if Yohannan might be Elijah or Moses, or even the Messiah himself. But Yohannan continually denied these thoughts.

With excited expectation, Yeshua sit out his own pilgrimage to the Jordan. He prayed as walked. "Be it to me as you have said. My soul glorifies the Lord. My life is yours. It is in your hands."

He remembered the words of scripture replied. *'Speak all the words I say to you, do not hold back. Even if only a few receive your words, speak them. You will be a stone that will make men stumble and a rock that makes them fall.'*

Yeshua was deep in thought when suddenly a viper launched itself towards him from the greenery along the path. Its fangs exposed as it flew at him. By sheer reflex, Yeshua cast his staff in front of him to hook the serpent mid-air. With one smooth whip of his staff, he flung the serpent away from him. The creature twist then rolled, recoiling to make a stand as if preparing to strike again.

Yeshua spoke to the menace. "You will get your chance to strike my foot. Just as I will get my chance to crush your head. To be sure we will meet again, but for now take your leave."

The viper swayed back and forth, hissing and spitting its forked tongue.

"Go!" The snake turned and slithered away at his command.

Yeshua had encountered this serpent before. It would appear out of nowhere, as if it followed watching him wherever he went. But never had it attacked with such intensity. Oddly enough, this encouraged Yeshua.

He realizes I know my purpose.

Occasionally, the serpent appeared in his dreams as a threat of intimidation. There had been nights, when he dreamed he was caught in a physical battle with this serpent. The serpent was strong. He could twist and turn in impossible ways. But Yeshua fought him to avoid his poisonous venom. He understood the dream came as a warning that some new temptation or struggle was coming his way. He called on his Father's name asking him to protect him, unsure of what danger might be near. These confrontations shook him, even as this one had today. Of one thing he was sure, this serpent was his enemy.

After Yeshua had passed, the creature stood to watch him go from a distance, muttering under his breath.

"I will soon have my way with you Yeshua Son of Elohim-Jehovah! I will delight in making you suffer when I do! You may think you will deliver your children from my clutches, but think again. They belong to me now, and so does this land. You may try to reclaim Jerusalem, that pitiful hill full of bleating sheep, but I sit enthroned on Mt. Hermon, the highest mountain of this land. I am worshipped here throughout this land. What are you but the son of man?"

Abruptly the serpent shapeshifted into a beast like creature, long in the face, with wicked looking horns. He had long been worshipped as Baal and by so many other names. Once he was the most beautiful of angels, he had held the highest of ranking. Now, he bore the appearance of an emaciated bull with sharp fanglike teeth. His arms hung low with large claw-like hands, his feet were cloven hooves. He wrapped his dark and tattered wings around himself, giving the appearance of a black robe. With a slight whirl, he disappeared leaving behind the scent of brimstone and destruction.

Yeshua moved on, making good time. When he arrived to the Way by the Sea, he caught a boat to the other side of the Galilean Sea, and grabbed a few good hours of sleep, unaware of what lie ahead. Before heading towards Salim, Yeshua heard that Yohannan had moved a bit south, making his camp on the eastern bank.

The morning was coming to life in the soft sunlight, a midst was rising from the river reeds, bird songs called above from tree to tree, in the sunny meadows dragonflies darted in dizzying circles, small animals collected their breakfast, and deer grazed. Mornings offered the illusion of innocence and safety, and the hope of new beginnings. The path traveled along the Jordan, where the river drifted southward towards the dead sea. The day grew warm.

Along the way, Yeshua recognized some trampled places where Yohannan had recently preached and baptized. He was glad that Yohannan was moving around from place to place. Still, if he could easily find him, then trouble could too. This was probably the reason he had moved to the eastern bank. It placed him just beyond the jurisdiction of the Sanhedrin.

He had been informed from the boat captain that people were coming to Yohannan from every walk of life. He described them as a parade of lost children, disillusioned, sad, and broken, searching for something to fill their aching emptiness and heal them. Healing began with Yohannan's words that pierced their hearts with the light of truth revealing to them their need to change. Those who fell under the conviction of his words entered the water for their sins to be washed away, and to give them a fresh beginning with God.

As he walked along the river path, Yeshua contemplated its current state of murkiness. Some days the water was clearer than others. At present , the water bore the dirty appearance of a sewer ditch, apparently carrying large mineral deposits within its depths.

He thought, 'It is as if it is carrying all the sins of the people down-stream to be buried in the heart of the Dead Sea.'

The salty sea, itself, was an unnaturally crystal-clear aquamarine, whose perimeter was trimmed with a salty white residue which added a beautiful contrast against the rock-face which surrounded it. The sea sparkled bearing no signs of anything so poisonous as the sin that had been deposited in its depths. Yet within there was no life to be found.

Sodom and Gomorrah had long before been razed and salted with a holy fire from heaven. From this the heavy residue of salt came the purification of the sediment of sin that was buried in the depths below.

Moses and Micah had prophesied, '*You will again have compassion on us; you will tread our sins underfoot and hurl all our iniquities into the depths of the sea.*'

All of the waters of Israel eventually found its way to this salt sea, the lowest elevation on earth. This included all the mikvahs in Jerusalem that flowed through the wadi to this place. He leaned over to stare into the mucky and cloudy water of the Jordan. A shiver of disgust traveled up his spine. He understood what his Father was asking him to do. He was to enter the foul looking waters and be immersed in it.

By doing this, he would be publicly making a new covenant, that he would take upon his self the sins of the people. He would be their lamb. Isaiah had written in his scroll: *'Surely, he took up our pain and bore our suffering; the Lord has laid on him the iniquity of us all.'*

The Psalmist wrote: *"The Lord is compassionate and gracious. So great is his love for those who fear him; as far as the east is from the west, so far will he remove our transgressions from us."*

Micah had written: *"Who is a God like you, who pardons sin and forgives transgressions..."*

He sat on a log watching the current travel sluggishly by, as if some sins clung stubbornly to the mud not wanting to flow into the salty sea to be eradicated. Unknowingly, this was what the people were seeking; someone who would remove their sins from them. Through baptism they trusted in the LORD to forgive them and reconcile them to a lasting relationship with himself. It made sense that only their Creator could purify them; and do for them what they could never do for themselves. Therefore, he would destroy the people's sins by taking them into the abyss of death. He thought of all the sins he had witnessed in his life: pridefulness, greed, impurity, unfaithfulness, evil oppression, perversions, hatred, malice, envy, prejudice, selfishness, gluttony, lewdness, slander, lies, abominations, and deceptions...

His stomach became nauseous as if he had eaten something that did not agree with him. Perspiration covered his forehead and the ground swam before him. Then the little he had hurriedly eaten that morning hurled itself out of him. Even as a child, Yeshua had often wondered why these behaviors did not affect others as it did him. It was as if they were blind to the destructive power within their behaviors.

After a few minutes, his vision cleared, and his strength returned. He stared down the river. He knew what he was to do when he came to Yohannan. He would commit himself to this specific saving work. Once he made this covenant of atonement with the people, there could be no turning back. From that moment on, the sins of the people would be laid upon him. He would have no choice but see his work of salvation through to the end.

He remembered the command the LORD gave to Joshua near this place. *'Be strong and very courageous. Be careful to obey all the laws my servant Moses gave you; do not turn from it to the right or to the left, that you may be successful wherever you go. Keep this Book of the Law always on your lips; meditate on it day and night, so that you may be careful to do everything written in it. Do not be afraid; do not be discouraged, for the Lord your God will be with you wherever you go.'*

These ancient words were instructive to him. He brought his water skin to his lips drinking deeply. He wiped his brow. He sat a few moments more with his walking staff planted firmly between his feet. Then he stood and resolutely marched onward to his destination.

~ 12 ~

THE IMMERSION

I, the Lord of sea and sky, I have heard my people cry.
I will make their darkness bright.
All who dwell in dark and sin my hand will save.
Here I am, I will hold your people in my heart.
Dan Schutte--Here I Am, Lord

...the Spirit of God descended like a dove, alighting on him.
Matthew 3:16

Yeshua found Yohannan standing to his midriff in the river. The line of people stretched waiting their turn along the river bank, with more arriving. Oddly, it reminded Yeshua of sheep lined up for their shepherd's cure. Yohannan received the confessions of the people, then laid hands upon their shoulders to lay them under the flowing waters to wash their sins away. Had Yohannan been in the temple he would have been laying the sins of the people upon their lamb or the bull of sacrifice. An act based in the persons trust for God's provision and in humble repentance, and the shedding of blood.

Yohannan took one person after another into the water and plunged them into the depths. His words were the same to each person when they rose up out of the water.

"Though your sins are as scarlet, today they are washed as white as snow. Seek the way of everlasting life."

Yeshua watched as each person came up out of the water refreshed in their spirit and reconciled to God. They clamored giddy and laughing toward the shore, their faces were full of awe and hope. Friends and family eagerly congratulated them on the banks with hugs, applauds, and cheers of celebration. They were so happy to have their burden of sin lifted from them.

In the bright flashes of light upon the water, Yeshua saw the Spirit of Flames and Wind dancing. He felt his Father watching from the clouds above. A gentle breeze blew at his back, lifting the tassels of his linen garment to tickle his legs as if gently urging him on. He slipped off his sandals, knowing this was holy ground. He was anxious to do what he had come to do. When his turn came, he stepped to the water's edge to take his first tentative step into the cold and murky water. The silty grit pressed up between his toes, sucking greedy at his feet as if to take him in.

Yohannan looked up just then, catching the sight of Yeshua standing at the shoreline. He came to a stand-still, holding up his hand to halt the people. His eyes slowly traveled up the familiar tunic that seemed to gleam unnaturally white and pristine against the muddy bank. His eyes widened and time seemed to standstill. Seeing the radiance of light play across Yeshua's face, the veil was suddenly lifted and he knew.

"It is you!" Yohannan whispered. He stood perfectly stilled, in awe. He wondered, how he had not known. After all the years of meeting together, after every conversation they shared at Qumran, why had it never crossed his mind? His memories raced backward, remembering all of it in rapid succession. He felt foolish, honored, and awestricken all at once.

Yeshua! Of course.

It all made perfect sense. He thought of Yeshua's supportive counsel and encouragement, never a slip of the tongue. Yet, he had never given a hint, but remained veiled from every eye, even his.

Now he realized, Yeshua was the most holy man he knew. There was really no one else like him. He could not account for even one small infraction, one blemish or defect of character. He was a perfect man. Yohannan could hardly take it in.

Yeshua waded out through the current to him. His expression was solemn and set.

Yohannan waited in confusion.

"It was not mine to reveal." Yeshua said, answering his unspoken question. "I know you understand. My revelation had to come according to my Father's timing."

He stepped toward Yohannan readied for his immersion to bind his people's sins to himself.

"What are you doing?" Yohannan stammered seeing Yeshua's intent.

"No." He shook his head, and backed up several fearful steps. "You have nothing of which to repent! You should be baptizing me! I am not worthy to do such a thing."

Yeshua approached Yohannan and touched his arm encouragingly, "It must be done this way for me to fulfill all righteousness. You don't want all of your good work to go to waste now, do you?"

Yohannan slightly shook his head, but his hands were frozen on the water's surface. Yeshua reached out to take Yohannan's reluctant hands lifting them to his shoulders.

Face to face, he said, "Yohannan ben Zechariah, you are God's chosen priest of the line of Aaron and Zadok. Do what the Father has purposed for you to do and consecrate God's chosen lamb."

Yohannan blinked, then slowly moved his hands to Yeshua's head. He watched wordlessly as Yeshua sank of his own accord into the depths of the water. When his dark curls were completely immersed Yohannan released him, waiting expectantly for Yeshua to splash back to the surface as people always did. But, the waters remained closed over Yeshua's head as it lay claim to him. Only then did Yohannan notice they had move further into the depths of the river. The currents swirled around him.

Buried beneath the water, Yeshua had stepped off the ledge of the rock hidden under the water. Losing his footing, he felt as if he was suddenly swallowed to an unfathomable depth. The sins of the people rushed violently upon him, one after another in rapid succession. They seemed to press him downward. In his airless vault, he heard muffled voices begging, sobbing, keening, a cacophony calling out for deliverance.

"God help me! Save me! Rescue me! You are all I have! My only hope. Save me from the miry pit. Rescue me from this evil. Save me from this body of death."

He was overcome by the people's pain and suffering, their desolation and confusion. His lungs burned with the threat of suffocation. In the dark depths, he experienced their blindness, deafness, and their mute inability to cry out. Feeling helpless, he blundered about to right himself searching for the glimmer of light that would lead him back to the surface.

The Voice spoke within him. "Yeshua, this is the misery of our people. Can you hear them crying out because of their oppression? They are drowning in their sins. Their sins are cruel captors. Do you feel our people's hopelessness, their helplessness, and their suffering? You are my essence sent to rescue them from the hand of the devil and to bring them up out of this miry pit into a good and spacious land."

Yes, Father. I feel their need. Lead me, I will rescue them. Your will be done.

He found his footing and burst up through the surface of the water. Gasping to take in air, he flung the water from his head in an arc. At that moment, the clouds parted to drench him in a brilliant ray of white light. The crown of a multicolored rainbow appeared within the light shining upon his head.

Yohannan could hardly take in what his eyes were seeing. He felt the rush of a refreshing wind. He saw what appeared like a snow-white dove coming down from within the rays of the light. It came to rest upon Yeshua's dripping head, landing perfectly within the circle of the rainbow.

The beauty of what he was witnessing held Yohannan spellbound. Only later had he understood, that Yeshua was being anointed and entrusted to fulfill the covenant of God's peace with his people. The rainbow had been given as a sacred sign to remind Noah of God's salvation. The sky rumbled heavily, ending in a lengthy and resounding boom. All the people looked anxiously into the sky.

Only two understood the words the thunder spoke. The Voice said, "You are my beloved Son. In you, I delight. I am well pleased."

Only two people saw the Holy Spirit descending from on high in the form of a dove to alight on Yeshua's head, melting into him and becoming one with him.

Yeshua felt the warmth of his Father's perfect and holy love envelop him. He had often longed to hear these words of affirmation and blessing from his Father's lips. He was 'the Son of God'.

Yohannan watched Yeshua stride from the water.

He bent down to refasten his sandals. He picked up his staff, and he hung his outer robe over his arm. He looked for all the world like a young god. His eyes shone and his damp curls sparkled with a coronet of light.

Yohannan felt the force of what had just happened. He sank to his knees in the waters. He realized, Yeshua had just received the full anointing of the Holy Spirit of God. He has received his Father's seal and approval.

The long-awaited Messiah is here! Today God's light has pierced the darkness just as the LORD has promised.

He watched while Yeshua strolled away into the wilderness. Others turned to see what held the Baptizer's attention. In wonder, he thought, 'I have known him all my life, yet I did not recognize him. Mysterious are the ways of God!'

In ecstasy, Yohannan began to laugh and clap his hands, breaking spontaneously into the song of praise written by Isaiah hundreds of years before.

'They will see the glory of the Lord, the splendor of our God. Strengthen the feeble hands, steady the knees that give way; say to those with fearful hearts: Be strong, do not fear; your God will come to save you. Then will the eyes of the blind be opened and the ears of the deaf unstopped. Then will the lame leap like a deer, and the mute tongue shout for joy. Water will gush forth in the wilderness and streams in the desert. Those the Lord has rescued will return. They will enter Zion with singing; everlasting joy will crown their heads. Gladness and joy will overtake them, and sorrow and sighing will flee away.'

So contagious was Yohannan's singing and rejoicing that all the people were compelled to join him in his euphoria, singing hardily with him. They did not know what had made Yohannan so ecstatic, or why their hearts were suddenly lifted up in such a powerful worship. But everyone experienced an overflowing sense of joy.

~ 13 ~

THE DESERT

Blessed is the one who perseveres under trial because,
having stood the test, that person
will receive the crown of life.
James 1:12

Yeshua walked away from the Jordan River caught up in his own state of euphoria filled with the presence of the Holy Spirit. His resolve in the face of his people's cries for help and pleas to be saved had left his emotions tumbling one over another.

Where previously Yeshua had felt his individuality and his freedom to choose, now he felt the weight of both the previous and the new covenant between God and humanity. They lay like a heavy mantle upon his shoulders. Death had taunted him under the water as if it were offering a preview of what was to come. The sins and captivity of the people were more terrifying than he had ever imagined. He deeply felt their predicament and burden. All of this he was experiencing along with the power of the truth and clarity of the Holy Spirit and overwhelming euphoria.

Now, with his covenant made there was no turning back. Hadn't he told his mother, that he was 'The Promise'? And this new covenant had greatly pleased his Father, of that much he was sure. It was too much to process. He needed time to think and to be with his Father.

Urgently he headed away from the people desiring solitude. The Holy Spirit led him into prayer as he always did whenever Yeshua felt he was out of his depth.

"Father, give me the wisdom to discern the spirits. Let your Spirit and your words forever lead me, remain alive and active in me. I know I will encounter enemies along the way, help me to overcome their schemes. Give me success so I may fulfill all of your promises. Let your hand rest upon the son of your right hand, the son of man which you have raised up for yourself. Show me your way, Father, in your faithfulness give me an undivided heart, that I may fear your name."

As he walked and prayed he was unaware of where he was going. When he finally looked up, he was surprised to find himself in a barren wilderness. A steep and rugged landscape stretched before him. He looked back, searching for the path. He saw nothing but rocks and inclines that seemed to go on for miles.

Fear jolted him until he realized, he was exactly where his Father had led him. He had brought no food or drink, no provision of any kind. Nothing but the clothes on his back. This was a wild and untamed place, a place of predators. He turned in a circle unsure of how he'd arrived here or which way to go to return.

He thought of Moses when he had led the Israelites out into the barren wilderness to a mountain. After ascending the mountain, Moses had been instructed by the LORD for 40 days and nights, without food or drink. How strange it was to find himself here in the wilderness. Was he to remain for instruction?

He tried to find his way back. But, after a time, he recognized that he had only walked in a big circle. The sun was deeply slanted, descending in the west. He looked eastward to see his own lonely shadow, remarkably large and surreal.

Have I come here to meet myself?

He looked around the glowing blood red terrain for a place to settle in for the coming night. He found the overhang of a large rock. It offered a small shelter. He checked the interior and found it empty. He lay down his staff. He wrapped his cloak around him and sat down, feeling suddenly exhausted, small, and vulnerable.

The sun disappeared in a blink, its warmth was gone. The gray twilight turned to darkness. He had no light and no fire. When it finally appeared, the moon was little more than a sharp sickle of light. His stomach gnawed. He wondered when had he last ate. The night grew cool. Yeshua shivered and pulled his cloak tight. He drew his legs up to his chest to reserve his body heat. He could hear wild dogs howling in the distance, then a terrifying silence.

He tried to sleep, only, his mind would not stop grinding over and over the events of the day and his present situation. He tossed and twisted, uncomfortable finding only a stone for his head. He remembered Jacob sleeping with a rock as his pillow on the run from his brother. He had dreamt of angels ascending and descending a ladder into heaven, and at the top of the ladder had stood the LORD to make him an offer too good to be true. He promised to bless Jacob, to multiply him, and to bless his descendants. He also promised to be with him on his journey, and in good time to return him safely to his father's promised land.

The memory made Yeshua smile. Of course, Jacob had recognized a good thing when he heard it. He had been quick to take him up on the offer. He immediately, set up the stone he had been sleeping on and pour oil over it in a spontaneous act of worship thereby acknowledging his agreement.

Now, in the dense darkness, with an abundance of distant stars visible in the canopy above, Yeshua felt himself a kindred spirit with Abram, Jacob, David, Moses, Elijah, and Daniel, and with every other servant of God who had found himself alone in the wilderness of this life. Even though he could not feel his Father's presence tonight, he knew his Father was with him.

As he reflected on this, he heard a slow gliding sound across the sand not that far away. He sat up to search for the source. Peering into the surrounding darkness, he could barely make out the form. That was when he heard the threatening hiss. Straining to adjust his sight, he could just make out the dark shadow of the coiled serpent. Its head wove back and forth menacingly. They sat staring at one another for some time.

Yeshua broke the silence, "I thought I felt your cold presence in this arid place."

"I wouldn't miss this. You are on my turf now. Just you with me as your only companion." The serpent replied in a singsong voice, darting suddenly toward him.

Yeshua asked. "Are you trying to frighten me?"

"You should fear me." Came a slow hiss.

Yeshua shifted his gaze up into the sky filled with dimensions both seen and unseen.

"Faith is being sure of what you cannot see." He said without looking at the serpent.

"You are mistaken, I am not alone."

He began to sing the ancient melody of the Ninety-First Psalm, sure that Satan would hate the song of praise to his Father.

'Whoever dwells in the shelter of the Most High will rest in the shadow of the Almighty. I will say of the Lord, He is my refuge and my fortress, my God, in whom I trust. Surely, the LORD will save you from the fowler's snare and from the deadly pestilence. He will cover you with his feathers, and under his wings you will find refuge; his faithfulness will be your shield and rampart.'

The serpent thrashed as if in misery.

"Stop!!" He shouted, trying to drown out the words. "You make an awful noise."

But, Yeshua continued singing the song of his ancestor—who had once been the lonely shepherd boy.

'You will not fear the terror of night, nor the arrow that flies by day, nor the pestilence that stalks in the darkness, nor the plague that destroys at midday. Though a thousand may fall at your side, ten thousand at your right hand, it will not come near you. You will only observe with your eyes and see the punishment of the wicked.'

Raising his voice loudly, the serpent shouted over his song, "Don't you know? The Exalted One sent me to you. Why else would you be here with me?"

Yeshua just kept singing.

Finally, when the creature could stand it no more, he fled into the darkness muttering to himself. "No matter! We have plenty of time to play games. Our time has just begun."

~ 14 ~

WHEN EVIL CROUCHES

"Watch and pray
so that you will not fall into temptation.
The spirit is willing, but the flesh is weak."
Matthew 26:41

The Tempter was back again. Day after day he came to Yeshua to cluck his tongue, to mock and bait him, to cast aspersions upon his faith, hoping to wear away Yeshua's resolve.

The Fallen One sent predators from the wild: a bear, a vulture, a jackal and a lion. But the creatures simply sat with Yeshua, as though recognizing his immense authority. The threat they were meant to arouse fell limp.

Satan disrupted his sleep at night, entering his dreams with terror. Yeshua tossed and fought his way back to consciousness.

At present, the serpent appeared to him in the guise of a beautiful woman perfect in form. She was dressed in shimmering white, a veiled perfection. The woman had the lovely appearance of Rachel who had lived in his village years before. Rachel's sweetness and beauty had made Yeshua long to stand under the nuptial canopy with her, to share a sacred bond, and to fill a home with children.

Marriage was an honorable covenant blessed by his Father. Enduring love was beautiful thing. But the words his Heavenly Father spoke to the young Jeremiah, urged him to refrain: *'You must not marry or have sons or daughters in this place.'*

Yeshua had understood this instruction was also meant for his life. So, Yeshua had remained far from Rebecca, avoiding her interested gaze. He stayed busy and prayed to will her from his mind, accepting his Heavenly Father's word to him. When her father approached Yosef with the proposal to make a contract between his daughter and Yeshua, Yeshua told Yosef that marriage was not his Father's will. Yosef had pressed him.

Yeshua had explained, "It would be the ultimate act of selfishness to take her as my wife and to bear children."

"I don't understand." Yosef had said.

"I would be like a man being ripped in two. She would become a stumbling block to me. No, of my need for celibacy, I am clear."

Yosef could see it pained Yeshua, so he took extra pangs to soften Yeshua's answer to her Father. Even so, Rachel never looked at Yeshua the same again. His answer had felt like rejection to her. There is no fury like a woman scorned. Her father betrothed her to another and the matter was closed.

Now, the woman walking towards him stirred his natural human longing to have a wife of his own. Yeshua felt the remorse once again that his refusal had caused Rachel any pain. The serpent whispered, tempting him.

"Hasn't your God commanded humanity to be fruitful and multiply. Her heart has always belonged to you."

But Yeshua saw beyond the veil, he glimpsed the seductive and haughty gleam in Rachel's eyes. He recognized the adulterous woman. Many men had stumbled and fallen under just such charms. He closed his eyes and prayed. When he opened his eyes she was gone.

Yeshua decided one night as he lay awake looking at the stars that this would be the way of the rest of his life, one temptation after another until his death. He would have to rely on all of the Scripture and his Father's Spirit that was within him, guiding him each step of the way. He would be surrounded by people: kings, priests, soldiers, friends, family, disciples or foes who would want to trick him, use him, or gain control over him. He must chart his own way in the strength of the Spirit. He could listen to no one but the Father, and he must constantly be on his guard.

After a good number of days had passed, the feeling of hunger left him, leaving a hallowed emptiness in its place. He prayed for the Holy Spirit to fill all of his empty spaces. His thoughts sharpened, even as his body weakened.

Satan was surprised at Yeshua's strength, but he still had tricks up his sleeve. Flesh was a traitor even in the best of the faithful. The voracious appetites and desires of these weak-willed humans forced them to thirst and hunger for things that become their downfall. It delighted him to prey upon them, while they frantically searched to fill their emptiness and cease their fears.

Just one slip was all he needed. He beat his dark wings in frustration, then repositioned them for his next ploy. This time he appeared in his fallen form, as a pathetic and horrifying creature stripped of all his former glory.

He made his appeal, playing upon his perceived weakness, "I know you are a man of compassion. This is why you will surely understand, I am just the lowly scapegoat of God. It is God that is forcing me to come against you. I am not really your enemy as you might believe. Rather, I want to be your friend. I know what it is like to be used by God, to be doubted, and lonely. It is a miserable lot to be forced to perform like a servant kept on a chain. Can't you see that I am just a victim, like you, I am forced to serve others. It is a miserable work."

His voice became soft and wistful, "I used to be a helper. I would like to help again. I am woefully misunderstood! Not really such a bad sort. Actually, I am rather pitiful! Shouldn't I deserve a second chance to prove myself trustworthy? If I were reinstated..." Satan drifted off, having chosen his words carefully, knowing that accusations and grumbling were a contagious disease. With enough negativity and constant grumbling others could be influenced to actually identify with the complainer's feelings and believe his words, allowing bitterness to seep into their hearts too.

"Haven't you ever wondered what you did to deserve this miserable task?" Satan asked him.

Yeshua gave no response. The old serpent hated him so much that he could taste his blood in his mouth. But he was not allowed to touch him, only tempt him.

Despite Satan's grumblings, the words of Ezekiel testified against the accuser. Yeshua began to speak the words out loud.

'This is what the Sovereign Lord says: You were the seal of perfection, full of wisdom and perfect in beauty. You were in Eden, the garden of God; every precious stone adorned you: carnelian, chrysolite and emerald, topaz, onyx and jasper, lapis lazuli, turquoise and beryl, denoted your high position.

Your settings and mountings were made of gold; on the day you were created they were prepared. You were anointed as a guardian cherub; for so I ordained you. You were on the holy mount of God; you walked among the fiery stones. You were blameless in your ways from the day you were created until wickedness was found in you. Through your widespread trade you became filled with violence, and you sinned.

So I drove you in disgrace from the mount of God, and I expelled you, guardian cherub from among the fiery stones. Your heart became proud on account of your beauty; and you corrupted your wisdom because of your splendor. So, I threw you to the earth; I made a spectacle of you before the rulers.

By your many sins and dishonest trade, you have desecrated your sanctuaries. Therefore, I made a fire come out from you, and that fire consumed you. I reduced you to ashes on the ground in the sight of all who were watching. All the nations who knew you, are appalled at you; for you have come to a horrible end and will be no more.'

"Ezekiel's lies." Satan shouted. "How dare you lay the crimes of mere men at my feet."

"The LORD does not lie." Yeshua replied. "Your day will come."

Yeshua reflected, prophecy was indeed a mysterious thing, speaking to the past, the present, and the future; and speaking to multiple persons at one time. But there was no doubt that Ezekiel had written those words to anyone under the power and influence of the Evil One.

Weeks flew past, and Satan had rather enjoyed playing his games with the Son of Man, but now the fortieth day was swiftly approaching, and still Yeshua remained faithful.

Satan felt his panic rising as his window of opportunity grew threateningly slim. In his physical state, Yeshua should have been easily defeated. Many holy men had fallen for much lesser things. Instead, the longer Yeshua fasted, the stronger the Spirit of Wisdom became within him.

Satan realized he had to act quickly.

~ 15 ~

TESTED AND TRUE

See, I have refined you, though not as silver;
I have tested you in the furnace of affliction.
For my own sake, ... I do this.
Isaiah 48:10-11

It had been well over a month since Yeshua had come to this barren wilderness. He had hollowed like one with a wasting disease. He stumbled dizzily when he stood, too weak to even walk. His throat was so parched that he could barely speak. His tongue clung like sand paper to the roof of his mouth. His eyes were sunken and his vision blurred, at times he saw double. He passed in and out of his days, not knowing if he was awake or dreaming. Was there really anyone there, or was he simply imagining it all? Was he going mad? His heart beat erratically in his chest as if his body was failing him. Death stalked him.

Mid-day, Yeshua panted like a deer longing for water, but the cool of the night provided no comfort for him. He shook, feeling the cold in his very bones. But worse was the dread of each new temptation to come. The landscape went nowhere, only one stone after another. They began to take on the appearance of loaves of bread to his starving eyes.

Noticing his desperate gaze, Lucifer drew near appearing as a dazzling angel of light sent to care for Yeshua and to bring him a message of reason.

"You must not waste away here in the wilderness. Your body will never be found. Obviously, your hunger has made you delusional and confused. You are not seeing things clearly." Satan said authoritatively.

Yeshua made no reply, his breath was rapid and reedy. He continued to stare out over the landscape.

Lucifer said, "Look, if you are the Son of God, just tell these stones to become bread. Why deprive yourself any longer of this one little thing that you so desperately need. You must keep yourself alive."

Satan knew historically hunger had caused people to do all manner of things. Some had even eaten their own children rather than perish. Starvation was a slow death, it didn't get much worse.

Yeshua covered his face with his trembling hands, searching within for the truth. He reasoned, 'I will survive this ordeal according to my Father's will. Obedience is my bread. Moses hungered forty days to receive the promises of God and he survived to an old age. As far as I know, forty days has not yet passed. Human appetites are like ravenous beasts. Even the desire for a particular kind of food has caused great downfall.'

Several examples came to mind. 'Didn't Esau lose his birthright because of his demanding appetite? And, Jacob used a bowl of savory stew to deceive his Father and to steal his blessings? Didn't Jael comfort Sisera with food and drink before lulling him to sleep so she could drive the tent peg through his head? And, of course for Eve, then Adam, temptation was the forbidden fruit.'

He resolved, 'I will fast until this spiritual battle is over, food cannot save me now. The power my Father gives me is not for my own desires, but for his will. My Father can provide for my physical need at any time. He can even raise me from the dead if necessary, but I must prove myself obedient. The moment I act by my own desires, the Spirit's power will disappear, or worse, turn against me. God only gives his power to those who trust his will.'

The words of Deuteronomy provided him counsel.

'*Remember how the Lord your God led you all the way in the wilderness these forty years, to humble and test you in order to know what was in your heart, whether or not you would keep his commands. He humbled you, causing you to hunger and then feeding you with manna. This was to teach you that man does not live by bread alone but by every word that comes from the mouth of the Lord. Know then in your heart that as a man disciplines his son, so the Lord your God is disciplining you. Observe the commands of the Lord your God, walking in obedience to him and revering him.*'

Yeshua uncovered his face and replied through cracked lips, "It is written: 'Man does not live on bread alone, but by every word that comes from the mouth of God.'"

The angel's façade crumbled, and his antagonism was laid bare. Then he spun around, unfurling his black and wicked looking wings.

Yeshua felt the earth falling away from beneath him, as he seemed to spiraled up through the air. Dizziness overtook him, so he closed his eyes. His feet landed heavily. It was all he could do to stand. Opening his eyes, he saw he was poised on the edge of a high wall. Looking around, he saw he was standing on the highest point of what had become known as Herod's temple. The courtyard lay below him on one side, while the Kidron Valley dipped precariously away on the other side.

He stood on the platform at the place of judgement, the pinnacle from which the Sanhedrin had previously cast condemned blasphemers to their death below in the Kidron ravine. To finish their execution, they hurled crushing stones down upon them. This was also the pinnacle from which the shofar sounded its warnings, and announced the holy sabbaths, the feasts, and the festivals of the Lord. From his vantage point above the temple courtyard, he saw people from every nation milling about. They were marveling at the grandeur of the edifice, but a sudden rumble under his feet forewarned of its ultimate instability.

Though heights did not normally bother him, Yeshua felt dizzy and weak. He swayed, struggling to steady himself. Below, he saw the high priest dressed in his decorated splendor, looking very pious indeed. The expectation of honor clung to him.

Yeshua wondered, 'How many priests have used my Father's house as their own pedestal of power? How many have exalted themselves before the people as if they were God, rather than God's servant?'

Under Roman rule, the high priest had to be approved by both the roman governor and Caesar Tiberius to keep the post of the religious leader of the Jewish people. He was expected to submit to Roman rule and pay the demanded tributes required by their oppressor, and make sure they upheld the pax of Roman. It was said, 'He serves at the pleasure of Satan himself.'

Satan made his logical appeal, "What better way to make yourself known or to advance to the throne than through the temple? If you are the Son of God, show the people who you are. Demonstrate your divinity, provide a miracle for them. Throw yourself down from here as proof. Doesn't the Scriptures say, 'He will command his angels concerning you, and they will lift you up in their hands, so you will not even strike your foot against a stone.'"

He offered a self-satisfied smile, having quoted from the same Psalm Yeshua had been singing on the first night of his testing. How fitting to come full circle. He was pleased to see Yeshua closely watching the priest. Religion was strongest temptation for righteous man. The sins of self-righteousness and self-exaltation came so easily to them along with the office.

Satan mused, 'Quoting scripture will trip them up every time. Especially, if it gives them what they desire. Surely, he will wish to prove himself before the priesthood! Humans are desperate to feel significant, always seeking to prove their worth to one another. They love to be esteemed and respected by their peers.'

Yeshua had caught the discordant notes within the tempters words, they sounded a warning within him. Wordplay was how Satan had seduced Eve. He thought, 'Beware a devil quoting scripture.' He shifted cautiously on the parapet, recalling the proverb: *'Pride goes before destruction, a haughty spirit before a fall.'*

He remembered, 'How often the pride of life and the need for approval, causes one to stumble and fall.'

He drew his cloak around his face, creating a space to reason. 'This is my Father's temple, where he alone is to be honored and glorified. From this humble threshing floor, my Father remains the true King among his people. And, *one* must never exalt oneself before a king.'

Yeshua sank to his knees, praying silently, 'Father, this is your kingdom, I am here to serve you. Didn't David wait twenty years after his anointing for you to recognize him as his anointed king? How could I do anything but wait upon you? You will make me known in your own way, and in your own time. I know who I am, that is enough.'

He opened his eyes to find the creature glaring at him with impatience. 'He knows who I am, or he would not have spent all this time tormenting me and trying to destroy me.'

Yeshua stood, his eyes stern. His brows furrowed with righteous indignation, he seemed to tower over his adversary.

"It is also written: Do not put the LORD your God to the test."

Surprise and fear flashed across the serpent's features. So, rarely had this ever happened to him. Job's victory presently came to mind. He was masterful in temptation. Surely, I can find an angle, a cause, some seemingly small infraction, or some sin with which to entrap him. What more can I offer him to cause him to sin?

Satan could feel the door of opportunity starting to close. He realized, 'There is only one more possibility, one more temptation he has not yet faced. I didn't want to go there. But it is all that is left. How ironic to offer the right to be a god, to God! Satan was fairly confident his last temptation would bring Yeshua to his knees before him.

With a snap of his fingers, the temple and the ledge disappeared.

The air changed. Yeshua found himself standing on the height of an icy precipice. The whole earth lay before him in the darkness below. The air was thin. It was the darkest moment, just before dawn. He felt as if the entire starry host watched him with breathless anticipation.

It took a moment for Yeshua to realize he stood on the top of Mount Hermon, the highest mountain in all of the land. Its snowy heights sourced the Sea of Galilee, the Jordan River, and the Dead Sea. Snow crunched below him; cold seeped up his sandaled feet and bared legs. He waited, shivering. His breath became a slow and frosty vapor before him. He wrapped his arms close.

Eventually, a dull light brightened the eastern horizon. The sky pinkened, casting a soft and misty light like a veil over the land. It looked other worldly, leaving the vague impression of a beautifully veiled woman.

In time, the air began to clear and the personified terrain revealed all her peaks and valleys. Israel had been metaphorically referenced as the wayward bride of God by the prophets. Sinai had sealed the marriage covenant with the LORD. Belonging to God, Israel became the constant desire of all the other nations. She had been blessed with every adornment and resource. Many of Israel's assets were obvious, but there were others still hidden in her unmined depths below. Israel was the most fought over property on earth, yet tiny among the other nations of the world.

The Mediterranean trade route wove like a silver ribbon through the green valleys below. To the south, lie the promise of newly budding trees, neatly laid vineyards, and freshly tilled fields, just beginning the procgression toward bearing summer fruits. There was a reason it was called 'The Promise Land'. The Mediterranean Sea spread out to the west like a rich aqua marine gown flowing away into lapis lazuli in its depths.

In the distance stood the City of Peace, Jerusalem. The Temple sat like a shining diadem upon her head. To the southwest lay the Negev, then the fertile valley of the Nile resplendent with its broad river and reeds. Was there ever a land so beautiful? His Father had promised Abraham that wherever his foot trod it would belong to his descendants.

Satan moved with a glide to his side, watching Yeshua take in the bedazzling sight. He inched closer still, until he whispered very quietly in Yeshua ear.

"All of this could be yours. Now. Without waiting, without suffering. You could rule it all." With a slight his serpent's tail, Yeshua began to see beyond Israel to every nation in the world. The beauty of all the nations were paraded before his eyes, each one colorful, rich, and exotic.

"Don't be foolish. You will never fulfill your calling. You cannot win against the odds. Just one little trespass and you are lost." Lucifer whispered. "It is a better this way. No battles. No suffering. Why deny yourself? It could be so easy. All of this, I will give you if you will only bow down and worship me."

Yeshua appreciated the dazzling landscapes, but distained the offer, 'Since the day of the fall, there has always been one man or another longing to rule over the earth out of selfish greed and ambition. The need to be exalted over other men is the greatest of temptations. With wealth and power, humans feel they have become invincible like God himself. Though, it is all a sham. With wealth and power they mistakenly believe they can satisfy every desire and have it all. And yet, to possess all of this, they forfeit the greatest and most satisfying treasure of all, their oneness with their Creator.'

He shifted his weight and adjusted his footing. 'How many have foolishly bowed before Satan in the guise of Baal, Marduk, Bel, Jupiter, Zeus, Apollos, Asherah, Ishtar, the Queen of Heaven, Aphrodite, Diana, whether on this mountain below or some other people willingly sacrifice to Satan everything that is precious, even their very souls. They cast their first-born infants into the fire to gain fame, power, and wealth. Behind them they leave a trail of oppression and heartache.'

He shook his head sadly. 'They know not what they do. Possessed by the beat of the drums, they drink potions that alter their minds; and they seek self-gratification. They break God's moral codes with temple prostitutes. They lash and mark their skin with knives and pierce themselves with needles making offerings of their blood to the gods of their desires, marking themselves with the images of their idols and oppressors who have profaned them. Their shame is permanently etched into their flesh marring their image.'

His thoughts turned to history. 'Time and again, Satan has raised up power-hungry men and women through which to rule the world. Cain, Lamech, Pharaoh, Sargon, Tiglath-Pileser, Ahab, Shalmaneser, Sennacherib, Nebuchadnezzar, Alexander, Antiochus Epiphanes, Cleopatra, the Caesars. They were nothing more than henchmen, slaves, puppets, pawns in Satan's war against God's reign.

In the end, every ruler comes to their own end, and are forced to lay down in death. From there, they will be called forth to stand before the supreme ruler, their Creator, to give a final account of their rule.'

Satan waited with baited breath, certain he had Yeshua this time. But then, Yeshua straightened with his final decision. 'The kingdom belongs to my Father alone.'

He turned and faced the beguiler, "Away from me, Satan! For it is written: Worship the Lord your God and serve him only."

At the command of his final word, his testing was ended. The serpent disappeared to nurse his failed attempts. Now, he would have to bide his time and wait for yet another opportune time.

Yeshua reeled weakly, finding himself standing on a ledge alone in the heat of the mid-day sun. He stumbled back to the shadow of his rock overhang and fell unconscious.

Angelic hosts rushed in like emergency medics from their stand-by positions, where they had been guarding him all along. They were relieved for Yeshua's testing to come to its end. It had been painful for them to watch. Now, they came swiftly to his side to lift him up into their arms. They began to minister to his greatly depleted body.

His parched lips were refreshed with a trickling coolness. 'Ah, water.' For some time, he fell in and out of a cottony consciousness. Whenever he was roused, he was surrounded by bright creatures, speaking in hushed and encouraging voices. Little sips at a time, spoons of a broth were given with healing herbs. Then, right back to sleep. They cleansed him, ointments were applied, his hair was washed and untangled, his nails were trimmed, his clothes were cleaned. They eventually fed him a tasty porridge, sweet with the taste of honey. He slept and slept, he was so very tired.

When his sedation lifted and his mind had cleared, he awoke to find two loaves of freshly baked bread with a comb of honey and a flask filled with refreshing water. The bread was sweet and tasted much like coriander. He ate. He looked around, but the creatures of light he did not find. He stood testing his strength and looking out from the shadow of his hovel. A clear path lay before him now, as if it had been there all the time.

With his strength renewed, he picked up the rest of the bread, and began a slow walk back to Yohannan's camp.

From his hidden realm, the Father proudly watched his Son leave the barren land behind.

"Yes! My Son has been tested and found true. No impurities have been found in him. He is a worthy warrior, donned with the Sword of the Spirit and my Word. He is ready to face any battle yet ahead."

~ 16 ~

COME AND SEE

"Say to Daughter Zion, 'See, your Savior comes!
See, his reward is with him,
and his recompense accompanies him.'"
Isaiah 62:11

When Yohannan saw Yeshua returning after so long a time, he called his two closest disciples Yohan and Andrew to him.

"Look, there he is, the one I told you about. He is the Lamb of God who takes away the sin of the world!"

"He is the one we have been waiting to see. He is the one who will supersede me, because he was before me. His ministry and work will be far greater than mine. I can't believe I did not know it was Yeshua. I did not know who this man would be, but I do know I was sent to baptize so this man might be revealed to Israel. He is that man!"

Yohannan's whole face was filled with wonder and excitement. Yohan and Andrew watched as the Baptizer ran to Yeshua. He was glad to see him given his disappearance without a word. Yohannan left his disciples at work, while he took Yeshua to his tent for rest and refreshment.

Yeshua's gaunt appearance told Yohannan that he had been through an ordeal.

"I am so glad to see you! I wondered, when you disappeared without a word what had happened to you. But I knew the Spirit of God was with you. Where did you go? Obviously, not Qumran. Word has been that they had not seen you there."

Yeshua shook his head with a tight smile, "I am not really sure where I was, though it appears it was not so far away. I was in such a state when I left. I guess I had to sort a few things out."

Yohannan nodded, not pressing the issue. He understood the importance of silence and solitude when it came to spiritual things. The LORD has his ways with his servants.

"You look the worse for wear. Stay here and rest in my tent. I will check in on you later."

Later, Yohannan gathered his disciples, who were equally anxious to meet the Messiah. He told them again of the vision he had seen when he had baptized Yeshua.

"He is the man upon whom I saw the Spirit come down from heaven as a dove to remain on him. I didn't know who he was until God revealed him to me. He appeared just as the One who sent me to baptize with water said he would. He told me, 'The man on whom you see the Spirit come down and remain is the one who will baptize with the Holy Spirit.' That day, I witnessed this very thing with my own two eyes! I can testify to you, this is God's Chosen One."

Yohannan's powerful testimony animated the camp with excitement. They understood, Yohannan was proclaiming Yeshua as the Messiah.

"If this is the LORD's anointed," Yohan whispered to Andrew, "who could be a better teacher in righteousness? We must align ourselves with him. This is what we have been waiting for. Now that the Messiah is revealed, we must get behind his efforts to usher in the kingdom of light."

Yohan added, "I have met this man and his family before at Passover. I think our mothers are related."

Andrew said. "Do you think he would consider taking us on as students? Maybe your family connection will give us a better chance."

"We better move quickly," Yohan said excitedly, "when everyone else finds out surely the others will flock to him. If you are not first..."

"...you could be the last." Andrew quipped.

Anxious to make his acquaintance, and make their request, the two men rose up early in the morning to wait by the river, hoping to be the first to approach Yeshua.

A little later in the morning, Yohannan saw Yeshua passing by on the rivers bank. He knew Yeshua wanted to get back to Nazareth. His sister's wedding was only a few weeks away. Yeshua stood on the bank, and touched his chest, giving Yohannan his nod of gratitude.

Spotting him, Yohannan guessed he was departing for Nazareth, he quickly motioned to Andrew and Yohan, who had been so excited the night before.

"There he is, the Lamb of God!" He mouthed to them pointing toward Yeshua.

The two ran after Yeshua not wanting to miss their opportunity to talk with him. When Yeshua heard them running up behind him, he turned and asked, "Can I do something for you?"

"Yes, we were wondering where are you staying?" Yohan asked anxiously.

Yeshua recognized their faces and not just from Yohannan's camp. Hadn't he seen them on the mountain? He saw their eagerness, and immediately understood their desires. He also noticed their youth, their strength, and their desire for adventure.

"Come and see." He extended his hand of invitation.

Andrew and Yohan looked surprised. "Now?"

"Yes, but of course I am planning to return to my home in Nazareth."

They looked at each other with surprise and confirmation.

"We would love that." They fell into step behind him, talking rapid fire. "We are from Bethsaida and we have been students of the Baptizer for a while."

Yohan added. "Rabbi, I believe our mothers are related. I remember in years past our families shared fellowship together in Jerusalem."

"Our families moved to Galilee from Jerusalem during the Essene persecution. Now we and our families are fishermen in Galilee. Though I am from Bethsaida, I spend most of my time in Capernaum working with my brother." Andrew said by way of introduction.

"We want you to teach us, Rabbi." Yohan ventured, "The Baptizer tells us you are the one we've been looking for."

Seeing their sincerity and boldness. Yeshua smiled. "Wonderful. Perhaps I should wait another day before we journey back to my home." He realized, the Father had begun calling men to him already. What better place than Yohannan's camp? Hadn't he even told Yohannan to prepare men for him? And, he would be glad for the company since his strength had not yet fully returned to him.

"In that case," Andrew said, "I will be right back. Yohan wait with the Rabbi, I will go get my brother."

"Simon would not want to miss meeting you." He shouted to Yeshua as he left to retrieve Simon up stream.

Andrew found Simon casting nets into the Jordan. "Simon, you won't believe this! Yohan and I have found the Messiah."

Simon shot him a skeptical smile.

"Oh yeah? How do you know he is the Messiah, is he wearing a crown?" He chuckled at his own joke.

"Yohannan told us he saw 'the sign'. The dove descended upon this man."

"Well, if the Baptizer saw a dove. But hasn't he been waiting for "the coming" for several years now?"

"Come and see him while he is here, Yohan and I are going with him tomorrow to his home."

Simon realized Andrew was completely serious. His brother really believed what Yohannan.

"Well, that is a bit sudden. Where is his home?"

"Nazareth."

"Nazareth? Andrew, really? The messiah?"

He was tempted to put his brother off since he was busy, but shouldn't he check out Andrew's messiah and see what kind of man his kid brother suddenly hitching his cart to. Yohannan was one thing, but what kind of eccentric might this guy be?

I should go, if only to expose the man's deception. Andrew should know the truth before he makes such a huge decision.'

Reluctantly, he drew in his small net and wiped off his hands. "Okay, let's go meet your messiah."

At first glance, Simon was not impressed with the man.

No great warrior here. The man is gaunt, maybe even anemic.

His sharp eyes raked over Yeshua critically, fierce like a hawks.

Yeshua read Simon's thoughts and understood his obvious attempt at intimidation. In what seemed like a swift flash of insight, Simon's future passed before Yeshua's mind's eye. He saw who Simon would become.

He smiled broadly.

"What's so funny?" Simon wanted to know.

"You are Simon ben Jonah. I will call you Rock."

Simon's craggy brows drew together warily, full of questions and surprise.

"Do we know each other?"

"Not yet but we will."

Simon wondered, 'What kind of man nickname's you at your introduction? Andrew must have told him of our Father.'

But Andrew appeared as surprised as Simon at Yeshua's words. Simon gave him a second assessing look, trying figure out his game. He took over the conversation, peppering Yeshua with challenging and direct questions, eager to blow the charade. Yeshua was apparently unconcerned by Simon's questions. He answered them just

as directly as Simon asked them. Although Simon professed himself a no-nonsense man. He claimed he had little time for studies
or ideologies like Andrew, but Yeshua could see he was far more
knowledgeable than he let on. Better yet, Yeshua sensed a passion
within Simon that was just waiting to be kindled. Andrew adored
his big brother, that was obvious. Both he and Yohan deferred to
Simon, listening when he spoke. Despite Simon's brusque personality, there was something tremendously likable about him. Yeshua
felt an affection for him immediately. He discovered Simon ran
a fairly successful fishing business in Capernaum. Andrew worked
with him, as did Yohan and his brother James.

When Simon stood to leave, he stretched and flexed his rather
muscular arms nonchalantly, apparently more relaxed.

Yeshua was nonchalant, "Glad you stopped by Rock."

Simon lifted his hands, "Sure. But just so you know, I'm not
looking for a teacher like these two philosophers. I have a business
and a family to get back too. I have no time to have my head in the
clouds. Still, Andrew is a grown man, I won't stop him."

"Yohan mentioned you might be heading back to Capernaum
tomorrow."

"Yes, that is my plan."

"Could we catch a ride to the other side with you?"

"Sure." He shrugged. "Why not?"

*This will give me another chance to check out this new 'Rabbi', since
Andrew is convinced he is the Anointed One.'*

He took note, the Rabbi had mentioned none of that.

Yeshua was elated. With little effort he had gained two followers.
His Father's plan for him was already underway. He remembered
he had seen Philip was in camp from Qumran delivering some food
supplies. He went looking for him. If he were choosing his own re-
cruits, Philip would certainly be one of them. He was an agreeable
man, even tempered, diligent to his work, with a devoted heart.
Philip responded well to God's authority, and asked intelligent and

important questions. He also had a heart towards evangelism and was quick to help others. Why not add him to his number?

Finding him, Yeshua could see Philip had heard the news.

"So, Yohannan has told us the news. It was you all along." Philip said when he saw him. "How did we miss that?"

Yeshua smiled and shrugged, "It wasn't time for it to be made known. But now it is. Philip, come and follow me. I am starting my mission. Yohan and Andrew are coming with me. Come and join us."

Having heard the Baptizer's messianic endorsement, Philip was thrilled at Yeshua's invitation. "Of course, I am in." Philip responded as if his decision had been made long ago.

Though he had not previously known who the Messiah was, Philip had always believed Yeshua was a very holy man. He was happy to accept his invitation on the spot. He remembered how Yeshua's words hit home every time in a way no one else's did. Why had he not recognized him? He was also acquainted with Andrew and Yohan, as well as Simon.

"Can you wait for me to go and get my friend Nathaniel? He will surely want to meet you." Philip asked Yeshua.

"Nathaniel? Yes, of course, I will wait." Yeshua nodded, seeing how quickly his Father's plan was falling into place.

Philip went to find his friend Nathaniel, who was a studious expert in the law of Moses. Most devout, Nathaniel excelled in the law and the prophets. Like Philip, Nathaniel was anxiously waiting for the coming Messiah. Philip liked him because he was scripturally knowledgeable and therefore very cautious in his judgements. He knew he would want to be on board.

Philip dangled the one carrot before Nathaniel that he knew would grab his attention: "We have found the One that Moses and the prophets wrote about. He is Yeshua of Nazareth, the son of Yosef."

Nathaniel lifted a skeptical brow, "Can anything good come out of that armpit of Nazareth?"

But Philip was persuasive, extending the same invitation that Yeshua had offered him earlier, "Come and see."

When Nathaniel came to him, Yeshua stepped forward to greet him with recognition lighting his face.

He said, "Ah, here is an Israelite who tells it like it is! There is no pretense in him!"

Nathaniel bristled with skepticism. "How do you know me?"

Yeshua said, "I saw you when you were under the fig tree right before Philip called out to you."

Awed, Nathaniel thought, 'There is no way he could know this, unless he has divine sight.'

He turned pink around his ears, remembering his critical words to Philip about Nazareth. But when he saw no defensiveness in Yeshua, only a genuine interest, he relaxed.

The fact that Yeshua had witnessed his private worship and prayers was enough to convince Nathaniel that Yeshua was indeed more than the prophet Philip had suggested. All of Nathaniel's skepticism was defeated.

Filled with wonder, he declared, "You are the Son of God, the expected Messiah of the Jewish people." He had no idea that now he was actually prophesying. His words seemed to surprise even him.

Philip slapped him on the back with a broad smile, as if to say, "See!'

"For believing that", Yeshua promised him, "You will see even greater things. You will see angels ascending and descending to do the will of God."

That was all Nathaniel needed to hear, nothing could keep him from following Yeshua now.

A day later, Yeshua and this four men climbed into Simon's boat. He set his course for the northern Galilee shore. Each man was excited for where this new adventure might lead them. Landing in Magdala, they prepared for the final leg of their journey.

Yeshua turned toward Simon, who was carefully rewrapping his ropes and preparing to sail on to Capernaum.

"Rock!" Yeshua called him by his new name.

Simon paused to look up from his work.

Yeshua touched his chest in gratitude. "You have been most helpful. Thank you for the crossing. I look forward to seeing you again soon."

Simon nodded, then watched Yeshua turn to go. The others trailed behind. Yeshua's words echoed oddly in his ear. Simon, felt a strange tug at his heart. He realized, he wanted to follow too. He couldn't help feeling a pang of jealousy for Andrew's new adventure. He shook his head in bewilderment, 'What is wrong with you? You are not a carefree kid. You cannot go running off on an adventure. You have a kid of your own, a wife, and responsibilities. Deborah will have your hide for being gone so long as it is now.'

Simon turned his boat back to the waves to head at home, but not without a second glance to watch them go.

~ 17 ~

CHANGED

When the set time had fully come, God sent his Son,
born of a woman, born under the law,
to redeem those under the law,
that we might receive adoption to become children of God.
Galatians 4:4-5

Miriam was frantic, Yeshua had been gone for over six weeks! She feared something had happened to him. Night after night, day after day, she prayed for his safety and his well-being. What else could she do? Yeshua had always been dependable, but she remembered how he had been gone longer than expected when he had gone on his prayer retreat. God had spoken to him and he had returned changed. Thereafter, he had immediately set on his journey to Qumran. Now, she could only hope that he would return to her once more as he did then. Inwardly, she feared what new change might come with him when he did.

When Yeshua finally returned, she had ran with relief to embrace him, so glad he had returned alive. But Miriam hardly recognized her son. His appearance had undergone another metamorphous. He had become surprisingly lean. His face had lost is softness, now it's plains seemed chiseled with determination, his cheeks were hollowed, his features were now more sharp and defined, his eyes seemed all seeing.

She couldn't help but stare at him with the shock of it.

Is that flecks of gray in his beard and at his temples?

"What happened to you? Have you been sick?" She asked searching his face.

She was so concerned by his appearance that she hardly took notice of the young men with him.

"Ah Ima, you are glad to see me." He smiled tiredly, trying to make light of it.

Despite his attempt at humor, Miriam could knew another metamorphosis had taken place. One which she could not approve.

He hugged her again, kissing her forehead.

"I am here now and I am fine."

Her look refuted him.

He took her face in his hands and said, "I am sorry I was delayed, but you need not make too much of it."

He was putting her off, and not giving her a real answer; intuitively she knew he had been something bad. But, she knew she would get nowhere with it. So she asked instead, "How was Yohannan?"

"Good. He sends his love to you."

"And tell me what you are doing with these young men?" She asked, looking at them for the first time. "Who are they? You will turn Hannah's head, by bringing them to our home."

Yeshua laughed. "Hannah will be fine, she is far too concerned about her upcoming wedding to pay them any mind." He assured her, then called forward each of the four men to introduce them.

"Have these men been with you all along?"

"Actually no, just a few days. But it would seem that Yohan and James are your cousin Salome's sons." Miriam looked around at the men searchingly.

"Salome?"

Yohan stepped forward and nodded. "Yes, I remember you from Jerusalem."

Miriam searched his face, seeing the resemblance.

"How are your mom and dad?"

"I guess they are alright. I haven't been home in a while." Yohan said. "I have been working with Yohannan."

"They took up following me a few days ago from Yohannan's camp, where he has been training them."

"There is water at the gate, if you wish to wash up before eating." She directed them all before returning to her task of kneading bread into loaves for their meal.

When Yeshua returned looking tired, she asked, "Are you really not going to tell me what happened to you?"

"Ima, I was led to take another retreat. It lasted longer than anticipated."

"Oh, my goodness, alone? I thought you were only going for a week's stay. Why did you retreat so long?"

"There was some unfinished business that drew it out. But see I am fine."

"I beg to differ. You should look in a mirror."

"It was business my Father wanted me to attend to. But your right it wasn't easy. bit you need not worry now." How could he explain the supernatural encounters he had experienced there? Or his fasting? Or the fact that he could not leave until his testing had ended. Such admissions would cause his mother unnecessary worry for his mental state of being.

Miriam wanted to berate him, but something made her hold back. She sensed the changes in Yeshua were far greater than the changes that had come before. His youthful persona had all but disappeared. The man who stood before her now emanated an authority, a solemn and holy gravitas, that breached no question or disrespect.

At the table, she stacked Yeshua's bowl as if she could fill out his frame overnight.

"James, how are your projects going?" Yeshua tried to make small talk.

"They are fine." He said tersely not meeting his brothers eye. He was clearly upset that Yeshua had brought four strangers into their already crowded home and added the pressure of unexpected hospitality. Stabbing into his stew, he thought, 'All I need is five extra mouths to feed.'

Long after the sun had set, the men talked around the fire about all that Yohannan was accomplishing, the growth of the movement around Galilee, and the ongoing conflict between the Sicarii and the Romans. It proved to be an informative evening.

Yohan offered, "I have heard that Antipas' wife Phasaelis has fled in fear to her Father in Nabataea with revenge in her eyes since Antipas has returned with Herodias. I also heard that Caiaphas was the officiant of the vows taken between them. It is unclear if either one was even officially divorced. But Caesar does what he pleases, why not his appointed leaders?"

"Can you believe it?" Nathaniel fumed. "This is the influence of Rome. The Herodians practice absolutely no discretion! They take and do whatever they want, caring nothing for the law of our people. They are pagans! Why are we surprised?"

"Meanwhile," Andrew added, "the Roman troops have been called in to hold the Nabatean border, while Antipas frolics with Herodias at his palace in Samaria. Apparently, Rome is not taking the impact of his indiscretions well. You know what happened to Archelaus!"

"Let's not get too excited, if they exile Antipas, you never know who may move in to take his place." Philip warned them. "Changes seem to be only for the worse, rather than better."

"Can they get any worse?" Nathanael asked.

"I have heard they can get worse." Philip mused.

Hannah hovered near Yeshua, listening to these political happenings that she did not understand. She was disappointed to share her big brother with these men. It was selfish she knew, but her opportunity of time with him was quickly disappearing. Even so, fascinated, she was glad to be allowed to listen in on the conversation rather than sent away like a child. Yeshua had never talked politics. But now he was listening intently to what the men were saying. She, too, sensed a drastic change in him. His focus had shifted outward towards the happenings of the nation, and she sensed to something more infinite.

"I have missed you terribly these past few years." She whispered to him, her disappointment evident. "Now my time with you will be so very short."

He looked at her sadly. "Yes, and I am really sorry about that. I really did not leave with that intent. But, it seems we are both being swept up by the winds of change."

"Yeshua, I am nervous about being married. What if Zerah is not pleased with me? Or I don't like him?"

Seeing her fears, Yeshua leaned toward her, "Let's take a walk tomorrow so we will have time to talk about this privately."

His suggestion pleased and assured her that she would get some of the private time she longed for. When it had grown late, she rose to go inside and Yeshua stood to embrace her. She held on to him longer than necessary, sharing her possessiveness.

"I have missed you, why did you stay away so long?"

"We will talk tomorrow, little one."

The next day, they took their walk. Hannah did not wait to revisited her parting question.

"Why did you stay away so long?"

"I was unexpectantly detained, I couldn't make it back." Yeshua explained. "When I left, I really thought I would only be away for a week, maybe two, but my Heavenly Father had other plans for me."

Beyond feeling piqued, Hannah realized that Yeshua was the only one she knew who referred to Yahweh as 'my Heavenly Father'. He had done it as long as she could remember. The sentiment had always caused her to love Yahweh all the more and to think of him as 'Father', as well. She realized for the first time that no one else but Yeshua called Yahweh by such a familiar name. Why would Yahweh withhold her brother from her in her need.

"I'm sorry for disappointing you, that was never my intention. I really thought I would be gone only a week." He stopped to look her in the eye.

"More and more my life is becoming no longer my own."

She looked at him oddly.

He explained, "My life is changing. The time has come that I must be about my Father's business."

"But you told James you did not want to take charge of the business." She pressed him.

Yeshua shook his head. "I don't."

She processed this, "You don't mean Abbas business, but Yahweh's business?"

"Yes. My Heavenly Father wants me to make the way for our people to enter his kingdom."

She raised her eyebrows in question.

"You will begin to hear things that may cause you terrible concern about me. My work will be difficult. You should know now that in the end some very hard and painful things will come upon me."

"What are you talking about? You are frightening me."

"You are not to fret, no matter what happens. Trust that everything is going exactly as it must, even when it seems you have reason to doubt and grieve. Especially then."

Hannah searched his face. Yeshua seemed oddly at peace with his words. She, eventually, gave a slow nod, even though his warning sounded ominous to her ears. Hannah was not privy to her brother's beginnings. Still, it was obvious to her that Yeshua was different from anyone else she knew.

"I have just one question."

"What is it?" Yeshua waited.

"Why do you call Yahweh 'Father'?"

"Because he is my Father." He said, matter-of-fact. Her expression was uncomprehending.

"What do you mean? Isn't saying such things blasphemy?"

"Not if it is the truth. It is just what it sounds like, I am Yahweh's Son."

"But, Abba ..."

"Abba claimed me as his son. I am his son. But I am not from his flesh, I was conceived in Ima by the Holy Spirit."

Hannah looked shocked, "How do you know this?"

"I just do. Talk with Ima about this, she will tell you. You are old enough to know the truth. You have been with me all this time."

"But Abba..."

"....raised me with Ima. They were God's chosen parents. Abba was Ima's chosen husband."

Hannah's filed through her personal memories of the past to search the things she had heard, seen, and not understood.

"Then you are, what? The Anointed One?" Her eyes widened and her words drifted away.

He nodded, glad that she had so readily seen it. Her mouth made a small 'o'.

"How come I didn't know? Is this a secret?"

"It has been a secret up until now, but this secret will now be made known. It is a secret that is already being told. Even so, there will be many who will never believe this to be true. You must decide like everyone else. Do you believe I am who I say I am?"

She gave a little shake of her head in her confusion, "Maybe. This is a lot to take in."

"I suppose it is. But, Hannah have I ever lied to you?"

She thought back over the years, "No, never that I can remember, but clearly up to now you have not told me everything. "

"Well then, let your thoughts start there."

~ 18 ~

A PROPHET'S RECEPTION

He came to that which was his own,
but his own did not receive him.
Yet to all who did receive him,
to those who believed in his name,
he gave the right to become children of God.
John 1:11-12

On Sabbath, Yeshua, his men, and his family went to the synagogue. After three years of absence, he found the meeting place un-
changed. While growing up, this synagogue had been his personal
refuge. The scrolls stored here had been his friends and vehicle
of self-discovery, opening for him his first understandings to his
true self.

After years of being away, some of the people of Nazareth
welcomed him back warmly. Others still viewed him and his family
through jaundiced eyes. Miriam and Yosef had never made a defense for themselves. They had long ago agreed that the origins
of Yeshua's birth must be kept secret for his safety, even at their
personal expense. Secrets are rarely a good thing. But in this case,
it had been necessary.

Rabbi Esli having seen Yeshua's devotion, admired the young
man despite the questions surrounding his parentage. He took him

at face value. He welcomed him back to the synagogue, happy to see his star student returned to Nazareth.

"Yeshua ben Yosef! I am so glad you have returned. I hope it will be for good. I could use your help with our older boys preparing for bar mitzvah this year, if you are willing? They ask too many precocious and difficult questions!" The Rabbi said, his brows arched hopefully.

Yeshua greeted his childhood teacher with an embrace. "Thank you for the kind offer. I would love to. I am afraid, I will not be remaining in Nazareth long enough to take the post. I have plans elsewhere. But I could offer some instruction while I am here."

"I was afraid you might say that." The old teacher said, "We have lost you to higher aspirations, but we will take what we can get. Speaking of that, perhaps, you could give the teaching today. Yes?"

Yeshua nodded. "For you? Of course, but aren't you already prepared?"

"I would rather hear your words." The old Rabbi said. That morning the Rabbi had brought out the gifted scroll Yeshua had brought him from Qumran on his last visit. Rabbi Esli called Yeshua to stand before the table. Giving a scant introduction to the congregation, he announced the reading for the day and handed the scroll to Yeshua.

Yeshua took the scroll and lifted it to his forehead with reverence and a prayer. Then he unrolled the scroll to the sixty-first writing of Isaiah. He noticed the text was a Messianic prophecy, and he felt in his spirit that this reading had been preordained for him to read on this day, in this very place.

Today in his home town his ministry would actually begin. It made sense. Why wouldn't he begin his mission here? Yeshua felt a rush of excitement. This prophetic declaration spelled out his Messianic mission to save his Father's people. He looked up searching faces to gage if the people were ready to receive the truth. If not now, then when?

He began to speak the passage to them: "The Spirit of the Lord is on me..." The way he said it commanded every eye to look at him. His voice resonated with the deepness of his personal conviction. "...because he has anointed me to proclaim good news to the poor."

He looked from one familiar face to another, noting the collective sharp intake of breath. His voice rose, full of authority, "He has sent me to proclaim freedom for the prisoners."

He waited for the people to absorb what he was saying before he went on.

"And, recovery of sight for the blind, to set the oppressed free, and to proclaim to you the year of the Lord's favor."

The eyes and ears of the assembly were fixed on Yeshua, waiting to hear what he would say next. He rolled the scroll closed, and handed it back to Rabbi Esli. He stepped from behind the table to take 'the seat of Moses'.

The people of Nazareth had no idea of the greatness of who now sat before them. This moment had been many generations in the making. Here was 'the Prophet' Moses had promised would come, 'the greater one'.

Yeshua made a bold declaration. "Today this scripture is fulfilled in your hearing."

Awe, like a charged current, shot through the crowd. Whispers broke the anticipatory silence. They understood what he was saying. "He was the One sent from God." The room became charged with emotions of joy, shock, denial, and disbelief. The voices began as whispers, and rose.

"Is he saying he is the Messiah?"

"I don't know. It sure sounds like it."

"Can it be?"

"That is Yeshua, back from his studies. He is most devout and knowledgeable!"

They leaned forward to hear what he had to share concerning these gracious words which he had just spoken. Others, however, were remembering his auspicious beginnings.

The skeptics whispered, "Wait, isn't this Yosef's son?"

Some of the elders said with an accusing eye, "He is too young to speak with such authority!"

"How can he say such things? He didn't even study in Jerusalem."

Yeshua looked around the room at all of the familiar faces of his childhood. Taking in their mutinous remarks, he felt the pang of disappointment.

Why am I surprised? These are the same people they have always been. Their hearts are as hard and cold as a stone.

He realized his audience would not receive his message to repent. But just as his Father had previously promised the people of this land, Yeshua would now speak the uncomfortable truth to them. It was the only way for them to realize their need for change and turn back to God. How else could they enter the kingdom? Prophets set the record straight, and he was sitting in the seat of Moses.

"Surely you will quote this proverb to me: 'Physician, heal yourself!'"

Half of the people nodded their agreement at his statement. He stood, walking towards them.

"And, you would demand proof of what I say, some sign of legitimacy."

Their eyebrows rose in expectation offering more nods.

He paused to consider his next words before he continued. "It is a sad truth that you will not believe me. But then, no prophet is accepted in his hometown."

He knew how great his people's hatred was for anyone they considered unclean or unacceptable. He knew how they maligned the surrounding Gentiles. He also knew how soiled was the reputation of all Nazarenes to all other Jewish circles. Yet, they thought they were so much better than the people who surrounded them; simply by the virtue of being 'a Jew'. His Father had commanded the Jewish people to be a light and example to all the other nations. How miserably they had failed at this.

Their ears were itching to hear the words from his lips, 'Come, join with me and let's annihilate the Gentiles.'

Yeshua returned to the seat of Moses. "Let us agree on this point, there were many widows in Israel in Elijah's time, when the sky was shut for three and a half years and there was a severe famine throughout the land. Yet, the prophet Elijah was not sent by God to any of them. Instead, God sent him to a widow in Zarephath in the region of Sidon, the region of the Gentiles."

The room responded with a sharp and collective gasp of outrage amongst the people.

He continued, "Also, if you remember, there were many in Israel with leprosy during the time of Elisha the prophet. Yet, not one of them was cleansed, only Naaman the Syrian who was also Gentile."

This was not the expected words of a Messiah! The jaws of the people dropped open sputtering with shock and indignation.

"He provokes us!" A Pharisee shouted.

"He is insulting us!" Shouted another. His words felt like salt in their wounds! Stinging and harsh. Some became so furious that they got to their feet shaking their fists and piercing him with their eyes.

The lead Pharisee said, "We can't allow him to get away with such disrespect! Who does he think he is?"

Rabbi Esli stood in shock; his mouth working wordlessly. He held out his hands in apology to the angry people.

A group of men came quickly forward to surround and take hold of Yeshua and push him toward the door. Once outside, the whole congregation spilled out behind them to watch or join the leaders in their agitation. The mob became even more angry, gnashing their teeth.

"Take him to the cliff of retribution!" The leader shouted.

The mob drove him out toward the rise beyond the town, planning to push him off the cliff to his death below. Their faces were contorted with an ugly rage.

Spittle spewed from their shouting mouths. "He has blasphemed the LORD!"

Reaching the overlook, Yeshua was reminded of standing on the pinnacles of his desert temptations. He was comforted that he did not die then; he would not die now. He became calm in the midst of their assault. Serene, he stood on the ledge looking out toward the valley below. He thought of the many of historic conflicts that had been fought in this very valley below. Peering into the future, he envisioned the final battle to come when he would end all conflict.

Like a demonic horde the mob pushed together as one, a driven stampede. The men who had taken him by force arrived to the cliff, only to be pressed precariously toward the edge right along with him. They strained to keep their footing. Fear gripped them that they might actually plummet to their death instead of the man standing calmly beside them. A shove caused one of the leader's feet to slip. He had begun to fall, when a strong arm reached out to retrieve him. Those on the edge started to push back and a scuffle took place.

A loud voice sounded, commanding them. "Be still! Come to your senses!"

An amazed hush settled over the people.

For some moments, they stood pressed tightly together on the ledge clinging to one another; unwilling to finish their goal for fear they too would fall.

Yeshua turned from the overlook to look into the eyes each person trapped in his close proximity. He didn't say a word. He didn't have to. They could read his thoughts. They pressed away from him, giving him his quarter.

This, is why Elijah had not come to the people of Israel. Pride, heedless human pride. It is God's own people who have historically taken the greatest offense at God's words of warning, though he would only wish to save them. Turning away from his words, they refuse to agree with God.

Yeshua looked at each man. They cast their eyes to the ground before his stare. He began to make his way through the crowd, everyone moved from his way, no one put out a hand out to stop him. When he broke free from the crowd, Hannah ran to take hold of his hand. Miriam solemnly trailed behind trying to calm herself and understand what had just happened. Behind her were all of Yeshua's frightened and angry brothers. Even his new followers behind at a distance exchanging traumatized glances. Everyone was silent, each one lost in a myriad of questions.

What just happened? Is this how it is going to be? Why was he so confrontative or his words so harsh? Why didn't he simply ask his village to support him and his leadership? If his own people don't support him, who will?

Yeshua had shocked them all.

His four followers said to one another, "Yeshua is more like Yohannan than Yohannan, himself." This was to be the first of many revelations for them. However, the one thing that had impressed them the most was, his calmness. It was as if he had no fear.

"He is more than the Messiah we had expected. He is more bold, more fearless, more righteous, more filled with authority than we could have ever predicted." They agreed. They could not guess what the future would bring; but, they were sure that Yeshua would inaugerate a new world order.

Once they arrived home, his mother and brothers could not contain their upset. Yeshua had confronted the whole village. What could they say to their neighbors? They had seen the fury and malice in the people's eyes. They were still shaken.

"What were you thinking?" James shouted at Yeshua as soon as they entered the courtyard. "Do you have some weird death wish? Why are you are bringing trouble upon our whole family."

"Did I not speak the truth?"

"Who made you the proclaimer of truth? Your truth! This was certainly not what the people wanted to hear from you. Even if you were not delusional, what kind of Messiah would build his kingdom by making everyone furious? Even Rabbi Esli was shocked by your audacity and you've been his favorite for years."

"Only God's truth can change people's hearts, not supporting people's prideful hatred of one another. The kingdom of heaven is built from within by submission to God's will."

"You come home and proceed to pass judgement on us all. You don't even live here anymore, Yeshua! But we do! These are our neighbors. What about us? Do you presume to judge us also?"

"It seems to me it is their judgement you are worried about. I am not judging anyone. My words are a warning. When you hear the truth, you must judge your own behavior by it. How can you rightly judge yourself, if you refuse to hear the truth? Shouldn't everyone examine the way they judge others? What does the Scripture say? 'To walk humbly and love mercy'."

"Yes, it is so easy for you! You think you are so very perfect! But now you have brought trouble on us all." James said bitterly. "Who knows what will happen next. It is best that you take your zealot friends and leave before you bring the ill will of this town down upon our heads."

The new disciples looked at one another uncomfortably finding themselves being blamed and caught up in the name calling as well.

James turned and stormed away.

Seeing James's anger and Yeshua's conviction, Miriam went quietly to Yeshua when everyone had settled. She spoke softly, "For once, James is right. This is Hannah's last week before we leave for the wedding, things are already tense. Perhaps it would be good if you lay low for a while. The towns people were really angry."

Yeshua nodded, understanding the people's desire for vengeance had frightened her.

Hearing this, Yohan spoke up "Your mother could be right." Andrew said, "Come and stay with us in Capernaum. Galilee is filled with devout people waiting for the Messiah. And, we are eager to introduce you to our family and friends."

Yeshua nodded, then looked apologetically toward Hannah.

She came and threw her arms around him. "I don't want you to go. I am not afraid."

"And, I love you for that, but maybe it is for the best that I let things sit for now."

Yeshua gave his sister a squeeze of affection. "Remember our conversation."

"I will."

"I will meet up with you in Cana, well before your ceremony."

~ 19 ~

THE HEALER

...for I am the Lord, who heals you.
Exodus 15:26

The next morning Miriam prepared a filling porridge. If Yeshua and his friends were leaving, she would send them off full. As she stirred the pot, she prayed for him. This new version of Yeshua frightened her, but what could she do? She must put him in God's hands now. He returned from his prayer time just as his followers were awakening to the delicious smell. She filled each bowl with a porridge, yogurt, honey, figs and nuts.

After breakfast, the men made ready to leave for Capernaum. Miriam stopped them, holding up her finger as if she just remembered, "Wait, before you go." An excited and secretive grin spread across her features.

She hurried inside to bring out a basket filled with the gift of new clothes she had made for Yeshua. She sat the basket before him, beaming, "For you! Your clothes are getting thread bare."

She removed the lid to bring out first some simple clothing lovingly made, simple tunics, and a new cloak dyed in the brownish red that was signature to Galilee. Reaching deeper, she pulled free the new robe she had pains-takingly made for him for the wedding. They were not a wealthy family, so hand woven clothes were a special gift of time, skill, and love. When Miriam held up the robe, Yeshua was taken aback by its beauty.

"Ima, you are confused. I am not the bridegroom!" He laughed, thinking the robe far too fine. But, seeing her happiness, her resisted his protest.

"Look!" He exclaimed fingering the many stitches of love she had sewn into it. The robe was a white wool tightly woven, and embroidered with almond blossoms and pomegranates on the sleeves and the collar. She beamed excitedly while he took the time to trace her handiwork with his fingers.

"This is too extravagant."

"Nonsense." She gave him a happy grin. "You are the head of our family."

"These pomegranates are like the capitals on the temple."

Miriam leaned her head to look with him. "Yes. And the almond branch and lilies."

She gazed earnestly into his face to let him know the symbols were of him.

"Look." She pointed out. "On one side of the robe I embroidered the name Jachin and on this side Boaz. The words are hidden among the vines and lilies. It means..."

"It means 'He will establish' and 'in Him is strength.'"

She nodded satisfied that he understood. "You will take Yosef's place as the head of our family. I want you to look distinguished and handsome. Here is your girdle to wear in the place of your belt." She offered the piece to him in her opened palms. I embroidered Yosef's tribal insignias on it. The lion of Judah for his tribe and a lamb for the town of Bethlehem. Miriam had embroidered them resting together.

She smiled looking at them, "It reminds me of when I made your swaddling clothes, I embroidered these same symbols."

He took the belt, examining her artistry.

"Exquisite, work. Thank you Ima, this is quite some gift."

Miriam was not finished, she reached within the basket to bring out a long finely woven linen wrap. "And, here is a turban for your head."

"Ima, I have never worn a turban in my life, they are for rich men who put on airs!" He smiled at it, unsure what to even do with it.

"Yeshua, just for this one day let me show you off." She pleaded. "You will look as resplendent as Solomon himself. Please, try it on for me! Let me see how it looks."

Though it was a request, he was not fooled. She would not take no for an answer. Yeshua gave an awkward chuckle, while his men watched him trying not to laugh. Their expressions told him he might as well go along with her, they had mothers too. His fingers touched the patterns carefully as he disappeared within. He had never owned anything so elegant. Material things meant little to him, but this was a gift from the heart. His mother's happiness touched him deeply. He changed into the wedding clothes.

When he reappeared, Miriam's breath caught and joyful tears welled up in her eyes. "You look so regal, so important, and handsome." Her lips quivered with emotion. Embarrassed, her hand flew up to cover them.

Yeshua laughed, "No one has ever told me that before!"

"But it is true!"

In his finery, he looked like a prince or a priest. Miriam's hand left her mouth to cover her heart. She thought, 'My son is beautiful. He is. He really does look like a bridegroom.'

"Doesn't he look beautiful?" She asked his men, embarrassing even them.

He held up the turban, "I don't know what to do with this."

Miriam made him sit so she could wrap it into place. It took her a few tries to remember how Zechariah had wrapped his long ago. "Later, you can use it as a scarf, or a prayer shawl."

"Don't you think this is a bit too much?" He asked touching the turban. But his onlookers shook their head, enjoying his obvious self-consciousness.

"Now make sure you bring your young men to the wedding too." Miriam urged him, as he started back inside to change for his travel. "It is not every day that we get to celebrate such a happy occasion."

She began to sing a bit of 'The Song' to herself, "'*Look at King Solomon wearing a crown, the crown with which his mother crowned him on the day of his wedding, the day his heart rejoiced.*'"

Yeshua turned to watch her, laughing at her happiness. He stepped forward and took her hand to whirled her around in a circle, singing the song with her.

"*How beautiful you are, my darling! Oh, how beautiful! Your eyes behind your veil are like doves. And, your hair is like a flock of dappled goats.*" His eyes went wide and he goosed her. Both of them burst into laughter at their silly display.

Their audience laughed at their merry making. Even James was forced to offer a tepid smile, shaking his head at their nonsense, although he did feel a bit jealous that Miriam had gone to such lengths to dress his brother in such an ornamented robe.

Arriving to Capernaum, Yeshua and his men went with Andrew to Simon's home. Andrew often lodged there, and he was quick to offer his brother's hospitality.

At Andrew's knock, Deborah opened the door just enough to talk, her expression distraught. "Andrew..."

"Deborah, what's wrong?" Andrew asked him, confused by her greeting.

"It's my Ima. She is very sick with fever. I am afraid for her and for us all. You know about the mysterious illness that has befallen many in Capernaum, and well, people have actually died."

"Oh no! What about you and Simon?" Andrew asked with concern.

"We are fine so far. But Ima is bad off. Simon is out fishing and trying to stay well. We don't need him to catch it."

"We were going to stay with you, but..." Deborah peered out at the others.

"Sorry. That's not a good idea."

Yeshua spoke up. "May I see your Ima?"

She looked at him perplexed. "I'm sorry, who are you?"

Yeshua smiled at her encouragingly.

She looked to Andrew.

"Perhaps Simon told you about our new Rabbi, Yeshua from Nazareth who we are following now."

"Why would you want to see her and endanger yourself?" She asked the teacher.

"Maybe, there is something I can do."

"Are you a healer?"

"We shall see."

She shrugged with exhaustion, desperation written on her face. "If you wish, but I am not responsible if you fall ill."

Andrew assured her, "He is the One that we have been waiting for."

She stepped back to look him over, seeing nothing impressive except the compassion in his eyes.

"Come." She led him into the inner chamber to her mother's mattress. Yeshua leaned over the poor unconscious woman, taking in the seriousness of her condition.

He stooped over her and spoke authoritatively to the illness. "Leave her!"

Deborah and his men looked at one another surprised by his command. Abigail stirred.

After a moment, she blinked her eyes open. She looked around in confusion. "What's happening? What is the matter?"

She turned to look Yeshua's way. For a moment, he appeared like an angel swathed in light. She shook her head, or was it the play of light shining through the doorway.

"Who are you?" She asked in a low whisper. "Have you come for me?" She reached toward him to take his hand. Remembering her sickness, her hands flew up to her head, throat, and chest. She was trying to understand how it was that she could breathe easily and felt fine now.

Seeing all the others standing in her room, she asked, "Am I alive? How can this be?"

Now, she looked more closely at the man beside her. "How...?"

"Ima, you have been very sick and I thought I would lose you. But look, Andrew's healer has made you well." Deborah explained.

"Healer?" She sat up to peer at Yeshua's face. He was the one. She beamed, "You?"

He smiled at her recognition. "I am Yeshua, Andrew's guest."

She took his hands into hers and squinted through thankful tears. "Thank you. You must be the man Simon has told us about." Seeing Andrew and the men behind them, Abigail moved to sit up.

"You are our guest? Then, I imagine you must be very hungry."

She rose up from her mat. She threw on her outer garment and hustled toward their food storage. "I must prepare for your supper."

"Ima, this man just healed you." Her daughter said as if she could still hardly believe it. "Are you really ready to cook? How can that be?"

"Yes. He really did heal me! I feel fine now. So yes, I am able to cook for him. I am so grateful." She said to him.

"But, I need a few ingredients to make a special dinner of thanksgiving for him. I will be right back." Abigail made herself presentable and scurried out to get some tasty herbs, oil, and a few ingredients. She saw her friend at the market. She couldn't believe Abigail's miraculous recovery. She had just heard that morning how badly Abigail was doing. Abigail could not resist telling her what had happened.

"Deborah told me I was as good as dead, and it was true. But now, here I am good as new." She spun around light of foot. "It is as if I were never sick at all, and now I am even able to cook." She whispered as if her secret would be kept between just the two of them. She did not consider that ten more people would hear of her miraculous recovery as soon as she left.

"Andrew brought a holy man to our house just in time. He healed me, just like that!" She snapped her fingers. "It is nothing less than a miracle. Andrew believes this man is the Messiah that everyone has been waiting for. After such a miraculous healing, I believe he is right. Since he is our guest, I am going to cook a special dinner in honor of him tonight."

Her friend was electrified by her testimony. Abigail rushed off, neglecting to tell her friend to keep this news to herself. Later, after preparing the meal, they sat down to eat. Abigail prayed the blessing, giving thanks to God for the food, of course; but more importantly for God having sent his Healer to her and to the people of Israel. Abigail lifted her head and smiled at Yeshua across their meager table. Reaching out to him, she squeezed his hand.

"I never dreamed I would live to see this day. But now I have! I was so sick, I thought I was going to die. But you, the Anointed One of God, have healed me and saved me from death. Thank you. Now, eat and enjoy!"

While they were eating, the news of the miraculous healing spread like wild fire throughout the village, along with Andrew's testimony that he had found the Messiah. By the time the sun was preparing to set, people were lining up at Simon's home begging to be healed too.

Yeshua went out into the street to lay hands on each person to heal them. By his command, their diseases and demons left them, some with loud shrieks.

"You are the Son of God!" One of the demons shouted as if with the intent to sound the alarm in the dark underworld 'the Redeemer was on the move'.

"Silence!" He commanded the demons. "You may not announce my presence."

That evening, the people began to believe he was indeed the promised Savior.

~ 20 ~

THE BIG CATCH

"I will send for many fishermen," declares the Lord,
"and they will catch them."
Jeremiah 16:16

After days of healing, preaching, and miracles, Yeshua prepared to go to Cana for the wedding week about to begin. He went down to the sea where his men had just come in from a frustrating night of work. Their boats were empty.

Simon was disgruntled as he waded ashore, securing his boat and preparing to clean his empty nets. He groused, "I have never had such a fruitless night!"

Andrew jumped over the side of the boat, splashing his way to Yeshua. "No luck today." He shook his head. "And Simon is in a sour mood."

James and Yohan came ashore behind them looking equally discouraged.

"I came out to meet you, since I am planning to leave for Cana today. You are all invited to come with me."

They hung their heads and kicked at the pebbles on the shore.

"We really need to bring in some income. But last night set us back. Perhaps we could come later in the week, in time for the wedding."

Disappointment filled Yeshua's face. He turned as if to go, but found himself face to face with a growing and expectant crowd.

He scratched his head and looked back toward the men. "Looks like I am not leaving quite yet."

As the crowd gathered, Yeshua began to teach about God's kingdom. The people were spellbound. They pressed close around him so they could hear all of his words. In time, more people came, filling the shore. Eventually he found himself pressed back into the water, while even more people came.

"I can't hear you!" A voice shouted from the rear quarter.

Yeshua looked around taking in his situation. He waded over to Simon's boat still moored at the edge of the water.

"May I?" Yeshua motioned towards the boat where Simon sat, still cleaning his nets.

Simon shrugged with a bit of reluctant. "Sure."

"Can you push us out a little ways from the shore?"

Simon thought, 'What is it with this guy? He has commandeered my boat twice now.'

But not wanting to be rude before the whole watching village Simon stood up and pushed out a ways from the shore. The watery surface began to amplify Yeshua's voice. He nodded his thanks to Simon. Simon took a seat and went back to his work.

Simon mumbled to himself with the realization, "Great! Now I'm trapped until he is finished."

Yeshua glanced back at Simon letting him know he had heard him.

Simon sighed ruefully, weighted with exhaustion and frustration.

Isn't it enough that Andrew regaled me with nothing but stories of this man all night long? It was like it was all he could think about. It appears this Rabbi is creating quite a stir.

He looked up to be totally amazed by the number of people filling the shore to hear this Rabbi teach. He paused to take note of the people's faces. They were fascinated, lending evidence to this new Rabbi's effect.

Andrew had said it was a lot of people I had no idea it was this many. Even Deborah and her Ima, in the few moments I've seen them, talk of nothing else but Yeshua. Suddenly he is everybody's hero. Meanwhile, I'm out on the lake fishing, cleaning, and trying to sell my fish to support my family. I haven't witnessed any of it.

Simon looked at Yeshua and noticed he was sitting a little too comfortably at the helm of his boat. Pushing away his frustration he looked down to continue working on his nets, forcing himself to focus on what the teacher was saying. After all, the whole town had come down to the shore to hear him with the expression of hope on their faces. The younger men, who often looked to Simon for advice were now looking expectantly to Yeshua, as if overnight he had become a father to them. This surprised Simon, he wasn't sure the man had even cleared the age of thirty. And yet, he acted like one much older.

"Repent, for the kingdom of heaven has come near!" Yeshua had begun his message.

Well that sounded familiar. The Baptizer begins all his sermons like this. Is he just another Yohannan?

Simon had been around the purification movement with Andrew long enough to guess what was coming next. He picked at his net, examining it to hide his reaction. It wasn't like he could argue with the words; he knew he needed to change his life. He had always excused himself, saying, *'I'm just a man. I try. Isn't that all we can do?'*

He sighed again thinking, 'I need to get out of here.'

He was held captive. Listening with one ear, Simon began to make a list of his many sins and faults in his head. Well he knew of his selfishness, crassness, cynicism and jaundiced eye. He had a short fuse; he was too controlling, too driven, too ambitious, and occasionally, a greedy cheat. He could stretch the truth, or out right lie and complain with the best of them. He was prideful, strong-willed, bent toward bitterness, and unforgiving when someone did him wrong. He could get a little mouthy, even aggressive when someone pushed him, especially if he was in his cup. And, even though Deborah was far more than he deserved, his eyes wandered like they had a mind of their own. His guilt pressed heavily upon him as he listened to Yeshua's message. The noise in his head was a cacophony of his personal faults.

'Uh-h-h!' Simon groaned under his breath in disgust.

Desperately, he wanted to run away from this conflict within. Yet, another part of him wanted to be caught, changed, and secured. Every since he'd met Yeshua, it seemed like a battle between two men had begun inside him. Today, sitting at Yeshua's back, he felt like his sins were being held up to a light for everyone in the village to see.

Simon moved on to wrestle another knot, caught up in his guilty thoughts as if he were a fish caught in the net. He was finally pulled from the depths of his deliberations when he heard Yeshua calling him by his new nick name, apparently for the second time.

"Rock!"

'Why does he call me that?' Simon wondered, 'I am not a stablizing or unmovable force. I wish I was dependable like an anchor, or a refuge for others in the changing tides of our times, but I am not. Sometimes I am the problem.' The revelation of this new desire surprised him.

Simon threw the net down and lifted his head to give Yeshua his attention.

"What?"

"The sermon is over."

Simon looked around surprised to see the people were dispersing.

Yeshua was watching him with a hint of amusement around his lips as if at some private joke. But he squelched his smile to peer pointedly towards the skies.

"It is a beautiful day, Rock! How about we take the boat out into the deep waters? I'd like to try my hand at fishing."

Simon snorted and shook his head. "No way. I am tired. I have been out all night. There is only one thing I want to do now. Besides, I thought you were on your way to Cana today?"

Yeshua, looked up to the sky, then, out toward the waves. "It looks like the winds are changing and so are the currents. Sometimes you just have to go with the flow and seize the moment."

Thinking the man was greatly mistaken, Simon looked out at the waters on the lake, only to see that Yeshua was right. He wondered, 'What is going on out there? The winds and currents had changed.'

Reminded of Ima Abigail's miraculous healing, he thought, 'How can I refuse this guy? I owe him.'

With the low bear-like growl Simon shook his head, bent down to lift the huge rock he used as his anchor. Noticing again the weight and dependability of the rock, he plunked it heavily into the center of the bottom of his boat, feeling its stabilizing effect. He neatly placed his rope around it.

Yeshua rewarded him with a beaming smile.

Simon couldn't help but grin back. "Where would you like to go Preacher?"

Yeshua pointed to the far side and Simon hoisted his sail.

On shore, his brother Andrew and the other men scratched their heads. "What is the Teacher doing now?"

Yeshua got comfortable. Reclining in the back corner, he propped his feet on a length of the bench. It was a lovely and temperate day. He luxuriated in the warmth of the sun, surrounded by the breeze coming off the cool crystalline waters. He drew a satisfied breath. The clouds were fluffy and few. They contrasted perfectly against the azure blue of the sky. Their soft reflections raced by on the top of the waters. A light breeze filled the sails tugging them on their way.

Once out into the deep, Yeshua leaned his head over the side of the boat, peering into sparkling depths, watching the light glimmer in the recesses below. 'This is good.' He thought, reaching down to let his hand skim the waters. It was indeed a moment of pleasure, but pleasure was not the only reason they were here.

Simon watched his bed and the Capernaum shore shrink into the distance. Surprisingly, a weight fell away with it. Rarely was he on the lake mid-day. It felt impulsive, like a kid playing hooky from his responsibilities out on a lark. He chuckled.

"What makes you laugh?" Yeshua asked.

"Oh!" He shook his head, "This was not how I expected my day to go."

Yeshua's expression questioned him.

"I mean, out for a sail with you. It is unexpected, that's all."

He cut his eyes to look Yeshua up and down, wondering, 'What does one say to a holy man? Do we have anything in common?'

Simons perusal was not lost on Yeshua. Nonchalantly Yeshua asked from his side of the boat, "So tell me Rock, do you like fishing?"

Simon shrugged, "A man has to do something to support himself and his family. It pays the bills. Well, sometimes, unlike today."

His eyes squinted at the sky with a mild grimace.

As if mildly curious, Yeshua asked, "But isn't there more to fishing than that?"

"Well, yes." Simon admitted. "I provide food for my village. People depend on me to eat. It gives me a sense of purpose. And, I like being out with Andrew and the other guys. They are my friends and partners, even if they can be knuckleheads."

He moved forward to loosen the sail just a bit.

He sat back again. "I like the thrill of the chase, securing a good haul. I can be pretty good at reading the signs of where to find fish."

He stared toward the shoreline. "But when it comes up empty, like last night, not so much."

He looked at his rough hands. "I know it is dirty work. My wife complains that I smell like fish no matter how hard I scrub." Then he chuckled, "But I tell her, 'It is the smell of money.'"

"Plus," He motioned toward his torso, "I like the physical labor of it. It keeps me fit. And Deborah doesn't mind that so much."

He offered Yeshua a sly look. "So, yes, I guess I like fishing."

Yeshua nodded his understanding. "It is a respectable labor."

"Anything else?" Yeshua asked as he glanced back into the water.

Simon shrugged, "Well, I mostly like being my own boss and running my own show."

"I can see that." Yeshua looked back to Simon. "You have always been your own man."

Simon wondered at the way he said that.

"What about you?" Simon asked. "Do you like being a ... Messiah?"

Yeshua coughed a little laugh at Simon's words of challenge.

"I like physical work also. I like to build things. It is satisfying to me to create beautiful works of art, things that function well, things that serve people. My Abba was a carpenter. I worked with him. Recently, my Heavenly Father, has put it in my mind to build something a bit different. But I think knowing how to fish could be very valuable skill as well."

This raised more questions in Simon felt comfortable to ask. Instead, he called out, "Stay low, we are coming about."

The boat bounced and the waves lapped at the side of the boat as Simon began to turn the rudder and loosened the boom. The boat lumbered for a moment on the waves, then he shoved the sail toward the other side. Yeshua ducked as the boom swung over his head. The wind grabbed the sail, pushing them on their way once again. Simon tied off the sail with a simple knot. The boat began to go faster, skipping across the waves.

With the return underway, Yeshua pointed, "Rock, swing to your left as we approach the shore. I will show you where to let down your nets."

Simon shook his head, jutting out his jaw stubbornly. Yeshua was going too far.

"No, man. I am telling you the fish are not running; we are well into the day."

Now he thinks he is the experienced fisherman?

They rode the waves in a peaceful silence. But as they made their approach, Simon could feel Yeshua's insistent gaze resting upon him. His eyebrows remained knit together in stubborn refusal.

He looked up again. Yeshua was still watching him. He shook his head stubbornly and he struggled to look away. But when he looked back a third time, Simon understood Yeshua was not asking him, he was telling him what to do. Simon's face twisted with annoyance, but his defiance soon deflated. He felt compelled to do as he said.

"Okay, I'm going to do what you ask, if only to show you I am right. But if we let the nets down, you must promise to help me haul the nets back in and help clean them when we get back, because I'm done."

He shifted the boat smoothly toward the place, pushing a heavy thatch of hair out of his face.

Yeshua nodded, "Agreed. See, I am wearing my old clothes today."

He thought, 'Fishing is not so bad, in fact I am having a great time. But, this Fish here is a tough one, he doesn't give in easily.'

Coming to the spot, Yeshua helped to drop the net. Simon made a little half circle to position it in the water. Yeshua leaned over the edge watching the net sink into the depths. Then he gave a little whistle, hardly noticeable.

Simon mocked him, "Yeah, that should do the trick, Rabbi."

But, while the words were still on his lips, the whole boat lurched pulling to the left. Simon's unbelieving eyes shot toward Yeshua. Grabbing for a hand hold, Simon stared disbelievingly into the waters teeming with fish. He had *never* seen a catch like this one.

Yeshua laughed, clapping his hands.

Now Simon let out his own low whistle of appreciation, trying to take it in. He and Yeshua began to pull on the nets, but the load was too heavy; there were too many fish.

Looking up, he gaged the distance to shore, Simon bared his teeth and gave a loud sharp whistle. Andrew, James, and Yohan looked up from their work to see Simon waving wildly in their direction. They jumped into their boat and shoved off to come quickly. Together they were able to lifted the haul, making their boats so full it seemed as if they might sink. Fish were flopping everywhere.

It was while the boats were lumbering toward shore that the truth of what just happened struck Simon. He realized he had grossly underestimated the man in his boat. Perhaps he was younger than himself, granted he was had the respect of being called "Teacher" and "Prophet", and no one could argue, that there was something both incredible and authoritative about this man; but that was the least of who he was.

Yeshua 'whistled' for the fish and they obeyed him. Only One Person can do that.

A dread fell over Simon like a weighted net making his legs feel too weak to stand. One word came to mind. *'God. The Holy Spirit and power of God was upon him.'* Simon clearly recognized the undeniable signs of Yeshua's anointing and divinity. Yeshua was the Holy One of God, the Messiah, just as Yohannan had said. Simon sank to his knees right there amongst the flopping fish, shaking with a reverent fear. Tears coursed down his sun-tanned cheeks.

What is this man doing in my boat? I am unworthy.

The tug on his heart overpowered him. It was a pull too strong for him to resist. Just like the fish captured in his boat, Simon heard his master's whistle. Simon had never been a follower, but he knew with certainty that this was what Yeshua wanted from him.

Simon cried out bitterly. "Go away from me, Lord; I am a sinful man! I am not the kind of man you are looking for."

"How do know what kind of man I am looking for?"

"But... Why would you want me? I am a horrible, stubborn, pig-headed man."

Yeshua planted his hand solidly on Simon's shoulder laying claim to him.

"I know." They stared at one another. Without any exchange of words, Simon felt Yeshua's acceptance. His winsome grin told Simon all he needed to know.

"Don't be afraid Rock; you will still be fishing and doing all the things you love to do, with all the people you know and love. From now on you will be fishing for men with me. Come and follow me."

Simon's eyes were intense and solemn under his fierce eyebrows. He nodded, then roughly he swiped at his eyes with the back of his arm. He didn't know how he could possibly do it, but he surrendered anyway. He felt suddenly vulnerable. Looking at Yeshua, he desperately wanted to measure up to Yeshua's ideal for him.

When they came ashore, Andrew came to help pull Simon's boat ashore. He noticed Simon's uncommon silence, his humbled demeanor, and his red eyes. He understood that something of significance had transpired out there on the lake between Simon and Yeshua.

Seeing Yeshua's joyful expression, Andrew laughed and hauled his big brother into his arms, pounding his back joyfully. "Welcome to our band of brothers."

Simon nodded, sniffing. He wiped at his nose and glancing timidly from his brother then back to Yeshua, too humbled to make his normally sarcastic response.

Yeshua told them, "Let us get these fish sold and off to market. We have a wedding to attend and Rock will be joining us."

James spoke up. "Well if Simon is going, Your not leaving me behind!"

Yeshua threw his arm around James' shoulder and said, "Of course, I just assumed you were coming too!"

Looking back, years later, Simon realized that was the day he stopped being his own man. From that day forward, the guys all called him Rock. Only on occasions of humbled rebuke or disappointment did Yeshua ever call him Simon again. Rock hauled his boat up on shore along beside James and Yohan's boat. They emptied their boats of the fish, and loaded them off to sell to the local market, leaving a plentiful provision behind for their families.

Simon went into the lake that day to be immersed into a new life. He scrubbed the fish away with Deborah's strong soap. Then, he kissed his wife, daughter, and mother-in-law. His departure felt bittersweet to Deborah. Seeing Simon's excitement, she wondered if she was losing her husband or if Simon was finally found.

Rock left following Yeshua, unsure of where he was going, where he would stay, what he would eat, or when he would return. Yeshua was in charge. He did not know a journey of a lifetime had just begun. Nor did he have any idea where his journey would ultimately lead him. He just knew he was happy to be going with the Yeshua.

~ 21 ~

A NEW HOME

My Father's house has many rooms;
have I not told you that I am going there
to prepare a place for you?
And if I go and prepare a place for you,
I will come back and take you to be with me
that you also may be where I am.
John 14:2-3

Yeshua arrived to Cana to find several tents readied around Zerah's home to accommodate visiting family and guests. Yeshua's disciples stayed in the men's tent. A new addition had been added to the side of Matthias' home for Zerah and Hannah. It had its own private outdoor space and a wedding canopy had been resurrected in front of the doorway. It was to be their private space where they would begin their family.

Yeshua had known Matthias and Zerah through Yosef's business dealings with Matthias. Both families felt this to be a suitable match for their children. The week-long celebration prior to the wedding was one of the ways families strengthened their bonds over the covenant of marriage.

Matthias greeted them, "Yeshua! The peace of the Lord be upon you! I am glad you have arrived early, so we can have time together before the other guests arrive for the evening festivities. We have a lot to catch up on. We are so excited to bring your dear Hannah into our home. I had such respect for your father Yosef, I am sorry he is not with us today. May he rest in the bosom of Abraham."

"I hope you don't mind that I have brought my students with me. I promise I will make them useful to you."

Matthias took in the six additional men. Graciously, he offered his welcome. "Yes, I have heard you are now teaching the way."

They spent the day in easy conversation. That evening a few guests arrived to share the meal and swap stories. Afterwards, Yeshua provided entertainment by treating the whole family to stories about famous marriages noted in scripture, leaving everyone to reflect on the meaning of this covenant, not only between a husband and wife, but also between God and his people.

Before retiring, Matthias approach Yeshua, "That was a wonderful night of storytelling. Your Abba Yosef would be proud. I wanted to ask you, I am hearing news of a young prophet in Galilee."

He looked at Yeshua closely waiting for his response. "You wouldn't know anything about this would you?"

Yeshua smiled and nodded, "You will likely hear more. It might be worth keeping your ear to the ground, but for now there is a wedding underfoot." He was determined that this sacred time be carved out for Hannah and Zerah and their wedding.

Matthias smiled and nodded his head also. "I will, I will, I do want to know more. Still, I agree with you. Let the children enjoy their wedding."

"Tomorrow we will go over the details of the marriage covenant Abba prepared with you and Zerah. We want all the promises to be fresh on Zerah's mind as he begins his new life with Hannah. Marriage is a sacred covenant to my Father."

"Of course. As it is to me and our family as well."

The next day, Yeshua read aloud the terms concerning the brides price, the expectation of monogamy, material provision, articles of faith and rituals, the requirements concerning anticipated children, resolution in the case of infertility, stipulations in case of divorce, agreeable disciplinary measures, etc. He took the time to interject important concepts to Zerah along the way.

Once the serious work was finished, they ratified the original agreement as it had been originally crafted. Then, Yeshua lightened the mood by sharing his favorite stories and details about his sister with the groom. Zerah took a ready interest in Hannah, asking plenty of questions along the way. His delight apparent.

Their morning ended with Yeshua saying, "If you will love Hannah with all your heart, Hannah will multiply your love in return and your whole family will be blessed. A good husband should be willing to do anything to preserve his bride, even lay down his life for her should it come to that."

That afternoon, the young men shared their funny stories and gave dire warnings.

"Don't expect Hannah to be the best of cooks! I ate burnt stew for a year and a half before my Sari learned to temper the flames."

"Don't believe for a second that you will be making all the decisions." Another added. All the men laughed, adding their agreement.

Another man said, "If you have married an intelligent woman, you will find that is not such a bad thing. She will be a great help to you. Women can see things that we men often miss."

"You will have to learn to live with her mother too." Simon added. "Mother-in-laws come with plenty of ideas of their own."

There was a round of moans and several spoke up to tell their mother-in-law stories. On and on the advice went, some purposefully meant to addle Zerah.

"Don't let the men terrify you," Yeshua whispered to Zerah. "They are just having a little fun at your expense. Watch them with their own wives and you will see the truth of their happiness." Yeshua chuckled and slapped Zerah on his back.

Zerah laughed with uncertainty. "Yes, they make me wonder what I am getting myself into."

Then he asked, "What about you? Don't you want a wife?" Yeshua gave an unconvincing chuckle before he grew serious. He got this question a lot. "In the worst of ways, Zerah. In the worst of ways. Someday..."

"What are you waiting for?"

"The bride I have my eye on is a little unruly. It might take some time."

Zerah was afraid to ask. "You must be a more patient man than me."

"Yes, patience is a great virtue."

The wine came out and the second night of feasting began. Later there was music and the men began their celebratory dances, a time of laugher and silly antics. Zerah quickly forgot his fears, and got caught up with the men in the celebration.

Meanwhile, Hannah was experiencing much the same in the women's tent. The mothers took turns talking with her. Jochebed shared with her Zerah's favorite meals, his temperament, his daily habits, his devotional attitudes, his good works in the community, his ability to work hard and to make good decisions. Miriam talked about women's purification rites, what to expect in the bedroom in the beginning, how to bring peace when tempers flared, and a few of her own excellent recipes. The other young maidens kept Hannah up late into the night, each one sharing their hopes and dreams for their future husbands. They, too, danced in friendship circles, shared stories, giggled and enjoyed delicious delicacies, feeling conspiratorially close.

The days and nights passed quickly. Then the day came for Hannah to enter the mikvah and to be anointed for her wedding. It felt all too imminent, too real. In the mikvah, the women gave her a special shampoo, smelling sweet like jasmine to use. She was immersed into the waters from head to toe, in a baptism of purification for her upcoming marriage.

Her mother spoke solemnly to her. "Hannah, today you are putting your childhood behind you. Your old life, and your childhood are washed away, forever gone. You become a new person to-day, you will receive a new life with your bridegroom. You become a wife. You enter your union with Zerah with a cleansed and pure heart."

When her purification was complete, Hannah came up out of the waters to be wrapped in soft white linens. Her mother anointed her face and shoulders with a sweet and spicy scented oil.

"Oh, Ima, this smells so beautiful."

"Yes," Miriam agreed. "It is a special and sacred scent. The oils will make your skin feel like silk. And whenever you smell it you will remember this your special day and the covenant you have made with your husband. Your body is consecrated to him alone. Like the temple unto the LORD, a holy vessel of new life."

Miriam paused, remembering how very different her own wedding had been to Yosef. When the angel had appeared to her to give her the incredible news, she was even younger than Hannah. There had been no special mikvah, or anointing of this sort. She had been anointed and consecrated by the Spirit of God instead.

I was giving birth when I was Hannah's age! I was so afraid when the birth pains began, so far from my Ima. She was not there to hold my hand. But Yosef was there for me. He was such a good man.

Tears escaped and ran quietly down her solemn face.

"Ima, what is wrong. Why are you crying?" Hannah asked concerned.

"Oh!" She said apologetically. "I am just remembering your Abba. Sometimes I miss him so much! Especially today. I wish he could be here to see you. He was such a good man, a wonderful husband. May Zerah be just as wonderful."

Hannah placed her hand on her mother's tenderly. "I'm sorry, Ima. I miss Abba too."

They shared a sad smile. Then going back to her task, Miriam began to silently pray over her daughter for every blessing with Zerah as she rubbed the perfumed oil onto her arms. She prayed for the family Hannah and Zerah would become and all that it would entail.

"You will make beautiful grandchildren for me to bounce on my knee." Miriam spoke confidently over her daughter.

"Ima!" Hannah blushed at the thought.

"It is nothing to be embarrassed about." Miriam said.

"The LORD has made women to be both delicate yet strong for this very reason. In your need, the Lord will never fail you or let you down." Hannah's friends began to brush out her long curly black hair, until it shined beautifully. It hung like a black curtain, waving over her creamy skin.

Then Miriam brought her the lovely white tunic she had toiled so lovingly over. The sleeves were embroidered with green grape vines and clusters of grapes, to bless her with fruitfulness. Her small form disappeared into the tunic of white, and a soft lavender robe was draped over it and secured with an embroidered belt. Finally, she placed and secured a delicately woven veil.

She was ready. Hannah could tell by the pleasant looks of all the women that they approved. "You look beautiful!!" They all cooed to Hannah.

Jochebed placed a kiss of blessing on her daughter-in-law's forehead, "My son will melt when he sees you. You have nothing to worry about. He will be a wonderful husband, gentle and loving like his Abba."

"And easy on the eyes." A bridesmaid added with an impish giggle.

That morning Zerah also entered the mikvah to be purified from his past and he was anointed as well. He wore his own new set of wedding clothes, readied to receive his bride. One of his friends played a happy tune on the flute and another played a stringed instrument to brighten Zerah's big day with songs and merriment.

The disciples passed the time, enjoying the lively tune. and trying out their dance steps. Yeshua watched them thinking of how Yohannan had called these men together and prepared them to be his disciples as if he was his best man. These men, along with other men and women, would join in the dance of ministry and participate in the divine life with him.

James awkwardly tried to match his steps but stepped on Yohan's then Rock's foot. Rock gave him a playful shove and shouted a few brusque words.

Yeshua smiled and shook his head, sure there would be a lot of mashed toes in this dance of ministry. He hoped eventually they would get their steps right and feel free to dance with abandon.

Yeshua stood then motioning to the groomsmen.

"Everything is prepared, it is time. I am going to get Hannah, get ready to bring Zerah his bride before he has an anxiety attack.

~ 22 ~

THE COVENANT OF NEW LIFE

Therefore, if anyone is united with the Messiah,
he is a new creation — the old has passed;
look, what has come is fresh and new!
2 Corinthians 5:17
I looked and saw the Holy City, the new Jerusalem,
coming down out of heaven from God, prepared as a bride
beautifully dressed for her husband.
Revelation 21:2

Yeshua stood outside Hannah's tent to call her name. Everyone was waiting for her. He would lead her out of the tent and down the path to the designated point where the groomsmen waited. From there, she would be lifted up and carried to the covenant chuppah where her groom would meet her for the public reading of the covenant.

"Hannah bar Yosef! My sweet sister! Come out to take part in this joyous day prepared just for you." He called in a lilting voice.

She leapt to her feet when she heard Yeshua's voice, fumbling to refasten her veil over her face, just as all women had done since the time of Rebecca. Miriam and Jochebed held open the tent flaps and Hannah came out to her brother shy but beaming. Seeing his sister dressed in her fine wedding clothes his eyes widened with surprise and his breath caught at her transformed beauty. For a moment he could not speak and tears filled his eyes.

Finally, he cleared his throat and spoke her name. "Hannah!"

She dropped her eyes with modesty, but she was secretly pleased by her brother's favorable response. Yeshua never put on airs. She knew she looked good, at least to him. Ceremoniously, Yeshua led the procession with the mothers and her maidens trailing behind. They walked slowly and the others dropped back, allowing a bit of distance for Yeshua to speak privately with Hannah.

She clung affectionately to his arm, his hand covered hers. Behind them the maidens giggled behind cupped hands, thinking Yeshua most handsome in his new tunic and cloak. He and Hannah shared their amusement hearing the sounds behind them.

Yeshua spoke soft words of assurance to Hannah. "I really like your Zerah. He is kind and sincere. And, you know I am a good judge of character, as well as Abba. You will be pleased."

He nudged her, "And, it must be said, it is always good to marry a man who has all of his teeth."

She elbowed him with a threatening arched brow.

"What? He has a very nice smile. I noticed he is smiling a lot this morning, because I have told him how wonderful you are."

He leaned toward her becoming serious, "He has a nice family and friends. And, he practices his faith in God carefully. He is excited to marry you."

He stopped walking for a moment to look directly into Hannah's face.

"Today, I understand the meaning of the Song."

"What do you mean?"

"The Song. Your eyes really are like gentle doves behind your veil, glowing and full of peace."

She blushed happily.

"How beautiful you are precious one!" He whispered to her.

"Thank you, Yeshi," She hugged him using her childhood name for him. Your opinion means the world to me. I know that Abba did his very best to find me a good husband. I trust his choice for me. I just hope Zerah will be satisfied with me."

Yeshua squeezed his sister's small hand. "He will adore you. I would be so pleased for a bride with a soul like yours."

Her heart filled like the sails of a ship. She beamed at him. Slanting her face towards his.

"Why have you never taken a bride, Yeshua? When I was younger, I thought you might make a match with Rachel, everyone knew she adored you." She searched his face.

"My heavenly Father has other plans for a bride for me. Like a patient son, I must wait for her. For now, there is much for me to prepare and do before I can receive my bride. However, I hope my bride will be like you. Happy about our covenant and ready to receive me."

"So, this is because of who you are?" She didn't name it.

"Yes, but do not worry yourself on my behalf. I will have the anointed bride."

Changing the subject, he whispered conspiratorially. "You do know that the groom gets a little nervous too, wanting to be well received, right?"

"I suppose." Hannah mused. "But it is different with men."

"Not as much as you might think, unless of course they are a brute. I think, Zerah is a little nervous about whether you will accept him too."

"Really?"

"Of course!"

Then Yeshua sighed with longing, "As for me, it may be years before I will be able to gather my bride to my home."

"I certainly hope not or you will be too old, you are pushing your limits now." Hannah laughed.

"Who knows, I may be coming to the marriage canopy with a very long white beard." Yeshua laughed.

"Uh, who wants to marry an old man!"

"Yes, I guess that could be a problem."

They approached their turn toward Zerah's home and together they peeked out to see all the party gathered together.

"There's the Bride!" Someone shouted happily. Yeshua kissed Hannah's forehead, leaving her hidden in the shadows with the two mothers.

He went to join Matthias, sending Zerah's young men to retrieve Hannah. Matthias called to his son to come out. Each patriarch played their part in weaving their families and friends together as they participated in the ceremony.

In his tent, Zerah paced back and forth. When he heard the shout of Hannah's approach, he bolted toward the flap to sneak a peek.

"Calm down!" His best man tried to sooth him. "You look like a horse waiting at the gate."

The music outside stopped, then changed its tune, and Zerah listened to hear his father's voice. "Let the bridegroom come out of his room." Matthias called to him, almost as excited as his son. Zerah straightened, turning nervously to his best friend and running his hands over his robes.

"How do I look?"

"You look better than I have ever seen you! Still, there is only so much new clothes can do." His friend laughed and straightened Zerah's turban slightly, then held the tent flap open before him. Zerah stepped out into the sunlight to take his place next to his Father and Yeshua who waited in front of the marriage canopy.

He saw his friends lifting Hannah upon her wedding seat as if she were a royal princess. Miriam and Jochebed led the bridal procession ahead of the young men, and taking their celebratory places. With a careful grace, Hannah stepped down to be led to her groom.

The couple solemnly and unapologetically stared at one another trying to gage the other's reaction.

The officiating Rabbi proclaimed, "The house of Yosef ben Jacob has entered into a covenant with the house of Matthias ben Zacchaeus to make a suitable match for their children. The bride price has been paid. The covenant has been sealed by their Fathers and their witnesses. Today, as promised Yeshua ben Yosef, has delivered his sister Hannah to be united to Zerah ben Matthias."

There was a perfunctory reading of the basic terms of the covenant. Hannah and Zerah listened carefully to every word of her Abba's legal agreement, noting his provisions for her. When she first met Zerah several years before, she had not understood that he was to be her husband, but she had liked him. When she was of age, Yosef explained her husband had been chosen. They met briefly to share a covenant cup. Hannah had been too shy to do more than steal awkward glances at him. Afterwards, she had been angry at herself, sure she had made a bad impression. Now she saw Zerah's joyful expression and was immediately comforted by her betrothed's obvious favor and his pleasant appearance.

Realizing she was staring, she lowered her eyes demurely, but only after catching Zerah's smile of encouragement.

Yeshua asked, "Hannah bat Yosef do you willingly enter into marriage with Zerah ben Matthias?"

Hannah nodded and answered approvingly. "Yes, I willingly take Zerah as my husband."

Yeshua kissed her hand then let it go. Then, as Jewish women had done for centuries, she began to walk in a circle around Zerah three times, as a sign of choosing him as her beloved for life.

As she circled, the Rabbi quoted the mysterious words of the prophet Joel over them, "The woman will encompass the man."

Then Zerah encircled her in the same way. Ending his third circle, he came to stand face to face with her to make his pledge.

"I take you, Hannah bat Yosef, to myself forever. I take you to me, in righteousness and justice, in loving kindness and mercy. I take you in faithfulness, and you shall know the LORD and I shall impart myself to you."

All her fears of his rejection or disappointment dissolved with his words of committed acceptance. This promise was meant to set the tone of their beginning together. Zerah placed a small bag of coins into her hand; indicating his confidence in her to establish their home. Then he placed a simple gold ring on Hannah's slender index finger. Her fingers curved to embrace his hand. Her eyes glistened and she smiled at him.

The Rabbi spoke the Blessings; one over the wine and one over their marriage. When the cup of wine to be shared was poured, the Rabbi's declared the first blessing. *"Blessed are you O LORD King of the Universe, who brings forth the fruit of the vine, and who has created all things including humanity."*

Then the second blessing, *"Blessed are you O LORD who makes joyful the Bride and the Bridegroom, and blesses Zion with children."*

He offered the cup to Zerah. Zerah drank from the cup and offered it to Hannah who lowered her veil to drink from the same cup signifying their union as one.

Then the Rabbi spoke the third blessing. *"Blessed are you O LORD who blesses the bride and the groom with joy and gladness, with feasting and singing."*

He wrapped a cloth around their shoulders together, signifying they were now of one flesh in the eyes of the LORD.

"Come." Zerah said smiling. He took Hannah's hand and led her under the chuppah, signifying to her and to all present that his home was now her home. He would now supply for all her needs.

Cheers erupted! Blessings were called out to them. The bride and groom uttered their first unofficial words to one another face to face, before being whisked away to enjoy the wedding feast.

Yeshua's heart overflowed at his sisters obvious happiness. The ritual of their covenant of marriage greatly moved him. The ritual and exchanges were the same as the covenant between God and his people.

"May it be so." He whispered.

~ 23 ~

THE BRIDE PRICE

"Surely you are a bridegroom of blood to me."
Exodus 4:23
"This cup is the new covenant in my blood,
which is poured out for you."
Luke 22:20

Hannah and Zerah sat happily together at the center of the celebration of their marriage. The banquet table was filled with delicacies. Wine was flowing. People were talking, laughing, and singing. In the midst of the joy, Yeshua recalled the prophecy: '*As a young man marries a young woman, so will your Builder marry you; as a bridegroom rejoices over his bride, so will your God rejoice over you.*'

Within the rituals of his sister's wedding, Yeshua was witnessing the various acts of becoming one in flesh as a metaphor or enactment of becoming one with God in spirit. These same elements were also found in the way of salvation: the Father's choosing, the contract or betrothal, the brides price, the announcement, the waiting, the anticipation, the preparations, the purification ritual, the individual choosing of the bride and the groom, the promises of enduring love, the seal of redemption, the dance of the Spirit, the encompassing, the public acknowledgement, the oneness, the joy, the beginning of a new and everlasting life as one, the out pouring of blessings, the cup of unity, the entrustment, the provision, the assurances, the giving of gifts, the private and intimate rela-tionship, and the all-encompassing embodiment. The prophets had understood, God's people were his bride.

Every human heart longed for something that could only become a reality by this joyous and faithful union with God. This covenant relationship with his people was the joy that was set before Yeshua.

Yeshua watched his sister and her husband's happiness. His longing laid bare on his face.

Noticing Yeshua's wistful expression, Yohan asked him. "Yeshua, do you ever wish for marriage?"

"I do." Yeshua admitted. "But it is not yet the time for a wedding feast for me, not like this."

"Celibacy, I think is easier for some than for others. The devoted of our sect has been criticized for it."

"It requires a special gift of grace and a heart-felt commitment. Still, celibacy frees one to serve in ways that others find difficult. Our ability to be single minded comes from our Father who has empowered us to stand alone in our consecration. And, there is a time and a season for all things." He said wistfully.

"And how about you?"

"There are other things I long for more than marriage." Yohan said. "I prefer to serve God undeterred. Still, I do think marriage is a rather lovely and mystical event, especially when it is well done."

"Yes, very."

Just then Miriam came up behind Yeshua. She tentatively touched him on his shoulder and leaned down to whisper, "Son, we have a rather embarrassing problem..."

Yeshua looked up waiting for her to go on. He took note of the servants standing behind her, wringing their hands.

"It seems we have run out of wine." She waited expectantly; her request was obvious.

Simon heard this and spoke up, shaking his head sadly. "That is a problem! Wine is a vital to the celebration, making all the hearts glad! Sips are to be taken with every blessing. A wedding without wine?"

"Dear woman, why do you come to me? This is not my time. I am not the Bridegroom of this day." Yeshua reminded her.

Miriam shrugged, "What can Zerah and his family do? They are on a tight budget. There are more people than expected." She looked at him pointedly. "We need your help."

What she meant was, 'All you have to do is ask.' His mother had clearly heard the rumors from Capernaum and meant to direct his abilities. She meant well, but had no knowledge of the stakes of what she was asking of him. This request was up close and personal and he was not a Genie in a bottle. He did not want to cross a line he wasn't meant to cross. But of course, Yeshua did not want Zerah or Hannah to suffer embarrassment in their celebration.

Yeshua lowered his head to think through the matter and to ask his Father, "Is there more to this miscalculation of wine and my mother's request for the children's provision?"

Miriam watched her son. She couldn't help but think how beautiful he was. Instead of wearing the humble and practical clothes of a laborer, Yeshua's new white robe gave him the appearance of spotless perfection. His curly black hair was glossy, and the whiteness of his teeth was highlighted against his sun-darkened skin and black beard. He really did look like the bridegroom of the day. Yet, seeing his reluctance, she intuitively she felt a pang of regret. Was she asking too much of him?

She reached down and squeezed his shoulder. "Yeshua, do what you think best. It's up to you."

To the servants, she said, "Do whatever he tells you to do." She walked away leaving the matter in his hands.

The servants remained by Yeshua's side awaiting his word.

He continued to deliberate over the situation, until he remembered the words of blessing the Rabbi had spoken over Zerah and Hannah, '*Blessed are You, LORD our God, creator of the fruit of the vine. The gladdener of Zion and of the groom with the bride. You created joy and gladness, you give delight to the bride and the bridegroom under the wedding tent. You provide a feast of singing.'*

He stood up to look around. He noticed six large water jars laying emptied from the ritual cleansings.

"Fill those jars with water." He ordered the servants.

The servants looked unsure. "Water?"

"Yes."

After a confused pause, they went on to do just as he had told them. They filled the jars to the brim, even though it seemed pointless. Yeshua unfurled his princely turban, turning it into a prayer shawl to lay across his shoulders. Approaching the jars, he privately he spoke words over them.

'Father, your children have no joy. Allow me to provide what is needed. I will redeem their lack and fill your people with the joy of life once more, so they may be married to us forever. Send forth your Spirit, that we may create the joy of life.'

He raised his face to the servants. "Draw some water out and take it to the banquet host."

They did as he directed, drawing the water out into pitchers. The water sparkled clear.

"Now take it to the banquet host and let him taste it."

They did as Yeshua commanded them, wondering about it as they went. Fear and surprise filled their faces when the water poured out a deep burgundy red. With surprise, their eyes looked to Yeshua.

He was about to retake his seat when his legs buckled under him and he all but collapsed onto the bench. Across the room, he could see the wine being poured into the cups. It sparkled red, appearing like the mixture of water and blood that filled the priestly waters during the sacrifices.

"Where did this wine come from?" A relieved banquet host asked them, thinking some of the supply had been overlooked, or only now bought out. The servants pointed to the water jars.

'Oh!' He thought cynically, 'They have mixed water with the wine to stretch it further.' Cautiously skeptical, the host took a sip to gauge its quality. He fully expected to taste a bitter cup. Surprised, his face broke into a joyous smile, savoring its pleasantly sweet after taste.

He waved his arms and called out to the wedding party. "Everyone brings out their finest wine first, and the second rate comes last. But you have saved the best for last!"

And he lifted his cup in blessing to the cheers of the people.

The disciples and the servants watched all of this with amazement, wondering, 'Who is this who has turned water into wine, humiliation and despair into joy and celebration?' The whole wedding party refilled their cups to offer an abundance of blessings upon the bride and the groom. Since there was plenty of wine, the celebration feast continued on past sunset.

After the sun disappeared, all the young maidens lit their oil lamps and held them aloft to light the way to Hannah's new home. Hannah was lifted up by the groomsmen to be carried to her groom anxiously waiting for her. Below her perch, Hannah was surrounded by a sea of dancing flames, it seemed as if she were being carried on a chariot of fire.

Joyful and worshipful love songs filled the air. Inside, the tented portal of her new home, the young maidens placed their oil lamps along line the walls of the tent. It glowed from inside with flickering candlelight.

Hannah's hand flew to her mouth, swept away by its breathtaking beauty. She whispered. "It is so beautiful."

She placed her hand over her heart as if to seal her happiness there forever. Zerah stood by the doorway, delight and eagerness filling his face. He stepped forward to scoop Hannah from her seat. His own eyes danced with the reflected light and twinkled with joy. He led her into the tented space, closing the flap behind them. Their friends called out their blessings and encouragement amid teasing laughter and songs.

Turning, the attendants left to rejoin the celebration, eager to enjoy the last remnants of the music and dancing. For a few more moments, Yeshua lingered near the tent mesmerized by the vision of light and love revealed before him. The two silhouettes were made visible by the warm glow of the lamps within.

Zerah stepped close to Hannah, anticipating the consummation of their covenant. It was the first of many nights they would lie down side by side together to hold and warm one another. Zerah reached to lift Hannah's veil so he could see his bride face to face. He took hold of her shoulders, rubbing them gently to warm and assure her.

Yeshua heard the whisper of low voices speaking intimately inside. "When did you become so very beautiful?" Zerah asked with a catch in his breath. "Look at you! You are perfect."

Hannah leaned toward him. Lifting her face to his, she radiated her joy and desire towards him. Zerah moved closer to touch Hannah's cheek softly. He bent slowly over her, tipping her face up to his. Inches apart, they stared into one another's eyes. Then he lowered his lips to hers tentatively for the first time. Then drawing back a breath, they gazed into each other's face, and whispered to one another words no one could hear. There came a nervous peal of soft laughter, joined by deeper sound of assurance. Then Zerah took Hannah's hand and led her onward through the wedding tent to the private space prepared for just the two of them, Hannah's new home.

Yeshua smiled wistfully as their shadows disappeared.

O, the ways of a man with a maid. Zerah is no longer alone.

~ 24 ~

A SACRED APPOINTMENT

'These are the Lord's appointed festivals,
the sacred assemblies
you are to proclaim at their appointed times:
The Lord's Passover begins at twilight
on the fourteenth day of the first month.
Leviticus 23:4-5
"Flowers appear on the earth;
the season of singing has come,
the cooing of dove is heard in our land.
The fig tree forms its early fruit;
the blossoming vines spread their fragrance.
Arise, come, my darling;
my beautiful one, come with me."
The Song 1:10-13

Passover followed quickly on the heels of Hannah's wedding. Yeshua's family came with him to Capernaum before making the five-day trek to Jerusalem. In Capernaum, Miriam became fast friends with Simon's wife Deborah and his mother-in-law Abigail.

The wedding had left everyone in a good mood. Now they looked forward to their time in Jerusalem. Passover was a sacred time of worship and remembering God's promises of salvation. These holy days were filled with communal fellowship, singing, and drawing near to God. However, under Roman oppression, whenever the Jewish people gathered together danger was never far away.

Andrew returned from checking on the fishing fleets with fresh concern. Taking Yeshua and Simon aside he whispered the foreboding news. The others immediately wanted to know what was the matter.

"The word on the street is that Rome will be flexing their muscle even more than usual. The Sicarii have murdered a few of Rome's higher-ranking officers, putting Rome on high alert. They are looking for revenge."

The men looked to Yeshua with concern.

Yeshua nodded. "Yes, I have heard the tensions are high."

"When are they not high?" James asked.

"Militia will be coming in force from Caesarea Philippi, we can expect to encounter them along the way. We need a plan to hide our weapons, they must not find a sword or a knife among us. We don't want to be identified as Zealots." Simon said.

"If one lives by the sword, they will also die by the sword." Yeshua uttered softly.

Andrew said, "Well, we don't want to become a casualty of 'the peace' of Rome'. Truth is, with all the pockets of Zealot and Essene communities in Galilee, we are all considered suspect. The Romans don't understand the difference between the mercenaries and the righteous ones. To them our communities are one and the same. They would just as soon kill us all. They know both communities are awaiting the Messiah."

Yeshua looked steadily at Andrew. "You have nothing to fear Andrew, we will travel safely."

He had just spent much of his early morning prayer concerning the safety of his group, and all pilgrims according to his Father's will. Andrew asked, "How can you be so sure?" Yeshua gazed questioningly at him. Andrew finally bit his lip and lowered his head, chagrinned that he too easily forgot who Yeshua was. He realized there were times when he treated Yeshua like one of them.

To his credit, Yeshua was subtle with his reminders.

When the group set out, it was a clear and breezy day. The wind tugged at their hair and whipped their cloaks around them. The trees swayed gracefully, stirred by the wind's rhythm. Bright blooms colored the red bud trees, delicate white blooms laced the fruit trees, and a soft peach covered the almond trees. Before them stretched a landscape filled with bursts of lavender, deep pinks, white and yellow. The freshened green fields were laden with bright red poppies and yellow chrysanthemums, and purple lupines, each meadow was a new feast for the eyes under the bright blue sky. The graceful movement of the trees made Yeshua think again of the swirling and joyous circle dances of the wedding celebration.

He recognized, 'Joy is an elusive thing. One cannot summon it of their own accord. It just is like an unexpected blessing, flowing like the breezes that buffet the swaying trees.'

Yeshua said, "Look, the trees are dancing today."

"Yes, just as you did some fine dancing at Hannah's wedding, my friend." Simon guffawed with amusement.

"Why do you laugh?" Yeshua asked as if he were offended but with a good-humored grin.

"You surprised me! I've never seen a holy man move like you."

Yeshua threw back his head with a laugh. "Why so surprised? Shouldn't a child of God always be filled with joy? I do love the communal dances. What can I say, it must run in the family. My ancestor David danced with all his might before the LORD."

"Well you were doing that! It is just that I always imagined the Messiah to be all stoic and dignified."

"Yes, David's wife Michal thought so too, but David rebuked her for that. Michal did not understand the joy of the Lord."

Yeshua pointed toward his sister and Zerah. "Look at those two, what can be better than a couple caught up in the first throes of love. It lightens the hearts of all who watch them. I tell you, their happiness reveals the joy of the ancient mystery of the marriage covenant for those with eyes to see it."

Simon was surprised to hear Yeshua waxing romantic. He nodded with his own nostalgic agreement, "When I look back upon that first year with Deborah, we were so happy, just the two of us. Time changes things, now we have Ana, and my mother-in-law, bills, and so many responsibilities."

"Yes, but these are the fruits of a blessed and faithful marriage. Do not resent your blessings." Yeshua said. "Despite your expanding number, you must recognize these gifts for what they are. Count your blessings, keep the joy alive with your beloved in the day to day living and all the ups and downs."

He motioned again, "Look at them. This is the very same union my Father in Heaven has longed for with the people of his creation. We want our people to live within the joy of our dance of love. Love is the very reason everything was created."

Simon was surprised at this turn in the conversation. No one had ever expressed something so beautiful about the Creator to him before. He was especially surprised to hear this message of love from the Messiah. Like others, he had always expected a warrior, not a lover. No, rather he had expected a king with a scepter of iron.

As everyone chattered around him, Yeshua continued to muse quietly on this mystery of love; watching his sister and her new husband, their entwined fingers binding their life together. They kept stealing glances at one another and sharing secret smiles. When they smiled at one another, Yeshua smiled too, echoing their joy.

The group came to a beautiful almond grove, filled with delicate pinkish-white flowers. They decided to stop for a rest and eat here, while enjoying the delicate blooms. Yeshua noticed Zerah and Hannah strolling among the blooms searching for a private spot for an embrace, thinking no one noticed. When they ducked behind a tree, he thought of the words from the Song. 'I delight to sit in my beloved's shade, and his fruit is sweet to my taste. Let him lead me to the banquet hall, and let his banner over me be love.' This was the love Yeshua felt for Israel. He hoped that soon the people chosen for him by his Father would be drawn toward his love.

The next day, an hour into their journey, they suddenly felt a rumbling beneath their feet. A battalion was coming on horseback. Everyone stopped and turned to one another with immediate dread, though this encounter was inevitable.

Yeshua gave the signal for his sister, and the other young women run and hide from view. The older women stood their ground so their sons and husbands would not come under the suspicion of the soldiers.

As the Romans approached, the group stepped off the road to make way for the garrison. They took a submissive stand, waiting, heads down to convey an attitude of deference, hoping the militia would keep moving. Each person, privately steeled themselves to take abuse if necessary, so no trouble would befall their families.

The ones with their hidden short swords and daggers, took up their stations nearest the women as they had planned. As the battalion approached, their commander scanned the group of travelers, taking note that there were several young men. He could not resist coming to a halt beside them. Without a word he scrutinized them. All, with the exception of one, had their heads down. One looked the commander in the eye, not with threat or belligerence, but with a certain confidence and interest. The commander glared at Yeshua harshly, prodding him to drop his eyes, or to react in fear or defiance. But Yeshua did neither. He stood unshaken before the great Roman militia.

Yeshua and the Centurion remain fixed on one another for several moments. Yeshua's lack of hatred or fear strangely unsettled Decimus. The Jew bore a calm he had only seen on those given great power and authority, but he wore no fine clothes or insignias.

"What is your name?" The Centurion finally asked.

"Yeshua son of Yosef."

"Where are you from?"

"Nazareth."

"Where are you going?"

"We are going for the Passover celebration in Jerusalem."

"Who are these people with you?"

"My family and friends, we travel as pilgrims. Our only intent is be reconciled to our God."

The commander took notice of their tasseled garments. Devout Jews. "Ah, yes. Your God is Yahweh. The God of the sacrificed sheep."

"Yes, Yahweh," Yeshua stated simply, "who longs to be reconciled to all men."

"All men?" The Roman asked sarcastically, rocking up in his saddle.

"Really?"

"Yes, as I said, all men."

The commander's eyes drilled into Yeshua's, as if posing him a challenge. "Does that include your Roman oppressors too?" He sent a stream of spittle flying to the ground, as if spitting out the bitter taste of their enmity from his mouth.

"Of course, Romans too." Yeshua said. "There is only One God, One Creator of all of humanity, he would be your Creator, too."

"Is that so?" Decimus' laugh was harsh with amusement. "But what of our Roman gods? Do they not count? What of Zeus, Apollos, and the others, are they nothing to you?"

Yeshua said nothing, holding the man's harsh regard. Everyone waited, feeling the tension. But suddenly, the Roman threw back his head and laughed uproariously. The readiness within his battalion eased a bit; and his men laughed with him, waiting for their commander's next words.

"Lucky for you, I am in a good mood for the moment; and in a hurry to get to the Antonia." The commander flashed Yeshua a surprisingly good-natured smile. Then he slapped his thigh and guffawed to his men, "Did you hear that? Yahweh loves Romans too, ha!"

Yeshua's open and good-natured expression did not waver with the man's amusement. He offered a pleasant smile in parting.

With a final glance toward Yeshua, Decimus gave a mock salute, then he twirled his stallion with a kick and gave the signal to move out. The soldiers passed swiftly, their Roman standard held high. Each soldier glanced curiously at Yeshua as they passed, wondering what he had said to put the Centurion in such a good mood.

Yeshua watched the retreating form of their armored leader, a faint smile tipped his lips and he uttered under his breath. "Yes, even Romans too." Once the Romans had gone, his disciples and family let out a collective sigh, surrounding him once more.

"That could have definitely gone quite differently." Yohan said.

Everyone fell back into step onto the road.

"Yes. Another miracle. What made you think to say such a thing?" Simon asked.

"What thing?" Looked sharply in Simon's direction.

"That Yahweh wants to be reconciled with Romans too. I am surprised that the Centurion didn't cut you down on the spot for insulting their Zeus."

"I said nothing about Zeus, I only spoke what is true. Our Heavenly Father loves people of all nations and doesn't want anyone to perish. You must learn to pray for your enemies, Rock, until they are no longer your enemy."

Simon stopped in the middle of the road, wondering, 'Is he for real? That's not possible! The Romans are enemies of God.' But then, Yeshua was not one to say things he did not mean. Why would Yahweh care about those cruel brutes? Confusion crowded his thoughts. Yeshua's words were contrary to everything he knew. Clearly, Yeshua saw things in a different light. Not wanting to be left behind, Simon hurried on to catch up. He decided to just be grateful they were all safe. He had not wanted to use his paltry little weapon against the Roman swords. He took a deep breath and walked on.

The group traveled on for several days, meeting another battalion, and encountering other pilgrims on the way. They camped by the side of the road at night, and sought out quiet sheltered places for their rest. When they drew near to Jerusalem, they came upon the grotesque and unsettling remains of those considered 'the enemies of Rome' hanging from trees along the side of the road. This was nothing new, but it shook them each time they saw them. Rome enjoyed terrifying the pilgrims with these grim reminders of what would happen to anyone who might hope to oppose their militant control or 'the peace of Rome'.

Beside one cross stood a man grieving. His distress overwhelmed him. Yeshua broke away from the group to approach him. He spoke gently to the man for quite some time while the others waited uncomfortably at a distance anxious to move on. After some time of conversation, Yeshua folded the emotional man into his arms as he wailed, raw and ragged cries of pain. Yeshua spoke more consolations to him.

When the man was quieted, Yeshua told him. "We cannot win our freedom with violence. Violence begats violence. Love is the only way to conquer evil. Light overcomes the darkness. Your friend died without cause. If you want your life to count, come and follow me. Help me reveal the very kingdom of God you are longing for."

Looking upon his friend's body, Simon, called the Zealot, wanted to stay to bury him. But no one was allowed to remove the bodies from the trees except the Romans. He felt a guilty cowardice. Still, should he be caught taking his friend's body down, it would quickly become his own cross. There were too many Romans patrolling the roads this close to Jerusalem.

"Let the dead, bury the dead." Yeshua had said to him, at the risk of sounding harsh, but Simon understood what he was saying and did not take offense. He was grateful to travel with this group so he would not stand out and be so easily identified. The group waited discreetly.

Finally, Yeshua returned to the group, bringing the grieving man with him. Looking back one more time, Zel realized he could just as easily be hanging beside his friend. He was not sure how he had escaped. Yeshua walked silently beside him offering him his comforting presence, so he would not feel alone in his grief.

Onward they pressed, to finish the last of their journey to Jerusalem.

~ 25 ~

A REFINER'S ZEAL

"Then suddenly the Lord you are seeking will come to his
temple; the messenger of the covenant, whom you desire,
will come," says the Lord Almighty.
Who can stand when he appears?
For he will be like a refiner's fire ...
He will purify the Levites and refine them like gold and silver.
Malachi 3:1-2

On the fifth day of the journey, Jerusalem came into view. Merging with the throngs of people their group began their up-ward ascent. As it supernaturally happened each time, they joined their voices together with the other pilgrims to sing the Psalms of Ascent. It was tradition to sing whenever they made their way up to the Holy City of God. Many sang with tears in their eyes, some sang with shouts of praise.

Even in his grief, Zel raised his voice to sing to God; passionately loving Yahweh, and believing him to be worthy of all praise. As the group compressed, people advanced as one body. Caught up in awe and worship, their voices reverberated as if one voice. Within that voice were solemn, mournful, desperate, longing, hopeful and joyful tones. All the emotions of God's people swirled and blended into one within their midst to become one collective cry to God.

The same prayerful songs had been sung for hundreds and hundreds of years, filled with cries for deliverance, worship and praise, supplications and proclamations of God's promises:

O LORD, hear my voice, be attentive to my cry for mercy.
I call on the LORD in my distress and he answered me....
Woe to me...Save me, O LORD
Where does my help come from? From the Maker of heaven and earth.
The LORD watches over us and keeps us from all harm.
Let us praise the name of the LORD.
Peace be within you, oh Jerusalem.
Praise the LORD, who has not let us be torn by our enemies' teeth.
The snare of our enemy has been broken and we have escaped.
Trust in the LORD. The scepter of evil will not remain.
Unless the LORD builds the house, the builders labor in vain.
Blessed is all who fear the LORD and walk in his ways.
May the Blessing of the LORD be upon Jerusalem.
If you keep a record of sin, Oh LORD, who could stand?
But with you is forgiveness.
I wait upon the LORD ...and in his word I put my hope.
Oh Israel, put your hope in his unfailing love.
For the sake of David your servant, do not reject your Anointed One.
Like precious oil poured on the head, let your Spirit fall upon Zion.

The sound of the voices magnified as they approached the large and beautiful gate of Jerusalem. Masses of people fused together like a flowing river, awe sweeping over them in waves. Their song reach to a triumphant crescendo as they finally entered the city walls.

The people cried out, *"Our feet are standing within your gates, O Jerusalem!"*

From that point, the pilgrims blended into a crowded beehive of activity, dispersed into a river moving purposefully in every direction.

Though Yeshua was exhausted from the journey, he felt the invigoration of having entered the city. His steps became light like a son away too long. He was not so much overcome by Jerusalem's physical beauty, nor the temple's impressive size; rather, this place was forever designated as his Father's footstool. This was where his Father was honored, where his people came to pray, and his Father's mercy was offered. His heart stretched towards his Father, as well as to all of the milling people here for that purpose.

"Abba!" His soul cried. He lifted his face.

For a moment, a breeze swirled around him lifting the loose edges of his hair pushing it back as if to see his face better. A sweet spicy scent wafted over him, despite the press of bodies and the droppings left by the horses patrolling the streets.

He headed to the mikvah to wash the dust and sweat away and don clean clothes. Afterwards, he headed towards his Father's house of prayer. His feet fairly flew up the great steps like those of a gazelle. His disciples struggled to catch up. Excited, Yeshua strode into the outer courtyard of the temple only to come to an immediate stop. What he saw was so unexpected he felt like he had been punched in his gut. His joy morphed into and expression of fury.

Everything is wrong! Instead of an atmosphere of awe, solemn prayer, and reverent worship, I find a bizarre? A common, filthy market place!

His fierce gaze took in the tables and booths, the lowing of cattle, the bleating of sheep, the beating wings of the caged doves, the clinking of coins, and the rude haggling of the merchants and money changers. So many booths lined the courtyard. Each manned by shrewd men who stroked their beards, and cut crafty and calculating eyes toward each person and animal. They were bartering the sacrificial sanctification of the people for exorbitant prices; their faces were twisted with an ugly greed.

A holy indignation arose from within him. He watched as one priest examined a fine specimen of a sheep only to reject it.

"This pink spot on his nose mars the animals beauty. We cannot approve this beast. You would offer this blemished lamb to God?"

The poor man was humiliated under the accusatory glare of the priest.

"But this lamb is in excellent health. We have hand raised him."

The man wrung his hands with distress. "He is the very best ram from my flock. Look at him, strong and sturdy."

Yeshua looked upon the flock of beautiful innocent animals being held in pins. He saw each tethered lamb being led away as unacceptable, only to be traded for another lamb at the hagglers unreasonable price. It occurred to him soon he would be the lamb they would haggle over, tether, and offer up. The day would come when the High Priest himself would count out the dirty money from these very coffers to receive the only acceptable sacrifice.

Yeshua felt himself begin to shake with righteous indignation at the injustice taking place before him.

This is not worship, this is a contemptuous assault against my Father's name and his house!

The smell of the animals feces commingled with the stench of spiritual corruption, made him feel nauseous. The words of the prophets came to mind,'*I require obedience rather than sacrifice!' This is not what my Father wants at all. This is what he meant when he said, 'Your sacrifices are a stench in my nostrils!'*

He turned toward his disciples, his eyes ablaze with such anger that they took a step back.

"Give me your belts." He commanded them, as he unfastened his own.

Confusedly each man untied their thin leather belts holding their tunics in place. They gave them over to Yeshua and watched wordlessly while his nibble fingers wove the straps together to form a handhold.

He put the straps to the test with a sharp snap. He turned toward the spectacle before him and moved purposefully forward, cracking the leather straps near the haunches of the unsuspecting animals. Startled, the sheep leapt forward, kicking as they ran. He opened the bird cages, swooped them up to empty them. Frightened birds fluttered wildly, then flew to freedom, coming to rest upon the remote heights to watch their rescuer below.

Yeshua ran towards the money changers tables, to grab them and throw the tables with their neat stacks of dirty money up into the air. The men seated behind them leapt quickly to their feet, only to dive protectively to the floor scrambling to regather their coinage. Frantic animals leapt over their backs. Men shouted to one another, calling for the temple guards. But the guards simply stood there dumbfounded with confusion, unsure of what to do.

Yeshua bellowed the roar of a lion. "You have made my Father's house into a market place, a den of thieves! How dare you blaspheme his name in this way! Get all of this out of here!"

"And you too," he shouted at the money changers as he snapped the straps toward them, "get this out of here, this is a sacred place!" They grabbed what they could and ran.

All the while, the disciples stood with their hands on their heads, clearly in shock.

Yeshua's newest recruit, Zel, became ecstatic and was caught up in the Spirit.

He testified, "This is the Anointed One who was foretold by David's vision, 'zeal for your house consumes me'. The Anointed One must be passionate for the LORD's house. Today, I am witness to 'the Zealous One' with my own eyes! The Zealous One is here!"

He lifted his hands in worship, praising God for his faithfulness. God had sent his refiners fire to his holy temple to set things right, to challenge the corruption and purify the temple just as foretold.

After the courtyard was emptied, one of the money changers ran to Annas, who called for his son-in-law Caiaphas. The two men lifted up their long, decorous robes to hurry to the courtyard, a Sanhedrin entourage followed close behind them.

"Who would dare to confront the work of the temple?"

No one answered, because no one would dare confront Caiaphas or Annas. They were not only above the law, they were the law. Money talked. The Roman government and the Herodians counted on their cut of the dirty money. Through their underhanded dealings they bought and held their coveted positions. This market place had created a dynasty and a great deal of personal wealth for them both.

The old priest growled with an ugly scowl, "Only a person who imagines themself an appointed prophet or a radical reformer would do such a thing. It must be one of those blasted Zealots or Essenes."

"Prophet?" Caiaphas questioned. "Could it be the Baptizer? He is a radical who stands against us. His following is growing. Would he do something this brash?"

"Surely, his father Zachariah taught him better than to challenge us in our own house!" Annas said.

They slowed their rush to walked with great decorum and authority out onto the elevated platform directly above the court-yard. Their higher elevation setting them apart from the common people, and allowed them to look down upon them.

In the emptied courtyard below they found a stranger stand-ing with his legs braced still searching the perimeter for lingering offenders. It did not appear to be the Baptizer, but the curls of his black hair obscured his face.

They called out to him. "You there! What do you think you are doing? Guards apprehend him!"

The guards started towards him, but Yeshua made quickly advancing steps toward them as if he were ready to run them out with the others. Something about the boldness and authority of the man caused them to halt and back up with an unreasonable fear.

Yeshua pointed to the animal droppings littering the people's courtyard and shouted to the High Priest. "Why have you defiled my Father's house?"

'Father?' Caiaphas' eyes became slits at his words. "By what authority do you speak to us this way?"

"As One sent from God." Yeshua retorted.

"If you are sent by God, you must show some proof. What credentials do you have?" Annas demanded to know.

Yeshua offered no answer.

Caiaphas agreed, "Yes, if you are from God, then show us some sign or miracle that we may know you!"

Yeshua glanced with recollection toward the highest point of the temple wall, recalling Satan's words. Then he turned and directed his sights upon the two men. Their malice was unmistakable.

"What proof do you have? You must show us some sign to prove yourself, if you are indeed a prophet of God."

A memory from Yeshua's youth was stirred and came to the surface. He had been twelve years of age. His Rabbi Eli had entered him as his star student to debate before a panel of scholars against other gifted students. The panel was meant to test their knowledge and understanding of Torah, and to goad the young men to pursue further studies under the great Rabbi's. Yosef had found it hard to refuse, knowing Yeshua was gifted with great insight in the Torah. Plus, Herod Archelaus had recently been exiled to Gaul.

During the testing, Yeshua gave clear and concise answers that impressed the panel of scholars. The panel had tried to stump him, but he had prevailed.

"I have never seen anything like him." The lead scholar Gamaliel had said to the other leaders.

They had asked him, "Boy, can you come back tomorrow to meet with the High Priest?"

Yeshua knew his family was preparing to return to Nazareth, but he thought, 'Now that I am of age, shouldn't I be about my Father's work?' Hadn't Abba even told him that his learning and faith were now his responsibility? While he prepared for his next round of testing, his family had thought the contest was over and Yeshua was simply among the other boys. They left assuming Yeshua was with them.

That day, Annas came to watch the panel test him. He was quickly surprised at the boy's knowledge. But unreasonably, he felt a malice toward him. The second day, Annas took over the questioning determined to find fault with his answers. He purposefully peppered Yeshua with questions that had stumped religious men for decades. Yeshua's humility and quick answers were faultless and beyond challenge making Annas look inept. The harder Annas grilled him, the more impressed the other scholars became. Annas refused defeat.

The testing continued to a third day. It finally came to an end when Yosef and Miriam returned to Jerusalem to find him still seated amongst the teachers. Apologizing profusely, they had pulled him away from Annas and the panel, reprimanding him harshly. That day for the first time, Yeshua had seen sheer terror on his parent's faces. He was immediately remorseful, realizing he had done something terribly wrong.

"What were you thinking?" Yosef had demanded, his whole body shaking with the concern that Yeshua may have unwittingly revealed himself right there in Jerusalem. "Son, you have never treated us with such disregard! Why would you do such a thing to us?"

"Didn't you know our caravan was leaving?" Miriam asked him, weeping with angst and relief.

That was when Yeshua understood there was more at stake in his identity than he had understood.

He tried to offered them his reasoning, "I only thought, I should be about my Father's work. Hasn't the Rabbi said I will make a great teacher someday?"

"Someday." Yosef had shouted at him. "But not yet! You must not draw this kind of attention to yourself! You are still under my authority and it is my job to keep you safe until the appropriate time. You must not act on your own accord, not yet."

Yeshua blinked back to the present.

Standing in the courtyard, he remembered that even back then, there had been a younger man by Annas' side, his protégé. During the questioning Caiaphas had frequently leaned in close to offer Annas his insights and his calculated questions. Caiaphas had been in his late twenties back then.

Now, Caiaphas stared down on Yeshua with the same arrogant jealousy. A vortex of a darkness emanated from both men. Yeshua felt the spirit of the Evil One upon them. These were Satan's chosen priests, who would gladly offer him up to death! Even as a boy Yeshua had felt their contempt, though he had done nothing wrong.

He wondered, 'Do they recognize me, now? Perhaps not in physical form. I was but a gangly youth all those years ago. But the darkness within recognizes me for who I AM. No amount of teaching, reasoning, or preaching will change their hardened hearts. Still, in obedience to my Father's love and mercy, I will speak words of truth to them and offer them the same chance for redemption as everyone else.'

A peace settled over him. Another piece of his Father's plan revealed.

In response to their disbelief and demand for a sign, Yeshua decided to give them only one irrefutable sign. And yet, despite that one undeniable proof they would still refuse to believe.

He stepped closer to the two men. Placing his hand on his torso, he said, "Destroy this temple, and I will raise it again in three days."

They were so shocked, they couldn't respond.

Yeshua turned to leave.

The religious leaders watched him go, having accomplished nothing. They knew only one thing, this man was obviously a threat. They turned to one another to cluck their tongues.

"Who was that man?"

"What was that all about?"

"Was he a zealot?"

"One of Yohannan's disciples?"

"Who knows? He was talking nonsense!" Caiaphas shouted over the den of voices. "It has taken forty-six years to build this temple into the structure it is today. Only an enemy or a madman would make such a statement!"

"Enemy or mad man, he just threatened our very way of existence. We must have a plan for the next time he appears. We will need to stop him. The sooner the better." Annas said with a spiteful resilience.

Some men dispersed, lost deep in thought, feeling in their spirits the weight of Yeshua's words. They wondered, 'What does his cryptic message mean?' They recalled his hand earnestly upon his own chest and they couldn't guess.

One devout Pharisee watched as Yeshua strode unchecked from the courtyard with his loosened robe and hair blowing behind him although there was no wind. His crude whip had dangled from his hand, making him look for all the world like of a mighty warrior, like a young David. His men followed him, hurrying to match his strides.

Nicodemus felt his draw. A peculiar excitement buoyed him.

Could it be?

Just then the strange breeze caught and lifted Nicodemus' own thinning hair. His eyes widened with wonder. He felt the intuition of providence. He knew, though he did not know how he knew, he had just heard words that would eventually come true.

While the other leaders continued their bluster, Nicodemus disappeared to follow the prophet at a discreet distance. He wanted to know where this man was staying. Outside the temple, he had to practically run to keep sight of him. But, Nicodemus was propelled by an irresistible desire as if some unfathomed part of himself had awakened to something quite wondrous. He laughed, feeling giddy as he went.

Yet even as he followed, he sensed the eyes of some hostile force watching him. For a moment, he stopped, scanning the perimeter for a face hidden in the shadows, but he saw no one. The hair on the back of his neck warned him otherwise. But finding nothing, he shook off the irrational fear to speed his steps, determined to learn where this prophet was staying.

~ 26 ~

THE RUACH

Who has gone up to heaven and come down?
Whose hands have gathered up the wind?
Who has wrapped up the waters in a cloak?
Who has established all the ends of the earth?
What is his name, and what is the name of his son?
Surely you know!
Proverbs 30:4

Throughout the week of Passover, word spread like wildfire of the strange new rabbi from Galilee. Stories of his numerous miraculous deeds were spreading abroad on the streets of the city. The festival attenders were excited, he had even challenged the Sanhedrin.

"A Prophet! A Healer! A Holy Man! Could he be the Messiah?"

People were asking. Their longing hearts stirred, for there had been no prophets found in Jerusalem for well over four hundred years. To them a Navi was almost a mythical creature. Perhaps now, they would hear from God! People searched for Yeshua anxious to hear his words for themselves. Those, who longed to hear him, searched until they found him. He far exceeded the teachers of Jerusalem. Yeshua's words reached into their souls and touched their deepest questions and needs. A supernatural power was at work within them.

"Surely he is the LORD's Anointed." Many agreed.

Yeshua spoke mostly in parables. He was shrewd enough not to proclaim his identity openly. Only those with pure intentions were given insights to his parables. Jerusalem's administration had historically held the reputation as persecutors and murderers of his Father's prophets. They would do even worse to God's Son.

He could no longer pass along the streets without covering his identity. His disciples were excited by his blossoming distinction. They were puzzled by his reluctance to claim his new found fame. Some urged him to embrace his popularity. Some felt fearful since his overt behavior at the Temple. The disciples were locked in a strong disagreement about this.

They were wasting their breath, however, because Yeshua did not ask their opinion.

"Why have you backed down?" Simon wanted to know. "Will we not go back into the Temple?"

"Rock, this is my mission, why do you question me?"

He looked around at the others. "I will make myself known all in good time."

Later, when Yohan returned from visiting some of his family members who were part of the Sanhedrin, he confirmed what Yeshua already knew.

"The Sanhedrin is offering a reward to those with information about you. As my cousin has put it, 'You have awakened a sleeping bear.' They are sniffing for your trail."

A good-sized crowd had gathered. Yeshua took noticed of a rather distinguished Pharisee watching him from a measured distance. The man listened thoughtfully with no trace of malice, only an avid curiosity. Once or twice the man nodded his agreement and understanding. Their eyes met. Yeshua smiled at the man and the man nodded back.

That night there came a furtive knock at the gate where Yeshua was staying. It was late and everyone was bedded down for the night. None of his men moved to go to the gate, the knock came again, louder this time. Still, no one answered.

Nicodemus knocked a third time, this time with loud and resounding determination.

One or two of the disciples roused irritably, but did not get up to answer the door. They waited for the knock to go away, or for someone else to answer it. Others remained sound asleep. But Yeshua's keen ears had heard each of the knocks.

Finally, not wanting the visitor to awaken all of his men, he got up and moved quickly to the gate. Clearly, the persistent person on the other side was not going away.

Rock was awake when the intruder knocked at the gate yet an audacious fourth time. He saw Yeshua was going to the door. He rolled irritably from his sleeping mat to stand behind Yeshua, his hand resting cautiously on his hidden dagger. Yeshua had drawn his cloak up over his head, casting his face in shadow.

"Peace be with you," the man said peering inside at the shrouded man, hidden by the shadows. "I am sorry. I know the hour is late. My name is Nicodemus. I need to talk with the Galilean Rabbi. Is he here?"

Yeshua recognized the same Pharisee that had been watching him from a distance, though at this late hour he was not in his pharisaical attire.

Rock gave Nicodemus a harsh once over, voicing his displeasure. "Do you realize what time it is? Everyone is asleep!"

"I know, I am sorry. I have questions that I must ask the Teacher. I need answers."

Nicodemus persisted.

Looking down with an awkward embarrassment, he said. "I can't ask him my questions during the day...."

Immediately suspicious of the man, Rock was ready to close the gate.

Seeing the man's discomfort, Yeshua placed his hand on Simon's hidden hand, said, "It is okay Rock, I will talk with him."

Yeshua drew back his cloak to reveal his face to the man.

"Go back to bed." He said to Simon over his shoulder, nodding towards his mat.

Simon reluctantly backed away.

Yeshua motioned for the man to enter and closed the gate.

Nicodemus whispered a second apology, acknowledging the hour.

Rock's bluster had awakened some of the others. Now they too were staring up at the intruder with annoyance.

Yeshua gave them the signal to return to their rest. Quietly, he led Nicodemus to one of the private alcoves overlooking the street below.

"You have connections in high places." Nicodemus stated, noting whose court yard Yeshua was staying in.

Yeshua grimaced, not wanting this to be widely known. "This is a relative of one of my students. He has been obliging to offer hospitality to us. I would appreciate your discretion."

Motioning to a bench, Yeshua took a seat and stated. "You are part of the Jewish ruling council."

Nicodemus was surprised that the Rabbi had recognized him and realized he had no reason to trust him.

"Yes, I dressed this way so I would not be so easily recognized. It could be dangerous for me."

Yeshua nodded noting the man's courage to make this clandestine visit.

"So, you have questions?" Yeshua's face looked open and relaxed, encouraging Nicodemus. With all the respect that he could proffer, he said, "Rabbi, we know you are a teacher who has come from God. No one could perform the miracles you are accomplishing if God were not with him."

Yeshua took measure of Nicodemus' words, while prayerfully pondering his motivations. He sensed Nicodemus was earnest and hopeful. Yeshua felt his Father's love for this man. He realized he had come wanting to know with certainty if he was indeed the Awaited One.

Yeshua stood and turned for a moment looking off into the distance.

He thought, 'I cannot yet entrust my identity to him directly. He is connected to the temple. Even if his intentions are righteous, whatever I say to him will likely be shared with the council.'

He wondered at Nicodemus use of 'we'. 'Caiaphas? I don't think so. He comes disguised under the cover of night with obvious fear.'

Nicodemus watched Yeshua with anticipation.

Yeshua reasoned. 'My Father is drawing him to me. Still, even if he doesn't mean to implicate me to the Sanhedrin, loose lips could implicate us both.

Yeshua returned to his seat and opened their conversation with invitation.

"So, tell me, what do you wish to know?"

"About the kingdom, are you…"

Yeshua cut him short. "I tell you the truth, no one can see the kingdom of God unless they are born again."

Nicodemus stared into the space before him as if searching for Yeshua's meaning.

He returned his puzzled gaze to Yeshua. "Born again? I am not sure what you mean. How can one be born again when they are old? Surely I cannot enter a second time into my mother's womb to be born again?"

Is he speaking of the pagan belief of reincarnation? No, no Jew would propose such a thing!

Yeshua allowed the question to hang between them for a few beats to give Nicodemus time to ponder his words.

"I am telling you the truth, no one can enter the kingdom of God unless they are born of water and the Spirit. Flesh gives birth to flesh, but the Spirit gives birth to Spirit."

Nicodemus looked even more confused. "Water—you mean baptism?"

"Are you really so surprised at my saying, you must be born again?"

The man stared at him blankly. "Well, yes!"

Suddenly a notable breeze swept over the wall of the portico, lifting Nicodemus' hair and beard. His eyes widened while he pressed his errant whorls back from his face.

Yeshua spoke another parable, to him saying, "Listen, a wind is blowing. Do you hear it?"

"Sort of..."

"Can you see it?"

"Well, no. I can't see it, but I feel it. I see the leaves quivering on the bushes."

"Right. You can feel it moving, but you cannot tell from where it comes or where it will go. So, it is with everyone born of the Spirit."

Nicodemus remembered how the wind had caught Yeshua's robe and hair at the temple, though it had not been a windy day at all. Then, he remembered how the same wind had caught his own hair too. It had felt like a caress. Wonder transformed Nicodemus' line worn face, and Yeshua prayed the meaning of his words would take root in the man.

'I should know this answer.' Nicodemus thought. 'Ruach - The Wind is the breath of life and God's Spirit. Ruach acts in mysterious ways. Prevenient are the winds of God's grace. Yahweh gives breath to sustain life. And, when life ends—the breath stops.'

Yeshua's spirit urged him on, seeing Nicodemus' wheels were turning.

Nicodemus asked, "How can this be?"

"You are Israel's teacher and do you not understand these things?"

Momentary disappointment flitted across Yeshua's face.

Nicodemus lifted his hands, his mouth open, embarrassed that he was a dull student.

Yeshua remembered Isaiah's words. 'They will be ever hearing, but not hearing, ever seeing but not seeing.' It was simply not

Nicodemus' time to see what he was saying. Yet, he was sure the Father was drawing this man to him.

Yeshua pressed on. "*We* speak of what *We* know, and *We* testify to what *We* have seen. But still, you people do not accept *Our* testimony. If I have spoken to you of earthly things and you do not comprehend or believe them, how then will you believe me if I speak of heavenly things?"

Now, Nicodemus wondered at the use of the word 'we'.

He blinked at Yeshua. 'What kind of heavenly things?'

Yeshua said, "I tell you the truth, no one has ever gone into heaven except the one who came from heaven, the Son of Man. Your council asked for a sign, and I have given them one sign. Don't forget the sign I have told them. He placed his hand on his chest, 'Destroy this temple and in three days I will raise it!'"

Nicodemus was working hard trying to gather in all of Yeshua's words to meditate on later.

Yeshua cleared his throat. "I will offer you another clue because of your earnest desire. Listen closely. Just as Moses lifted up the snake in the wilderness, just so will the Son of Man also be lifted up. Whoever sees this sign and believes on him will gain eternal life in God's kingdom."

Yeshua made a silent intercession, 'Father, help him to see the truth in my life, death and resurrection. Let this sign open his eyes when the time comes, so he may see.'

Nicodemus felt the conversation was coming to an end, so he rose a bit uncertainly. He didn't know what to say. He still felt completely lost and foolish. Dejection drew the lines of his face. Even so, he nodded his head respectfully towards Yeshua, whose rest he had disturbed.

Yeshua reached out to touch Nicodemus sleeve, motioning him back towards his seat. Nicodemus sat down, waiting.

"Keep this one thing in mind, Nicodemus."

He waited, inclining his ear intently.

"Despite what it seems. I have not come to condemn, but to pre-serve life. I have been sent to be a light. But, some love the darkness and hate the light."

Nicodemus thought then that he was referring to his coming to him under the cloak of night. "I know how bad this looks," He whis-pered urgently, "I really don't like hiding my actions or sneaking around, but how else could I be sure? My reputation is on the line; this could easily cost me everything, and perhaps you too. I have taken the greatest of care in coming tonight. But, unscrupulous men are in power."

Yeshua clarified, "What I am saying is this, men love darkness because their deeds are evil. They do not want their deeds to be exposed. But whoever loves the truth, enters into the light, so they may see clearly all they have done in the sight of God."

He reached out to squeeze Nicodemus' shoulder encouragingly, "It has taken courage for you to come out of the darkness to seek the light tonight. Keep seeking the light."

Nicodemus nodded his head, this he understood. But he had hoped to learn more about the coming kingdom! He wanted des-perately to ask, 'Are you the Messiah?' It was why he had come. But now he was embarrassed to ask him.

Shouldn't I know?

He arose again and thanked Yeshua for his time. He stepped lightly around the sleeping bodies, disappearing through the gate, closing it behind him. Once again he was ensconced into the dark-ness of the night, but he still stood before the words of light. Yeshua had given him a lot to think about. He felt sure his answers were there, if only he could make sense of them. He couldn't wait to tell his friend, Yosef. Maybe they could decipher the answers together.

~ 27 ~

HYPOCRITES

Do not sit with the deceitful,
or associate with hypocrites.
Psalm 26:4

Yeshua was not ready to openly declare his identity. Yet, each day he could feel his Father's words of truth burning inside of him, as if they urgently needed to be declared. People could not see their need for salvation, if they did not know the truth. The crowds had grown so large that he began to use the temple steps creating an auditorium. It was a daring move given the hostility of the temple leaders. Spies were constantly present, reporting everything he said and did. The crowds became his protection.

It became clear to him that some witnesses had misconstrued his miracles and gracious words, thinking their sin was inconsequential. There was no need to revisit their behavior or to turn from their sin. They assumed his Father had somehow changed his mind concerning his previous covenant of law as if he had made a mistake. His Father's words never changed as if he had uttered them in error. The covenant was literally written in stone.

Yeshua clarified his Father's intentions declaring, "Do not think that I have come to abolish the Law or the Prophets! No! I tell you: Unless your righteousness is greater than that of the Pharisees and the Teachers of the Law, you will certainly not enter the kingdom of heaven."

His listeners were askance, "What then? Who is more righteous than the Pharisees? What kind of righteousness does God demand?

He continued. "Do not be like the hypocrites who love to pray standing in the synagogues and on the street corners to be seen by others."

Bewildered, the people shook their heads wondering, how could one prove their piety to others without public prayer?

Reading their minds, Yeshua went on, "Pray in private, so your prayer is just between you and your Father in heaven. When you seek him privately in praise and thanksgiving, when you ask for his advice and counsel, he will hear your every word and thought. He will reward you for bringing your concerns to him. Ask him what you should pray for; he knows your needs and the needs of others better than you do. He knows what you need before you even ask."

This made sense, so the people nodded their heads. 'Personal prayer is better than public prayer.'

Yeshua walked along the step, then stilled. "Don't fast to be seen, or put on long faces as if you are making some huge sacrifice that others should applaud you. Keep your physical desolation between you and your Father in heaven."

"Stop seeking after worldly wealth that is fleeting and temporary. Instead search for ways to store up heavenly treasure. Out of the heart flows generosity to reveal what is most important to you. Just as out of your heart also flows selfishness and greed to condemn you."

Many people turned away when they heard this. For they didn't want anything to come between them and their money, not even the kingdom of God. Some of the poor nodded, they counted themselves more blessed than the rich in receiving the kingdom of God.

He pointed to one of the narrow gates of the temple.

"Enter through the narrow gate, it is the way that leads to life, though it be different from the gate of crowds. Seek the narrow path. Crowds will lead you astray. It may feel lonely at times to break away from the crowd, but follow the way to life."

The tide of people, ebbed and flowed. Some remained, straining to hear every word. Some paused curiously as if he were but an entertaining side show. When they found nothing to impress them, or heard an offensive word, they moved on their way.

"Who should we follow in Jerusalem?" The shout come from within the crowd. Yeshua ignored the question.

Instead, he said, "Watch out for false prophets. They dress up in sheep's clothing. They have the look, but underneath they are ferocious wolves. You will recognize a false prophet by the fruit of their labors.

"When looking for wisdom, remember, your foundation matters. The wise man builds upon a rock, but the foolish man builds upon shifting sands. When the storm comes he gets swept away."

Spies from the Sanhedrin listened. He did not challenge the Sanhedrin directly, but his inferences were understood. His words infuriated them all the more. Constantly the conversations amongst the Sanhedrin focused on ways they could be rid of him. He became their obsession.

The Passover celebration was coming to an end. Yeshua decided it was judicious to leave Jerusalem before the leaders could get their plan organized.

On his last day of teaching, a man approached to make his acquaintance.

"I am Judas son of Iscariot. Rabbi, I have never heard such enlightened teaching as yours."

Yeshua politely allowed the man to talk. All the while, he knew what Judas ben Iscariot was doing. His words were flattering and pleasing to the ear. Judas was subtle, he understood the clever things that easily impressed gullible people. He demonstrated a certain kind of emotional intelligence. The man could very convincingly repeat his words back to him. Yet, Yeshua found no evidence of their intended effect. Something felt off with Judas, he was hollow, produced, artificial.

Yeshua noted Judas' watchfulness of those around him. He had shrewd and crafty eyes, constantly monitoring people's underlying motivations. Judas calculated each person's connection and apparent worth like a commodity. He was not surprised to see Judas had already ingratiated himself amongst some of his disciples before having even approached him.

But the clincher for Yeshua was his recollection of having seen Judas in the temple courts. He had been among the money changers when he had driven them out of the temple. Yeshua felt the slippery, oily truth of this man. He would very likely trade his own mother for a bag of silver. Judas' big smile, overflowing compliments, false humility, and social intelligence bore all the signs of one very convincing manipulator. He realized he had become Judas' target.

"Rabbi, I know you know nothing about me, but I would love a chance to study under you." Judas declared. "I have learned so much this week from your teaching. It has given me so much to think about. Would you consider taking me with you as one of your students? I could be of great assistance. And, I have some useful ideas about the expansion of your ministry and fund raising."

Love of money.

Yeshua stared into an all too familiar face.

Fearing he had gone too far, Judas humbly added, "Or whatever you want."

He shifted his gaze away from Yeshua's scrutiny, to wave to acquaintances passing by, calling out his greetings as if to impress that he had connections.

Yeshua had been expecting Judas. He was after all a crucial part of his Father's plan. There had to be a 'traitor', a consummate actor or hypocrite who would be capable of double dealing him to the Sanhedrin.

"Yes, Judas. I believe you will be of great benefit to my ultimate mission." Yeshua offered a slight smile that did not reach his eyes. "In fact, I am sure your skills will be most helpful."

Judas' face beamed as one who could not believe his own good fortune.

If this guy reaches his potential, he will become a lucrative money maker as the Messiah. People are already hanging on his every word. And, should he somehow miraculously become the King as they hope, I could be in charge of the coffers!'

Yeshua nodded toward Judas, "We will be leaving tomorrow. By the way, have you been baptized?"

"Baptism? Of course." He smiled, then turned towards the other disciples as they welcomed him into their group.

In truth, Yeshua was sure Judas did not subscribe to the holiness code, nor was he particularly zealous. He cared little for the Jewish law unless it worked to his benefit. He understood money and power. He was an opportunist, who made it his habit to position himself near those who could benefit him most. Judas saw him as his money ticket.

Judas talked charmingly to the other disciples. He was the perfect hypocrite, an actor skilled in playing his role. Another piece of his Father's plan had fallen into place. Two-faced people often cause serious problems for everyone. Until the appointed time, he'd have to keep his eyes on Judas. One can never trust a hypocrite; they are nothing if not trouble.

~ 28 ~

THE GROOMSMEN

The bride belongs to the bridegroom.
The friend who attends the bridegroom waits
and listens for him, and is full of joy when he hears
the bridegroom's voice.
That joy is mine, and it is now complete.
John 3:29

Yeshua talked with his brother James, "Things have become too dangerous for us to remain together on the journey home. The Sanhedrin is plotting against me. It will be safer if we split and you take the family home."

James, was once again upset, "Yes, you have certainly stirred up the hornets' nest once again. What were you thinking to challenge the High Priest and the Sanhedrin?"

"I did what had to be done."

"Are you trying to get yourself killed? You know how ruthless the Sanhedrin are, and what about us? It puts us all in danger as well, is that what you want?"

"No, it is not. You need not worry. You should know that."

"You make trouble, Yeshua! You think you know better than anyone else! Trouble follows you around. Who are you to judge others?"

Yeshua did not answer him. He felt the old familiar aching in his heart. His brother seethed with bitterness towards him.

"I promised to work something out for Ima. She has become fast friends with Rock's mother-in-law. I have talked with her and she agrees it is good to give you space for your own family. So, we have arranged for her to remain with Deborah, Abigail and Rock's family, until I can establish a home base where she and our brother Si can live. Rock will be on the road most of the time with me. I can keep an eye on Ima as we come and go. Would you return Ima and the women safely to Simon's home?"

Imagining his privacy, James quickly relented. "Of course."

"And travel with Hannah and Zerah to Cana and make sure they are settled. It is only a little out of your way."

"Zerah can manage his own family."

"Please." James knew this was not a request.

He nodded. "Where are you going?"

"Another way." He did not say more. "From now on, I will be keeping my distance so you will not be endangered on account of me."

The next day, Yeshua and his disciples struck off through the barren eastern side of Jerusalem. It was a dangerous and narrow road, with steep drop offs, lots of rocks and no shade to be found. The landscape reminded him of his time of testing, when he had become suddenly lost and disoriented. He was grateful now that the road lay plainly before him.

Yohan said, "Will we be seeing the Baptizer on our journey?"

"Yes, I am sure we will. We go this way to escape the prying eyes of the Sanhedrin. Once we have traveled up into the Jordan river valley, we will spend time helping to baptize new believers and share the good news. Many of the people I have been teaching in Jerusalem will come to receive baptism. I will be teaching. You who have been trained under Yohannan can train the others. It will take all of us."

Yohan looked surprised, as did Andrew. "But that has always been the Baptizer's job."

"You have been baptized and watched Yohannan baptize. You are trained to do this work. Your family is also of the priestly line. But that matters little, because everyone who believes in me becomes a part of my royal priesthood."

The men were surprised at these order changing words.

When they arrived to Yohannan's camp at Aenon near Salim, they found the water abundant there. Yeshua and Yohannan embraced one another, exchanging the words of peace.

"Cousin, you are a sight to behold. How is your ministry?"

"The numbers are growing daily! People are searching for the kingdom of heaven and for you!" Yohannan laughed.

"I have brought some of your old disciples to help get the job done."

Yohannan raised his eyebrows in question. "To help?"

"Yes, get ready for an onslaught of people anxious for the baptism of repentance." Yeshua said. "People will be coming from the Jerusalem festivals."

"Ah! You have been busy."

"Yes, we had quite a time in Jerusalem."

"So, I have heard! It has not been safe for me to go to the festivals for some time. Still, I wish I could have seen you taking them on with the whip!"

Yohannan gave a hardy laugh. "I wish I could have helped you."

Yeshua offered a wry humor at Yohannan's comment before they both grew serious.

"I could not contain my outrage when I saw how they were desecrating my Father's house. They make a mockery of its very intent. How can people take what is holy and grace filled, and transform it into something so evil?"

"I heard you challenged Annas." Yohannan's face beamed at the thought.

"And Caiaphas as well. He has finally gained his turn to be High Priest, as you know, since Annas has ran his course with all his sons for the office."

Yohannan's lip curled, "Yes, Annas refuses to relinquish his power. And Caiaphas has always been like his pet dog. Still, he had to wait to take his turn until Annas' sons had held the position."

"I remembered Caiaphas from the year of our Bar Mitsvah." Yeshua nodded. "Do you remember he was a disciple of Annas even then?"

"Yes, he has been groomed as if he were Annas' own son. Annas could never manipulate his own sons quite like he could Caiaphas. Changing the subject, I hear tell, that you have been healing people of their afflictions in Capernaum."

Yeshua nodded. "I plan to base my ministry out of there. But you better get ready to start baptizing."

"Is that so?" Yohannan's eyebrows shot up with happy expectation.

"Yes, you still have work to do." Yeshua assured him with a hardy pat on the back.

"Come then and wash up for the evening meal. Though I am not sure what the men have scrounged up for us to eat."

"I hope they were fruitful, since I am not so fond of locust." Yeshua quipped.

The next day, people began to arrive early in the morning like a flood that had just broke its restraints. Yohannan and his men were amazed by the numbers. They realized Yeshua was right, they could not keep up with the demand. Yeshua's disciples moved further upstream and began to baptize people also. It did not take long before a dispute broke out between the two groups of disciples about the baptism rite itself. Yohannan's men complained that Yeshua's disciples were not discharging the baptism correctly.

Yohannan's disciples complained,"You must do it exactly like Yohannan does it, they must be plunged all the way under. Not just poured or scooped."

"And, you must say the right words."

"You should be sending them to us for baptism if you are not of the priestly line."

Yeshua's disciples argued, "Yeshua says anyone who believes in his name are of his royal priesthood. Some of us are from priestly families anyway. And as to the particulars, Yeshua trusts our instincts. "

Ultimately, Yohannan's disciples were jealous for their teacher's ministry. They came to him with their lists of complaints.

"Rabbi, the one who was with you by the Jordan—the one you testified about, is baptizing, or at least his disciples are! They are not performing the baptisms correctly!"

"Yes, and that is not all; now all the people are asking for their Rabbi. People are going to him to hear your message and to be baptized!"

Yohannan sighed heavily at their complaints, searching for the right words, "Listen to me, my ministry is not of my own doing, but of God. It has been my pleasure to serve at the will of the King of Heaven. You have heard me say it time and time again that I am not the Messiah. I was sent to prepare the way for him. It is the bridegroom who makes the bride his own, not the friend of the bridegroom! My calling was to prepare the way to him. I was to wait and listen for his voice. And, I did hear it, just as I told you! Now as one who goes before him and as his servant, I rejoice when I hear his voice. And, I long for his happiness."

His disciples were surprised by Yohannan's relinquishment.

Yohannan's face took on the light of inspiration, remembering Isaiah's texts.

"Yeshua is the Bridegroom, I am his friend and my happiness for him is overflowing. He must increase among the people, while I get out of the way. The One who comes from above is the One who is over all people. I can only tell you of earthly things. Yeshua comes from heaven, and he testifies to us of what he knows from his Father. The One whom God has sent speaks the words of God.

His Father is giving to him his Spirit without limit. The Father loves the Son and has placed everything in his hands. Yeshua is our way to salvation. He far surpasses me because 'He Was' even before I was. His words are filled with grace and truth. Our job is to assist him in his work."

So Yohannan got up and went to Yeshua.

"Our men are in conflict. What would you have us to do?"

Yeshua said, "Cousin, I must train up these men. Many of whom had their beginnings under your influence and ministry. You have begun the work, now I will complete my work in them. All of these men will have their own part in the mission too. They will be entrusted with the responsibility my Father entrusts to them for the kingdom, just as it has been for you. Your work is not yet complete. Return to your camp and continue, we will route any overload of people to you and your men for baptism. Let us complete this work together."

Yohannan agreed. The two men hugged in the sight of all their men and everyone closed their mouths. When the numbers began to wane, Yeshua knew their work at the Jordan was drawing to an end. It was time to move on and leave the rest of the work to Yohannan.

~ 29 ~

A BROOD OF VIPERS

Rescue me, Lord, from evildoers; protect me from the violent,
who devise evil plans in their hearts and stir up war every day.
They make their tongues as sharp as a serpent's;
the poison of vipers is on their lips.
Keep me safe, Lord, from the hands of the wicked;
protect me from the violent.
Psalm 140:1-4

Members of the Sanhedrin rode along the Jordan Valley, searching for Yeshua. As it was, they happened into Yohannan's camp
hoping to find Yeshua there.

Yohannan stood up, recognizing Caiaphas seated on his mule as
if he were a general. He surmised, after what had happened in Jerusalem, he was probably not the target the Sanhedrin pursued. He
prayed on the fly that neither Yeshua nor his men would happen
into the camp. His uplifted palm and his fierce look commanded his
men to silence.

The temple guards dismounted, coming to stand threateningly
near Yohannan. Caiaphas leveled his gaze on him from his mule.
This was not Yohannan's first confrontation with the Sanhedrin;
but Caiaphas had never deemed to make a personal visit. Yohannan
recognized the intimidation tactic. He waited.

"Who are you?" Caiaphas demanded as if he didn't know him at all.

Yohannan's fierce glare said as much, but he remained mute.

"Are you the Messiah?"

"I am not." Yohannan stated evenly.

"Are you Elijah?"

"I am not."

"Are you the Prophet?"

"No."

"Then, who are you? By what authority are you preaching and baptizing these people?"

"I am the voice of one calling in the wilderness, 'Make straight the way for the Lord.'"

Caiaphas gave him an incinerating look, his party muttered to one another at these words of Isaiah. The holy ones had long been a thorn in their flesh. They were considered fundamentalist, outdated, radical, and even seditious to the new order of the temple the Sanhedrin had implemented. Yohannan's holiness movement threatened their advance. This was why Yohannan had rejoiced when he had heard of Yeshua's confrontation in the temple courts.

Now, Yohannan felt that same holy fire rising up from within his being towards these thieves standing arrogantly before him. With a quick intake of air, he opened his mouth to find his preaching voice.

"You brood of vipers! Who warned you to flee from the coming wrath? Produce fruit in keeping with repentance. And do not think you can say to yourselves, 'We have Abraham as our father.'"

Yohannan came to his feet, motioning to the stone he had been sitting on. "I tell you that out of these stones God can raise up children for Abraham. The ax is already at the root of the tree, and every tree that does not produce good fruit will be cut down and thrown into the fire. You cater to the desires of that fox Antipas! A lawless man, who is living in adultery with his own brother's wife!

You not only approve, but you have even officiated the ceremony for this illegal marriage!"

Yohannan paused long enough to regather another breath. "Humble yourselves before the Living God! Strip off your fancy robes and come on in. I will baptize you with water for your repentance. Because I tell you now, after me comes one who is more powerful than I, whose sandals I am not worthy to carry. He is the one who will baptize you with the Holy Spirit and fire. Already, his winnowing fork is in his hand prepared to clear his threshing floor gathering his wheat into the barn. Then he will burn the chaff with unquenchable fire."

Despite Yohannan's pointed inference to the threshing floor, his meaning was lost on Caiaphas. Instead, at the mention of Antipas' wedding, Caiaphas' eyes glinted dangerously.

"Another one comes after you? Who? Tell me who he is, and where I might find him." Yohannan was sure Caiaphas already knew who. He had come hoping to find Yeshua here. Only then did Yohannan realize, he had said too much.

"If the Messiah was here, he would be speaking to you, not me. As it is, he is not here. But you will know him when you meet him! No doubt, you will blaspheme him as you blaspheme the very God of Heaven. Unless you have come to repent, what more have I to say to you?"

Caiaphas took note of the large crowd of witnesses. He would deal with Yohannan's insolence, but not publicly. He and his company of the Sanhedrin left the way they had come.

Yohannan drew in a deep breath of relief and let air out cautiously. He was thankful their caravan did not go in Yeshua's direction. Still, they would not stop looking for him. It was not safe for Yeshua to remain in Judea. Yohannan stepped from the water, waiting long enough to know they were really gone. Then he personally ran to Yeshua's camp, not leaving the job to another.

When Yohannan arrived, it took a moment for him to catch his breath. He blurted out. "Yeshua! You must leave immediately!

The Sanhedrin just came to my camp looking for you, if they have found me, they will find you too. Caiaphas is leading the charge. His guards and political supporters were with him. They did not come in peace. Cousin, Judea is not safe for you any longer."

Yeshua put his hand on his cousin's shoulder, glancing down the road that Yohannan had just traveled. He had done what he could to help with the blitz of people from Jerusalem. Now that the flow was waning, Yohannan would manage the rest.

He looked into his cousin's eyes. "What about you? Our ministries are tied together, we share parts of the same mission from my Father."

"I won't pretend I am not concerned." Yohannan said. "But haven't I always known the danger of my work and message? I will complete the work given to me, I trust God with my future. Besides I am not the target, at least, not today. You go away now, far from here, remain safe so you can finish your work. I will try to buy you some time. They will continue to sniff around here and send spies to watch for you, believing you are here hidden among us."

Yeshua saw the wisdom in his words. "You are right. We will leave under the cover of darkness tonight."

With that, the two men threw their arms around one another as if for the last time, each one sorrowful but resolved to complete God's will. Yeshua squeezed his cousins neck.

"Yohannan, I love you."

"And, I love you." Yohannan replied as they looked at one another eye to eye, then released with a determined nod.

When Lazarus heard Yeshua was preparing to return to Capernaum to flee Caiaphas, he came to him saying, "Lord, I must return to my home in Bethany. I wish I could go with you, but for now I think it best that we return." He nodded toward his sister Martha who had braved the excursion with him to be baptized. Yeshua understood, Lazarus was concerned for his sister's well-being because of the danger that may lay ahead.

"Yes, take Martha back to safety. I am glad for the time we have shared the last few days. I have missed you since Qumran. Once your sister is settled feel free to come find me, come follow me."

"You know I would love to go with you." Lazarus apologized with a shrug, but my father has handed off a portion of the family business to me to handle.

Yeshua was aware there were many things holding Lazarus back, having nothing to do with Martha at all but with material wealth. So it was with so many people. Not everyone was willing to leave everything behind to become his disciple, especially where wealth and position were concerned.

"Promise me one thing." Lazarus said to him.

"What do you ask?"

"Promise me that from now on whenever you come to Jerusalem, you will stay with us in Bethany. It will keep you just out of Caiaphas' reach and provide us a chance to meet regularly, away from all the watchful eyes."

Yeshua accepted this as Lazarus' offer to serve him. Yet, Yeshua knew even this would eventually put Lazarus and his family in the line of fire. Yeshua loved Lazarus, and his sister Martha as well. He felt he could trust them and they had a large estate with plenty of room to accommodate him and his men. It was a good offer. Yeshua nodded his head in agreement.

"Yes. Thank you for your gracious invitation. I will take you up on your offer and I look forward to the next time we meet."

While saying goodbye to them, Yeshua was reminded of Lazarus and Martha's concern for their estranged adoptive 'sister' who they called Mari. Apparently, she was in Jerusalem. They had explained how time and space had distanced them all from one another. They were worried for her, because close as it was, Mari had not come home in years. As with so many families, it was easy for misunderstandings to drive people apart, and for someone to get lost. He was always most concerned for the lost sheep of his flock, for those who found themselves alone.

"I will pray for your sister."

"Thank you."

That night, Yeshua and his followers traveled under a mere trace of a waxing moon, on a darkly shadowed path.

Yeshua acutely felt the presence of his old nemesis lurking in the blackness. He half expected him to come snapping at his heels yet again. After some time, he heard the hiss from the side of the trail.

"You cannot escape me, you know."

Yeshua did not reply.

"Why are you going to Samaria? They will eat you alive there?"

He did not answer to Satan, only his Father. His own men had asked him the same thing. To which he had simply replied, "I have to go through Samaria." When one is dealing with serpents, one has to be as shrewd as a serpent. No priest or Pharisee would travel through Samaria for fear of their own lives. Rightfully so, the hatred between the Samaritans and Jews was unrelenting. By going the way of Samaria, he would escape Caiaphas and his henchmen.

So, Yeshua led his men into the very heart of the one place they would never choose to go. Samaria.

~ 30 ~

THE CORRUPT SHEPHERD

Son of man, prophesy against the shepherds of
Israel;
prophesy and say to them:
'This is what the Sovereign Lord says:
Woe to you shepherds of Israel
who only take care of yourselves!
Should not shepherds take care of the flock?
Ezekiel 34:2

Herod Antipas had ruled Galilee and Perea as Tetrarch for over thirty years. Yet, despite the most recent celebration of his reign, Antipas was far from satisfied. He still felt the long shadow of his father.

'The Great King Herod' he had named himself and no one had argued. His father's energy, cunning, and iron fisted cruelties had been unconquerable. That was until mysterious and pain filled illness struck him down. No one had mourned Herod's passing. Even his family was glad his reign of terror had come to an end. No one was more joyful than Antipas.

Herod the Great was a privately a polygamous, supporting numerous women, but keeping one queen. Antipas' mother was the fourth of the five official wives of Herod. She was a Samaritan beauty, but her heritage earned Antipas no favors. For many years, Antipas and his brother Archelaus received only scraps from their father's table. Wisely, Antipas kept a low profile, spending most of his time in Rome. By biding his time, he had remained alive. Over time, his father executed his favorite wife, then her two sons, then the son of his first wife, perceiving each of them to be threats to his throne. It was said, "It is better to be Herod's pig, than one of his sons."

Although Antipas had longed for his father's approval, he feared the constant threat of death that came with it. Mellowing with old age, his father had only deposed, divorced, and exiled his third family, sending his namesake Herod I to Rome and his wife to Bethany to her father. No one was irreplaceable or above his suspicion.

Eventually, Herod divided his kingdom between his last three remaining sons and a small sliver to his sister, Salome. Making sure no one person would rule his all the provinces of his kingdom, less they supersede him.

Judea was left to Archelaus as the Ethnarch. But when Archelaus was removed from his rule, Antipas hoped for a brief moment to expand his reign over Jerusalem. But by that time, Caesar considered the city too volatile. Instead, he sent a hardnosed governor to enforce Roman rule. Antipas knew better than to oppose Tiberius Caesar. So he chose for himself the desecrated city of Sepphoris in Galilee as the site on which to build a beautiful palace. Mimicking his father's great building projects, he exacted tax from the Galilean people to build it. He named his palace The Autocratoris, 'the ornament of Galilee'. He also inherited his father's fortified palace on the eastern side of the Jordan named Manchaerus and the fortress of Masada on the western side.

The governor was given Herod's palace in Jerusalem, but Antipas kept a smaller compound in the city for the Festivals. For years, his political marriage to the Nabatean princess Phasaelis served to expand his borders to the northeast. In the end, he had ended up with a pretty sweet inheritance.

When Antipas received an invitation to visit his half-brother Philip in Rome, he should have known something was up. It was by design rather than fate that Antipas was seduced by his brother's wife – Herodias. Under the tutelage of her Great Aunt Salome, Herodias had grown powerful in Rome. She felt cheated of her rightful royal status when her husband had been disinherited to become only a high-ranking Roman citizen. Philip had even abandoned his Herodian name. He had long found Herodias to be tedious, treacherous, and unfaithful. When she set her wiles on Antipas, Philip considered it his lucky day. He was happy to assist. Finally, he had found a way to be free of the woman and the child he was quite sure was not his.

Herodias excelled at her craft, he would give her that. She had a brittle beauty, along with intelligence and strategic cunning. With little effort she convinced Antipas that a match with her would make him more acceptable to the Jews because of her Hasmonean bloodline and to Roman for her connections. Antipas was bored in his middle age, ripe for the picking. Forbidden, his affair with Herodias excited him. She employed her wiles of persuasion on Caesar Tiberius to gain approval for the match. When Antipas returned with Herodias to Galilee, his wife Phasaelis fled to her father King Aretas seeking asylum.

Installed as Queen, Herodias set the tone for the lifestyle in which Antipas lived. Pagan, decadent and even perverse. Antipas approved of it all.

For this reason, when word reached Antipas about a prophet crying out in the wilderness against immorality, he felt the threat.

"Who is this man?" He asked his adviser.

"It appears he is a prophet."

"There have been no prophets for well over four hundred years. I thought prophets were obsolete. Just like all the rumors of a Messiah have repeatedly come to nothing."

"Well, while you have been away large numbers your subjects have been going to the Baptizer 'to be purified of their sins'." His advisor told him.

Antipas realized a moral movement could not be good for him. Such movements reeked of a possible uprising. He didn't need any more trouble. Rome barely tolerated the Herodians by virtue of their citizenship. They were allowed to reign only if they were successful in keeping the peace. Antipas was already under Caesar's scrutiny because of the current conflict over the Nabatean border.

Antipas called for his best advisors.

"Is this one of those underground organizations, connected to the Sicarii?" He asked trying to hide his shudder of fear.

The Sicarii were reputed to be sleuth mercenaries; they struck quickly and unexpectedly with a deadly cruelty that was unrivaled.

At their mention, his advisor tugged uncomfortably at his collar. "There is no doubt that a variety of people are going to the Baptizer, some could be considered suspect. However, there has been no violence from Yohannan ben Zechariah."

The other advisors nodded their agreement.

"The Baptizer is closely associated with the Essenes, who keep to themselves. I wouldn't make too much out of it."

Antipas recalled the Essenes had refused to compromise their beliefs even under duress during his father's reign. Though persecuted, many had escaped to Galilee and the Jordan keeping their own counsel.

"To what purpose does he baptize?" Antipas probed.

"He preaches to prepare 'The Way'."

"What is 'The Way'?"

"The Way', is a term for returning to God through Yahweh's long-awaited Anointed One—the fabled Jewish Messiah. The Baptizer is convinced the Messiah is here and will soon appear. He is calling out to Jews to be spiritually prepared for his arrival. It is the stuff of tall tales, sir. Still, I hear, even Roman soldiers have gone out to listen to the wild man and some have even been baptized."

Antipas' expression turned incredulous. "Romans?"

"Yes. He preaches moral holiness and justice. But like I said, I wouldn't worry too much. Even if a leader rises up, their days are numbered. Who will challenge Rome? It will blow over in no time."

Herod chewed a hang nail as he listened, concern gnawing on the inside. The people's desire for a holy ruler did not bode well for him. His first instinct was to send out his own mercenaries to shut down this 'Baptizer'. His father would have done it and not looked back. But times were different now, such a move would come back to haunt him. The people of the land might rise up to revolt against him believing Yohannan to be a prophet sent from Yahweh.

'No', he thought. 'It is prudent to wait for Rome to handle the movement. What is baptism anyway, but a little water?'

~ 31 ~

THE WELL OF HUMAN NEED

Need My people have committed two sins:
They have forsaken me, the spring of living water,
and have dug their own cisterns,
broken cisterns that cannot hold water.
Jeremiah 2:13

For most of the night, Yeshua and his men continued moving, until they were utterly exhausted. Only then did they unroll their bedding off the side of the road for two hours sleep. All but Yeshua, he kept vigil over his men while taking the needed time to pray over all that was pressing him forward. He prayed, until the night morphed into light again.

He woke his men, having them eat quickly, unwilling to tarry. His men still wondered, what they were doing there on the road to Samaria. Yeshua had not told them much. He wanted them to learn to follow him without question, to trust him in every circumstance, to grow in faith without sight. He'd found that the more his followers knew, the more likely they were to inject their own preferences and ideas, or do things to complicate his plan.

The road to Samaria was curvaceous, with steep paths, sharp cliffs, and rock outcroppings. The soil was red, loose and gravelly. At times, they glimpsed beautiful vineyards and orchards in the distance. Neither was along their road, nor did they find a water supply.

By the time they approached Sychar, they were hungry and thirsty. The day had grown unseasonably hot, and they had drained their water skins.

Yeshua was limping in pain, having bruised his heel on a sharp stone. His lack of sleep was catching up with him, and he was developing a pounding headache that made him feel nauseous. He knew this feeling, dehydration. There was literally no shade in this otherwise exposed valley. Yeshua looked ahead to a well surrounded by a short rock wall. He limped to it looking for a water pot. There wasn't one. He sat down in the sparse shadow of the low wall.

"I think I will rest here." He said.

His men were apprehensive, noting that he looked unnaturally pale.

"The town is just ahead. Can't you make it?"

"Shall I stay with you Yeshua?" James asked longing to plop down beside him.

Yeshua shook his head. "No, go on ahead into the village and find refreshment. I will wait here and rest until you return. But take care, Samaritans don't trust Jews. Remember if you are insulted, turn the other cheek. We don't want any trouble." Yeshua expected little hospitality for Jews. Simon, James, and Yohan could be easily offended and apt to lose their tempers.

"I think we should all stay together" Simon said decisively.

Judas looked toward the village, already planning a way to barter for what they needed, with a plan to skim a little extra for himself.

"No, no. I will be fine." Yeshua waved them onward.

"Who is going to come out to the well at this time of the day? And if they do, maybe they will have mercy on me and draw some water for me from the well. Go." He ordered them wincing.

"I will wait for you here." Though they exchanged concerned glances, but he waved them on. They went on their way, traveling up the cart path into the town.

Yeshua slouched against the low-lying northern wall of the well. He looked towards hazy Mt. Gerizim rising up steeply on one side, then toward Mt. Ebal on the other side. He considered what he knew of this location. It was to this very place that Moses had instructed Joshua to bring the Israelites after they crossed over the Jordan River and entered the land. In this place Joshua led a worship service commemorating God's covenant relationship with his people. They were to celebrate God's faithfulness to deliver them out of Egypt and to bring them safely to this land. He had kept all his promises. That worship event was to set the tone for the future possession of this land.

Why here?

Yeshua had noticed on their approach, that from a distance these two mountain peaks rose up out of the terrain like two breasts, side by side and perfectly matched. The valley between, where he now sat, was considered to be the heart of the land.

He tried to imagine the massive number of persons filling this valley. The Israelites had been instructed to build a monument here of twelve stones, which they had carried from the Jordan River. The priests had brought the Ark of God's covenant and set up their site for worship. The stones were to be plastered together, and on the plaster they were to inscribe all of the promises of God.

Years later, after Israel's many moral failures, Ezekiel had prophesied that the nations heart of stone would become a heart of flesh. That prophecy was now being fulfilled. That heart of flesh beat in his chest. He was the fulfillment of everything within the ark and all that was engraved on the stones.

The Ebenezer had been placed, so the people would not forget God's promises, and to remind the people that their hearts were to belong to the LORD alone. On that day, Joshua had one half of the tribal leaders go up to stand on Mt. Gerizim to declare the covenant of God's blessings over the people below. The other half of the tribal leaders went up to stand on Mt. Ebal to proclaim the curses, which would surely come if they failed to keep the covenant. They were to never forget the words carved here. But, they had.

In time, both mountains had become the home of the pagan high places of the northern kingdom. Each with shrines to the golden calves, the Baals, and eventually every Canaanite god, as well as the other nations. But how could it not? In a hidden act of subterfuge hundreds of years before, Rachel had stolen her father's household gods and brought them to this very place. When Jacob found out, in anger, he had collected the idols from Rachel and all the members of his household and buried them under the great oak tree on Mt. Gerizim.

Like evil seeds, the idols were planted into the land like a cancer waiting to spread. A doorway for evil had been opened there. Neither Rachel, nor Jacob, had any idea of what they had done. From that time until now, the enemies of Israel had assailed them. The land and its people struggled from one disaster, affliction, or evil after another.

Yeshua thought, 'What fellowship can light have with darkness? People have no understanding of the evil seeds they unthinkingly plant into their lives, their marriages, their children, community, government and even into the land itself!'

He leaned back. His temples were pounding. He desperately needed a big drink of water. If only someone would come and draw for me a drink of water! During the heat of the day, only woman of low reputation drew water. His own mother often went for water at that time to avoid the nasty looks of the other women in Nazareth. Fetching water was the work of women if there was no slave. He was teased mercilessly as a boy when he had helped his mother with this task. It was well known a remote well was not always a safe place; women had often been accosted there. Without friends, it was a lonely place. He marveled at the generous women who freely offered to draw water for strangers and even their camels as an act of good-will.

Moses rescued Zipporah and her sisters at the well. Rebekah compassionately provided water for the slave of Abraham and his camels. Which, as it turned out, became the very same camels that carried her to Isaac—her beloved and chosen husband, and to blessings and promises. Rachel provided water for a weary Jacob before she knew the besotted man would literally strive fourteen years to become her husband. Each of these women had met their husbands at the wells, and became the mothers of a nation. The well sustains the most basic human need. It offers life.

Yeshua laid his head back against the large stones behind him. His eyes closed, shutting out the brightness of the day. Soon he had drifted off to into a most needed sleep.

~ 32 ~

THE WATER OF LIFE

As the deer pants for streams of water,
so my soul pants for you, my God.
My soul thirsts for God, for the living God.
Psalm 42:1-2
Although our sins testify against us,
do something, Lord, for the sake of your name.
For we have often rebelled;
we have sinned against you.
You who are the hope of Israel,
its Savior in times of distress,...
You are among us, Lord, and we bear your name;
do not forsake us!
Jeremiah 14: 3, 8-9

Yeshua awoke with a start to the sound of a pot being indelicately hoisted upon the stone wall. He listened, hopeful that now he might get a cup of water. He was about to push up when he heard a growl and a string of profane mutterings.

Someone is in a foul mood.

Peering around the well, he found a woman beaded with sweat, fastening a large clay jar to the rope. He stood just as she released the rope carefully into the recesses. She stared at him daring him to speak to her. She gave him the once over. Her expression was rude and indicated she found him unimpressive.

Lo-Ruhamah thought, 'Ah a Jew! No need to worry! He will want nothing from me. Besides, what could he take that has not already been stolen from me?'

Her fierce brown eyes bore into his. She was a small and wiry woman wearing a scowl as evidence her life had been a bitter cup. She made no move to cover her head in the traditional show of modesty.

An echoing splash sounded in the depths below. It was exquisite to Yeshua's ears. He licked his dry lips.

She waited for the jar to fill, then began to haul it up. It was heavy and she was giving it considerable effort, tugging hard hand over fist.

"I could help you with that." Yeshua said pleasantly to her.

She ignored him.

"I was hoping you might give me a drink of water?" Yeshua said, his need obvious. He didn't mind asking since the water was free to the community. It would cost the woman nothing to fill his water skin.

She glared at him, stating the obvious. "You're a Jew."

"Yes." He said mildly.

"In case you haven't made the connection, I am a Samaritan, and a woman." Her voice was angry and defiant.

"Yes, I suppose you are." He stood waiting.

She glanced up into his pained face, "Why would you ask me for a drink? Isn't that beneath you? We don't share the same cup."

Yeshua was jarred by the bitterness in her answer. It was such a simple request, politely given.

He answered her. "If you knew 'the gift of God' and who it is that is speaking to you, you would have asked him and he would have given you living water."

She offered a skeptical glance. "Is that so? Where, pray tell, is your jar, O Man of the Living Water? Where is your rope? This well is deep! How are you going to give me 'living water'?"

Yeshua caught and held her gaze. He had long known the eyes are the door way of the heart and soul.

"Oh wait" she snapped her rough and dirty fingers, touching her forehead as if she had just remembered, "you must be greater than our father Jacob, who gave us this very well. In fact, now that I think of it, he was even able to draw water from this well and drink from it for himself. As did his sons and his livestock." She cocked her head, her taunt sassy.

Despite her cattiness and venom, Yeshua felt sorry for her. She was so angry and defensive. A withdrawn and protective pain emanated from her. In that moment, he recognized her.

Here she is; the very the embodiment of the spirit of my people, Israel.

Despite her rancor, he couldn't help but admire her pluck. After all the ways life had pushed her to the very bottom of the social ladder, she was not going down without a fight. He liked her feisty tenacity. His lips tipped upward like a parent not quite able to hide their incensed humor and chagrin at the ridiculous audacity of their ill-behaved child.

"What's so funny?" She snapped, giving him the evil eye. She pulled hard, with stubborn determination, until she had pulled the heavy clay pitcher over the side of the well by herself. It landed with a thud on the wall, splashing a bit back into the well. He watched it go with regret.

Looking pointedly at the very inviting water, he said, "You know, everyone who drinks this water will be thirsty again, but whoever drinks the water I give them will never thirst. Indeed, the water I give them will become in them a spring of water welling up to eternal life."

Is this guy for real? I've seen snake oil dealers before. Will he try to sell me water? Does he really believe me that gullible?

With an overly dramatic earnestness, her eyes went wide in exaggeration, she said, "Sir, please give me this water so I won't get thirsty and have to keep coming here to draw water!" She let out a snort of sarcasm, feeling quite clever.

The irony was not lost on Yeshua. He was after all a thirsty man asking her for water, while offering her living water at the same time. No wonder, she did not trust him. The difference was she was the one who was really thirsting to death.

In a flash, the woman's whole life passed before him. He swayed on his feet, holding on to the wall. For the first time the woman looked at him with concern. When he had steadied himself, he said to her, "Go and call your husband."

Her head snapped up with so much pain filling her eyes that he could feel it inside his own chest.

He'd had no choice, this was how hearts are transformed, the stones have to be broken; truth has to be spoken and acknowledged before one could receive a new heart of flesh. Like salt to the wound, it was not a painless process.

She dropped her head to hide her flaming cheeks. How does he know the very thing that torments me; that I am unloved, unwanted, that no one really cares about me? If I went missing, my master would only be upset because his dinner had not been prepared. Yeshua saw a chasm of despair in her painfilled eyes. She was a slave and not a very good one. She took her beatings in stride, always wondering when she would land on the street yet again, and sure that she would.

"I have no husband." She mumbled, her bravado gone now. Unwanted tears glimmered at the corners of her eyes. She turned quickly on her heel as if to run away from him as well as her pain, just as she had tried to do all her life. She did not want him to see her cry.

Yeshua called out to her. "The fact is, you have had five husbands."

She stopped dead in her tracks, an overwhelming feeling of dread filled her.

He sees me; he knows me. How can this be? Could it be that this is not an ordinary Jew? Who is he?

"And the man you live with now, he is not your husband. What you have said is quite true." Yeshua said softly matter-of-fact.

Lo-Ruhamah turned slowly, her mouth hung open in undisguised awe. She reappraised him as if for the first time, taking in every detail. The intensity and compassion of his eyes pierced her. His black curls escaped from under his head covering, his skin was bronzed, his teeth white and tassels hung from the four corners of his tallit. She noticed the pattern in his prayer shawl. Then, she noticed his dirty and worn feet.

He looks like a holy man. Can it be?

She had recently heard the rumors of a prophet in Galilee. People were saying he was the long-awaited Jewish Messiah. They said he was filled with the supernatural power of God.

But why would he come here?

She searched his face for ridicule, blame, or accusation; but she saw there was none. Instead, she found compassion and a sympathetic sadness.

He sees me.

Wonder enveloped her. "Sir, I can see you are a prophet. Our ancestors worshiped on these mountains, but you Jews claim the place where we must worship is in Jerusalem."

Lo-Ruhamah had never been to Jerusalem. It might as well have existed on the moon. Her mind was racing quickly now with everything she had ever heard about Yahweh! She had so many questions about Him rushing into her mind all at once. How am I to worship a holy God? What is truly right or wrong? Could God even care about me? Even after all I have done? Questions came gushing up from within her that she never knew she had. Yeshua could see her questions and awe flitting across her features.

"Woman, believe me when I say a time is coming when you will worship the Father neither on this mountain nor in Jerusalem." She listened, hanging on his words. "You Samaritans worship what you do not know; we worship what we do know, for salvation comes through the Jews."

Her eyes narrowed and a slight frown knit her brows together.

Oh, back to that again.

But to her credit she did not say it.

"Yes, a time is coming and has now come when the true worshipers will worship the Father in Spirit and in truth, for they are the kind of worshipers the Father seeks. God is Spirit, and his worshipers must worship in Spirit and in truth."

Her eyes widened with wonder.

Is he saying, I could have access to God? I could worship God and it would be acceptable?

She paused to take in the words "in Spirit and in truth, pondering the meaning of his words. Obviously, the man before her knew all of her truth. He spoke authoritatively, and his words were believable.

She stuttered over her words, "I-I-I know that Messiah is coming. When he comes he will ex-explain e-everything to us?"

Yeshua moved closer to her, and held out his hand palm up towards her and placed his other hand to his chest. "I, the one speaking to you—I am he."

A burst of joy bloomed on her face. How could it be that the Messiah was there and talking to her? But she knew, absolutely knew, it was true. She grabbed his forearms and began jumping up and down in a dance of holy ecstasy, she laughed like a little child. Fearfully, she covered her mouth as if trying to hold on to her joy, to contain it, as if it might escape and disappear. But she could not hold it back.

Her happiness transformed her whole person from head to toe.

Yeshua laughed with her, sharing in her joy.

"The Messiah is talking to me!" She squeaked in awe.

A little bit later, the disciples came down the hill from the town, Yeshua and Lo-Ruhamah were still in an animated conversation; amazement radiated from her. She finished her conversation, then turned to rush away, but before she had gone but a few steps, she turned back to throw herself into Yeshua's arms giving him a huge hug. Yeshua laughed and hugged her back. Then she launched off again.

"Yes!" She turned and shouted emphatically.

"Yes, what?" Yeshua called after her.

"Yes, you can share my cup." She motioned to the pot of water she had left behind.

He beamed, watching her run toward her village. His men marched right past her hardly glancing her way, treating her as if she was invisible.

Yeshua watched them wondering, 'How could they miss her contagious joy?'

He, glanced towards the water jar still standing by the well as a testimony to the power of his living water. He went to the pitcher and took a very long drink.

"You seem to be miraculously enlivened and refreshed" James said to Yeshua.

Rock offered him a roll of bread filled with humus spread and vegetables.

"We brought food to strengthen you!" Yeshua took the food appreciatively, praying his gratitude.

Looking at his men, he said laughing, "I have received food that you know nothing of."

James asked Yohan. "Who brought him food?"

"My real food is to do the will of him who sent me and to finish his work." Yeshua clarified, stuffing in a big bite, he chewed while pacing back and forth.

He kept looking toward the city expectantly, while his men sat down to eat and drink.

"Are you expecting someone?" Andrew asked him

"A village."

It wasn't long until the first of many people appeared coming hurriedly toward them from the village where the woman had disappeared. Then others appeared, as if in a race. Others appeared with slow and steady steps. Yeshua turned to his men, and motioned toward the approaching people.

"Look around you, the harvest is coming. I tell you, open your eyes and look at the fields! They are ripe for the harvest. Even now the one who reaps is drawing her wage, she harvests a crop for eternal life! Today the sower and the reaper will be glad together! Get ready, it is time to go to work men."

The towns people came to stand around Yeshua, just as they had once come to stand before Joshua and the ark of God in the heart of the valley nestled between these two mountains.

Lo-Ruhamah finally returned satisfied she had called everyone, she was happy to join them. She looked luminous and just a bit out of breath. Her whole being was transformed. Yeshua began to share the good news of God's promises that were being fulfilled on that day, along with his Father's desire to bless them all. He warned them of the curses that come from a life devoid of his Father.

Many believed, because of Lo-Ruhamah who had the courage to tell her neighbors, "A man has come to the well who knows everything about my life. He has opened my eyes to the truth about myself, could he be the Messiah of God?"

But after he had been there for two days, the people told her, "Now, we know for ourselves; this man really is the Savior of the world!"

~ 33 ~

A GREAT LIGHT

In the past [the LORD] humbled the land of Zebulun
and the land of Naphtali, but the day is coming
when he will honor Galilee of the nations,
by the Way of the Sea, beyond the Jordan—
The people walking in darkness have seen a great light;
on those living in the land of deep darkness
a light has dawned.
You will enlarge the nation and increase their joy;
they will rejoice before you as people rejoice at the harvest.
Isaiah 9:1-3

Yeshua left Samaria with all his disciples, having added more people to his caravan, both men and women who followed to hear more of his teachings. Mid-afternoon, as they approached the city of Nain, they came upon a large funeral procession. Numerous people walked behind the bier, but only one person caught and held Yeshua's attention. A singular older woman who leaned on another with graying hair like hers, a sister or a friend. He could see that the woman was devastated.

"What a horrible loss. What will happen to Naomi now?"

The mourners wailed as if expressing Naomi's sorrow for her.

"How hard to lose her only son, her only family."

Yeshua waited respectfully as the procession came close to pass him.

Death! How he had always hated death!

Looking closely at the dead man passing by he noticed he looked only a little younger than himself, and he was striking in similarity. His Ima had always said, 'It is not right for a mother to have to bury a child.'

The woman still held the appearance of shock. She trembled, an obvious turmoil building within her like a dam threatening to burst. Her friend was trying her best to console her. But no comfort reached her. He felt the woman's emotional trauma washing toward him in waves. He saw the first of many tears glistening on her cheeks.

Haven't I come to overcome death? To take back those who are my own?

As the mother approached him he spoke gently to her, "Don't cry."

The woman stopped, looking strangely at Yeshua. He really was startlingly similar to her own son.

"That is exactly what my son would say." She whispered.

Yeshua gave her a sad smile. He stepped to the bier looking at the man laying rigidly still. He reached out to touch the bier, and the bearers came to a standstill.

With authority, Yeshua spoke to him. "Young man, get up!"

A collective gasp went up from those around them.

At that very moment, Yeshua felt himself swallowed up in a deep darkness, a frightening nothingness. It was a fleeting impression. Quickly the darkness dissipated, and his vision cleared, the exchange complete.

The dead man stirred as if coming out of a good night's sleep, slowly at first. He moved with growing awareness. Whispers of awe shot through the crowd. When he opened his eyes, he looked wildly around in utter confusion. He sat up. He had no idea where he was, nor did he recognize the stranger standing beside him, watching him.

"Where am I? What is happening?" he asked then searching the faces of all the people around him, then once more at Yeshua.

"You were dead." Yeshua said, "But now you are alive."

Bewilderment filled the man's face. Only then did he realize he was on a bier. He leapt quickly off of it, as though distaining all it stood for. His friends sat it down quickly, eager to welcome him back, astonished and laughing.

"Only you, Tobias, would attend your own funeral!" One friend said to him.

The mourners said, "How can this be?"

Some looked from one to another suspiciously.

Yeshua stepped forward to lead the man back to his mother. "I give your son back to you, just as you requested."

The woman fell upon her son's neck with sobs of relief and joy. "How can this be?"

"You prayed, did you not? You begged God to give you your son back."

Wonder filled her eyes, she asked,

"Who are you?"

Yeshua said, "Why do you ask me who I am?"

Her knees gave way at the wave of recognition and awe which overcame her. Naomi sank to the ground and bent her face to the earth before him, taking note that his feet were covered by the dust of his travel that had just brought him to her! All morning she had been pleading with God. Though she had said nothing out loud to anyone, she had cried out to God for her only son.

Now his question filled her with wonder, 'Why do you ask me who I am?' She remembered Isaiah's words from the LORD.

'My people will know my name; therefore, in that day they will know that it is I who foretold it. Yes, it is I.'

Naomi was totally overcome. Tears of gratitude dripped upon his dusty feet. She was certain that God was standing right in front of her. Who else could have heard her prayer or bring the dead back to life? She reached out and took his feet in her worshipful hands, touching her forehead to them.

When she had finished worshipping, Yeshua offered his hand to lift her up. She searched his face with wonder, and whispered through her tears, "Thank you, Thank you. Thank you."

All of the people were filled with awe. They were praising God, saying, "A great prophet has appeared among us."

But Naomi boldly proclaimed, "Today, our God has come to help his people."

News of 'the man raised to life' spread quickly throughout the surrounding countryside.

Some said, "It is a ruse, the man was not really dead."

Nevertheless, the news continued to spread and crowds continued to grow. His disciples were inspired by all they had seen.

The power of The Anointed One continued to increase day by day. Nothing was impossible for him. Rock, James, and Yohan remained ever near Yeshua like puppies jostling for his attention. Which, he gave to them liberally like a good-natured father. Yet, he was quick to correct them when they acted from their old nature. Not wanting to disappoint him, his men watched everything he did and tried to mirror his actions. Each disciple was unique, possessing individual gifts, needs, strengths, weaknesses and responses. He studied each one of them for what they needed next.

Philip clearly tried to anticipate what Yeshua needed next and he was anxious to serve and support others. Nathaniel marveled at the prophesies of scripture brought to life day by day. Yeshua had promised him he would see greater things, and he was not disappointed and he often drew the correlations. Rock was taking on greater responsibility, as was James and John. They were all growing into their places of their intended effectiveness.

Even Judas found ways to be useful and carried his load. But still, he saw the healings, signs, and wonders as one assessing a commodity with great potential. He could not figure out Yeshua's end game. He realized that if enough people believed he was the Messiah, the profits could be huge. And yet, whenever people offered a tribute to Yeshua, he simply told them to go make a thank offering unto the LORD.

It was as if Yeshua had no interest in money at all. Their money bag remained lean. Judas grew frustrated, but clung to the hope that eventually Yeshua would see the need. It would take a lot of money to gain the power needed to build a kingdom. Instead, it was nothing short of miraculous that they seemed to have everything they might need, but with very little fluff. Judas wondered if Yeshua had some hidden source of income that he knew nothing about. Still, he refused to allow Judas to take up a collection or fund raise. Who had ever seen a king with an aversion for money? Still, Yeshua's lack of interest certainly made it easy for him to skim a bit off of the top.

Day by day, the disciples found their community growing and evolving into something even more awe inspiring. They worked, problem solved, argued, challenged one another, failed, and succeeded together. Their rough edges showed up daily, needing to be worn away. Yet, they were still formative. The team had not yet reached the easy relationship needed to weather the storms and challenges they would have to face without Yeshua's constant presence and mediation.

~ 34 ~

MAN WITH AUTHORITY

I looked, and there before me was one like a son of man,
coming with the clouds of heaven. He approached
the Ancient of Days and was led into his presence.
He was given authority, glory and sovereign power;
all nations and peoples of every language worshiped him.
His dominion is an everlasting dominion
that will not pass away,
and his kingdom is one that will never be destroyed.
Daniel 7:13-14

Stopping in Cana, Yeshua had the chance to check on his sister. She was blooming with young womanhood in every way. And she was surprised when he arrived, with a caravan of followers.

"Why are there so many people with you?"

"These are the people who wish to be reconciled with my Father and I am leading them to him."

"Rumors have circulated of your confrontation with the temple leaders in Jerusalem. I could hardly believe it. YOU! As if you are some sort of outlaw." She gave him an uncomprehending look. "You have changed."

"Have I?" Yeshua challenged her.

"Why would you do such a thing in the temple of all places?" She wanted to know.

"James is fearful the repercussions might reach us, your family. What will they do to you when they catch up with you?"

"Hannah, do you think me a criminal?"

"No, of course not, but…"

"There are forces at work here that will be hard for you to understand. Remember I told you that you would hear rumors about me?" She nodded, realizing she had been too busy to consider Yeshua's confession right before she married. He reiterated the conversation again.

"You will hear all manner of things about me, some true, some false. You must sort that out for yourself. You know me. Even if things end very badly, even if it ends in my death. You must not be afraid for me. I am doing what my Father in heaven has called me to do."

She swallowed. "What do you mean, 'death'. If you are God's son then why are you trying to get yourself killed? I saw for myself what happened in Nazareth and now this. You say things that anger people."

"It is unfortunate that people don't take kindly to the truth."

"Apparently, they don't like your truth."

"Versions of truth do not exist. There is only one truth. Light and darkness have nothing in common."

They sat together in a silence, while she considered what he had told her, as if for the first time. Memories of her parents engaged in hushed whispers concerning Yeshua, niggled the corners of her mind. It was as if they had always been watching for dangers where her brother was concerned. Their secretive and fearful glances had confused her; and when she had asked questions, she was shooed away like an impertinent child. She realized now, Yeshua had truly always been different. She had simply taken his peculiarities in stride. He had always been her favorite person. Whenever he referred to God as his 'Father in heaven', innocently she had found it endearing. Only now did she recognize the audacity of it. Stranger still, even though Yosef was a stickler about proper reverence, he had never corrected Yeshua when he said it. But he did grow angry when James and Jude mocked him for it. Why?

And now people were whispering about a man of God, the Messiah from Galilee who was doing all manner of miracles. Zerah's family had asked all sort of questions concerning Yeshua, that she couldn't really answer. She looked up to find Yeshua's eyes on her, as if he was reading her thoughts. For the first time, she saw the dangerous truth in her brother's face. She saw it in his countenance, a holy mixture of sadness and joy. She was surprised to realize this combination had always been there. How had she not seen it?

Yeshua smiled tenderly at her. Hannah leaned into him and buried her face in his shoulder drawing in the familiar scent of him.

"I'm sorry! I just don't want anything bad to happen to you!" She told him, holding to him with intuitive fear.

"Don't you worry." He leaned in and kissed the top of her head.

"Now tell me all about married life." Hannah looked at him and blushed, her eyes glowed. He laughed at her satisfied that all was well.

After some days of teaching and healing in Cana, Yeshua prepared to return to Capernaum, when there sounded a rumble of horse hooves. A Roman official escorted by a small company of soldiers rode purposefully into the town. He paused to question a terrified bystander, who pointed toward Yeshua. The town's people scurried to find their loved ones and to get out of the way. Some of Yeshua's men closed rank around him, unsure of the commander's intentions, but fearing the worst.

Noting the people's distress, the Centurion raised his hand. His men came to an immediate stop some distance behind him. The Centurion continued right up to Yeshua's party. His dismount was in one fluid motion. He began to approach Yeshua, but suddenly stopped. His eyes widened with recognition.

"It is you, the Nazarene!"

Yeshua recalled their encounter on the way to Jerusalem. The Centurion had questioned him. "Yes, we meet again."

Humbly, the Centurion came forward and touched his chest, his head bowed as a sign of humility and respect. He wasted no time cutting to the chase.

"Lord. Stories of your miracles have circulated throughout the Galilean region. Just a few days ago, I heard you raised a man from the dead! Truly, you have been given great authority by your God."

Yeshua waited, remembering he had referred to his Father as 'the God of the bleating sheep.' He sensed the man's desperation. "My servant, my adoptive son lies at home paralyzed. He is suffering terribly, fevered, and close to death. I have come to ask if you would heal him?" He dropped to one knee as he made his request.

"You want me to come to your house?" Yeshua asked.

"Yes." Decimus said. "But I realize your people will looked down on you if you enter the house of a Roman. Lord, I do not deserve to have you come under my roof, but if you will simply say the word my servant will be healed. I understand how authority works. For I, myself, am a man under authority and I have soldiers that do my bidding at my command. I say go and they go..."

Yeshua's expression reflected his genuine surprise that this Roman understood his authority better than his own people. He nodded his assent. "Then, it will be done just as you believe it will. Your son will live."

The Centurion was overcome with emotion, and the peace of belief settled over him. He was profoundly grateful that his request had not been rejected. He stood then and took a step back bowing once again, confident the deed would be done.

People watched from their concealed vantage points, surprised by this Roman's show of humility and respect. Decimus bowed his head once more before Yeshua, touching his chest in reverent gratitude. Then he turned as if he had been dispatched to his duty. He regathered to his stallion. He offered a lingering salute and an appreciative smile before he galloped away.

On his way, he held on to Yeshua's words within his heart.

Yeshua watched the man go. He inhaled deeply looking heaven-ward to worship his Father for his work in the Centurion's life.

Miles away in Capernaum, the young man's fever broke and he began to regain consciousness.

Nathanael stepped to Yeshua's side, "I can't believe that just happened, a Roman Centurion came to you for healing. You are a Jew and he is our oppressor. I can't believe his pluck."

"Nathanael, people will do anything for those they love when they need help. Why shouldn't he ask me? I tell you the truth, I have not found anyone in Israel with such a great faith."

Nathanael frowned, unsettled to hear these words of praise for this gentile commander, or the words of rebuke for his own people. Then he remembered Nazareth. He was reacting just like the people there. Old prejudices ran deep. A pained and confused expression crossed his face.

However, Yeshua did not notice. Suddenly, a melting weakness buckled his knees. He reached out to brace himself against Nathaniel, who helped him to the ground. Power had gone out of him, and now the illness was being gathered in.

Occasionally this happened as if to remind him of how he would pay for healing the people. In fact, at the appointed time every healed affliction would fall upon him all at once to crush him under their weight. This momentary exchange marked the deeper purpose of his mission. 'The healing of the cross.' Moses had recorded God's promise to heal his people in the Torah. "I am the LORD, who heals you."

Even the disciples recognized Yeshua could be as strong as a lion one minute, only to become as weak as a lamb the very next. They were awed at his power, then concerned for his weakness. This confounded them and drew them to him, knowing he was the Anointed One of God who suffered their same pain and weaknesses. They failed to understand it all. But, they knew, through him, God was with them.

Half way home, the Centurion encountered messengers bringing him the great news. "Sir, your son is recovered! He pulled through and is doing well! He has had a miraculous recovery!"

Decimus closed his eyes and bowed his head sending up his words of thanksgiving. The Nazarene had healed his son, just as he had believed he would.

Wondering at the timing, he asked, "What time was my son was revived?"

The messenger confirmed it was at the hour he was with the Nazarene. Decimus wanted to travel back to give his thanks to the Healer, but he wanted to see his son and his mother first. He traveled on to Capernaum, believing he would see Yeshua again soon enough.

Assured his son was recovered, the Centurion shared his miraculous story with him. He gave glory to the One who possessed the power to heal. He moved on to testify to his whole household, and later he told all the men who served immediately under him. The good news spread. Yeshua did not spurn the needs of the Romans.

That day, Yeshua was placed unofficially under the Centurion's personal protection within the Galilean region. Allowing him to travel about largely unhampered by the Roman soldiers. The service of protective freedom was the most tangible tribute the commander could offer the Man of God who bore authority over life and death.

~ 35 ~

LION OR LAMB

I wait for your salvation, Lord,
and I follow your commands.
Psalm 119:66

Caiaphas traveled to Herod Antipas's compound on the east side of the Dead Sea. The matter of the Baptizer needed to be handled expeditiously. Herod was currently at his eastern fortress embroiled in a boundary conflict with the Nabateans. Having broken his marriage covenant with Phasaélis, her father King Aretus was trying to reclaim the land he had given Herod as a wedding gift.

Caiaphas did not make social visits. Antipas assumed he came bearing bad news. Their sparce conversations had always been held in Jerusalem. He chose to receive Caiaphas in his throne room dressed like a roman Caesar with Herodias beside him. Both peered down upon the Jewish priest to discomfort him. This charade made Caiaphas' mission all the more repugnant to him. He entered with only a curt nod his head.

Antipas greeted him. "Caiaphas this is a surprise."

He held out his hand for Caiaphas to touch, albeit awkwardly.

"What brings you all the way to Manchaerus?"

Before he made his appeal, Caiaphas made polite inquiries of Antipas and Herodias' good health.

"Never better my man." Antipas assured him, glancing at Herodias.

Caiaphas took a breath ready to stir the hornets' nest. "As your friend, I have come to personally share some very disturbing and dangerous news."

"Then it must be very dangerous indeed for you to travel all this way." Antipas narrowed his eyes with concern .

"The Baptizer is publicly pointing his finger at your marriage and calling it incestuous and unlawful! I heard him with my own ears."

Antipas gave a snort of indignation.

Caiaphas rushed onward, "Think of what this kind of propaganda will do to your popularity and reign. It is said he has connections to the zealot organizations. At his word, the zealots could rise up against you. I hear the Sicarii has been very active as of late. Even now, they may have infiltrated your ranks, you could both be at risk. We wouldn't want history to repeat itself. You remember Jehu of course. Never doubt the determination of a mercenary, or those who will gather with them. The movement is growing. Even now, another man named Yeshua from Nazareth has joined forces with the Baptizer and is beginning to draw numbers of his own."

He glanced toward Herodias, hoping to invoke her fear.

Antipas considered Caiaphas' words, obviously concerned. The two men had never been friends. More aptly, they were uneasy enemies who were forced into a necessary political liaison as the need arose. Antipas' forehead wrinkled with worry and his jaw worked. 'Obviously, Caiaphas has his own problems with the Baptizer's movement. He must really need resolution if he has come to me.'

Antipas reluctantly agreed, "Caesar hates unrest and demands peace at all cost. I do not want to suffer his wrath, because of this Baptizer. "

"This man is your enemy. The people consider him a real prophet, so his words are powerful. And, he resides in your territory." Caiaphas warned him.

Antipas gave a nod, sending for the commander of his guard. When the commander appeared.

"Take a few of your best men and go to the region of Salim. Covertly look for the man they call the Baptizer. I want you to extract him at night away from the crowds. Bring him to me. Do not take any other captives. I am interested in him alone. We want as few witnesses as possible."

The commander was clearly eager for this mission. "I will be happy to take care of the man."

Noting his wicked expression, Antipas added with warning, "Bring him to me in one piece, unharmed. I want to be able to talk with the man when he arrives."

His commanders grin deflated.

Antipas said to Caiaphas. "A movement can't survive without its leader. I will deal with him."

"What do you intend to do with him?" Caiaphas wanted details.

"Execute him." Herodias interjected with a deadly smile.

A shiver ran down Caiaphas' spine at her harsh words. He considered Herodias for the first time happy for her alliance, but even happier she was not set against him.

"Leave this to me, I will make the decisions concerning this man." Antipas told his wife. He was willing to face the peoples reaction if he should kill a prophet. Better to proceed with caution.

Days later, they brought the Baptizer before Herod Antipas. Herodias appeared at his side, wearing her gloating curiosity. Her headdress was styled a good eight inches in height. Her kohled green eyes glinted unnaturally, giving her an almost serpentine appearance.

She was disappointed to find nothing remarkable about the dismally hairy man standing before her. Between the two mountainous guards, he appeared smaller than she had expected. He was dressed in his wear worn brown homespun tunic with his camel hair mantle dyed blood red. It was as simple and hairy as the man himself. Without an audience to hang on his every word, Yohannan appeared deceptively benign.

He watched Herodias size him up while returning her gaze as if to challenge a viper.

"I have heard you are spreading negative words about my recent marriage." Antipas queried him.

"I have heard that you have married the latest Jezebel and you have become the new Ahab! You have spent too much time among the Roman dogs. The ways of Tiberius have rubbed off on you. Any real Jew knows your adulterous and incestrous marriage is unlawful! You defy the living God. Shall I recite the law to remind you?"

He began to list Antipas' infractions, "Let's see how many you have broken. You are not to have a sexual relationship with your brother's daughter, nor your brother's wife. You have broken your covenant of marriage with your former wife to make your liaison with this married woman. You have dishonored both your father, your brother and God by being overwhelmed with your desire for more power and your sexual lust."

Antipas' face registered surprise. He laughed loudly, taken aback by Yohannan's harsh assessment of him. At the same time, he had to admire the man's conviction and willingness to be so bold with such truth. No one had ever spoke to him like this. Oddly, Yohannan's unsettling verdict only served to provoked Antipas curiosity to hear more.

Yohannan turned his accusing words toward Herodias, "Woman, do not think your incantations have completely bound Antipas to you. Even now, he has taken an interest in another."

She drew a sharp breath at his audacity and waited to hear Antipas refute his words. But Antipas shrugged nonchalantly, as if he could not deny the allegation.

"Who? Who is he talking about?" She spoke in a low threat, for the first time doubting her powers over he husband.

Feeling her sudtle rage, Antipas shrugged again, "He is not a sane man. Why do you believe him?"

Her eyes could have pinned Yohannan to the wall. He met her angst head on without flinching.

"I want this man dead!" She shrilled like a shrew.

"No! I know my people, let me handle it!" Antipas told her, despite her outrage. "For now, to quiet the prophet's voice was enough."

For reasons he could not explain, Antipas was intrigued by this man. Holiness seemed an impossible feat to him. He wanted to see what holiness looked like.

An unexpected knock came at the door, bringing everyone to attention. Thaddeus peaked out, then opened the door recognizing two of Yohannan's men. They had clearly come bearing bad news.

"We have come looking for your Rabbi with urgent news of Yohannan." They furtively glanced around.

"What has happened?" Yeshua came forward clearly shaken.

"Yohannan was taken captive by Herod's special forces. We followed them at a distance. He is being held in the fortress at Manchaerus. Our community has scattered to avoid further trouble!"

The other man added, "People kept coming. So Yohannan refused to leave. He had not expected Antipas' men, but he was concerned about the Sanhedrin"

"One viper or another? Won't they share the same pit?" Yeshua asked.

"From the intel we have recieved from Chuza, apparently Caiaphas took Yohannan's threats and criticisms about Herodias to Antipas. Antipas fears any uprising in his territory. Also, Caiaphas may stirred some trouble with Antipas for you as well. We all know Caiaphas was really hoping to get you along with Yohannan."

The other man cut in, "After Yohannan refused to cooperate, Caiaphas was sure to make him pay. There has been bad blood between them for years. I am sure Caiaphas was hoping to get both of you in one raid, but Yohannan's words gave him what he needed to get Antipas involved."

Yeshua could feel Caiaphas' unrelenting malice even from far away and he understood that anyone associated with him was endangered.

"No. Yohannan wouldn't tell him anything, even if he knew it." Yeshua said confidently, "Yohannan has lived bravely under the threat of the Sanhedrin his whole life."

Yeshua hung his head, feeling the pang of responsibility. Truth and salvation were weighty commodities. Even if he had not gone through the Jordan Valley, trouble was sure to come to Yohannan by virtue of his prophet's tongue. Every prophet is eventually brought before the king to speak God's fiery message to them. If Yohannan had not warned him and sent him on his way, they would both be sitting in prison awaiting a trial.

"What will you do? Yohannan told us to come to you for direction should anything happen."

Yeshua understood what they were hoping to hear. They wanted him to gather the forces to go to release Yohannan. He saw it in every man's expression. They expected a military leader to take up arms and lead the charge, to spark an uprising, to unite the people. Many had hinted that all he had to do, was to whistle for the Sicarii and the Zealots. They would gather to his side to do his bidding. Their standard would be the Lion of Judah. They had been waiting for a messiah who would be military leader like David.

Yeshua would face plenty of battles, And, like David he would have his own Goliath to defeat, but his would be a very different kind of battle. The day of retribution could not come until later.

The men held their breath.

But he said nothing, looking each man in the eye, knowing he could not play to the approval of men. He would not free Yohannan, nor the world through military might.

'Not by might, nor by power, but by my Spirit...,' Zechariah had said. *'By my Spirit'.*

This was how he would defeat the kingdoms of this world. A greater peace would be purchased at a much higher price and he would pay it. Yohannan was born to a prophet's mission, he was under his Father's authority as was he. And his own mission would be even harder and far more encompassing. He had to trust his Father's way. As Yosef once said, 'Everyone will ultimately perish from this world anyway.' And he was right. It was the second death that Yeshua had come to defeat. Still, he knew it was hard for people to understand the work of God.

There will be a lot of collateral damage. Plenty of sanctified and dearly loved men and women will suffer with me and lay down their lives for the salvation of others.

It occurred to him, it was time for him to have a serious talk with his disciples, but not tonight. Everyone was too shaken, himself included. He needed time to think and pray. Soon he would sit his disciples down to explain to them what they must be willing to suffer for his name sake, just as his Father had shown him. They must know the truth about their part in the mission. They must be free to decide where their own sacrifice was concerned, just as he had chosen his own.

Yeshua looked to the messengers, "I will continue in the mission to which I have been sent." The whole room exhaled. Some in frustration; some in relief.

One messenger said, "But, what about Yohannan? He sent us to you. Are you going to do nothing on his behalf?"

The other added, "Yes, you are the only one who can help him now. He believes you have the power to save him. Is it true or not? We all want to know, are you the One that we have all been waiting for? Are you the Messiah?"

"What did the prophets say?" Yeshua retorted.

"The prophets? What do you mean? 'Remember the prophets', what can they do for us now?" They felt insulted.

"Yes. The blind receive sight, the lame walk, those who have leprosy are cleansed, the deaf hear, the dead are raised, and the good news of the Kingdom of God is being proclaimed to the poor. These things are happening. So you will have to decide."

The two men looked at one another as if testing these words. Hadn't they heard Yohannan quote that scripture?

Yeshua said, "Blessed is anyone who does not stumble on account of me."

These were scriptural code words concerning the Messiah, words that Yohannan knew. He had even prophesied these words over Yeshua; they were words his men should also understand.

"Now, you must stay and refresh yourselves, you are welcomed among us." He offered cordially.

He passed through the door, stepping outside for some fresh air and a moment of solace. He walked toward the shoreline. Passing the fishing boats, the smell of the lake and the fish hung in the night air. The empty shoreline seemed to match his mood. The air hung heavy with humidity that seemed to match his building sorrow. A rumble sounded in the sky.

"Father," he prayed, "May your words speak to these men and to others, but especially to Yohannan." A large rain drop fell on his up turned face, then another.

Soon it was hard to tell the cool falling rain apart from his own hot tears. Still, he interceded, allowing the rain to wash over him. When he returned to his men, Andrew brought him a towel to dry his dripping hair. He took off his wet outer cloak and sat down by the warm hearth to dry.

Yohan and Andrew came to sit with him, bringing their concerns, and seeking consolation. Yohannan had been more than their teacher, he was their friend and mentor.

Yeshua spoke to all of their questions. "I tell you, among those born of women there is no one greater than Yohannan. Yet, the one who is least in the kingdom of God is greater than he."

They looked around puzzled, wondering, 'Who was the least in the kingdom of God?'

Yeshua prayed the day would come when they would remember what he had just told them and understand what he meant. The glory of God is only seen from the back side.

"Yohannan bears the spirit of Elijah. Just as Elijah faced down Jezebel and Ahab for their wrong doing, Yohannan is telling God's truth to Antipas and Herodias."

They nodded, recalling Jezebel's sworn threat to put Elijah to death by way of the sword. It was a distressing thought for them all. They were all greatly tormented with thoughts of Yohannan being held captive by Antipas, but no one more than Yeshua. Unbidden, the premonition of Malachi's prophetic words spoken concerning Yohannan at Qumran stirred in his memory. He felt sure that Yohannan's imprisonment would not end well. Prophets are put to death for their words. Who knew what Yohannan might suffer at Antipas' hands?

Later, when it stopped raining, Yeshua went out to pray again. "Father, protect your servant Yohannan from undue suffering at their hands. Show him your mercy to him, let his death be swift and painless when the time comes. Preserve him for new life. Clear his confusion. Show him the truth about me—about Us. His life has always been in your hands and empowered by your Holy Spirit."

He paused, turning to his own portion of the mission. "Father, Caiaphas is already seeking my life. Give me courage to remain on the path you have made for me. Give me the time I need to complete my mission, help me to finish my work! My days are passing swifter than a runner."

His thoughts turned towards his followers. The numbers remaining near him had grown large and unwieldy, making it hard to move from place to place without notice. And, It was impossible to personally invest in so many. It was exhausting him to be the only source. He remembered that Moses had a similar problem. He had set a leader over each tribe, one chosen and especially trained by him. The twelve tribes of Israel were now scattered, but the choosing of twelve leaders made good sense. He could not afford to waste even another moment of his fleeting time. The choosing and training of his disciples had to take precedence. Then he could quickly multiply his work and accomplish more of what he had come to do.

"Father, show me the twelve I am to choose, men I can entrust with our message. Show me what is in their hearts. Let them be men who will stay their course through to fulfillment. Too much is at stake now. Help me to see them and know what is needed. Let me see who they will become. You know all things, show me that I may choose well."

In the silence of the night, a wild dog howled not so far away. A predator on the hunt. He heard the threat. He spoke into the darkness.

"Yes, I know you are there. You come to steal, kill, and destroy. But you will have to come through me to get to them."

~ 36 ~

WHAT HOLDS YOU BACK

I urge you do not receive God's grace in vain.
For the Lord says,
"In the time of my favor I heard you
and in the day of salvation I helped you."
I tell you, now is the time of God's favor,
now is the day of salvation.
2 Corinthians 6:1-2
We had to celebrate and be glad,
because this brother of yours was dead and is alive again;
he was lost and is found.
Luke 15:32

Yeshua passed a certain Roman tax booth regularly. Day after day, whenever he passed the tax collector looked up just in time for their eyes to meet. He noticed, the man wore the longing look of a prisoner chained to his block, wistful of a freedom he sensed more than understood. Frequently when he taught, the tax collector came and stood at distance listening with a pained expression, as if he thought he could never be accepted. It was clear the man sincerely pondered every word. At times, he hung his head in shame. He did not beat his breast physically. Yet at times, he closed his eyes as if in shame and he held his chest, as if his heart was hurting. It was as if he was recounting his sins and beating the man within. At those times, his lips moved as if he were begging for mercy under the distress of his conviction.

Once again, as Yeshua passed, their eyes met.

The man paused to watch him pass, his scribers pen poised in mid-air.

"Come on, let's get on with it!" A customer barked impatiently. "What are you looking at?"

"Where do they find these traitors, anyway?" The man behind him commiserated.

Matthew quickly handed the waiting man his change.

Then prepared to serve the man who had spoken so harshly of him. He was a social pariah among his own people. He had long suffered their taunts and rudeness quietly, taking their constant stream of bitterness.

Matthew had once thought working with money would use his skills and make him happy. He had also thought having plenty of money would provide him everything he needed and wanted. He had been wrong. Trusting his instinct, Yeshua doubled back to Matthew's booth. He noted Matthew wore the insignia of the tribe of Levi.

Matthew stumbled over his words of greeting.

"Can-can I help you, Lord?"

"Are you not a son of Abraham?" Yeshua asked him challengingly.

Matthew stammered, "Well, y-y-yes." Shame scalded him. Bewildered he thought, 'Will the Rabbi berate me also for doing the Roman's bidding?'

The people waiting in line grumbled at Yeshua, "Hey! Wait your turn! We are in line. If you want to talk to him, get in line."

Ignoring their complaints, Yeshua said to Matthew, "You have been watching me day after day."

Matthew's eyes widened, and he nodded. "Yes, well I..."

"You have come to listen to my teachings, ... and you have heard my message."

Matthew nodded guiltily.

"And, you have been praying!" Yeshua eyes softened.

"Well, yes, I...I....I"

"You have also been to the Jordan to be baptized." Yeshua tilted his chin up as if to challenge him.

"Yes." He swallowed. "Before the Baptizer..."

"Yes. So, I have just one more question for you."

"Excuse me?"

"What is holding you back?"

"What do you mean?" Matthew asked, wondering, 'How does the Rabbi know all of this?' He'd practically hid himself in the margins of the crowd, trying not to draw attention to himself. He was unprepared for what followed.

"Come and follow me." Yeshua said holding out his hand to him.

Something in the way he said it sounded like a command, one that brooked no argument.

Bewilderment, then pure joy spread across Matthew's features and his lips lifted up into a beauteous smile.

"Me? You want me, to follow YOU?"

Yeshua nodded, "Yes, of course! That is, if you want to?"

Up until that moment, Matthew had not known that was what he wanted. Having heard the words, he knew it was true. It was more true than anything anyone had ever said to him.

"Your heart is exactly what I am looking for." Yeshua looked at him as if appraising his good qualities. Matthew stood rather clumsily to his feet, his eyes fixed on the teacher. The fact was not lost on Yeshua that Matthew did not wait to gather his coinage, instead he left it all neatly arranged in the box inside. He stepped out from his protective booth, onto the street to grasp Yeshua's outstretched hand.

The Roman guard for the booth, stepped up to shout at Matthew. "What do you think you are doing? You can't just walk away like that!"

"Yes! I can." Matthew said excitedly, running back to hand the guard the key to his strong box.

"He has told me to follow him."

The guard stared after Matthew in confusion.

Yeshua released a peal of happy laughter. Taking Matthew's head between his hands, he planted a kiss in the middle of Matthew's crinkled forehead as if he were a child who had just greatly delighted his father.

Rock and Andrew looked at each other astounded. This was the very same tax collector that they had previously paid their ridiculously high taxes when they sold their fish.

James grumbled to Yohan, "Great, just great, now he has added a tax collector."

Yeshua heard the comment and shot them all a stern look.

The guard shouted behind Matthew, "You will regret this. Your booth will be given to another! If you leave, you are finished, you can never come back."

Matthew waved a hand to quiet him. The guard couldn't do anything more because this rabbi was secretly protected. Even so, he dreaded making the report that this tax collector just up and quit. Matthew was a diligent tax collector, exacting and legible in his accounting. As far as anyone could tell, he had never tried to skim a mite.

Matthew looked at the other disciples with a sappy grin, too delighted to be brought down by their less than happy expressions. Not knowing what to say, he looked from face to face, and then back to Yeshua. Then an idea came to him.

"Lord, may I honor you with a banquet at my house tonight? I will invite a few of my associates. I want them to hear what you have to say. Up until now, I have had nothing worth celebrating or sharing with them."

"Certainly, may I bring a few of my friends with me?" Yeshua asked motioning to the men behind him.

"Of course!" Matthew beamed, hopeful that among their number he might find a place of acceptance and belonging.

The disciples looked at one another with disbelief, who would Yeshua invite next? He seemed to have no boundaries as to who he was willing to accept into his circle of grace. So far, he had sought a multitude of the sick and demonically oppressed, a slew of people from Jerusalem, a Samaritan woman and her village, a grieving mother and her son, a Roman centurion, and not to mention four fishermen, a scribe, a student of the law, a zealot, and a financial opportunist.

On that day, Matthew spared no expense on the best foods Capernaum had to offer, along with an abundance of wine. He hired a musician to play joyful and lilting music of flutes and lyres. His house and courtyard were filled to overflowing with the disciples, various followers, and other tax collectors. Even a few of the Roman guards attended, escorted by their wives or favorite prostitutes.

Matthew's house shone like a bright candle against the twilight of the sky, filled with the sound of music, and a welcoming hospitality. In so many ways, the lavishness of the party reminded Yeshua of his sister's more modest wedding feast.

Matthew proudly installed Yeshua in the seat of honor next to him.

After the dinner, he stood. "Friends I have invited you all here to celebrate with me my great fortune and to introduce you to Rabbi Yeshua of Nazareth, who some of you may have also heard is Israel's savior. He has asked, me..." Matthew's throat suddenly became thick with emotion. His eyes filled and his voice croaked.

After a few awkward restarts, he was able to finish. "He has asked me to follow him and to be his disciple. I still don't know why."

He laughed a weak laugh, holding his hands out in wonder, but his face glowed. "There is nothing I am more honored to do. Since you are my acquaintances, I have asked him here to meet you and to provide for us a teaching in honor of this joyous occasion."

His large portico glowed with the light of many lamps scattered throughout the corners and on the large table in the center so every face was illuminated. Yeshua stood comfortably in the middle of the large room of reclining people. He realized this was not the time for preaching, so he began to tell a few parables to incline their ears towards him.

"Suppose one of you has a hundred sheep and you lose one of them." He began. "Tell me, wouldn't you leave the ninety-nine so you could go find your lost sheep?"

Some shook their head, "Of course not."

But several from herding families spoke up to agree. "Yes, herds tend to remain together and are safer than a drifted animal, lost and alone."

Yeshua nodded. "Exactly. And when your sheep is found, wouldn't you call out to all your friends and neighbors and say, 'Rejoice with me that my sheep is found'."

Heads nodded sagely. "Yes, to the shepherd every sheep is a valuable." One young man called out.

"That's right." Yeshua said. "In that same way there will be more rejoicing in heaven over one sinner who returns back to God than over the ninety-nine righteous persons who do not feel they are lost."

Everyone nodded, aware that their lives were full of things that needed to be changed.

"Wouldn't you do the same thing, if you lost something precious to you?" He asked them. Everyone thought of all the precious things they had lost, things life had stolen from them.

"Thus, it is with God. He searches for those who are precious to him." The people listened quietly, pondering the meaning of his stories. He gathered in their rapt attention, and his subtle words touched their aching and needy hearts. Some were sure that they were the lost one who no one cared to find. They had been tossed aside by this world. They had no social standing, no group. They were all outcasts to the righteous society, worthless, and unworthy. Their sadness and longing lingered in their eyes.

He took his message deeper. "There was a Father with two sons. The younger man said, 'Father, give me my share of the estate.'

"The Father, with great sadness, divided his estate and gave this younger son his share. Suddenly independently wealthy, the son felt no need of his father, brother, or family connections. He longed for his own life. He had no need of things like rules or authority. So, he packed up and went to the far country. There, he began to live a life of pleasure and excess."

His audience sat up and leaned forward listening. "Many people admired him for his wealth. They attended his parties hoping to enjoy a share of his inheritance. He bought whatever he wanted, only the best in life was good enough for him. The wine flowed, the music played and the women were willing. All too quickly, he had squandered away his whole inheritance. He looked in his purse and all the coins were gone."

Yeshua looked in his own travel bag, his face remorseful. The people were captivated. "He was bankrupt." Yeshua looked around a room of solemn faces. He allowed a few beats for his words to soak in. Some leaned back, having felt the truth in these piercing words.

The disciples listened, hiding their knowing smiles. They watched Yeshua weave his story that clearly targeted these sinners. They waited for his to call to repentance. They cut their eyes smugly from one to another, while Yeshua addressed the tax collectors and the flamboyantly dressed women resting on their arms of the Romans.

Their smile quickly disappeared when the story took a sudden and unflattering look at the older brother, who was every bit as selfish and guilty. They swallowed their smiles.

Yeshua made the point, "Yes, the brother was still by his father's side, but secretly he coveted his father's estate. He was just hanging on and waiting for his father to die, so the estate would be his. In fact, he was already behaving as if his father's estate belonged to him." Now their looks turned sheepish.

By the end of the story, Yeshua could see guilt, humility, and the hope for second chance written on each and every face. Satisfied he had reached his goal, he concluded, saying, "The younger brother was inside being celebrated because he had returned to his father and sought forgiveness for his deplorable behavior. The Father rejoiced and brought his wayward son who had been as dead back into his good graces and blessing. But now the older brother remained outside in the dark angry because his Father was reconciled to his brother.

"'Come in and rejoice with me,' the father begged him, 'come in and enjoy the celebration, because your brother who was as good as dead is now restored back to life to us.'" Obviously, the father wanted everyone reconciled to him and to one another.

Yeshua ended his story abruptly with the father's invitation dangling. Would the brother refuse to join the feast? Would he refuse to forgive and be reconciled to his brother? Would he remain alone in the darkness? Would he accept his father's plea to celebrate his happiness? Would the elder son bravely confess and be forgiven too? Would they become a family, bound by the bonds of love and respect once again?

~ 37 ~

A SWORD

"No student is above their teacher,
nor a servant above his master.
...expect that if the head of the house
has been called Beelzebub,
how much more so the members of his household!"
Matthew 10:24-26
"Do not suppose that I have come to bring peace to the earth
...but a sword. A man's enemies will
be the members of his own household."
Matthew 10:34-35
For the word of God is alive and active.
Sharper than any double-edged sword...
Hebrews 4:12

When the Pharisees and the synagogue leaders heard about the banquet at Matthew's house, they searched for Yeshua and his followers. Approaching Simon first, they directed their contempt and criticism toward him.

"What is this we have heard? Your teacher eats and drinks with tax collectors and sinners!"

Simon felt immediately defensive, but how could he explain what he had witnessed the night before? These pious men would never understand. A few of the other disciples joined him.

246 ~ K. S. MCFARLAND

One Pharisee shouted, "How can your Rabbi be a holy man when he fellowships with those who are impure?" They all began to talk over one another, their loud voices were punctuated by raucous laughter. They mocked the disciples as if they had all been deceived.

This rankled their pride. They turned to one another, searching for a fitting response. Matthew was mortified to see he was the cause of this dishonor against his rabbi.

"And, while we are on the subject, why do you not purify your hands before eating?"

Now it wasn't just Yeshua that the Pharisees maligned, they were also being called impure. The men had no rebuttal to offer.

"Or for that matter, why do you not fast and pray in the synagogue like we do. Do the laws of holiness mean so little to you? Even the son of Zachariah and his disciples held to these practices!"

The disciples looked at one another with self-doubt and confusion. Rock clinched his fist and ground his teeth, wanting to defend himself, if not with words, then with his fists.

But Yohan grabbed his tunic and held him fast. "Let it go, Rock. They just don't understand."

"Why are you following this man?" They goaded Simon, sensing his short fuse. "He is no holy man!"

Having allowed it to go on long enough, Yeshua stepped from the shadows behind them, parting his men as if the waters. The bright morning sun light reflected blindingly off of the white of his tunic, making his face radiant, as if he were lit from within. He placed his hand on the back of Matthew's neck as a father would a son who he was truly proud of. He paused, giving Matthew a reassuring look of pure pleasure and a reassuring squeeze. Dropping his hand, he moved toward the accusing delegation shielding his men behind him.

In a voice that sounded like the low rumble of thunder, he assured them, "I am not here to call the righteous, but sinners so they may enter into a new life in God."

These religious and powerful men thought of themselves as righteous. Each held impressive educational titles and public esteem. The tassels on their robes dangled long, practically dragging on the ground, as if to testify to their supreme holiness. Their clothing was expensively and decorous created to set them apart from the common people, indicating their service to both synagogue and temple. They appeared clean and well groomed, but Yeshua knew what they did behind closed doors. He discerned their attitudes and thoughts. He knew what they conspired in the shadows and imagined within the dark corners of their minds.

Power brokers never confessed their own unworthiness or sins, not even to God, especially when their sins were against the public. And, since they taught the law, they became confused and thought they had become the law. They were totally blind to the fact that the only righteousness they could ever put their hope in was his righteousness, which they were currently refuting.

Yeshua said to them, "As to fasting, it is inappropriate to fast at a wedding if you are the friends of the bridegroom. There will be time enough for my men to fast when sorrow overwhelms them, when the bridegroom is taken from them."

He moved closer to them. "You remind me of children sitting in the market place and calling out their silly, memorized rhymes to others. 'We played the flute for you and you did not dance. We sang a dirge and you did not mourn!' You serve yourselves, calling all the shots. You forever manipulate the rules to suit your own purposes. Yohannan came in holiness, and you accused him of having a demon. The Son of Man comes banqueting with others, just as you do, and you accuse him of being a glutton and a drunkard. You should take care with your accusations, because wisdom is proved right by her actions."

The Pharisees gnashed their teeth, feeling the barbs of his words. They shouted, "His words reek of lunacy and deception."

One man took off his shoe and held it up toward Yeshua's face, showing his disdain and rejection.

"We want no part with you!" the man shouted, ejecting drops of spittle.

Another shouted. "You are not of God! You must be of the spirit of Beelzebub! Look at the company you keep and the people who keep coming to you!"

Yeshua answered, "If the miracles you have been privy to were performed in the cities of Tyre or Sidon, they would have repented long ago in sackcloth and ashes. But you Capernaum, don't expect that you will be lifted up to the skies! You will be plunged down to the depths. It was more bearable for Sodom on the day of their judgment than what will come upon you!" He turned back towards the door and motioned to his men to go back inside, he entered behind them and closed the door with a resounding thud.

He said to his men, "Don't let them bother you. They are just a horde of bothersome flies."

On another Sabbath, Yeshua was in the synagogue teaching. He noticed a man who was the son of one of the officials of the synagogue around the age of seventeen struggling with an impure spirit. The demon was plaguing the young man with unclean thoughts making it impossible for him to hear or understand what Yeshua was saying. The demon kept dragging the man's mind away to thoughts sex and lust. These thoughts weighted the young man day and night. He could think of nothing else until he was filled with self-loathing, and even desperate thoughts of suicide. He knew something was very wrong with him.

Finally, seeing the distracting spirit, Yeshua paused to walk to the young man. Standing before him, he confronted that impure spirit.

"Come out of him." The spirit departed with a lewd sound.

The boy's father stood up ready to make an objection believing he was confronting his son. But Yeshua held up his hand towards him. He sat back down again without further interference. From that day onward, John Mark was freed to receive the teaching and to follow Christ.

Another Sabbath, he noticed a man in the assembly with a shriveled hand. Ashamed, the man kept trying to hide his affliction and keep his hand concealed.

"You. Come up here." Yeshua motioned to the man. Timidly the man did as he was told, fearing he would be humiliated for his affliction. He had long believed his hand to be a sign of his unworthiness.

"Hold out your hand." Yeshua reached out his palm to take it in his.

The man obeyed, extending his hand his hand. He placed in Yeshua hand. It was healed immediately.

"Look!" The man said moving his hand toward the others as proof. "My hand is healed!"

Most of the congregation was delighted by Yeshua's work of mercy. But the leadership was infuriated with jealousy.

"It is unlawful to heal on the Sabbath." They accused him.

After the people emptied the synagogue, the leaders called Yeshua aside for a discreet meeting. "We have asked you time and again to stop healing on the Sabbath. Since you won't stop healing, we can no longer welcome you to Sabbath worship."

"Yes, your actions are disrupting the worship service."

"You don't know what you are doing." Yeshua said.

Yeshua clarified Sabbath law to his men as they left the synagogue. "Sabbath is meant for exactly for such things as healing. The Father heals his people when they draw near to him and listen for his voice. He restores their body and mind. He puts discernment and a right attitude within them. People are not made to serve the Sabbath. The Sabbath was meant to serve God's people. It is a day of mercy, rest, and healing. It is a day when my Father works his goodwill on the behalf of his people and destroys spiritual oppression. It is a day to praise God for what he is doing in your life."

Yeshua did not stop teaching or healing, he simply changed his venue to the open areas. People gathered to him wherever they could find him. Even still, the conflict with the synagogue leaders continued to increase.

One sabbath, the people found Yeshua at the home of Simon. Yeshua sat in front of the house, teaching to a large crowd that had formed a tight band around the home's entrance. Pharisees gathered to spy on what he was doing. Four people arrived carrying their friend on a litter.

They cried out in a loud voice. "Let us through! Let us through!"

But the crowd was too large, too compressed for them to get to Yeshua. Desperate for their friend's healing, and confident that Yeshua would heal him, the man's friends shrewdly went around to the back of Simon's home. There they searched out a foot hold. One of their number, then another, climbed up the back side of Simon's house, then hoisted their friend up onto the roof. They positioned him, then began to dig through the thatched roof. They proceeded to strip away a section large enough that they could lower their friend down into the room below.

"I'm sorry! I'm sorry!" The man called down to the astonished faces below, while his friends lowered him through the opening.

Four faces stared down to the people below, begging for their friend to be healed.

Abigail and Miriam called out to Rock and Yeshua who were standing just outside the portico. Turning to see the commotion that was interrupting the teaching, Yeshua was surprised and oddly pleased by their bold action.

Rock rushed into his house, "No, no, no, what have you done to my home. Have you no respect?"

Looking down from the roof, the friends spread their hands, "We are desperate to help our friend."

"Bring the man out into the light." Yeshua ordered his men. The disciples brought the man out before the crowd. Everyone whispered to one another, wondering what he would do. Yeshua stepped to the humiliated man, then squat down to look him in the eye.

"Son, your sin is forgiven." The man looked greatly relieved at his words, grateful that the healer was not angry with him, but then he realized he was not speaking of the roof. His smile broadened when he realized the Healer was forgiving him of everything he had ever done.

The man nodded through grateful tears, thinking, 'That alone would be enough.'

The Pharisees and the teachers of the law began to mutter to one another, greatly offended by his words.

"No one but God can forgive sin!"

Seeing their angry thoughts, Yeshua stepped towards them.

He asked, "Which is easier? To say your sins are forgiven? Or, to say take up your mat and walk?"

He took his time to look each one in the eye. They did not answer him. Of course not, how could they? They did not understand the crippling seriousness of sin.

"Well then, so you will know that I have authority on earth to forgive sins..."

He turned back to the paralyzed man, "I say to you, stand up and take up your mat."

With amazement, feeling began to flood into the man's legs and feet. He moved clumsily at first. Then, he scrambled to a squat expecting to find shaky legs. Instead, he found a miraculous new strength. Coming to his feet, he could not believe he was actually standing. He simply stood for a moment taking it in and trying his feet. He had forgotten what it felt like to move like this. Remembering Yeshua's command, he hurriedly leaned over to scoop up his mat, pausing to roll it up. He turned in a circle with a smile of delight before all the people, before trying out his new mobility. He moved forward to try his legs, only to find himself blocked by an unmoving Pharisee.

They stared at one another. The healed man was momentarily confused by the Pharisee's apparent opposition.

Finally, someone else moved allowing him to walk through the crowd to sighs of amazement. He hurried off, much like a child delighting in his newfound freedom.

Awed onlookers began to rejoice and praise God, but the Pharisees left complaining to one another about yet another Sabbath healing. Through gritted teeth, they complained, "It is time we bring Herod Antipas into this. Didn't he just take captive that dreadful Baptizer? We must rid our land of this man who opposes our rules!"

Hearing the leader's words, Miriam made the decision to call together Yeshua's brothers to discuss the conflict building around Yeshua, and to stage an intervention. Yohannan's capture had greatly increased her anxiety. Knowing he was held captive in Herod's fortress, she believed Yeshua would be the next target, then who be next James, Jude, Josés?"

"Ima, we must try to stop him." James agreed. "I fear our brother is not of sound of mind. All of this will come back to haunt us. We will all be implicated with him. We have already had to leave Nazareth because of him. Our business dried up as a result of his insults to the whole village. Now, both the Herodians and Sanhedrin will be searching for him. We must reason with him. He is not thinking clearly. His delusion has to end now before it is too late."

The next day, Miriam and her four other sons found Yeshua teaching at Matthew's house. Nathaniel came to the door.

"Please tell Yeshua his family is here to talk with him. Please have him come out to have a private word with us." James said.

Yeshua heard his brothers voice, knowing he had come because of the conflict the day before. He knew what his family had come to do. He spoke out loudly, so his family could hear him through the open door. "Who are my mothers or my brothers?"

He paused before answering his own question.

"My mothers and brothers are those who do the will of God." He cast his family a direct and trenchant look.

Hearing his harsh retort, his brothers began to argue with Nathaniel that Yeshua was not thinking clearly. He was putting himself in grave danger and they had come to take charge of him.

Yeshua motioned to Rock and Philip, who stepped forward to softly close the door, putting an end to the disruption.

Yeshua continued his teaching. But outside the door, he could hear his brother's raised voice.

"This is your fault." James accused his mother irrationally.

"My fault? I am the one who asked you to help me." Miriam's voice was outraged.

"If you and Abba had not filled him such grandiose fabrications to hide your own indiscretions, he would not be living out this lie. Do you see what you have done? He actually believes he is the Messiah. I blame you for his delusional behavior. If he dies, it will be your fault!" James continued.

"Yosef and I did not lie to him or anyone else. You speak of what you do not understand." Miriam said in a low and even voice, her eyes flashing. James' bitter accusations were all too repugnant. He had never attacked her so directly. How she wished Yosef was here. He would take James to task, and talk sense to Yeshua. Ever since his death the family had been at odds. But what could she do if Yeshua refused to talk with her? She was desperate. Now, his students backed him all the way.

Miriam grabbed James arm and tried to reason with him, "I know you don't want to believe it. He is the Messiah, I just don't want him to be captured by Antipas, or killed, not yet."

Miriam's youngest son spoke up, "Well, I believe he is who he says he is, and I am going in to listen to what he has to say."

Si opened the door, and gave Yeshua a conciliatory greeting. He went and sat down.

Inside, Yeshua gave pause, realizing he was the source of division within his own family.

Satan continued to seek new paths to make him doubt himself, trying to turn him back. Today it had been his family, those closest to him. But, it was more than that, painfully he recognized he would be the cause of division and separation for every person who professes belief in him. He would bring divisions deep enough to provoke a murderous rage in people. He heard the sound of his family arguing and his mother crying outside the door. A chasm was growing between them all as his mission advanced.

Even though he had warned his mother, and she knew who he was, and what he had come to do, she was still struggling to accept his destiny. She would have to accept it sooner or later. It pained him that he was forced to speak a truth to her that had the power to pierce her heart with so much grief, but he could not change Father's will. It was for her own good.

Outside the door, Miriam wondered, 'Will my own son really renounce me and my legitimate concerns as his mother?'

Prophetic words that had been uttered to her many years before resounded in Miriam's memories.

"This child is destined to cause the falling and rising of many in Israel. He is to be a sign that will be spoken against, so that the thoughts of many hearts will be revealed. And a sword will pierce your own soul too."

'Is this what Simeon had meant?' She wondered with bewilderment. 'One thing is for sure, there will be no stopping Yeshua. To even try is to risk our relationship. It will be severed should I try. I cannot stop a prophecy which is preordained. If Yosef were here, he would tell me not to battle against God's will for his son. But how can God demand so much from me?'

She laid her hand on James arm, and said, "There is nothing we can do. We can't stop him. Neither, can we stop the conflict he is stirring. He is following a path that we do not know."

The door opened and a student stepped out. Yeshua's eyes met Miriam's. She saw his staunch determination chiseled on his features as if written in stone, and yet she saw a glimmer of his compassion towards her. A wail of despair escaped her.

James took his mother by the shoulders to lead her away. He volleyed an accusing look toward Yeshua. "If he is determined to get himself killed, he can't say we did not try to reason with him."

Yeshua turned back to his disciples to continue the teaching.

~ 38 ~

LIFE AND LIGHT

Thus says the LORD:
'He who scattered Israel will gather them
and will watch over his flock like a shepherd.'
Jeremiah 31:10

Yeshua's family had adjusted to their move to Capernaum from Nazareth glad to be free of the persecution they had experienced for years. Cleopas and Mary had remained to oversee the family's home, where his youngest brother Si often visited.

Things were better overall in Capernaum, but they still felt the ongoing effects of Yeshua's ministry. Between his popularity and his conflicts they felt they were under a constant surveillance, even though Yeshua kept his distance so they could find some measure of peace.

Even under the protection of the Roman Centurion, Capernaum was becoming fraught with constant hostility for Yeshua.

"It is time to leave Capernaum." Yeshua told his men.

They offered no argument, they had accepted their mission would take them out on the road. Only Rock felt the reluctance to go because he had to leave Deborah and Ana behind. The others were excited to get out on the road, agreeing it was best to get moving.

Rock had been anticipating this, and had devised a plan that would allow him to frequently return to Capernaum to see his family.

"What if we use my largest boat to travel from place to place? It would be just big enough for us all. We can store our travel packs on the boat. It would beat carrying everything around on our backs from place to place. We can fish to eat. And, you can conveniently deploy the boat as your speaking platform. Think of it as a floating auditorium. Most of the towns along the Galilee shoreline, have individual pockets that we can easily slip into and out of, making it easy to keep moving. It will give us separation from the officials. They will never know where we will show up at any given time. It will be harder to track us and make it easier to escape. And we can reach out to a variety of villages and regions."

He stared at Yeshua waiting for his reaction.

"Well done, Rock." Yeshua beamed at him.

"You have certainly given this some thought." He slapped him on his back, offering a broad smile of appreciation to reward Simon's initiative and generosity to offer of his boat. Rock's fore-thought and resourcefulness would be a useful to the future of the movement that was forming. Yeshua encouraged him at his effort. The others became excited about this new plan, too.

So they traveled, Magdala today, Bethsaida tomorrow, and so on. This worked quite well, for a while. Eventually, the crowds grew larger as people became more savvy, watching their travels patterns. Along with the crowds came friction with local fishermen and businesses as well. They complained of the masses trampling their towns and seashores, making it impossible to get their fish and other products to market.

Yeshua made adjustments in an effort not to over burden the towns, but the influx of people remained too impactful. When the barley harvest had been reaped, Yeshua found a large gleaned field overlooking the sea away from the towns and villages. As it just so happened, it was a fallow year and no more crops would be sown for a year. So, he was able to gain access for the use of the field for a while without conflicts.

There he harvested souls and taught important kingdom principals.

"Blessed are the poor in spirit, for theirs is the kingdom of heaven..." He began.

His words were beautiful. He painted a portrait of a totally different kind of rule and reign, a Spirit filled kingdom that offered comfort, mercy, forgiveness, fulfillment, peace, adoption, family, an eternal inheritance. Yeshua taught what it meant to be holy, to have salvation, and to live according to the laws of love and grace.

"This is good news!" the people told others.

"He has clarified God's expectations for us." Said another.

"Now I understand holiness and he has made it desirable."

Judas was standing next to Rock watching Yeshua teach. His face mirrored the peoples admiration. "The Rabbi grows more popular every day. The people love him."

Rock reflected. "They come to hear him because he tells them how to find a fruitful and blessed life. A beautiful life."

Yohan added. "He speaks with unquestionable authority."

Judas looked at the rapt faces of the masses. "How has he come to know so much, having come from a cesspool like Nazareth? Jerusalem is where all the great Rabbis have studied."

Rock fixed Judas with a sarcastic stare. "Have you ever heard of anything like that coming out of Jerusalem?"

Judas considered Simon's question. "I suppose not. Still, look at him, he never studies. He carries it around in his head. His words flow from his lips like a fountain."

"You are wrong to think he has not studied. From what I can tell he has been preparing for this all of his life. Yeshua is serious about the truth. He understands spiritual concepts and he is far more passionate about his Father's words than any of the Sanhedrin. He has been given a knowledge no mortal man could offer him. His authority comes from his pure and righteous heart. Truth simply lives in him. It is... as if..." Rock paused to think before continuing, "as if Truth itself has been spoken aloud from his lips since the very beginning of time."

"All I know is, people are mesmerized by him." Judas' eyes sifted through the crowd noting the diversity of caste, education, wealth, experience, gender, race, nationality.

Turning to Simon, Judas asked, "When do you think he will make his move?"

It was the question they all pondered.

Simon shrugged, understanding at once what Judas was asking. "I don't know. He has never spoke of making a move, not in the way you mean."

"Really? I am sure that if he is the Messiah, he has a plan of action! Are you saying he has never shared his plan of ascending to the throne with you? Aren't you his right-hand man?"

Simon searched the ground before him, feeling suddenly small and unsure. "I don't know. Why would you say that? He has never placed any of us above another. And, he has never spoke to any of us about a plan to ascend the throne."

"Really? Are you sure about that?"

Simon was surprised by the challenge. He didn't answer, but wondered, 'Why hasn't Yeshua told me his plan? If not me then who?' He looked around at the others, wondering if anyone else kept a greater confidence.

"Surely he has a plan." Judas urged him. "Why would he keep it hidden from you of all people?"

Before Simon could find his rebuttal, Yeshua's words interrupted their conversation.

Judas heard the word 'money' and he moved closer, listening intently to Yeshua's words. His ears were tuned and receptive, waiting with a great excitement. After so many controversial subjects, finally he is speaking about money! A smile flashed broadly across Judas' face.

Yeshua said, "The love of money is a root to all kinds of evil. Some people, eager for money, have wandered away from the faith and pierced themselves with many griefs."

The bubble of Judas' smile burst. 'So just tell them to give their money to us.' He thought grounding his jaw.

Yeshua directed his gaze toward Judas, saying, "No one can serve two masters. Either you will hate the one and love the other, or you will be devoted to the one and despise the other. You cannot serve both God and money."

Judas drew a sharp breath, feeling as if his thoughts were discovered. He turned away, while Yeshua moved on to another topic. Disappointed, he turned back toward Simon ready to continue his probing, but Rock had walked away.

Simon eyed Judas with a discerning eye. 'Why does he get under my skin so easily? Better yet, why am I so easily swayed? One minute I am in awe of Yeshua and the next Judas has flooded me with doubts. It is disturbing. Yet, the moment I turn my attention back to Yeshua my doubt dissipates as if it were but a temporary mist obscuring the truth.' Disgusted with himself, Simon shook his head trying to erase all of Judas' words.

Meanwhile, Yeshua was saying to the crowd, "You gain connection to God by his Spirit, by way of God's reign, by seeing things through his eyes, by sharing your life with him. The more you deploy God's words in your own life, the more of God's Spirit will be given to you, the more the kingdom becomes manifest in your life.

"Don't settle for common or profane things, the Glory of God's kingdom will be yours when you follow him and his will. Take his path, even when others refuse to go with you. It will be the harder, narrower, and lonelier path but it will lead you to a place of great beauty, the kingdom. Crowds take the broad, easy, and well-worn path but they will never find the kingdom."

People could tell he was speaking out of what he knew first hand to be true. Simon glanced again towards Judas, noticing for the first time an emptiness, a void in his eyes. Judas was bored; he was not at all interested in the teachings. He listened, but it was as if he did not hear. He clung to the margins, removed, and busy with his own thoughts.

Simon wondered why Yeshua had chosen Judas, but he would never question Yeshua's decision for fear the responsibility of the money bag might fall to him. He knew that what Yeshua had said was true, money was a trap. He did not want that temptation.

He rejoined to listen. "To build a solid and lasting life of blessing, you have to build your life on the right foundation. Even before you begin to build upon that foundation, you should sit down and estimate the cost of what you plan to build. What will it cost you?" Yeshua paused giving people time to ponder his unspoken questions.

'What have you built your life upon? Vanity? Popularity? Prestige? Material wealth? Admiration? Physical beauty? Pleasure?'

After a pause, Yeshua continued, "Everyone who hears my words and puts them into practice is like a wise man who builds his house upon the rock. Their house is strong and will not fall, because the foundation is rock solid."

"But everyone who hears my words, yet refuses to put them into practice is like a foolish man who builds his house upon the sand. When the adversities of this world come against him, his house will fall with a resounding crash."

Simon realized he had previously built his life on all kinds of the unstable things.

So, why did Yeshua ask me of all people to be his disciple?

He had no idea. There was absolutely nothing special about him, except perhaps that God had been gracious enough to include him. He smiled to think of all the times Yeshua called him "Rock." That silly nick name made Simon try all the more to be dependable, stable, and strong. But as he thought on it, he realized that Yeshua was the real rock.

He wondered, 'Maybe someday, if I stick with Yeshua, I will be as solid as a rock too?'

All day Yeshua preached, casting such graphic and imaginative visions of what life could be with God. By revealing his heart to the people, they could see God's kingdom was beautiful and good, and much to be desired.

~ 39 ~

THE DARKNESS WITHIN

Instead of your shame you will receive a double portion,
and instead of disgrace you will rejoice in your inheritance.
And so you will inherit a double portion in your land,
and everlasting joy will be yours.
Isaiah 61:7

Mari awoke to a headache from another restless night. She lay there with no desire to move, though she had a full day scheduled. The headache left her dull as if she had drank too much wine. All night an unexplainable anxiety had held her captive. Her heart had hammered and a terrible dread pressed upon her. Would she never be acceptable, ever enough? Her mind was racing over everything she had said and done recently. She felt unsettled. Her feelings of doom had been triggered by a small but unexpected criticism concerning one of her lessons. The gossip, as gossip always does, had found its way to her. Her slanderer was a trusted friend. The accusation had felt like a betrayal and it stirred up all the dark emotions she kept buried inside.

Once the darkness took over, all her feelings of abandonment and betrayal threatened to cripple her yet again. She felt unworthy, like a fraud, and unable live up to her own standard of perfection despite all her efforts. Her standard was higher than any person could hope to obtain. She longed for a perfection and an approval that was never to be found. There were places in her heart that felt barren and empty. A loneliness permeated her and left her feeling her life was ultimately meaningless.

Susanna entered her room, opening the curtain. She sat a fresh glass of pomegranate juice on table near her bed.

"Good morning." She chirped happily. "I have set out a fresh tunic for you, and cleaned your gold sandals that match."

Mariamne, who everyone knew as Mari, sat up to take a sip of the refreshing sweet-tartness to wash her thoughts away.

Susanna left and returned with heated water for her morning bath.

"Were you up late last night?" She asked. "You look tired."

"Oh, I woke up and couldn't go back to sleep. A lot of old memories came back to haunt me."

"Did you have your nightmares again?"

Susanna knew Mari suffered from bouts of sadness, anxious thoughts, and depression from time to time.

"It was not exactly a nightmare, but it was the same old type of dream. This time I was standing in the temple and it was empty. Everyone had disappeared. I couldn't find my way home or find anyone I knew. I felt lost as if I had somehow been left behind."

"I would call that a nightmare. You know I am always here for you."

"Yes. I do know and I am so glad. This anxiety is like a sickness, I never know when it will lay me low. But I am a survivor, and I must not let it get me down. Besides, I am too busy for that. This morning the women are depending on me to bring them the teaching. Plus, I have an appointment with my women about the use of a new dye color just in from Ethiopia."

"Sounds like a busy day. Maybe you should try to find some time to rest this evening."

"No, I have been invited to dine with Joanna."

"Ah, she has news to share of the Herodians then? What do you think it is?"

"Yes, I do expect some news about Herodias and how things are going with her marriage to Antipas. Funny, even after all these years of being so distanced from all of them, I still want to know what they are doing. Finally, after all these years my sister's dream is coming true, she gets to be a queen."

"I don't know why you bother, they are such awful people. Maybe some think blood is thicker than water, but I don't know why. Still, I suppose it is natural to want to know something of those who are kin to you. Do you think your sister will try to find you?"

"Of course not. Why would she? She never has before. Herodias was against me even as children. We were never close. She resented that I was chosen to marry the heir and be the next queen. And, even though that didn't happen, I have been told that when I disappeared she was quite glad I was gone."

She sighed sadly, "My identity has been kept well hidden and I plan to keep it that way. Besides, Herodias has been living in Rome for years under the tutelage of my grandfather's sister, Salome. She is a dreadful woman! I heard that Herodias even named her daughter after her. Trust me, I am the last person Herodias would hope to see. Still, I'm curious."

"If you ask me it is an odd curiosity. Why care?"

Mari knew she was right, but for some reason she still did.

She stared into space remembering Herodias when they were children. A cold shiver traveled down her spine. She wrapped her arms close as if to contain the old memories.

"If she believes I am dead, that is a good thing."

Susanna shook her head, unable to understand the Herodians, and just as glad that she was sent with Mari when she disappeared.

Mari finished her juice and abruptly stood as if putting those thoughts away from her. Staving off the heaviness in her chest, she searched for an uplifting thought.

"Oh, there is one thing." Mari threw a hopeful glance toward Susanna. "Word has been buzzing around about that new prophet that I heard on the teaching steps from Nazareth. I have heard he has been teaching to huge crowds out on the side of a mountain in Galilee.”

“Oh?”

“His message is so uplifting. People are excited for God’s coming kingdom and rumors are, he is the Messiah. His teachings intrigue me. I feel hopeful when I hear him speak. Some others have made the trip."

“I have heard good things too, but Galilee? That is a long way to travel for his teaching. Galilee is not Jerusalem! Won't he come back to the city soon.” Susanna asked.

“I have heard, the authorities in Jerusalem are against him. So, I doubt he will return to Jerusalem anytime soon. Susanna, you have to hear him, no other teacher speaks with such authority. His words make sense of our lives and I need that.”

Susanna saw Mari eyes were vulnerable and ringed with circles, evidence of the battle within. She also saw Mari’s determined hope. “When shall I begin to pack?”

“Start preparing right away, and I will make arrangements.” Mari set her jaw the way she did when she had made up her mind. She needed to leave Jerusalem and her dark thoughts behind.

“I will invite Joanna to join us on our little adventure, too.”

In Galilee, a shabbily dressed man stood on the periphery watching Yeshua teach. He was sweating under the dark brown cloak of his disguise. He had no recourse but to swelter, unwilling to risk recognition. It didn't help that Caiaphas was fuming.

The rumors of the healings and the massive crowds were true. In fact, this Galilean’s popularity and influence far exceed his imagination. Before him was a field filled with Jews, Samaritans, and even Gentiles. It was apparent that many had traveled great distances to hear his words.

Caiaphas' hands balled into fists and his jaw clenched. He wanted nothing so much as to challenge this man’s legitimacy. But, he carried little influence here among the Galileans. These were not the politically swayed people of Jerusalem. This ethnically diverse crowd was far too enthralled.

He wove a tight serpentine path in and out of the outer fringe of the crowd. He hid himself from view to judge the situation spread before him. He recognized several religious leaders from the surrounding areas. He tried to determine their attitude toward this rabbi.

'Concerned or hopeful? For or against? Allies or enemies?'

He was surprised to see so many Roman soldiers flanking the perimeter of the crowd, watchful and interested. He assumed they were there to keep the peace. He couldn't know that a good number were posted there as protection by Decimus, while others were there because they wanted to hear his words for themselves.

Caiaphas came to a rise nearing the outcropping where Yeshua was teaching. From that vantage point, his eyes raked through the crowd searching for familiar faces. He was surprised to find the ethnic adornments of Assyrians, Decropolis, and Jerusalem. All of them were captivated.

Just then an elegantly tinted splash of color caught his eye, appearing like a particularly delicate almond bloom found in a field of grey stubble. He sought a better vantage point to view the beautiful woman wearing the delicate scarf. His breath caught. He leaned forward. She was a bit taller than average, slender, well-formed, and well-dressed. Her stance appeared regal. His eyes narrowed with an interest he had not felt in many years, if ever. He was surprised when he realized her face was familiar.

Ah, yes. She teaches in the women's court. She is the youngest daughter of 'The Leper'. Why is she here of all places? Curiosity? Or, has she become a follower?

Intuitively Mari glanced his way, having subconsciously sensed his stare. He turned quickly away.

She did not glance back, she was too caught up in the Galilean's words.

She must be following his teachings.

268 ~ K. S. MCFARLAND

Caiaphas snorted, with indignation, thinking, 'This is the very reason women are not to be trusted in matters of the religion, they are so easily beguiled! She will surely take this man's teachings back to the women of Jerusalem. Annas always said, one could never underestimate a woman's power to cause trouble.'

Caiaphas knew this all too well, being married to Annas' own meddling daughter. His wife constantly tried to intrude in temple affairs. The daughter of a High Priest, she reveled in the politics of the temple and coveted her brothers involvement. It was all he could do to keep her at bay.

He was surprised in his sudden interest, he had never previously given this woman a second thought. Perhaps because of the long standing frictions between her family and the House of Annas.

He thought, 'Herod made a mistake by allowing Simon ben Boethus to settle so near to Jerusalem. His reach still has too much influence in the politics of the Sanhedrin, even if it is from Bethany.'

Caiaphas dredged what he knew about the Boethus family. Simon was now very old, older than Annas. People joked he would out live them all. Yet, he was still one of the most politically august patriarchs amongst the priestly families. His connections and alliances spread far and wide. Back in the day, even King Herod the Great had feared Simon's political weight among the Jews.

Simon's son's had succeeded him as High Priest when he was removed. Eleazar was still very active in the Sanhedrin, and had recently begun to groom his son Lazarus. Simon's son Joazar was a prosperous business man who remained a leader in Jerusalem's shadow groups. So they played both sides of the divides.

The women of Simon's family had all held positions of influence as well. His eldest daughter had been the third queen of Herod the Great, she was crowned as Mariamne II. After some long years, Herod had divorced her on accusations of treason. She had been deposed along with her Simon, and Herod II was exiled.

Eleazar's daughter Martha married Joshua ben Sie, who won the bid to became high priest against Annas. His priesthood was short lived however. He had mysteriously fallen ill and died, the suspicion was poisoning. That rumor had also mysteriously disappeared. He smiled at the thought. No one tried to cross Annas after that.

Martha became a very wealthy woman at Joshua's death, moving back to Bethany, she had built her own wing onto her grandfather's compound in Bethany, which she now managed for the family. She held the respect of a good many priestly wives in Jerusalem. Caiaphas' wife was not one of them. But, Martha's social gatherings during the Festivals were well known. She too, was a beauty.

Mari, Simon's youngest daughter was more of a mystery. She was highly educated in the law, taught by Simon himself. Her clothing line had become popular among the women in Jerusalem. But not much more was known of her, except that Mari had never married. She lived independently in Jerusalem. She had gained the unofficial title of 'Rabba nit' amongst Jerusalem's women despite her bypass of a priestly marriage.

'Why hadn't Simon married her off to make for himself another political alliance?' He wondered.

Caiaphas observed Mari listening to the Galilean's teachings. Her lips were slightly parted with a kind of wonder and anticipation of what the Nazarene would say next. It was as if she were breathing in his words. She was with two other well-dressed women and a manservant. The older woman with her wore the insignia of the Herodian household.

Unaccountably, he felt a surge of desire for her such as he had not felt for any woman for years. He wanted to snatch her away and take possession her. Had he ever had any such thoughts?

In his state of confusion, Caiaphas mistook his covetous envy of Yeshua as lust for the woman.

He forced his thoughts back to the Nazarene. 'If only I could find some law to twist into a weapon against him. But what?'

He listened for several painful hours before he gave up. He found nothing he could use to condemn the man. Finally, he could bear no more. At least he understood what he was up against. He had to find some strategy to take the Nazarene down. He motioned to his body guards, then took one more lingering look towards Mari.

Yes, I will find a way to take that woman as my own.

~ 40 ~

KEEPING SECRETS

Oh, how I wish that God would speak,
that he would open his lips against you
and disclose to you the secrets of wisdom,
for true wisdom has two sides.
Job 11:5-6

Back in Jerusalem, Caiaphas tried to concentrate on a strategy to deal with the Nazarene. But try as he might, his thoughts kept turning back towards Mari.

What is wrong with me?

He watched for Mari's return. He devised ways to encounter her. He found vantage points from which he could observe her when she taught in the women's court. He could not account for his sudden obsession with her. Caiaphas had been careful to leave no indiscretions in his married life. But this fixation was different, unnatural, and far too consuming for a pragmatic man like himself. Some men his age had dalliances, but he had little interest. Mari had become like salt on his tongue, leaving him restless to satisfy his craving.

His investigation had yielded little information. Except the fact that Mari had been adopted to Simon's family. Still, Simon was old enough to be her great grandfather.

'But who were her birth parents?' Caiaphas wondered.

Caiaphas sent an invitation to Simon for a small honorary feast. His wife was shocked when he gave her his small guest list.

Without explanation, he said, "This is strictly business. No women will be attending."

"Why the Leper?" She asked, he is not our ally.

"You never know how he might be useful." Caiaphas answered her vaguely.

When the invitation was delivered to Simon, he was surprised and immediately wary. But in the end he could not resist the mystery of it. Besides, although they were political opponents, Caiaphas was not a person to insult. If his years had taught him anything, it was to beware of friendly enemies, and to keep them close. Obviously, Caiaphas had some ulterior motive.

"Simon ben Boethius, father" Caiaphas said solicitously, "you must take the seat of honor next to me tonight." Simon offered a reserved smile, expecting no less.

Once they reclined around the table, the old priest's cup was filled with the best of unwatered wine. Caiaphas made pleasantries while waiting for Simons lips to sufficiently loosen. Simon cautiously feigned little sips from his goblet, aware that wine was never a wise man's friend. How many men had given away their secrets while in the cup?

After a full hour of prattle concerning political issues, Caiaphas broached his intended subject, "Your daughter, Mari teaches in our women's courtyard. I understand you have done a remarkable job training her. She is quite popular among the women."

"I can't take too much credit for her knowledge." Simon said. "But I will say, Mari was my most enthusiastic disciple. She has gone far beyond all my teachings now."

"Few women have any understanding of the law. Tell me about her."

Simon cast him a quizzical eye, pretending a moment of aged confusion. He had learned affecting an addled mind often gave him time to slow down and think. Although, these days he could be more easily confused. "Why this interest in Mari? I believe you already have a wife. Aren't you married to Annas' daughter?" Simon arched a sardonic brow.

"You are not interested in making a switch of wives like Antipas are you?" He laughed provocatively, glad for the opportunity to make a derisive pun concerning Caiaphas' involvement with Antipas' marriage.

Caiaphas also laughed, but more so at the old man's cheek. He could see the old fox was not as imprudent as he'd hoped.

"I would only like to help advance her ministry, but I need to know more about her before I do."

"I'm pretty sure she doesn't need your help. She has certainty not needed my help for quite some time. She is quite capable." Simon countered, knowing few powerful men advanced a woman's cause, unless there was something in it for him.

In his earlier life, hadn't he stooped to similar measures with his own daughter by forcing her into a marriage that gave him the political advantage.

He smiled benignly. "Usually, it is the High Priest's wife that chooses and elevates the women's teachers. You should have invited your wife. I am curious, however, what would you like to know about her."

Simon popped a large olive in his mouth, extracting the seed with his fingers.

"I am interested in her origins. I understand she is adopted."

"I can't see what difference that might make, she bears my name. That was a long time ago. I wonder, how did you come to this insight?"

"I have asked around."

"Ah! I see! You are investigating her." The old man rubbed his chin.

So, he is sniffing after Mari's secrets.

Simon's defenses rose.

How can I satisfy Caiaphas' curiosity without giving her away?

Caiaphas explained. "It is strictly a technicality. I can't stick my neck out to recommend her ministry to the women unless I know all the facts."

Simon took command of the conversation by veering into the past. "My daughter Mariamne was a kind woman. She cared about people. The girl appeared at our gate when she was nine, orphaned by a tragedy. My daughter was lonely. In her compassion, she took Mari in as her own. There is really nothing else to tell. The girl needed a home; and my daughter needed a child to love. When my daughter died, I adopted the girl as a daughter. She is my daughter now, Mari Bat Simon of Bethany."

Simon was satisfied with the truth in his words. Caiaphas motioned to his servant to fill Simon's cup once more, though it had been barely touched. Simon stared pointedly at his cup.

"She is a real beauty, isn't she?"

Caiaphas did not respond.

To steer the conversation away from her, Simon began to ramble in the seemingly nonsensical ways of the elderly.

"You are too young to remember the days of Herod the Great."

"I was in my late twenties when he died, but..."

Simon motioned his hand to shush Caiaphas.

"He was a calculating and dangerous man, I knew him well. During his reign there was constant intrigue at court. His household was a veritable pit of vipers, all too happy to devour their own. Not only was Herod dangerous, but his whole family as well. It was supremely dangerous to be associated with him in any way. Nothing was sacred to Herod but Herod."

He paused and looked at Caiaphas meaningfully. "Perhaps, you have seen some of the family traits in your friend Antipas, yes? Herod was paranoid. He had good reason to be. His sister Salome was conniving to the core. She coveted the power of her brother's throne. While, Herod would as soon kill you as to look at you, the malice and deceit in Salome constantly played to his worst instincts. Herod fell for her ploys time and again. She caused a lot of trouble for the members of his household."

Simon recalled the look of hatred Salome reserved for his daughter and grandson, Herod I. He shivered. He slowly shook his head, lowering his eyes to hide his feelings of regret and shame.

"I didn't realize how ruthless the Herodians were when Herod was looking to replace his former queen. Had I been more informed I would have been wary. He wanted the daughter of a priest to preserve his balance of power and influence with the temple, but looks mattered too. Whoever he married, her father would become the next High Priest. An associate put in a word of my daughter's beauty. I was not as highly ranked as Herod would have liked, but he could not resist coming to meet my Mariamne anyway. Perhaps he hoped to find another woman as beautiful as Mariamne I, his murdered wife. Indeed, my daughter was named after the great queen."

Simon's mind seemed to be wandering in a field of guilty thoughts.

"We were trapped, how can one say 'no' to the King of Israel? It was like making a deal with the devil. My daughter despised Herod at first sight. But once he saw her, he wanted her. Mariamne begged me not to go through with it, but I feared the repercussions. So, I tried to make the best of it."

"I comforted myself, imagining Mariamne as our modern-day Esther and I, her Morticai. But, after we came to Jerusalem the Sanhedrin applied pressure for Mariamne to provide information of Herod's activities. Vainly, I had thought I could save Israel. Back then, I was like you, Yosef. A man in his prime and hungry to build a name and dynasty for myself."

Caiaphas frowned at Simon's familiar use of his given name, not appreciating the comparison at all.

Simon stared into space. All three of the Mariamnes, I, II, and III, swirled in his mind's eye: the murdered queen, his deposed daughter, and the orphaned girl. They seemed to blur together as if they became one in his memory.

Caiaphas waited, noting Simon's tremble of regret.

"What does this have to do with Mari?" Caiaphas finally asked, trying to redirect Simon's thoughts.

"What? Nothing." He stared blankly at Caiaphas. "I am sorry, I suppose this visit has stirred up the ghosts of the past."

He recovered. "Knowing how Mariamne I of the Hasmonaeans had been executed, my daughter knew to stay clear of the court's intrigues despite all the pressures to turn informant. She couldn't trust anyone. Salome was constantly contriving traps for those not aligned with her. All of Herod's children feared her. It seemed safest to ally with her. She eventually planted malicious accusations targeting Mariamne, hoping to inflame her brother's paranoia.

Luckily, I was able to convince him there were no proof against my daughter or our family. I convinced him to let us go quietly. I am still not sure why he relented, except that God heard my prayers. Herod divorced Mariamne and forced me to step down from my position and leave Jerusalem."

"Yet, you didn't go too far away." Caiaphas said, his jutting chin dared any rebuttal.

Simon laughed and shook his head. "No, that was my one concession."

Caiaphas tried again, "So why did you adopt Mari? She could have easily become your daughter's handmaiden instead."

Simon simply smiled at that absurd thought, thinking, 'Not likely.'

Then looking at Caiaphas, he gave him the real reason. "We all loved the child. She became a part of my family. Mari was young, alone, endangered, and in need of protection. She appeared by the front gate. Mariamne was glad for her companionship. She became like a daughter to her and a granddaughter to me. When my daughter died, I made it official. Wouldn't you do the same?"

"But, who were her parents?"

Simon held up his hand, setting his boundary. "Why dredge up her humble beginnings? She is my daughter now."

He remembered, how the girl had been discreetly delivered to Mariamne for safe keeping. Only five people knew where the princess was hidden. She had been but a child. As her guardian, Archelaus wanted the girl kept safe, just in case he needed her to become queen at some future date. That had never happened.

When his daughter died, Simon and the girl remained bound together by their common grief. Simon had promised he would never divulge Mari's identity. Not even the other members of his family had any idea of her auspicious parentage.

Caiaphas' probing questions did not sit well with Simon. I should send a warning to Mari and invite her to visit.

Why has she kept such a prolonged silence? Didn't I do right by the girl?

His voice became tremulous. "I don't get out much these days. Thank you for your hospitality, it has been..." He squinted at Caiaphas, "an interesting evening. I fear I have over done."

He motioned to his servants to assist him to his feet. He and his youngest son, Eleazer made arrangements for their departure.

Caiaphas watched Simon go, feeling he had been stonewalled. 'Is he hiding something? He certainly stirred Herod's ghost, what with all of his talk of the court intrigue. Does Herod have something to do with Mari? Or was that just an old man's ramblings? Afterall, wasn't she with a woman from Herod's household?'

Despite his suspicions, Caiaphas was still only grasping at straws. He had learned nothing new about the identity of Mari.

~ 41 ~

THE CHOOSING

You did not choose me,
but I chose you and appointed you so that you might go
and bear fruit—fruit that will last...
John 15:16

Yeshua carefully observed his followers, taking note of those who consistently and most closely followed him and his commands. He noted: who asked questions, who seemed to understand and modeled his kingdom principals, who were the most devoted, determined, and able to persevere though hard times?

Now, it was time to choose his twelve leaders. The clock was ticking, his time with them would all too soon come to an end. It was time to train the core team; and take his trusted inner circle deeper into the ministry.

Plenty of people came and went easily curious, sometimes inspired. The commitment of most remained shallow. They preferred to stay at arm's length. He zeroed in on the steadfast, the ones who had remained the longest and made the biggest sacrifices, and who had shared the hardships of his life daily. Who left behind their comforts, businesses, jobs, and families to follow him? Which men were supportive of others and did the work? Who were hungry and thirsty for righteousness? Who was courageous enough to face the dangers?

It stood to reason that his most intimate relationships had developed with those men willing to suffer with him. They believed in him and his leadership and embraced his mission. They remained teachable. Into that twelve he would pour all of his energy and time like a farmer pours out his best seeds into a fertile soil. He needed bountiful seed bearers who were able to yield their own crop of dedicated disciples. The seeds of his Father's kingdom would be scattered by them into the four winds, multiplying until the whole earth was permeated with his kingdom.

Skills could be honed. Spiritual gifts could be supernaturally given. But Yeshua was looking for something more essential. He was looking for a certain kind of heart, a very rich soil, into which the seeds of truth could flourish. Yeshua thought back over the kind of people his Father had chosen to serve His purposes as leaders and prophets throughout the years. They were created with purpose and anointed with God's spirit. None of them might have seemed very impressive at first glance. But each one had a certain sensitivity to the things of God. They naturally sought a government that was better than this world offered them. They were independent thinkers, who were able to discern good from evil, and who intuitively understood their dependency on God. They knew the ideal kingdom could not be built by human hands. They made God's rule their priority.

One night while resting from their busy day, Yeshua posed what seemed like a nonchalant question to his men.

"What kind of people did my Father call to serve him and Israel? Think of the great servants of God, how would you describe some of them?"

His question sparked their curiosity. They took a moment to ponder this.

Rock answered first. "They were willing to go where God called them to go, like Abraham."

"Yes. Good. Thank you, Rock. What else?" Yeshua looked around, watching the faces within the circle encouragingly.

"They trusted in God's promises and believed what God said." Thaddeus said quietly.

Wheels began to turn; each man began to focus.

"They were courageous, like David." James said.

"They persevered, like Jacob." Said Thomas.

"And loved God, like they all did." Rock said.

"They were humble, like Moses." Nathaniel chimed in.

"They listened for God's voice, and followed the LORD's commands, like Samuel and Elijah." Andrew added.

"They were set apart from the world around them and obedient to God's command like Noah." Yohan said.

"They were receptive and excited about God's calling like Elisha." Phillip said thoughtfully.

"They endured unfair suffering, like Job and Joseph, but still believed in God." Matthew added.

"Yes, yes, outstanding!" Yeshua said.

Turning pensive he asked, "So then, how can we account for the fact that these same men were also at times fearful, weak, or fell to sin? Some were young, and some were old. Some were the least of their brothers, some took abuse, some were sold into slavery, and some were totally discounted and disowned by others?"

The men looked uncomfortably to one another. No one answered.

Yeshua continued, "They were chosen as a display of God's glory, not for their own. None of their paths were easy. They understood their most important need."

"What's that?" All eyes were on him.

"They understood their need for God, their dependency, and they knew how to pray in power. Success comes through God's will and for his purposes, not through the purposes of man." Yeshua answered.

"They aligned their hearts with God's. They wanted what God wanted. The desires of men are self-driven. But the Father's desire is different. He always wants what is best for all of his children.

Your desires will lead you astray. Seek God's heart, let him give you the desires of your heart."

He looked around the large circle of faces. "Which of you will commit yourselves to my Father's will and allow the Father to place his desires for you in your hearts? I will be praying tonight to choose twelve of you as my servants. You will be my core leaders. I will train you for leadership. I ask you to be praying as well."

After everyone was asleep, Yeshua got up and went out for his time of prayer. He prayed fervently throughout the night, considering each man before his Father.

"Father, show me who is to be chosen. Show me what lies within, show me their hearts and who they will become."

As he considered each man, he found it was not so difficult to make his choices as he first thought. When his work was done, he prayed.

"Help these twelve to remain with me when I don't fulfill their preconceived desires. Strengthen them to remain to the end. And at the right time, Father, reveal our plan to them."

He continued, long in prayer, until the darkness fled and birdsong ushered in the first rays of day. Light streaked the distant horizon with faint peach, framed by the black shadows of the distant trees.

The sky quickly transformed, brightening as if splashed with brilliant red flames. Although the sunrise was beautiful. Yeshua understood it was a sign of foreboding. About that time, Simon, James, and Yohan appeared on the rise of the hill headed his way.

"There you are!" They clamored as if they had been searching for him. Their faces reflecting the bright warmth of the red sky.

"You know I go out to pray, why are you looking for me?"

"Yes, about that..." Yohan said. "You mentioned prayer last night..."

"Would you teach us to pray like you do?" Simon finished Yohan's sentence.

Yohan shot Simon an annoyed look and continued. "We realized after what you said about prayer...well we could use some help. Could you show us how you do it?"

Yeshua smiled broadly, as if something important had just been confirmed to him.

"Of course, but let's go back for breakfast first. I am starving from my rigorous night."

After breakfast, he began his teaching. "When you pray, acknowledge the Sovereign Majesty of God as your heavenly Father. Acknowledge that he is rightly sovereign and exalted high above you. Worship his name, for his name is the greatest of all names. He deserves all of our praise. Ask for his will to be accomplished in everything, everywhere and at all times, pray for his will over every concern, and need."

He wiped his bowl. "Then, ask for what you need for that day, and for the needs of those around you. Confess your wrong doings, and ask your Father to help you set your wrongs right. Be open to the Father's direction and examine your behavior in the light of God. Ask for God's forgiveness of those who have wronged you, ask that you will also be able to forgive your offenders in your heart. Ask God to keep you free from bitterness, temptations and distractions. Ask to be shown the right way to go, the right thing to do, and for help and strength to do it. Ask also for deliverance from evil, for evil is always crouching at your door. Proclaim the praise of God for his goodness and holiness. Proclaim his knowledge, his sovereignty in all things, his power, his holiness, his eternalness over life and all things".

"And do all this privately because your prayer is meant to be between you and your Father. You can bring anything to him. From his trustworthiness, he will answer you. When he has done this, remember to give thanks."

His teaching was done for the day, he had business to attend.

"I have made important decisions and will be taking some of you away from the larger group today to talk with you, individually and then we will gather all together."

That day, Yeshua came to his chosen twelve one by one, asking them to come meet with him. He shared with them their strengths and their weakness and explained what he demanded of them.

"Are you willing to make this kind of commitment to the future of my mission? Will you take into account the dangers and conflicts, and follow anyway?"

Judas watched with partly shuttered eyes, waiting to be summoned. Yeshua had yet not called on him. He needed to be a part of the team. Yeshua said he would choose 'twelve'. When Judas had counted out eleven, he saw that Yeshua was headed toward Matthias. He quickly came to his feet to intervene, saying, "I am ready for my turn Master."

Yeshua scrutinized Judas for an uncomfortable moment. His lips flattened.

"Yes, but I have something to say to Matthias first."

Judas drew in a deep breath. He waited, sure he was about to be excluded. Yeshua returned with Matthias, then he said to Judas. "Okay, come with us. Matthias will tag along also."

Yeshua knew there were two things that Judas loved more than God's kingdom; it was money and doing things his way. These would ultimately be Judas' downfall. Still, he took Judas along as his one of his chosen, knowing that Judas had his preordained purpose.

Yeshua told them all, "Time is fleeting, and there is much more work for me to do. The Sanhedrin has been pressing close to us recently. Danger is increasing making it harder to travel as a larger group. We must become less stationary, more strategic, with schedule places to meet and preplanned time.

"Pack your bags; from now on we will be on the road, moving from place to place. Foxes have dens and birds have nests, but the Son of Man will have no place to lay his head. I am asking the twelve of you to travel with me.

"I have chosen you to be the ones I will send out into the various regions to preach in my name. Tonight, we will leave this region under the cover of night, otherwise the crowds will try to follow us. We need to reach others. This is why I have come."

They peppered him with questions about the logistics, but he held up his hand.

"I will tell you as you need to know. For now, the Feast in Jerusalem is fast approaching. When we return to Galilee, we will begin to implement my plan."

The Twelve looked excitedly at one another, Yeshua had chosen them to be his leaders. They had a lot to learn about what that meant. But to each man the honor was real, and they couldn't help but feel special, each one imagining themselves his favorite.

Yeshua continued, "Meanwhile, I want you to look seriously at my life. We will be constantly on the move. Our mission will become even more dangerous than the days past. In the years to come, your lives will be no different from mine. If people hate me, they will hate you too. If they hunt me, they will hunt you too. Now is the time for you to count the cost, and decide if you want to remain with me."

He told them, "If you remain with me, I will remain with you. If you are to follow me, you must be determined, strong and courageous because the hardest days lie ahead."

They looked soberly around their group, each one thinking of the constant conflict that followed Yeshua. They did not voice their fears, but each one wondered, 'If things get worse, am I willing stay the course? Yohannan still languishes in prison. If I follow Yeshua that could be me.'

They questioned themselves, 'If I am not willing to fight to re-establish our nation and God's kingdom on earth, then who will do it? God's kingdom is my heart's desire! Yeshua is the only one who has what it takes to inaugurate that kingdom on earth. How can I fail to do my part in this?'

They had only just begun to realize just how serious their call really was. Despite Yeshua's dire warnings, they filled their back packs to follow him back into the lion's mouth of Jerusalem.

~ 42 ~

IN THE CHAOS

Now the earth was formless and empty,
darkness was over the surface of the deep,
and the Spirit of God was hovering over the waters.
Genesis 1:2

After the sun set, Yeshua and The Twelve departed quietly to the boat. The night felt eerily heavy and all too silent. They did not speak as they picked their way stealthily down the path to Simon's readied boat.

"Everything is set to go." Simon said. "But Lord, I don't think that we should."

His fisherman instincts were on high alert. He knew this lake and the weather.

"Rock, we will be okay. Have a little faith!" Yeshua cast a pertinent eye towards him with a knowing smile, remembering the mornings teaching on prayer. Prayer was an exercise in faith. Faith would be their strength in all of the storms ahead.

Simon set the course southward toward the landing near the mouth of the Jordan River. There was no breeze, his sails hung limp. But knowing the currents as he did, Simon turned the rudder and they paddled towards them hoping to pick up speed within them.

"It is as dark as ink out here." James commented.

"Yes, a great evening for sleeping." Yeshua said. He curled up into the bow of the boat, exhausted from his vigil of prayer the night before.

"Wake me up when we reach the other side." He told them, letting them know he was not in a talking mood.

Simon was finding it hard to gauge his location, his only indicators were a few flickering lamps in the distant village along the western shoreline. The darkness grew thicker still; he could feel a dangerous pressure building in the clouds above, filled with unspilled rain. Remembering the red sky that morning, he was sure they would not make it to the other side in time. His jaw worked with frustration. Squalls could be deadly on this lake. Many boats had gone down in the storms.

Why was Yeshua so adamant about leaving tonight? I tried to tell him.

Suddenly they heard a loud pop over-head, the bright flash of lightning made them all duck for cover. A jagged white light slashed its unpredictable path through the sky to hit the mountain to the east of them, exploding in a loud ground-shattering strike. The earth resounded its loud complaint, a rumble traveled into the depth of the earth. Then another flash and Simon sprang to his feet counting off the seconds until its sound. The storm was coming fast. No longer able to see the lights of the shoreline he could only guess they were in the very middle of the sea, the worst place to be.

"Wake up, get ready. This could be bad!" He shouted his warning to those awake enough to listen. Helplessly, the men heard a loud clattering marching menacingly towards them, sounding like the advance of battle hooves. Simultaneously, two brazen thunder bolts split the sky. A sudden surge of water flowing into the sea from the highlands behind him made the current sway and buck, building quickly into large waves, then swells. Again, the lighting flashed through the sky just behind them in a blinding arch, landing a direct hit again this time to the west, the charge of ions still hung in the air overhead.

"Get the sails down. Hurry!" Simon barked.

Andrew, James, and Yohan each took hold of the ropes to release the sails, pulling it down quickly, just as a wall of rushing wind grabbed as if to jerk the sail from them. The men quickly threw themselves upon the billows to keep the sail from being blown away. The boat rose and pitched violently.

"Hold on." Simon shouted. Each man grabbed for a hand hold. The torrent of rain hit so hard they could scarcely gather in a breath without the intake of water. The sea turned into a convulsion of unpredictable chaos. Each man fought with all their strength not to be swept overboard. Meanwhile, Yeshua was still asleep like a dead man under his cloak in the protective curve of the bow.

Seeing Simon's terrified face, Yohan squatted down precariously to shake Yeshua arm.

"Master, wake up!" He shouted over the roar. "Wake up!!"

Yeshua came awake suddenly, tossing his drenched blanket aside.

Simon spoke urgently. "Lord, we are being swamped. We are going to drown."

Yeshua came to his feet, calmly assessing the chaos swirling around them. His hair was plastered to his head, his tunic clung to him. He stretched out his hand toward the wind, the rain, and the sea, speaking like a father who had been disturbed from his peaceful sleep by his rambunctious children.

"Quiet! Be still." At the force of his words, everything halted in mid-air. The rain ceased, the wind evaporated into a slight breeze, and the tossed boat landed with a gentle splash upon the collapsing waves.

The wild-eyed men stood motionless in their dripping clothes, slack jawed. Pulling their eyes from what had been a storm, they turned their full attention toward the man standing in their boat.

Yeshua rubbed his eyes sleepily. "Brothers! Didn't I tell you! 'You have to have faith!' Where is your faith?"

Clearly he felt they should have been able to take care of the situation themselves without waking him. His eyes met Simon's with an unspoken rebuke. Then he shivered slightly in the night air, grabbing up his wet cloak to wring it out. Then lay back down into his nest in the bow of the boat.

The men, stared at one another wordlessly as if they needed confirmation of what had just happened. The stars and the moon appeared in the night sky to light the way. Finally, a shaken and rebuked Simon raised the sails. They had been blown off course toward the eastern cliffs.

None of the other men went back to sleep. Instead, they replayed what had just happened in their minds, a different fear at work in them now.

They took turns staring at Yeshua, each one wondering, 'Who is this man that even the wind and waves obey him?'

Only One has that kind of power.

~ 43 ~

DELIVERED FROM CHAOS

For great is your love toward me;
you have delivered me from the depths,
from the realm of the dead.
Psalm 86:13

Yeshua directed Simon toward the Gerasene shore to cook their fish for breakfast. Simon looked at him quizzically. Every good Jew knew this western shore was home to the Gentiles and their pagan gods. The far side was off limits, every parent warned their children against their perversions and impurity.

As if greatly refreshed, Yeshua leapt out onto the sparce and rocky beachhead when they landed. Expectantly, he looked up towards the steep incline.

"Hello, is anybody up there?" He shouted towards the heights, then waited. No answer. "I have come! I am here." he called out into the air.

His men looked at him with confusion.

"Are you meeting someone here?" Simon asked.

When Yeshua didn't answer, Simon took closer measure, bringing his hands to his hips. "Ah, I see. Is that why you wanted to put in here? Lord, this is a bad place! Do you know where we are? I feel defiled to even step onto this land." He shivered with long held superstition.

"Really?" Yeshua scoffed, with a laugh. "After last night on the sea, I would think you would be only too happy to let your feet touch even this ground?"

Simon did not banter back. Instead, he solemnly hunched his shoulders looking up at the menacing terrain.

"This doesn't feel right." He grumbled under his breath, sensing the evil in this place.

The men set up their small cooking fire quickly, ready to complete their task of breakfast and move on quickly. Once the flames were hot, they placed some skewed fresh fish over it.

Meanwhile, Yeshua stood like a sentinel watching the steep paths leading from the rise expectantly.

The disciples exchanged glances with one another, wondering what strange thing to expect next.

This time it was Matthew who asked the question, "Lord, are you expecting someone, or something?"

Yeshua looked his way smiling, giving him a terse nod, offering no explanation. This made everyone wary.

They were about to sit down to eat when abruptly they were interrupted by a sound of that like a wild beast bellowing its warning. Looking up they saw a man running down the steep and narrow descent from the ridge. He groaned in guttural tones as if he were held in a choke hold. His hair and beard were matted together and standing wildly from his head at odd angles; it was as if he had been pulling on it and twisting it in some kind of agony. His sun darkened and dusty skin was proof that he had not bathed or worn clothes for a very long time. The man looked less than human. His nails had become long and dirty claws. Unbelievably, he ran with a determined lope towards Yeshua as if he were awkwardly dragging a whole mob behind him.

Yeshua could tell, this is the man he had dreamed of last night, chained and huddling amongst the tombs, his soul desperately crying out for God to help him.'

Still manacled, the putrid smell of pig slop wafted from him. Despite his dangling shackles, Yeshua knew it was not the physical chains that held the man captive—but Satan and his demons. Desperation filled the man's face. The newly appointed Apostles stood nearby, their hands upon their weapons in fear. The man stumbled, falling at Yeshua's feet. A threatening growl came from within him.

"What do you want with me, Yeshua, Son of the Most High God? I beg you, do not torture me!" The man said. He was holding his bloodied wrists out towards Yeshua imploringly. His chains jangled together.

"What is your name?" Yeshua asked the demon.

"Legion," came the fiendish growl. Many demons had taken control over the man, with hysterical groans they begged Yeshua not to send them into the Abyss. Unmoved by the threatening sounds or pleas, Yeshua had no sympathy towards the evil spirits. He looked around for a proper place to send them. The spirits would simply find new persons to torture, if he did not bind them to something, but what?

His eyes lit upon a large herd of pigs feeding on the hillside above.

"Yes, send us into the pigs." They begged.

Yeshua raised his hand over the man. He spoke in a low and authoritative voice, "Come out of him. Leave him and go into the pigs."

The man was thrown to the ground as if he was being trampled by unseen forces. The demons departed one by one for the pigs. When the last one had departed, suddenly without warning the whole herd began to squeal and run with fear and confusion. Together the herd rushed from the cliffs above. They tumbled head over heels from the heights into the sea below. They ran blindly as if trying to rid themselves of some unseen agony. Some died immediately, others swam frantically into the depths of the seas as if escaping a horde of hornets. When they grew exhausted, they sank into the abyss below.

The pig farmers witnessed it all, and saw the spirits entering their swine and their immediate madness. Terrified, they ran away to tell the owners of the pigs what had happened.

Now in his right mind, the man explained to Yeshua how he had been taken captive. He had been taken into the Roman militia as a slave. There one horror after another had happened to him or to those around him. With each abuse and terror another demon had taken hold of him.

He had finally escaped the Romans to return to his home, but the atrocities he had experienced remained to haunt him, causing him to react angrily, and to lash out at the people he had once loved. Eventually, he was chained hand and foot by the towns people. But his servitude had made him unnaturally strong. He broke his restraints so many times, that the people finally drove him away from the village. Homeless, he found solace among the tombs and the dead. The towns people feared him and avoided him at all cost. He admitted that under the influence of the demons, he was not even sure of all the evil things he had done. But to Yeshua, he confessed what he could remember.

The disciples took Isair out into the water where he was baptized. He was scrubbed clean with the strong soap Deborah had made for the men. A tunic was given to him to wear. One of the apostles took a sharp knife used to cut bait. He cut the tangled mess from his head and face. They gave him oil for his cleaned head.

After Isair was cleansed and clothed, he sat peacefully with the disciples. They invited him to share their meal. It was his first proper meal in a long time. Yeshua explained to him about the rule of God. He listened to all Yeshua was saying, his words brought him a feeling of peace and reconciliation with God. Despite all the horrors of his devastated life, he knew hope once again.

The pig farmers returned with some of the town's people. They were astounded to find the man they had feared and thrown rocks at, sitting calmly at Yeshua's feet, dressed like one of the Hebrews.

Although this was a miraculous thing, the people raised their fists to shout at Yeshua from a distance.

"What have you done to our pigs?"

No one drew near. They remembered how they had treated this man because of his violent fits. They feared him. They had been cruel and abusive towards him. Why wouldn't he retaliate?

Yeshua waited, knowing these people also had a great need for healing. But no one stepped closer, no others came to ask for his help. Instead, they picked up rocks as if to throw them at Yeshua.

"Return to the place you have come from. We don't want you here. Look what you've done to our livestock!"

Isair begged Yeshua. "Please, let me go with you." He feared the towns people, as well as the demons who might try to return and overtake him again.

Yeshua explained their boat was already overloaded. Furthermore, they were headed to the Feast in Jerusalem.

Yeshua placed his hand on Isair's shoulder to reassure him. "Do not be afraid! When the Son sets you free, you are free indeed. You've been healed! For now, return to your home and tell everyone how much God has done for you. I will pass by here again soon enough to check on you."

Isair nodded, reluctant to see Yeshua go. He remained on the shore watching until the boat had disappeared from view, thinking of what had happened.

The God Who Heals came here today just for me. Even though, I am the only one willing to receive him, he came here for me anyway. He heard my cries for help and he came.

Grateful tears of joy ran down Isair's face. He glanced down at his wrists healed from which the shackles had fallen, and lay now on the ground. Not even the scars from the manacles remained. His nails were trimmed, cleaned and smooth. He fingered his new clothes and touched his head and face. He felt more like his old self. It was as if Yeshua had made him all new. He bent down and took hold of his manacles, only to cast them out into the sea with the pigs.

Isair returned to his family's home to tell them of his miracle. In fact, he told everyone who would listen. People stepped away and stared at him with fear, but his joyful smile quickly drew them near to hear his story. They could see it was true, he was set free from the internal chaos that had scrambled his thoughts for such a long time.

In the boat, the men asked Yeshua questions about the demons and what they had just witnessed. It wasn't as if Yeshua had not already been delivering people from a variety of demons. But today, the healing had been up front and personal. There was so much about spiritual oppression that they did not understand. It was easy for them to understand the people's fear of that man who had so clearly lost control over his mind and his life. No one else had ever done what Yeshua was able to do! Healing the mind and the emotions, delivering people from chaos.They realized there was a lot they did not know about the supernatural world.

"Was Isair the reason you wanted to land there?" Simon asked him then.

Yeshua's smile was enigmatic, "Could you not hear his cry for help?"

"Well yes, but only when he ran bellowing down the mountainside."

"He has been crying out for a long time, but there was no one to listen to his cries or to deliver him."

"I have never seen so many demons in one man. Why were there so many?" James asked.

"And, why did you send them into the pigs?" Yohan asked.

"These are all good questions. You do deserve some answers." Yeshua said, leaning back against the side of the boat.

"When an impure spirit comes out of a person, it wanders through arid places—places devoid of life—seeking a person to rest upon. When it does not find a home, it says, 'I will return to the house I left.' When it returns, it finds the house unoccupied, swept clean and put in order. When it reenters, it brings along with it seven other spirits that are even more wicked than itself, and together they take over that life. They enter with lies meant to control the person's way of thinking. Once there, they bring chaos to their thoughts and they manipulate their reactions. The captured soul grows weak and unable to find its way out of the lies. In the end, the final condition of that person becomes worse than the first. It is best to never allow the devil a foothold."

"What do you mean?"

"A foothold is an unacknowledged or unconfessed sin that you allow to remain in your life, a faulty thought that one stubbornly holds on to. Like unforgiveness, or sexual sin, or violence. People have a tendency to double down. Once a lie has taken root, it begins to grow in power, inviting other lies and bad behaviors to enter." Their eyes grew large with fear.

He explained, "That is how it will be with this wicked generation. But when the presence of the demons is replaced with the truth and a right spirit before God, the truth of God takes up residence within them and becomes a shield from within. Truth has the power to bind and break the strongholds the demons create. Dependency on God's truth keeps the demons at bay."

They nodded, this made sense. "Then, how easy it must be to fall into bondage. " Thomas offered.

Yeshua spoke a low warning. "Doubt and a lack of faith is very dangerous. By this people reject God's word. Without the word and the Spirit, each person is fighting a battle they cannot see or win. They are like an empty house swept clean. There is nothing within them to shield them from the evil spirits or to keep the demons from bringing in even more lies. This is how people are taken captive by the evil forces at work around them.

This is why we must share the good news of God with those who have been delivered. The truth of God is their one sure defense, otherwise our work is useless in the long run.

"Was it his fault or the fault of others that he became like this?"

"Captivity is complicated. There are many pathways for evil to take hold of people, sometimes it begins because of the sin or the misdeeds of others. The company you keep is important. You must not be complicit or easily swayed. You must know and believe God's word is always right. Mostly, however, captivity comes by way of one's own sin and actions. So many lack any knowledge of the truth. Ultimately, however, there is only one way for a person to be completely set free."

None of them wanted to become like the man they had just seen. They promised themselves they would hold on to the truth of God, leave no room for doubts, nor allow such spirits to gain access to their lives.

They perceived, it was unwise to remain ignorant of the influences or the fight. They had to grow in faith and in spiritual sight. They all trembled at the thought, because keeping the faith was sometimes very hard.

~ 44 ~

THE TRUMPET SOUNDS

Blow the trumpet in Zion; sound the alarm on my holy hill.
Let all who live in the land tremble,
for the day of the Lord is coming.
It is close at hand.
Joel 2:1-2

Their caravan arrived to Fall Festivals just in time for The Festival of the Ingathering that began at sunset with the sounding of the rams horn. Yohan and James had family connections in Jerusalem in one of the more elite neighborhoods. Several tents of hospitality were contained within its wall.

"Thank you for your generous welcome." Yeshua told their host.

"We are glad to receive you and Zebedee's sons. We don't see our family nearly enough. However, I urge you to please use discretion. I have heard members of the Sanhedrin are watching for you in the temple area." Tobias told him.

"Our family is already suspect to those in power, we do not want any trouble."

Yeshua nodded acknowledging the dangers and added. "We value your discretion as well. I am planning to remain hidden during the Days of Awe to spend a special time of teaching with my closest followers."

"Not a problem, I have heard how the crowds follow you, giving you no quarter. Your privacy is of as great a concern for me, as it is you." Tobias winked.

The disciples were greatly relieved when Yeshua told them he planned to remain concealed.

"We will focus on deeper insights to God's kingdom to prepare you for your work when the festival is over. Get ready for your rabbinical schooling." His look was serious and for ten days they hunkered down to study the work of calling people to repentance.

The trumpet sounded ten days later to announce the Day of the LORD, the Atonement Day. It was a day known for its fear of God's wrath. On that day, each man pondered the meaning of God's judgement and grace. A meager dinner was eaten before the time of fasting and prayer began. At sunset, the city ground to a halt in observance of this special Sabbath. It was a time of confession, prayer, and supplication before the LORD.

In the temple, the Sanhedrin began their all-night vigil. Especially chosen priests guarded over the High Priest to make sure he kept himself pure for his communal duties the next day. The priest read the scroll of Levitcus and Deuteronomy out loud to him to remind him of each detail in the offering of the sacrifices. They made sure Caiaphas did not dose off as he prayed or inadvertantly do something to make himself unclean.

Atonement Day was a long twenty-four hours for the high priest and the other priests officiated over the fifteen temple sacrifices. The first began just as the sun peaked over the horizon. To show their devotion, people gathered to the temple observing the sacrifices and to pray that the priest would be heard.

Caiaphas began his duties of slaughter, prayer, submersion, dressing in new clothes repeatedly between each sacrifice until sunset.

It was a day of blood.

The sacrifices were executed in a specified order with great care and anxiety, remembering when Aaron's errand son had been consumed in flames. During the course of the day, Caiaphas entered the inner sanctum of the Holy of Holies four separate times, each time to cleanse the altar with incense and blood; once for himself, once for the priesthood, once for the people, then again to purify the altar from all the sin of the past year just before the new year was ushered in.

Yeshua watched it all, interpreting the meaning in every act. He despised the calloused way Caiaphas wrangled the animals, including the ease with which he slit their throats and drained their blood. It made him feel nauseous. He couldn't help but think, 'No matter how many times you wash your hands and feet, your blood guilt has yet to be removed, it is only temporarily appeased.'

After each entry to the Holy of Holies, Caiaphas stood before the people to pray the prescribed prayers in the Hebrew language now rarely used. He asked for the absolution of sin for the people. When the last sacrifice was complete, all of his actions were duly noted.

Yeshua sighed with relief, understanding the final absolution would not be complete until the Great Day of the LORD yet to come.

Finally, with all the sacrifices made and the last embers removed from the inner sanctum, an exhausted Caiaphas immersed himself once more in the mitvah of blood tinged water. He put on fresh clothes, relieved the bloody day was over. At sunset, he presented himself in the women's court to announce that all his duties had been discharged. The priest was still alive.

The people cheered their relief before turning to leave for home, eager to break their fast and to celebrate God's provision of grace.

Yeshua was also spent. He didn't feel like celebrating and he wondered who could? The day's sacrifices had left him somber and unsettled, still reflecting on the meaning within the sacrifices.

Five days later the Festival of Tabernacles began, Yeshua ventured out of the compound taking Yohan with him to the healing pool near the Sheep's Gate. It had a lovely portico with five grand columns.

The pool was renowned for its healing properties. Some believed angels descended and ascended on this pool to stir its waters. From time to time, the waters would mysteriously bubble and swirl, indicating a healing miracle would be given. People came to the pool hoping to be the first one into the waters to receive their miracle. Walking along the pool platform

Yeshua saw all kinds of needy people, but one man in particular caught his eye. He was lying slumped against one of the columns rather awkwardly. It seemed as if he had been poorly placed by his helpers; or perhaps his weakness had caused him to slide down until his shoulders and neck were left uncomfortably crumbled against the column. He looked miserable.

"What can you tell me about that man?" Yeshua asked a servant, pointing to him.

"Paralyzed. He has been like that for a long, long time. Two people bring him and leave him here regularly. They leave and go on about their business. The man is left to fend for himself. He is not much of a talker and as far as I know, he has never asked anyone else for help."

The servant added. "He doesn't seem to even try anymore. It is like he has given up. As if he doesn't believe God wants to heal him. He just lays there waiting for the people to come and carry him home again."

Yeshua cocked his head, studying the man.

What disappointments and indignities has he suffered? Why doesn't he ask for help? Fear of drowning? Disbelief or lack of faith? Or, does he find satisfaction in being a victim? Hm-m-m. There is only one way to know for sure.

Yeshua squatted down next to the grimacing man to ask him,

"Do you want to get well?"

The man squinted toward the knees of the one bent down before him, as if Yeshua was an intruder to his misery.

"What?"

"Do you want to get well?"

"See here, I have no one to help me into the pool when the water is stirred. Everyone else always beats me to it."

Yeshua stood and told him. "Stand up!"

The man flinched, wondering at the audacity of such a command. He craned his head, trying to see the man standing before him to know his authority.

"Pick up your mat and walk." Yeshua's words sounded weighty and unarguable.

Then it happened, Reuben began to actually feel his legs. He reflexively twitched at the intruders voice and his foot moved. Awe swept over him; feeling began to flood into his limp legs moving upward through his hips and lower back. He gave it a try, he was able to push himself up and draw in his knees. He was able to reach down to touch his now enlivened feet.

'Who was this man ?' Reuben look up toward Yeshua's face. But it felt as if the sun were blinding him, making it impossible to see his face.

So instead, he looked at his healer's feet. He wore the sturdy sandals of a working man, worn from travel as if he had come a long way.

Pulling his feet up under his body, Reuben tried to rock to his feet. He was a bit clumsy, but after a try or two he was able to stand. Now upright for the first time in thirty-eight long years, he stared with confusion at his own two feet. 'How had this happened?' He turned searching for the man who had urged him to stand, but no one was there.

Reuben wondered, 'Did an angel come to me after all?'

Looking around he saw only the onlookers clamoring with excitement. Reuben reached down and picked up his mat. He began to walk, totally absorbed in his movement. His attention was quickly interrupted, however, when some people began to shout angrily at him.

"What are you doing? You are breaking the law by carrying your mat on the Sabbath."

He was immediately irritated, how dare they take him to task for carrying his mat.

"Look! The man who just healed me told me to pick up my mat and walk. I am simply doing what he said."

"Who told you to do this?" A Pharisee inquired, already certain it was the Nazarene. Everyone had been watching for him the past eleven days.

"I have no idea who he was, but he had a powerful voice. I had to obey him, when suddenly I could feel my legs for the first time since I was a boy."

"What did he look like?"

"I am not sure. I couldn't really see his face, the light was blinding me. But it appeared by his sandals that he had traveled from far away."

When they went to search the colonnade, there was no sight of Yeshua. But, all of the people were excited and word was spreading about Reuben's healing. Later that day, Yeshua found Reuben walking in the temple court, looking around curiously. This was the first time, Reuben was free to enter into the Temple, a place long forbidden to him.

Seeing him, Yeshua approached offering him a happy smile, "Look! Now, you are well!"

The man stopped at the sound of Yeshua's voice. Fearful, he moved away from Yeshua. No testimony or joy graced his lips. Instead, he wondered what Yeshua might demand of him now in exchange for his healing.

Yeshua's smile faded. He came close, almost eye to eye with the man, he said privately. "Stop sinning or something worse may happen to you."

Stepping past Reuben, Yeshua moved on.

"How dare you talk to me like that!" The man mumbled, "Who do you think you are?"

He grabbed the first person he came to, "See that man, who is he? "

"Yeshua of Nazareth, a prophet." They answered.

Indignant, Reuben went to inform the authorities, offering them his healer's name.

Hearing that Yeshua was on the temple grounds Caiaphas came out onto the platform, scanning the people before him. He spotted Yeshua and moved quickly in his direction, his cronies trailing behind him like crows.

"You have broken the Holy Sabbath laws!" Caiaphas called out to him. "You healed a man on the Sabbath, then told him to carry his mat."

"That is right, my Father and I are always at work! And, tonight, this man will have a place to sleep."

"Are you a mad man? Are you now claiming God as your Father? Do you claim to be equal with God?"

Yeshua moved towards Caiaphas giving him his full attention. All the bustle in the court slowed to listen. Not wishing to be guilty by association, people simultaneously moved away anticipating a confrontation. They left him wide berth.

Calmly, Yeshua amplified his voice so everyone could hear. "You want the truth, so I will tell you. The Son can do nothing by himself. He can do only what he sees his Father doing. Whatever the Father does, the Son also does. For the Father loves the Son and shows him everything he is doing. This healing is just the beginning. Just as the Father raises the dead to give them life, in the same way the Son gives life to whomever he pleases."

Caiaphas' men gathered with him—a united front.

Yeshua continued, "The Father has entrusted all judgment to the Son, so that all may honor the Son just as they honor the Father. Whoever does not honor the Son does not honor the Father, who sent him."

Caiaphas understood Yeshua was claiming to be the Anointed One of God. Rage coursed through him. But he remained silent, knowing people were watching him. He could not afford to lose his self-control in his well proffered position. Only the gnashing of his teeth gave him away. He lifted his face haughtily, literally staring down his nose at Yeshua. The men with him shouted their objections, and called out accusations of illegitimacy. Caiaphas stood still, his face set like stone.

Yeshua stepped closer, speaking directly to Caiaphas. "I tell you the truth, whoever hears my word and believes the Father has sent me has gained eternal life. They will not be judged."

He held out his hands to Caiaphas in invitation.

"The moment they believe they cross from death to life."

Hatred radiated from Caiaphas.

"I am telling you the truth," Yeshua assured him, "a time is coming and has now come, when those who are dead will hear the voice of the Son of God. Those who hear and receive my message will live. For as the Father has life in himself, so he has granted the Son also to have life in himself. The Father has given him authority to judge because he is the Son of Man."

Even though, Yeshua was plainly laying his identity before him, Caiaphas' resistance only grew in strength. Because, when one resists the truth, the lies planted within them become all the stronger.

Pleading from his heart, Yeshua said "I am telling you the truth, a time is coming when even all who lie within their graves will hear the Son's voice and come out. Those who have done what is good will rise to live. Those who have done what is evil will rise to be condemned."

He drew a frustrated breath. Looking around at all of the hardened faces surrounding him.

What more can I say?

Yeshua searched for the right words to shatter Caiaphas' barrier. It was now or never.

He pressed on with his hands extended to Caiaphas.

"Look, by myself I can do nothing. I judge only as I hear. My judgment is just, I am not seeking to please myself but the One who sent me. If you refuse to listen to my testimony, then at least listen to the One who testifies on my behalf. Surely, you know the words of his testimony, and his testimony about me is true."

He was not surprised, the current priesthood did not hold to the prophecies of Isaiah or any of the other messianic prophets, having decided these prophets must have been mentally imbalanced persons. To those in currently in power their prophetic words had become irrelevant, aimed at the past alone.

Caiaphas thought, 'I am hardly ignorant the testimony of Scripture. I study it daily. Messiah? Certainly, not a man like this! And if Rome would ever allow a Messiah of the people to arise, wouldn't it be the High Priest, in the manner of the Hasmonaean Dynasty before Herod? If there is to be a Messiah for the nation, why not me? Haven't I come to power for such a time as this?'

He dug his heels into the stone beneath him stubbornly.

Yeshua continued. "You went to see Yohannan and he has testified to the truth. Believe what he has said! Yohannan's lamp has burned brightly to provide you light. And now, my testimony is weightier than Yohannan's. Listen! The works that the Father has given me to finish—the very works I am doing—testify to the fact that the Father has sent me. The signs are recorded in the Scriptures. My Father who has sent me testified through the prophets concerning me."

Caiaphas said nothing.

"Does his word not dwell within you? Why do you not believe the One he sent? Your life has been dedicated to the study of the scriptures. You study the Scriptures because you think that by studying them you have eternal life, but you miss the whole point of the scriptures. I am the point. These very scriptures testify about me! In pridefulness, you refuse to come to me so you may have life."

Will he not stop trying to convince me?

Caiaphas could take no more. The Galilean had struck his every nerve. Even though his men thought Yeshua was speaking to the lot of them, Caiaphas knew that he was speaking directly to him. It was insulting to have this Nazarene talk to him, the High Priest, this way. He turned to leave.

Yeshua called out to him. "I am not asking you to glorify me. Human praise means nothing to me; but I know you."

Caiaphas stopped, though he did not turn around. Fear filled him with a knowledge that Yeshua did know him.

Yeshua lowered his voice, and spoke with sadness and longing. "I know that you do not have the love of God in your heart. However, you should not worry that I will accuse you before the Father."

Caiaphas turned back towards him, ready to make a testy retort.

Yeshua continued. "No, your accuser will be Moses, on whom you have set your hopes. If you had ever really believed what Moses said, you would believe me. Moses wrote about me. But since you do not believe what Moses wrote, how are you ever going to believe what I say?"

Yeshua watched Caiaphas retreat, unwilling to dignify him with even a retort.

He wondered, 'What more can I say or do? He has made his choice. I have told him the truth, now all that is left is for me to suffer for telling him the truth.'

~ 45 ~

UNRIGHTEOUS INDIGNATION

There is no fear of God before their eyes.
In their own eyes they flatter themselves too much
to detect or hate their sin.
The words of their mouths are wicked and deceitful;
they fail to act wisely or do good.
Psalm 36:1-3

Caiaphas stormed into his home, not bothering to speak with his wife as he rudely passed her by. She stared after him. He kept no confidences with her. Instead, he passed through the portico that attached his home to the home of Annas, an even more expansive mansion conveniently connected to his own. The door servant moved quickly to usher in the son-in-law who was closer to Annas than his own sons.

Having been announced, Caiaphas entered the room with a petulant exclamation, "Father, the Nazarene is here!"

He paced the room like a caged tiger. "He humiliated me before the people and claimed to be the Son of God."

He paced the length several times before stopping to look at his father-in-law.

"What amuses you about this?"

Annas shifted his soft and sizable girth. "Come now, you knew he would be back. His kind do not cave in easily."

His eyes narrowed perceptively on Caiaphas, giving him the appearance of a shrewd weasel. His gray and yellowish complexion reflected his jaundiced soul.

He asked, "Did you approach him? Or did he approach you?"

"I did what I was required to do, I simply charged him with his crimes as they were brought to me. He healed a man today and it is Sabbath. Worse, he told him to carry his mat. The man was found wandering around the temple courtyard, carrying his mat with him."

"Did you really need to engage the Nazarene? Don't you have others who can do this for you?"

"He openly broke the law!" Caiaphas ground out the words as if speaking to a simpleton.

"Ah! I see. You just couldn't resist a power struggle with him. I thought we had talked about this. So, tell me, what did he do this time?" The old man asked calmly, taking measure of how rattled Caiaphas was.

When Caiaphas opened his mouth to explain, he was so mad that at first only unintelligent sputters were produced.

How can I even repeat his words? They are too offensive to even utter.

Gathering his thoughts, he bit his lip so hard that he tasted blood. He uttered a string of unholy words.

"You are shaken." Annas wrinkled his brow with concern. "He has gotten to you. What did he say?"

Caiaphas admitted nothing. Taking a deep breath to gain his composure, he spoke as calmly and lowly as he could. "He as good as proclaimed himself the Anointed One. He talked of Yahweh as his Father as if they were one in the same. He called himself the Son of Man! He healed a man who had been paralyzed for over thirty-eight years."

"Oh." Anna shook his head and pursed his lips. "The healing, is it real or just a ruse?"

"It has been confirmed by the healed man's parents and the witnesses at the pool."

"Such bold and boastful talk! Blasphemous too, unless of course it is true." Annas stroked his beard.

"It can't be true. Wouldn't I the high-priest know if it were true?"

"Not if it doesn't fit your chosen narrative." Annas chuckled, clearly amused at Caiaphas' high opinion of himself.

"What do you mean?"

"Come now, you are not talking to one of your underlings. Remember at whose breast you have supped. I know you." Annas chortled.

Caiaphas face went grim, "He said those same words, 'I know you'."

Annas flinched hearing that, though he couldn't say why. "How did you react?"

"I did not reply to him, even though I wanted to kill him with my bare hands, I said and did nothing at all. I couldn't think of one convincing thing to say to him. It was so humiliating being talked down to like that."

"Ah, you could not trust yourself to speak. Then it is good that you said nothing. It is never good to allow your words to betray your emotions. Besides, by remaining calm, you will make him look as if he were the unreasonable one."

"It was worse than that. I simply could not speak! He would not stop talking! He kept trying to convince me; he ranted like a mad man. It was as if he really believed everything he was saying. He made it seem like I was the offender because I would not believe him! The man has absolutely no respect for the office of High Priest."

"Historically, prophets offer little respect for our office." Annas said. "Although, besides the Baptizer, there has been no prophetic voice to challenge us."

"Are you saying you think he could be a legitimate prophet?"

"Caiaphas, wake up. He could be exactly who he says he is. Why are you so surprised? The scriptures say he will come at a designated time, which would be now. Herod believed there was a

Messiah among us; look at the lengths he expended to be rid of him. And, look at the Essences they have been preparing for his coming. According to prophecy, it is time. The Messiah is expected to appear. But what is that to us?" Annas looked at him pointedly.

Caiaphas looked undone, "Every person in the temple heard what he said and I could tell many believed him!"

A bit of spittle flew from his mouth, landing on Annas' luxurious robe. Annas looked down in disgust, pulling a handkerchief from his robe sleeve to wipe it off.

"It is this simple, we have to stop him." Annas said gazing out of his large window overlooking the city below, as if looking into the not-so-distant future.

Without turning he asked. "Did you send anyone to follow him?"

"No. I didn't want to be that obvious. Otherwise, the people will blame me if something happens to him. I can't afford to have the people turn against me, my priesthood has only begun. But, I can't be the only person that feels this way about this man. It stands to reason, he would have many enemies amongst our peers." He drew a sharp breath as if his chest was constricted.

"Just breathe Caiaphas! Take a deep breath." Annas spoke soothingly, "I know you."

Caiaphas felt the power of those words echoed once again.

Seeing Caiaphas' expression, Annas rushed to explain. "What I mean is, surely you have been thinking of a plan to bring him down in the eyes of the people."

"I have gone to every extent. Still, I have come up with nothing. We need to entrap him somehow according to the moral law of Moses. Then, who will question our motives?"

"What have you been thinking?"

"I am not sure. So far, I am unable to uncover any moral offense in him." Annas stroked the length of his beard.

"I hear he is known for his compassion? Perhaps you can turn his compassion against him in some way, entrap him in a moral dilemma. Pit compassion against the law. He will appear either completely lawless or far too judgmental. Either way, you will score points against him with over half of the crowd."

Caiaphas held his fist over his mouth, mulling Annas' words. "That's good. Let me think on this."

Even as he said it, Mari came unbidden to his mind. 'Strange. Why am I so plagued with thoughts of this woman?'

He tried to push his thoughts away, but to no avail. The image of her listening to the Nazarene with such engrossed attention came to mind. He wondered, 'Perhaps she is even now listening to him in the women's court, or on the teaching steps.'

A fit of jealous envy overwhelmed him. He forgot all about devising a plan. He left to go watch for her departure towards her home. Why should she follow Yeshua and his teachings? She should serve me instead.

~ 46 ~

BACK STORIES

You say, 'I am rich;
I have acquired wealth and do not need a thing.'
But you do not realize that you are wretched,
pitiful, poor, blind and naked.
Revelations 3:17

Mari was in the temple, in the women's court when the news came, "Did you hear about the confrontation between Rabbi Yeshua and Caiaphas today? The Rabbi openly announced that he was the Son of God to the High Priest. Caiaphas fled with his tail tucked."

She could hardly believe it. Her mind sped into overdrive, trying to reconcile this news about the teacher she was so enthralled with. Rumors were circulating. It was true, he was unlike anyone she had ever heard.

"Did he really say that?"

"Well...not directly. But trust me everyone knew what he was saying."

Mari's mouth made a solemn "O".

"You know Caiaphas won't stand for that!" Her informant predicted.

Caiaphas was the most powerful man in the temple besides Annas. She could only imagine the sparks that must have flown at Yeshua's words.

"I wish we could have been there to hear his words." Mari said, resenting that women were not allowed beyond their courtyard.

"Caiaphas challenged Yeshua for breaking the Mosaic Law to heal a man on the Sabbath. The man was reported to have been invalid for thirty-eight years."

Mari wanted to cheer for the poor man, whoever he was. Even if Caiaphas had the power to do such miracles, she was sure he would never use his power for the good of a crippled man, without extortion. After years of living in the presence of 'the priesthood', she knew there were only two things they cared about, being exalted and money. Mari had developed a cynical eye. She worked hard to steer clear of men like Caiaphas.

Now, here was someone willing to stand up against the lot of them, and to call them to account for their treachery and injustices. The leaders could put on airs and pretense all they wanted, but the Sanhedrin wield 'the Law' as a way to lord themselves over the people. They happily move the covenant law aside to create new man-made laws to drive the temple's agendas. In recent years there were so many laws it was oppressive, a constant stumbling block.

This was one of the reasons that she had become interested in the study of the law. She loved the rightness and the justice of the law. But even though she loved the foundational laws, she still found them hard to keep. And, she was stuck in a purgatory of loneliness because of the law. When people asked her why she had not married, she simply answered 'I have dedicated my life to God.' This was true but not the whole truth. Perhaps that made her as pretentious as the rest of them. It wasn't that she even wanted to marry. Still, she would have liked to have some choice in the matter.

What would people think if they knew the truth of who I am? I don't even know what might happen if the truth were to come out now. Only Simon, Susanna, and Joanna know my real identity.

Mari was the daughter of Aristobulus and the granddaughter of Mariamne I. At birth, she became Herod's favorite granddaughter because of her bloodline, appearance, and name. Her father was executed shortly thereafter and her mother placed in another political marriage. King Herod made himself the guardian of all of Aristobulus' children. Perhaps it was a murder's remorse, but Herod had in mind to appease his guilt putting her grandmother to death by making her namesake the future queen of Jerusalem. Mari young as she was, would be married to his successor. This had made her a lightning rod within the Herodian power struggle.

Although, it was illegal to make a marriage contract for a girl before the age of twelve, Mari's pedigree made it of legal necessity for the fruition of Herod's plan. She was under marital covenant twice before she was eight. Her Hasmonean blood made potent the throne of his successor, just as her grandmother had strengthened his own position when he became king. No one dared to argue against Herod's unrestrained power.

In the end, Herod's plans came to nothing. Her first husband, Antipater was executed by his father for treason. Her second husband, Archelaus was to become ethnarch, but since Mari was still too young for marriage Archelaus took his executed brother's wife to begin his dynasty.

Herod's sister teamed up with Glaphyra, Archelaus' wife. Looking down the years with great concern that the girls beauty would eventually turn Archelaus' head and uproot Glaphyra, they conspired to rendered the child spoiled by devising her abuse and humiliation.

Her grandfather had his doctors refuted the allegations, but Mari knew the sordid truth. Only later did she realize something precious had been stolen from her. The memory haunted Mari. She had never spoken of it to a soul. Yet, she struggled with the untenable feelings of trauma, shame, and unworthiness. She tried to bury the event in the dark recesses of her mind, believing what they had done to her was best forgotten.

After the Doctor cleared her, Archelaus agreed to keep his rights to the girl. When his father died, it was his right to do what he wished with her. But things happened, women died in childbirth, or failed to produce heirs, or became treasonous. Mari was held as insurance. Should the situation dictate, Mari would indeed become queen in Glaphyra's place. But when it was discovered that Mari's life was endangered, Archelaus covertly arranged for the girl to simply disappear.

He sent her to an old ally, Mariamne II, for safe keeping. He trusted the deposed queen's discretion for the child's benefit and financially he made it worth her while.

Mariamne had always favored Mari as a little girl. Who better understood the danger to the girl's life. She was happy to protect Mari, and foil Salome and Glaphyra's schemes.

Later, as a young woman Mari learned the truth, Yahweh had mercifully spared her from not only Archelaus' harshness, but also from the whole godless Herodian household. The LORD had placed her in the priestly household for something better. Though, she wasn't sure what or why.

She grew up with Eleazar's children Martha and Lazarus. Mariamne was a mother figure to all three children. Mari suffered a great loss when Mariamne passed away, leaving Mari in the care of her family. Eventually, Martha came of age and was married to the priest Joshua ben Sie, who became High Priest. Lazarus went to study in Jerusalem, under Joshua. Mari remained in Bethany alone with Simon and the servants. When Archelaus was exiled, Simon pulled strings to solidify Mari's identity as a daughter of his house.

It became Mari's goal to become an independent woman, knowing Simon would not live forever. She could not marry, since no divorce was ever given. And, no priest could marry one who had been married before anyway. Marriage was not to be her fate. Even so, Mari felt she was finally free of the Herodian threat. Her marriage to Archelaus would never be fulfilled. Financially well off, Mari would not be anyones chattel again, or so she thought.

But, every once in a while, when Mari passed by the beautiful Mariamne watchtower in Jerusalem, she stopped to gaze upon it, wondering about her once celebrated grandmother. What would it have been like to be a queen so beloved by the people? Then, she would remember where it had eventually led her grandmother, and she quickly shook off the thought. Still, the tower inspired her to somehow live up to her grandmothers good name and reputation. She wanted to be able to stand tall like the tower, with her head up, unafraid to stand upon the truth.

Meanwhile, Simon had indulged Mari with the finest religious education. It was a benefit few women were allowed. He personally tutored her in the law, enjoying her questions and keen wit. Eventually, she became a respected Rabbi nit within the women's court. The title was proffered to her in honor of her knowledge even though she was not married to a priest. She was the daughter of a priest and that was good enough.

When her ministry got underway, Simon gifted Mari his apartment in Jerusalem which he no longer had needed. It was conveniently located near her shop and the temple. Susanna who had been with her since her childhood came with her. She began a business to help women who were alone with no substance. When it grew in size and success, she developed her own line of women's fine clothing and contined to hire single, divorced, and widowed women who needed a means to support themselves and their children. Her reputation proceeded her among Jerusalem's poorest women, as well as some of its most elite. Her work gave her a strong sense of identity and it flourished under her strategies and hard work. Mari was nobody's chattel now.

Because hers was a cottage industry, Mary had been able to avoid Annas' business consortium, but as her success grew so did its visibility. Annas had not only instituted markets within the temple courts for 'convenience' sake, but he had also built a business alliance among the Pharisees, which eventually forced everyone to pay yearly tributes to the consortium. This was another reason that Annas and his sons had the most lavish homes and lifestyles in Jerusalem. She worried that it was only a matter of time. The Sanhedrin had now even required tributes from the distant synagogues of the diaspora.

Annas' consortium was a powerful force in Jerusalem. Who would dare go up against him or his cronies? It would be financial suicide. Mari had never heard of anyone with the courage to publicly challenge the High Priest or the Sanhedrin, until the Galilean.

She wondered, 'Who is this Rabbi from Galilee? The long-awaited Messiah? I can't wait to tell Susanna the news!'

~ 47 ~

WHO WILL SAVE ME?

Beauty has beguiled you and lust has perverted your heart.
This is how you have mistreated the daughters of Israel,
with force and fear.
Susanna 50:56-57 NRSV

Mari left the temple walking at a good clip. She was excited to tell Susanna what the Rabbi had done. She didn't even notice when Caiaphas appeared out of nowhere to call her name.

"Mari bat Simon!" She paused to turn uncertainly his way.

His hand offered a greeting.

Mari was momentarily confused and looked around as if he must be talking to someone else. Seeing no one, she motioned to herself with the look of question.

He nodded.

'What could Caiaphas want with me?' She wondered. She had never been formally made his acquaintance.

Noting her wariness, he offered her a compliment, "I understand you have a successful following in the women's court."

She gave him a nervous nod, waiting.

"And, you also have a thriving business, I am told. It is becoming quite popular for your fabrics and quality creations"

"Yes, it provides work for women who need income."

Her shoulders lifted, her internal intuition on high alert. She suspected he wanted his cut from her business.

"I can't imagine why you would be interested in such lowly things, Lord."

"Oh but I am very interested."

She wanted to hurry away, but that would be rude. "You should not waste your important time on such things or let me take up your time." She lowered her gaze toward the ground in deference.

When he did not move on, she gave a small bow said, "Please have a good day."

She moved to go her own way, for the sake of her own reputation. She could not be seen speaking with this married man. Quickly his strides caught up with her, blocking her attempt to leave him behind.

"You might be interested in what I have to say. I have taken an interest in enhancing your success."

His offer was far too solicitous. She'd done nothing to warrant his attention or interest. And, the families of Annas and Boethus stood opposed to one another.

"Why would you want to do that? We are not of the same house." She dropped her polite pretense, she stopped to face him. "We should not even be seen talking. It is improper."

She maneuvered around him to continue on her way. Once again, he blocked her path, bringing them eye to eye.

Mari's heart began to pound with fear, seeing his face hardened with determination.

"Come let us reason together. Woman, I can either enhance your work or I can shut you down. It is completely up to you."

Shock registered on her face. "What is this about? Why are you doing this? I am a daughter of a high priest, a teacher of women, and you are married. Your interest does not feel honorable. If you have something to talk with me about, we should meet with my father."

"Come now, don't play coy with me. It will do you no good. We both have things to offer one another. We can make a good trade."

She backed another step away from him as if readied to run. "I don't know what you are suggesting, I have dedicated my life to God."

"I have done my homework. I know the truth about you. The Boethus family is powerful, but ultimately they must also bow to my demands."

'What truth is he talking about?' She searched his face for meaning.

"I assure you that you are only an orphan girl to Simon ben Boethus." Caiaphas smiled a grim smile.

Mari's eyes widened at the inferred betrayal. Too late, she realized he had meant to inflict pain upon her to confuse and manipulate her.

Caiaphas smiled knowing full well that brokenness made people vulnerable. Their places of pain was easy to use against them.

Despite the jab to her heart, she asked. "Who told you such nonsense."

He smiled an indulgent smile, "I recently had dinner with Simon."

She could hardly believe this, "What are you talking about, you are political enemies."

She thought, 'Simon would never give away my secrets, especially to this man. Unless, what he says is true and he really is angry with me. How much does Caiaphas know?'

"Now, I will keep your secret, if you play nice. We could be good together. Surely, you do not want to live your life all alone."

"What secret?"

Fudging he said, "That you are not who you say you are. You are not a Boethus."

"That is ridiculous. And, what about the law? You are a married man."

"What is a little broken law between friends? Why God himself has brought us together."

"We are not friends. I will not be bullied or blackmailed into a liaison with you. You are a priest!" She said this as if his post should mean something to him.

Caiaphas' eyes were black and hard like a reptile. He grabbed her wrist, holding it fast, he pulled her close and whispered, "You may want to think about what your future at the temple might look like should you deny me. I will not take no for an answer. I hold your future in my hands, as well as your esteemed family members? I demand your answer by tomorrow. Come to my private office at the temple by mid-morning. I will be waiting for you."

He tipped her chin towards him, his smile was lecherous registering her fear and anger. It pleased him; he might enjoy a little fight. Perhaps it would make things more interesting. He dropped her arm and walked away holding his hands piously before him.

Mari remained rooted in shock, watching to make sure he was really gone. She pulled her head covering tighter around her face and shoulders. She felt dirty because of his touch and she was shaking. Full of disbelief, an awful mixture of dread, anxiety, and shame clawed its way up through her chest, practically paralyzing her mind. In that moment, Mari hated the vulnerability and injustice of being a woman. This unexpected aggression made her feel helpless, like a lamb cornered by a predator.

She wondered, 'What can I do? How can I fight the High Priest of all people?' Her mind was spinning and she felt dizzy.

Who can save me from this threat? If Simon has broken his promise and shared my secret, who can I go to? Martha is widowed. And Lazarus, who knows where he has gone?

She had not seen him in Jerusalem for some time now. She had allowed all of her adoptive family disappear from her life. Of course, they had not pursued her either. She couldn't stop the devastating thought, 'Have they all forsaken me too?' Simon would be very aged by now. Had he grown feeble? She should know, but the years had quickly passed while she had focused on building her solitary life. Now she felt all too alone and defenseless. Her nightmare had suddenly come true.

That night Mari hardly slept. When she did drift off, she dreamed she was running from something or someone, some creature of immense evil. While she sensed its presence, she could not see the creature's face. She awoke screaming with terror. Her heart hammered wildly in her chest and she gasped for air.

She got up to think. 'Perhaps I should at least try to take this situation to Simon. But even if he tried to help me, what can he do against Caiaphas?'

She imagined her business barred and closed. She thought of not being allowed to enter the temple. She felt suffocated by these thoughts. She peered desperately about in the darkness of her room. "What can I do? LORD, who can save me but you?"

Her tortured thoughts kept tumbling over and over like dice, only to come up empty of any answers. How could it be that at his whim, Caiaphas held sway over her existing life, the life she had worked so hard to build? If her business was taken from her, she would lose her independence. What would she have then? And what of the other women who depended on her help? Her fears overwhelmed her. The life she had thought would protect her she now found to be far too fragile.

"What is the matter?" Susanna asked while she twist Mari's long black hair up into a low and modest chignon, pinning it securely.

Pale, Mari replied. "Please pray for me. I am confronted by a very difficult dilemma today. I struggled all night, but have found no answer. What it is, I simply can't say. But please pray for me today."

"That sounds ominous. You are scaring me!"

"It is ominous."

Mari stood abruptly searching around the room. 'This is my home! My work. My mission to needy women, my provision. Can that monster really steal my life from me, just like that? Do I really

not have any choice in this matter? I just can't see anyway out?'
Desperation blocked all helpful thoughts. She felt trapped. Her
circumstance felt surreal.

   She glanced at her bruised wrist that bore the marks of his forceful fingers. Though she didn't understand why, Caiaphas' threat
was very real.

~ 48 ~

ABLE TO SAVE

The fingers of a human hand appeared and wrote on the wall,
near the lampstand in the royal palace.
The king watched the hand as it wrote.
His face turned pale
and he was so frightened that his legs became weak.
The inscription read: Mene, mene, tekel, parsin.
God has numbered your days;
you have been weighed on the scales and found wanting."
Excerpt Daniel 5

Entering the temple premises that morning, Mari saw the Nazarene Rabbi already on the teaching steps surrounded by a hopeful gathering. Her eye was drawn by the brightness of his simple white tunic. Was it just the way the sun shone on his garments? Or was there actually an aura of purity surrounding him? The authority of his words and the strength of his baritone reached her, even from their considerable distance.

"Come to me, all you who are weary and heavily burdened, and I will give you rest. Take my yoke upon you and learn from me. I am gentle and humble in heart, and you will find rest for your souls. For my yoke is easy and my burden is light." Yeshua glanced her way. Their gazes caught and held.

Mari's foot was poised on the next step where she had come to a halt. 'Is he speaking to me? Does he know what I am about to do? No, of course not! How could he?'

"Whoever finds their life will lose it, and whoever loses their life for my sake will find it." He continued, still looking her way. His hand remained aloft, extended toward her as if he were bidding her to come.

Confusion flickered across her face. 'No, he doesn't even know me...that is just part of his oration.'

She turned and walked stalwartly up the remaining steps.

Sensing Mari's desperation, Yeshua blinked, then lowered his hand sadly. He had the impression that things were about to go from bad to worse. He watched her go, then turned back to the others.

Mari took an indirect path to the office of the high priest. Only because of conversations with Simon and Lazarus did she know the way to Caiaphas' private office. Her feet felt like lead.

Surely God will understand, I have no choice.

Arriving to the chamber, she stood at the door with a mounting distress. Mari felt sick knowing she was selling herself off like a slave. Once she had submitted to his demands she could ever go back to being who she had previously been.

I will be no more than a temple prostitute. He will rule over me. Who knows to what torment this might lead me into?

The question kept running through her mind, 'What choice do I have? If I want to keep MY life?'

Caiaphas got up from his couch where he waited for her. He opened his door with a smug smile of victory. She had actually come. The fact that she was there at all told him his intimidation had worked. He motioned her in.

"Well?" He said as he walked to a waiting jug of wine and poured a goblet. He brought it to her, pushing it into her reluctant hand with a satisfied gleam. She nervously looked around his private apartment.

"Shall we toast to our new arrangement?" he asked salaciously.
"I..."

She looked down into the cup he had placed in her hand trying to find her voice. She felt queasy to find a fly floating on the surface. It appeared as a cup of abomination to her. She sat the cup down on the table beside her. Caiaphas stepped closer to her, sitting his cup on the table as well.

"Well?" He repeated. He wanted to hear her say it.

Her mouth worked but she could say nothing. She looked down at her hands.

Her fearful muteness delighted him. Now at last he could take her and drive her from his mind.

Mari was preparing to beg him to relent, to explain that she didn't want to be that sort of woman. Hoping to play to some sense of rightness and sympathy within the man.

Abruptly, he reached up taking hold of the delicate fabric that covered her head, fingering it for its quality before he pushed it negligently from her head. It landed in a puddle on the floor. He prodded her chin upward to take in the long arch of her neck, running his fingers over her skin roughly. The cloying scent of his priestly oil mixed with the foulness of his breath made Mari feel even more nauseous.

He licked his thick lips as if anticipating the taste of her.

The scent of the oils made Mari think of Simon and his betrayal. She was devastated to think he had told her secrets to Caiaphas his enemy. 'Why would he tell my secrets after all these years? Is he that angry at me or feeble? Shouldn't she know?'

Caiaphas reached for the twist of her hair and roughly pulled it free from its restraints. Scattering the pins on the floor. Her hair fell in a heavy curtain down her shoulders to the curve of her back. He lifted the strands. Tangling it within his sprayed fingers, he appreciated the glory of her hair. Loosened, she had the look of a wanton woman.

Mari backed away, bringing her hands to her head.

"What are you doing? Surely, you don't imagine here or now?"

"Where else would you suggest?" He moved towards her.

"But, I haven't given you my answer. I am not ready. I have just come to talk."

"Oh, but you have made a decision. You are here. This was your decision. What is there to talk about? Would you retreat now?"

"I need more time to think." Her eyes darted about for an escape. She moved back a step, trying to find her voice and stay his grasping hand. But horror seized her throat allowing nothing but a hysterical squeak to escape. She raised her hands defensively.

"Come my little orphan, you can belong to me. I will be like a father to you." Caiaphas pressed forward upon her. His fingers dug into her forearms roughly as he guided her toward his day couch. Then, as if a something evil had taken possession of him, he reached up and gave a violent jerk to the neck of her tunic ripping the delicate fabric.

She mewled like a frightened child, her hands beating against him.

He buried his face in her neck like a wolf going in for the kill.

Finally the strength to fight surged through her and her voice found its release. She began to scream at the top of her lungs. Forcefully, she dug her nails into his beard, leaving bloody trails. She pushed and flailed to break free from his restraint. Violently, he flung her onto the couch and made the move to overpower her. Mari instinctively drew up her leg to block him, she kicked as hard as she could. He let out a cry of agony, bending helplessly.

Two temple guards came bursting through the door. Finding only Caiaphas and the woman in the room. Caiaphas was clearly in pain, and the woman was regathering her bodice.

Quickly they assessed the scene, staring at one another in speechless shock. They were unsure of what to do with this unexpected turn of events.

"Is everything okay my Lord?" They asked solicitously, as if he was the one assailed.

Thinking fast, despite his pain, Caiaphas said, "No. No, it is not. I came in here and caught this woman in the act of adultery."

"Is that so?" Malchus chuckled knowingly, emboldened by their family ties. "Where is her lover?"

"The man has escaped." Caiaphas breathed heavily, offering him a pointed look that brooked no argument.

Despite their surprise, both guards understood the situation. They took in Caiaphas' face and the woman's clothes. The truth was quite clear. Still, they were paid to protect Caiaphas, they awaited his order.

Mari rebuked him. "You are lying! Why are you doing this to me?"

He backhanded her, sending her reeling backwards on to his chaise lounge.

"I am the High Priest you are talking to. Would you dare to challenge me?" He said, looming over her.

Her ear was ringing and the room swayed. She tasted blood from her torn and smarting lip. Blood ran down her chin onto her tunic. Her lip immediately began to swell.

All the desire he had known for her was transformed into a seething hatred. He despised her. He wanted to beat her with his fists, to destroy her. He laughed to himself thinking, 'Does this little orphan really not understand? My men will never go against my word.'

A chilling and sinister smile appeared on his face. Finally, he had an idea; it was so perfect that he chortled out loud to himself.

He looked to his guards and pronounced his verdict upon her.

"This woman has sinned against the law of Moses. She has been caught in adultery. I will go to gather the council." The look of horror on her face, satisfied him in a way that having her never could. He enjoyed watching her wilt with trembling desperation.

"Malchus, go and summon that new Rabbi from Nazareth. And put out an order for the guards to bring the buckets of stones. When everyone has assembled, take this woman down to the ledge of judgment. We will let the Nazarene pass the verdict for her death there."

"You would do this against the house of Simon?" She asked incredulous.

"I won't be the one rendering judgement on you, so I will have done nothing against Simon. No, it will be your 'Messiah', who you followed out to Galilee. Let him judge the adulteress."

He savored her fear and devastation.

"What? You don't want him to know what you are? I hear he favors prostitutes. Besides, isn't he supposed to be Israel's savior?"

He began to laugh at her. "You think he will save you? I am the only one with the power to save you!"

The guards were all too willing to oblige Caiaphas. After all, his favor was the cream on their bread. They laughed, grabbing Mari harshly by her arms, purposefully trapping her torn garment to leave her shoulders bare. She was guilty of seduction, let her look the part.

"I will have the council meet you at the place of judgement. Let's see how the Rabbi's mercy may benefit us today."

Caiaphas smirked, as the guards pulled her away. He straightened his linen tunic and golden girdle. He donned his priestly turban and smoothed his beard, his face stung from the slash of her nails. Before he left for the courtyard, he lifted her untouched goblet swishing the red wine around in his mouth as if to erase the taste of her. He poured some of the wine out onto his handkerchief to dab at the cuts on his face.

He grimaced at the waste not only of the wine, but of the woman as well. But Mari had made his choice for him and now he could use the situation to finish off that upstart. How quickly his desire for her had disappeared. He left to gather the council from their chambers. His eyes glowed, ecstatic with anticipation at this unexpected and fortuitous opportunity to entrap them both.

Yeshua looked up across the court yard to see the council coming his way. Temple guards walked menacingly behind them, lugging buckets of large stones.

This cannot be good.

At first, he thought they were simply coming to stone him until he saw the same woman who had halted on the steps. She was now pressed between two guards, being forced along like a guilty convict. Her previously modest appearance was now quite ruined. Her garment torn, her tussled and undone hair made it obvious that something terrible had happened to her. In her eyes, he saw her terror, regret, and shame. Her lip was bloodied and swollen.

Yeshua understood all too well, this was a trap.

He looked up to see Caiaphas watching from the platform above at a safe distance. He was holding a handkerchief to his face. He would not draw close today.

The two guards pushed the woman forcefully toward Yeshua as though they were discarding a mangled lamb. Roughly the woman landed on the dirty pavement in front of him, scraping her hands, knees, and toes in the process. Her previously lovely tunic was now destroyed, covered with dirt and blood.

One of the teachers of the law addressed him, "Teacher, we have a dilemma. This woman has been caught in the act of adultery. The Law of Moses commands us to stone such a woman. But, tell us what do you say?"

Yeshua glanced her way. The woman did not even lift her eyes, as if she felt there was no hope for her cause. She stared at the ground trembling with fear.

"Well?" The spokesman demanded impatiently.

The guards moved through the gathering crowd, handing out stones to those who approached like invitations to a party. Yeshua saw it for what it was, 'The whole situation is wrong and unjust. How quickly these men are readied to condemn this woman without knowing the facts, without naming or apprehending her supposed partner in crime. They offered no testimony or proofs. The council condemned themselves.'

The mob gathered, happy to heap on this accused woman their own sins, happy to administer to her a harsh justice. Large stones were balanced in their readied hands.

Women gathered at perimeter of the women's court to see what was happening.

"Who is it?" They asked.

"I don't know, I can't tell."

"What are they saying?"

"She's been caught in the act of adultery."

"I can't believe it! It is Mari!" They cried in disbelief; shocked to see their beloved teacher in such a state. A few women began to weep and cry out on her behalf. Others were already condemning her behind the cover of their hands. Others turned quickly away unwilling to share her guilt.

Yeshua searched the crowd, taking a moment to think of what was really behind this spectacle. Saying nothing, he knelt down on his knee and began to write in the dust, barely glancing toward the woman.

Feeling his gaze, she was embarrassed to meet his eyes. But she peeked to see him writing in the dirt.

The officials harassed him, demanding, "Give us your answer!"

Others joined in. Yeshua did not look up, but continued at his task. Onlookers strained to see what he was writing, though it was clearly some sort of ancient script no one could identify.

As he wrote, people were gripped by a holy kind of terror. The story of a hand that had once wrote judgement upon the Babylonian wall came to their mind.

'Mene, mene, tekel, parsin,' When the onlookers had been warned they were falling under judgement.

"What is he writing?" Someone shouted.

Everyone else became unnaturally silent. Each person felt the script rising up from the ground to condemn them personally.

Even Caiaphas felt a sudden trembling fear from his distanced position.

Though, they did not know what the script said, they were terrified.

Finally, Yeshua straightened himself clapping the dust from his hands. He looked up from the words to each man. A raven curl hung loosely over his face, but they felt his eyes burning upon them none the less.

He spoke deeply, in measured tones, "If any one of you is without sin, let him be the first one to cast his stone."

Again, he bent down to continue writing. After some moments he began to hear the dull and heavy thuds of stones dropping to the ground one by one until the only sound left was that of the woman's sobs.

He stood, taking a step towards her, "Woman, look. Where are your accusers? Is there no one left to condemn you?"

Looking upon her, Yeshua thought, 'Here she is ... a woman caught in adultery, 'the very image of my people Israel. My Father's words wrote about her.' Hadn't Hosea been ordered to marry such a woman? And, whenever she had run away from him, he had gone after her to bring her back to him. She had such a hard time receiving her husband's love for her.'

He blinked, seeing before him the woman's brokenness.

Her slender hand pushed back the thick hair that hid her crumbled face. She looked cautiously around holding together the fabric of her bodice with her other hand. She could hardly take in all the stones lying on the ground. She was astounded. Tears coursed down her cheeks. She swiped at her eyes to see clearer. She couldn't believe it! The men were gone.

She looked then at the teacher. Emotions of fear, hope, wonder, questions, and shame traveled across her ravaged face. She did not move.

"Th-th-there's no one... but you sir."

With a tender verdict, he said, "Well then, neither do I condemn you."

He took off his outer cloak and placed it over her head and shoulders, to hide her torn garment and her loosened hair.

He said softly. "Go home now, and leave your sins behind you. Entertain them no more."

Mari was surprised to see that his eyes were gentle upon her. She nodded, casting her eyes down demurely.

Oddly, she noticed his feet planted as if he could not be moved, exuding his strength. Mari wanted nothing so much at that moment as to throw herself upon those feet as one would when honoring a benevolent king or a conquering hero. She wanted to kiss them with gratitude and relief for being there. Single handedly this man had vanquished all her enemies. But she was too exposed, undone, ashamed and unworthy. She turned and fled the temple courtyard.

As she fled down the temple steps she stop to laugh, realizing that despite Caiaphas' mocking words to her, this Messiah—*her* Messiah had been able to save her from a certain death.

~ 49 ~

THE REPENTANT WOMAN

Rend your heart and not your garments.
Return to the Lord your God,
for he is gracious and compassionate,
slow to anger and abounding in love,
and he relents from sending calamity.
Joel 2:13

Mari returned home stunned with shock. The trauma of the morning had left her weak and unsteady. Her mind was dominated by one thought, 'Scandalous. I am scandalous!'

She was so ashamed, her good reputation was left in tatters. How had this thing happened to her? Now, she was marked as an adulterous woman and what could she say? Even though her circumstance had befallen her against her will; even though Caiaphas had bullied her with force and attacked her; and even though he did not complete his intent, now Mari's reputation was left in ruins. Perception seemed to be everything. How would she face the women of her ministry now? Her business would likely fail.

Still, the truth was, her fear of losing everything had driven her to consider the abominable and in the end she had lost it all anyway and almost forfeit her life.

"What happened?" Susanna cried running to Mari when she stumbled numbly through the door shaken to her core. Her face was bruised and swollen, and when Mari lowered the coarsely woven cloak Suzanna saw her tumbled hair and torn tunic.

"Was it a Roman?" she whispered with hysteria.

"No, it was our High Priest!" Mari doubled over in grief.

"High Priest? Caiaphas? But, what did he do to you?" Susanna was confused and appalled. She took Mari in her arms and the two sunk down into a puddle of shock. Susanna let Mari to cry until her sobs abated.

"He has taken everything from me." Mari whispered. "Why has this happened to me? I went to him to try to reason with him. He wanted to make me his mistress. Instead of talking, he tried to force me right there and then."

"Caiaphas?" Susanna clarified, still aghast at the thought.

"I should never had gone to him. But his threats yesterday had frightened me and I... And apparently, he knows all my secrets from Simon."

"Secrets? What secrets?"

For the first time Mari tried to remember exactly what he had said.

"He knew I was adopted." Only then did she wonder 'But did he know the rest?' He had not said, anything more than that, except that Simon had told him. But, what if he didn't? And if he did, would Caiaphas have done what he tried to do? She didn't know.

Shame covered her yet again. She could not bring herself to admit what she had thought she might do to save the life she had built. She had not been thinking clearly, she was driven by fear.

"He tried to have me stoned to death for adultery!" Mari finally told her.

With sorrowful recrimination, she said, "I should have gone to Simon and asked for his help. I should have begged him to intervene. I should have stood up to Caiaphas when he demanded an answer this morning. He purposefully gave me no time to go to Simon or to think. Now the whole family will feel the shame of what I have done!"

"Mari, where was your faith in God?"

Susanna's question surprised her. She realized the truth of it. "I know, I shouldn't have gone."

She recalled the way the teacher had held out his hand. She should have gone to him.

"Why would Caiaphas accuse you? Look at you, didn't all of this implicate him instead? Isn't both the man and woman to be stoned for their sin according to the law?"

"We are talking about Caiaphas! Of course, no one would charge him. He twist the truth to accused me. And, despite the obvious evidence, the people accepted with his words without question, even with my scratches on his own face!" Mari looked down to see his blood under her fingernails. She shook her head, still trying to process it all.

"And worse yet, no one even asked about the man. No one questioned my torn tunic or my bloodied lip. No one asked for my testimony. I was just condemned as guilty. The council surrounded me with stones ready to kill me."

Then she added as if seeing something for the first time.

"It was the strangest thing that happened after that. Caiaphas placed my judgment in the hands of the Rabbi we went to see in Galilee! Why would he do that? The Rabbi has no standing in the temple amongst the leaders. Caiaphas hates him and the Sanhedrin has put a price on his head." Her eyes widened with the sudden realization that Caiaphas had hoped to put both her and the Rabbi to death at the same time.

"The Nazarene Rabbi? No!" Suzanna sputtered.

"Yes."

"But why?"

"Good question. Now that I think of it, it felt like the Rabbi was on trial as much as I was. They surrounded us both. Their stones seemed to be readied and aimed at him as much as me."

"What happened then?"

"The Rabbi bent down and wrote something unrecognizable in the sand."

"He wrote in the sand?" Suzanna thought Mari's story was growing stranger by the minute.

"Yes. He wrote in the sand for an awkwardly long time. Meanwhile, the leaders kept pressing him to give his verdict. They kept shouting at him, but he just kept writing in the sand! After some time, he stood up and looked around. He said 'Whoever has never broken the law was to cast the first stone'. Then, he bent back down to continue writing in the sand. I can't explain it, but something started happening. I heard a thud. At first, I thought someone had actually thrown their stone. Instead, it was just someone dropping it. Then another and another fell, until the only person left standing there was the Rabbi."

Susanna stared at Mari some moments before asking, "Did he say anything to you?"

"He asked me, 'Where are your accusers?'"

"And there was no one?"

"No one."

A light dawned in her eyes.

"He did not condemn me Susanna. He saved me from a painful and certain death, even though the law demanded it. It was a truly a miracle! I still cannot believe it. What kind of Rabbi, is this?"

Susanna wondered too.

"When it was over, he covered me with his own cloak to cover my shame. He has to be the Holy One of God." Mari said with surety. Mari's face took on a wondrous expression and she remembered her compulsion to kneel at his feet.

Only then did she realize she was still clutching his cloak to her.

She looked down at it quizzically. 'God?'

What she held was a very humble garment, coarse, but tightly woven and handstitched. She rubbed her hand over it. The fabric was rustic and died a strange brownish red, the color of blood.

"Oh, I am sure he must need this. I must find him. Judging from his teachings, I am not sure he would even have another cloak readily at his disposal. I must thank him properly and return his cloak.

"What does this mean for you now?" Susanna wondered. "What will happen to your teaching ministry or your business?" She knew how much they meant to Mari.

"I don't know. Though, my life is in shabbles and as good as dead, here I am alive; that is all that matters for now."

She looked at Susanna, "I have got to find him. Please, go and see if you can find out where this Rabbi is staying. Someone must know. But be discreet. Meanwhile, I will think of a fitting way to show my gratitude. If I gave him everything I own, it could never be enough."

While Susanna was away, Mari washed, dressed her wounds, and dressed in clean clothes.

Susanna returned with news of the Nazarene's location. Mari had not been prepared for the shock of it.

"The Rabbi has departed for Bethany. Priscilla said he has strong connections to Lazarus, the son of Eleazer. It appears he and his men have gone to your brother's home." Susanna reported.

Mari's eyes widened perplexed.

"Lazarus? The Rabbi has gone to Bethany?"

"Yes, and I was told that Martha lives there now too."

Mari was stunned. "How strange is that? What do you think they would say if I should show up there now, after today? It has been years since we were together?"

Susanna shrugged, "It has been a long time, but you were close once."

Mari said, "This is too much to be a coincidence. But what will they all say when they hear of my disgrace? Ugly words travel fast."

"Don't be a coward!" Susanna said. "Besides, what can they do but kick you out."

"You are right, this is my one chance to show a proper gratitude to the man who saved me before he returns to Galilee."

She was afraid to delay. It was time to return to the home of her adoptive family, the only real family she'd had. She hoped they would still have her.

She wondered, 'Why did I stay away so long?'

She changed her focus, 'What can I do to show my gratitude? What would be costly enough? Meaningful enough?'

She went to her bedroom and moved her bed aside. She pressed her foot on the floor until she found the loosen floor board. She began to remove the boards one by one, uncovering her secret storage space. She bent down to lift out a heavy chest from within. It took a few tries before she was able to haul it up from its hiding place. She stared at the box that held the secrets of her past. She had not looked in this box for years. She ran her fingers over the intricate gold shield carved into the olive wood.

Looking inside, she lifted out a tunic of luxurious silk and gossamer. It was elaborately embroidered with a matching cloak that shimmered with gold threads woven throughout. It was finished with gold embroidery on the label and the sleeves. She had never seen anything like it. It had been her grandmother's gown, the fabric was woven with gold brought from the far reaches of Ophir. She set it aside. Gingerly, she removed a box holding her jewels and a crown meant for her coronation day. She did not pause to admire the magnificent stones. They had no meaning now.

Underneath, she found another intricately carved wooden container. She opened the lid. It contained two identical unique and expensive alabaster bottles. Each was filled with an oil of combined spices blended to make a perfume uniquely purposed for the anointing of the king according to the ancient recipe. It had been prepared for her to anoint Archelaus on the night they would have begun their life together. This oil was meant to bless the couples union with God's presence as they prepared to rule together. The second bottle of anointing oil was to be kept safe for the day of her husband's burial. Neither seal had ever been broken. They had remained as closed as her heart. She had no hope of ever using it. Still, it was very rare.

With Herod dead, and Archelaus exiled, there was no longer a king in Jerusalem or Israel, but only a Roman governor. But now she wondered, 'Is that true? Was this Rabbi the long awaited and rightful king who had been promised. He was being called the Son of David, the Son of God. Can it be he is God's saving King, the Messiah who everyone has been waiting for, the one rightful and true ruler of God's people? She believed that he was. Everyone wondered what the Messiah would be like when he came. She was sure, he would be unlike anyone else, a mystical person indeed.

She looked down, 'Now this nard can find its purpose after all.'

Sitting it aside, she found the corner at the bottom of the larger chest and tripped the spring to open the false bottom. There lay a small fortune of tightly wrapped stacks of large gold coins shiny and untouched. This was her bride price meant to set up her house-hold. She lifted a gold coin, weighing it in her hand. She would give him this as a tribute to help fund his ministry. For now she wrapped it back and closed the false bottom.

She picked up the alabaster container, admiring the smooth white simplicity of the jar. She could not imagine how expensive it was. Mari pressed the perfume to her heart, hoping this gift would be extravagant enough to show the depth of her appreciation and willing service. She placed it into her leather carrying bag to set out for Bethany.

The climb up the Mount of Olives gave Mari plenty of time for doubts. She pressed on nevertheless to arrive to her childhood home at twilight. The lavender-pink sky was making its transition toward lapis lazuli. The homestead was unexpectedly changed, as if time had moved on without her. The oldest and familiar part of the structure was the same. But now there were new additions. The family compound had grown impressively. It seemed to sparkle with plenty of well-placed lamps to illuminate the front of the house against the darkening canvas of the sky. The gate still stood open to receive the evening's guests. A servant manned the gate.

What to do?

A chilled breeze shook her from her memories, and she recalled why she had come. Unsure of her reception, she did not dare to walk through the front gate. Circling toward the back of the property, Mari searched for the familiar low-lying branch that hung near the back wall. She pulled herself up onto the branch, then climbed higher. She worked her way over the wall and moved to other limbs. Finally, she crouched, suspended just above the yard. Grabbing another limb, she swung loose from her branch to land on a patch of soft grass below. She took a moment to catch her breath. She was not as flexible as the younger version of herself.

When she was composed, she entered through the servant's quarters. They were all busy serving dinner in the banquet hall. Pressed against the wall, she could clearly see the faces illuminated by candlelight. It was a good-sized party. Probably not the best night for what she had come to do. But who knew when the Rabbi might leave, and she could not miss her chance.

While hiding in the shadows, Mari beheld the members of her adoptive family for the first time in years. Guilt assaulted her, making her want to turn around and leave. At the head of the table sat her adoptive father as patriarch. She was reminded how long she had been away. Simon, had always loomed large to her as a child, though he was really a small man. He seemed to have shrunk, and was a former shadow of himself. His thinning white hair hung oiled, stringy and at odds with the regal beauty of his robe. To his political enemies Simon was known as 'the Leper'; but Simon still wore the refined clothing of a wealthy priest. His two successful sons Joazar and Eleazar sat on each side of him.

The Rabbi sat with Lazarus as his guest. She noted a variety of humbly dressed men were at their end of the table as well. She took note of the easy conversation between Lazarus and the Rabbi. They were obviously friends. She thought, 'Maybe Lazarus has found the answers his soul has yearned for after all.'

Peering to the far side of the room, she saw Martha in the seat of honor at the women's table, holding her own conversations. She couldn't help wondering, 'What had transpired in her life?'

"Martha smiled brightly at something someone said, then leaned forward passing a basket of bread.

Seeing the peaceful celebration underway, Mari felt her resolve begin to slip. Her very presence would disturb the harmony of this gathering. Just then, Yeshua glanced up from his conversation catching her movement in the shadows. Wary of unforeseen danger, he looked closer. Recognition lit his features. He waited to see what she would do. It was the directness of his gaze that finally gave Mari the courage she needed to surge into the room clutching her bag to fulfill her mission.

The banquet fell into a stunned silence. Her name was frozen on everyone's lips. The rumors had already arrived, she could see she had been the topic around the tables.

Undeterred, Mari moved quickly toward her savior. She dared not look to the right or the left. She took out the beautiful container, and cracked the seal to release the stopper of the nard. A weighty, sweet, and mysterious scent wafted into the air. She stood behind the Rabbi and poured a portion of the anointing oil upon his head to convey a great blessing. The exotic richness of the scent ran down over his dark curls into his beard, then dripped onto his robe.

Yeshua inhaled, taking in the exotic scent with pleasure.

"Blessed be the One who is God's Salvation." She said to him, overwhelmed with gratitude and emotion.

She fell at his feet and began to sob her worship. Prostrated, she made the point of her submission to him. Her tears fell upon his feet, tracking through the dust of that day. She poured out a liberal amount of perfumed oil into her hands. then poured a liberal amount of oil over his feet. With her hands, she spread the oil, rubbing it into all the callused places. This was something only the lowliest of servants might do. All the while, hot tears poured from her eyes falling warm upon his feet to mix with the oil.

The onlookers were surprised that Yeshua did not try to stop her. But, Mari was so completely bent upon her worship that Yeshua was totally captivated. No one had ever honored him in such a lovely or worshipful way. The mixture of Mari's sorrow and gratitude flowed over him like the oil of blessing and adoration. The act seemed to transcend time. It was the anointing of God's saving King of Israel and the true husband of God's people.

As Mari had previously longed to do, she pressed her face to his feet as a sign of her obeyance. She covered the arch of each foot with the kisses of her devotion, an act of such honor and intimacy, that it stole his breath away.

"Thank you!" Mari said over and over, "Thank you. Thank you, for your great mercy, for your wisdom, for saving my life, and returning my freedom."

She acknowledged his righteous intention, "I should have come when you held out your hand to me."

She made no excuses, nor offered any explanations to him for what had happened. She felt sure he already knew. She offered all she had, her broken heart and all of her gratitude.

The room of onlookers were hushed, mesmerized by Mari's lavish yet scandalous adoration, so intimate that it seemed they were the only two persons in the room, all others were simply voyeurs.

When Mari saw she had poured an overabundance of oil on his feet, she realized the need for a towel. She could have used her head covering or her cloak; but that seemed gauche. Instead, she reached up to slip the pins free that held her hair in place. It fell in a dark pool before her. She grabbed its length, and wadded it up like a towel, she began to painstakingly wipe his feet free of all the excess oil and grime. When his feet were finally cleaned and dry, she laid her face and her lips upon them once again, holding his feet reverently in her hands. She placed one final kiss to the top of each arch. She lifted her eyes to his and whispered for him only to hear.

"My Lord, I am at your service."

The spicy-sweetness of the nard clung to both Yeshua and Mari, but the beautiful scent filled the whole room.

Gripped by her tear-streaked repentance, Yeshua felt the depth of her sorrow, her pained and aching heart, as if the sorrows of this day had connected back to all the sorrows of her whole life up to the moment. His lashes and cheeks glistened as if he shared Mari's tears.

This was it, the invaluable gift his Father had promised—mutual love. Mari was a sign to him of what was yet to come and as such, she was sealed on his heart. Adoration, true repentance, and worship. But what was so beautiful and precious to him, was repugnant to the old priest who watched the woman with a bitter and jealous eye.

"You!" Simon sputtered angrily, outraged by this seemingly wantoned spectacle.

He pointed his crooked and shaking finger at her. "I heard what you did. Has your lust gotten the best of you? Have you fallen so low that you would come and throw yourself upon this fellow? Would you humiliate me in my own home? After all this time with no word from you, and after all the things I have done for you!"

The old man wheezed in agitation. "I allowed you too much freedom. This is how you repay me? You abandoned us to become willful and independent. You should have long ago returned to show your gratitude and to honor for me. If you had, perhaps you would not have made such an exhibition of yourself and been caught red handed! Now that you are in trouble, what? You come to humiliate my table! To make an extravagant display of yourself before us all with this wandering Rabbi!"

"Grandfather!" Lazarus called out harshly. "Yeshua is my esteemed guest, he is a great teacher, and I believe he is the Holy One of God that was to come. And, Mari is our sister. Please do not treat her this way. Whatever she has or has not done, she is our family! We have not even heard her side of the story. You know how Caiaphas is! And, you know nothing about what has happened today. Won't you show her mercy?"

Lazarus' words quieted Simon.

It was true. Simon remembered Caiaphas had been up to no good, asking inappropriate questions about Mari. But he had failed to follow through to warn Mari. He had failed to protect her. Perhaps, he was wrong to accuse her after all.

"No." Mari spoke up, sitting back on her haunches. She looked to Simon, seeing his fragility and remembering his kindness to her.

"Our father is right, I have not done right by him or by our family. I have been too independent. After so long a time, I was afraid to return." She said shame faced and regretful.

She looked down at her hands. "What has happened has brought shame upon me and this house. I apologize. I was wrong."

She said with a sob. "Nor can I honestly justify what has transpired most recently. It seems like a nightmare. But..., I am very, very, sorry for not believing I could come to you."

Speaking those last few words, she turned her eyes back towards Yeshua, "Please forgive me."

Discomfited, Simon turned the focus away from himself to back toward Yeshua. He said, "Do you even know who this is that is touching you, or what kind of woman she has become? Hasn't she this very day been caught in sin before you? Why would you allow her to touch you?"

Yeshua swept his eyes over Mari.

"Yes, I know who she is." He offered her a barely perceptible smile, as if he knew a secret.

"I will call you Magdalene." He said to her. "For, you will become a watch tower that will stand tall in time, just like the Mariamne Tower in Jerusalem."

Mari's eyes grew wide with surprise, 'He knows me!'

Filled with awe at his insight, she remained at his feet like a well-heeled dog. Her eyes on him, she waited for her masters next words.

Yeshua continued, "Whatever kind of woman Mari has been, all I see now is the woman she will become."

Turning back towards the old man, Yeshua said, "Simon, I have something to tell you."

Simon's scowled at this familiar use of his given name.

"By all means teacher, I give you the floor." He motioned sarcastically.

Yeshua began a parable, "Two people owed money to a certain moneylender. One owed him five hundred denarii, and the other fifty. Neither of them had the money to pay him back, so he forgave the debts of both. Now which of them will love him more?"

Simon replied, "I suppose it should be the one who had the bigger debt to be forgiven."

"Yes, you are right. That is how it should be." Yeshua said nodding.

He motioned toward Mari, "Let us consider this woman. When I came into your house. You did not offer me the oil of blessing for my head, or a pan of water for my feet. Conversely, she has blessed me with an anointing, wet my feet with her tears, and wiped them with her hair. In comparison, you did not offer me a polite kiss of welcome. Yet this woman, from the moment she entered my presence has not stopped kissing my feet."

Simon gasped astonished at Yeshua's audacious words, too stunned to speak. He wondered, 'Who is this outspoken friend of my grandson's that he would dare to point out an old man's lack of polite hospitality. Who is he to publicly criticize a man of his stature and age?'

Guilelessly Yeshua continued, "You did not offer oil for my head, but she has poured a royal perfume on both my head and my feet out of respect for who she believes me to be."

Yeshua locked his gaze on Simon, a long-time member of the religious ruling class. His position of power had made him a prideful man. Even after his long years of exile his pride had hardly diminished. Simon thought himself righteously above repentance by virtue of his title. He did not see or acknowledge his own sinfulness. His sin remained unresolved. It was no surprise that Mari's show of gratitude toward him had made Simon uncomfortable and angry.

"Therefore, I tell you, all of her sins have been forgiven—just as her outpouring of love has shown. But whoever has been forgiven little loves little."

Speechless Simon dropped his head to escape Yeshua's scrutiny. He realized he was partly to blame for the events of the day. He had done nothing to protect Mari. He should have at least forewarned her and offered his protection. He also knew the distance between them was as much his fault as hers. He had not reached out to her but expected her to come to him.

Yeshua leaned toward Mari. "Your sins are forgiven."

In a fatherly gesture he reached out to wipe away her tears.

Simon's sons, Joazar and Eleazer, along with some of the other guests around the table whispered amongst themselves. "Who does he think he is that he forgives sins?"

Yeshua offered a smile of encouragement to Mari. "Your faith has saved you. Go in peace."

Reluctantly, Mari stood, pulling her long hair up into a tussled bun. She recovered her head scarf. Reaching into her satchel she handed Yeshua back his cloak. "Thank you for covering me."

She put the stopper back into the perfumed oil and carefully placed it into her satchel for safe keeping.

When she reached the doorway, she found herself caught up by Lazarus and Martha. They signaled their many thanks across the room to Yeshua. Then they whisked their sister away for a proper welcome home. As strange as all this was, Yeshua had fulfilled their previous request, he had reconciled their sister to them.

Simon shook his head with resignation. His grandchildren saw the world through different eyes. Hadn't his favorite, his grandson Lazarus, invited this young Rabbi to the family compound? With all his bluster spent, Simon was just too tired to care. He was helped up and to his room.

He fell into a restless sleep, to the words, 'Whoever has been forgiven little loves little.'

In his dreams, he felt humiliated by the thought that after so many years, he still might not understand love at all. Later, he awoke to blink sadly into the darkness. His mind drifted back over his earlier after he had taken his post in Jerusalem. He had naively thought he could make the temple right again, because he had been elevated to serve God in a greater capacity. Still, he had felt close to God then. At that time there was much anticipation of a savior, a 'Messiah'. Influencial people whispered about it. The Essenes were adamant about it, saying the time of the Messiah was nigh. He had begun to privately study the Scriptures. He had cautiously talked with those who were thus persuaded; even though he served at the favor of Herod.

When kings from the other nations came to town saying the King of all Kings was born, Herod had called Simon to his side to offer his consultation concerning a newly born Messiah. Herod had been frightened by the thought. Simon offered little bare facts of what he knew to appease him.

On that same day, a couple had entered the temple to dedicate their first-born child. Something had taken hold of him at the sight of the child. He had became ecstatic and caught up in the Spirit. He was sure he held the key to God's salvation in his arms. He had began rejoicing. And, he had never felt so alive. Then Anna, the old prophetess drew near in the midst of his worship. When she looked up on the child she had been overcome too. They had worshiped God together and spoke words over the child!

He tried to count back the years. Astonishment swept over him. 'Could it be?'

When all were asleep, Yeshua still lay awake. His thoughts kept returning to Mari's anointing.

The scent permeated his senses.

He thought, 'I have glimpsed her once again, the very image of my people who I have come to save—the children of Judea, of Israel, and all of those out of every nation who are yet to be grafted in, each a part of the whole.

Faces of the past year of his public ministry passed before him.

Every so often, it would happen that he would catch a momentary impression of the gift his Father had promised to him. Face after face, person after person, each one was a precious child created by his Father to become a part of 'the gift'! The vision of 'the Gift' was always before him. But today the Gift became real, manifest in this woman who had been condemned as 'an adulterous woman'. Her worship was a only a foretaste meant to encourage him.

Prophets of old viewed both Israel and Jerusalem as married to the LORD. But the people could never be true, they were faithless, 'adulterous wives', always choosing other gods, they always ran away doing things their own way. This metaphor of the Bride of Christ would shift into 'the ecclesia' in time. He imagined all the people scattered amongst the nations waiting in desperate need of mercy and truth, harassed just like Mari; a remnant here, a person there. His father never gave up on his people. Neither would he; simply because he loved them and held them in his heart.

Falling asleep, Yeshua entered into the kingdom of light. Again the cosmic vision of a beautiful woman appeared, the bride his Father had promised him before time began was before him. His church was effervescent in beauty and purity. His dream changed, suddenly she was being pursued by evil and he saw she was in grave danger. With covetous jealousy, a dragon pursued her to devour her in his flames. The woman ran with terror in her eyes, reaching her hands towards him, beseeching him to save her, her eyes filled with sorrow and shame. He moved towards her ready to save her from the beast, but the path was blocked by a gnarled and ugly tree. Moving one way, then the next, he could not get to the woman and she could not get to him.

He looked up at the dreadful barricade. He recognized the tree of the knowledge of good and evil, it was immovable. Yeshua realized the only way to get to the woman was to climb up and over this pain filled tree. Its limbs stretched out grabbing at him with splintered fingers. He started awake.

'I know this tree.' He thought.

How often had he seen this very tree along the Roman roads?

He remembered his Father's words to him.

"You are their only way, Yeshua. Only you can save them."

~ 50 ~

LEAVING THE PAST BEHIND

If anyone is in Christ, the new creation has come:
The old has gone, the new is here!
2 Corinthians 5:17
Daughters of kings are among your honored women;
at your right hand is the royal bride in gold of Ophir.
Listen, daughter, and pay careful attention:
Forget your people and your father's house.
Let the king be enthralled by your beauty;
honor him, for he is your lord.
Psalm 45:9-10

During the holy days of Tishri, Mari ate and drank in every word Yeshua spoke. This greatly irritated her sister Martha, who was thrilled to have Mari home. She longed to share Mari's sisterly companionship in her daily activities. They had a relationship to rebuild and stories to share. But Mari was far more focused on learning the realities of God's kingdom. Mari was filled with questions. Yeshua's answers were powerful to defeat the lies of her past.

As the days passed by, Martha began to resent Mari's obsession with Yeshua's teachings. She was jealous of both her questions and her fascination. Irritated, Martha, finally came and stood before Yeshua.

"Lord, are you really going allow my sister to sit at your feet day after day without helping me. Look at all I have to do to prepare meals for so many guests."

Yeshua took measure of the situation. "Martha, you have a lot on your mind. Mari has just one thing on her mind. Between the two of you, Mari has made the better choice." His expression and nod indicated that she should join Mari at his feet. "This is more important."

Martha felt rebuked and upset that he would side with Mari. She was not used to not getting her way, didn't he understand how busy she was? And everyone just expected her to do what must be done. Martha released a sigh of frustration and walked away.

It left an opening for Mari to screwed up the courage she needed to make her outrageous request.

"I know this may sound bold; but when you leave, I want to go with you as one of your disciples." She held her breath, her eyes on his.

"I would not deny you your righteous heart's desire. I can see, this desire has been given to you. But first you should know how hard it will be to be my follower. We will be constantly moving, from place to place. Our mission is fraught with discomfort, danger, and long exhausting hours. We often travel in harsh conditions. Also, a diverse group of men follow me. They won't make it easy for you. They will likely resent your presence."

"But how can I know more about God's kingdom if not from you? I am willing to rough it, just don't leave me behind. To-morrow, come with me and Susanna to Jerusalem, I want to show you something."

The next day they left for her apartment. There she brought out her trunk and placed it before him.

"This can support your ministry, along with me and the women I will bring with me. I won't be a weight. Allow me to learn your ways first hand."

He recognized the seal on the chest.

She opened the lid.

"This is your betrothal box." He said eyeing the rich fabric on top.

Momentarily, Mari's whole life passed before him

"This gown was meant for your wedding day."

Mari nodded, "Yes, this box was given to me by my Grandfather."

She lowered her head, "As you probably know, I have no need of these things now. I was sent away long ago, never to be recalled. No one bur Archaleus knew where I went. Through provendance I was entrusted to Mariamne and adopted into Simon's flock. I only keep this dress because it was passed down to me from my grandmother, Mariamne I. I am her namesake. It is the only family heirloom I have, though it will never be used. The silk was embroidered with gold from Ophir. There is no telling the value of this dress."

She went on, telling him her story. He listened while Mari opened to him her past devastations. It was good for her to speak her truths out loud. As she spoke he absolved her shame, leaving a healing acceptance in its place. By bringing her story out of the dark shadows of her memories into his light, the power of her secrets over her was neutralized.

"My identity has been hidden; and, I want to keep it that way. I am pretty sure you already knew who I am."

Her chin shot up with a challenge for him to deny it.

"Yes. Magdalene, 'The Watchtower' after your grandmother's tower. She was a political pawn, too. But it is not the only reason I call you that."

Mari looked at him quizzically. But he said nothing more.

She continued. "Joanna told me what she knew about the intrigues of court. She said I was spared from many dangers and she should know. Still, I am forever tied to a man I don't even know. Archelaus never thought to provide me a certificate of divorce when he was exiled. So, I remain bound."

"A technicality until his death."

"Yes, but it is enough." She shrugged as if she cared little.

"Early kingdoms are full of intrigue and dangerous to navigate, especially for children. I am sorry for what has happened to you. Still, rejoice, for you have been spared for a better kingdom. And, things are different in God's kingdom. In time, you will receive your reward."

Mari raised her head, hopeful.

Yeshua said, "Things are not always what they appear to be. Here, you see things dimly. In heaven, you will see face to face. Trust in God. All good things in God's timing. Keep this dress. Let it remind you of a better time coming. This life is not the end of your story.

Mari dug out a gold coin from below and handed it to him.

His eyes narrowed on it and he looked at her, "This dowry is your husband's provision for you. Keep it to set up your household for your future." He placed it in her hand and curled her fingers around it.

"I recieved a similar box as a tribute when I was born. My mother still has the box. But it is only filled with memories now. The gold served my family when we had to escape to Egypt from your Grandfather. The gold given to us financed a place to stay."

"I want to contribute something. I have the means."

"Okay then, I will allow a tithe of your business profits to our mission."

She placed a number of coins in his hand. Then at least take this to help finance your family's needs and to set up your head-quarters."

He placed two back in her hand. "Foxes have dens and birds have nests, but the Son of Man will have no place to lay his head. But this will help my family, so thank you."

She nodded. "And, I will find a place for me and my friends in Capernaum."

She placed the dress back in the box.

Yeshua turned back to the topic at hand, "It won't be easy to follow me. There will be pain and suffering in it."

"But, there will also be joy, right?" She said smiled hopefully.

He stared at Mari knowing she was unsuspecting of what lie ahead.

"Yes, there will be joy." He assured her. "It is for joy, that I am set apart by the Father to do his work. The work must come first, before the joy. My passage here will be short-lived."

She frowned, not understanding what he was saying.

"Short-lived?"

"I am Ani Lo, devoted to the LORD. My life will not end in popularity. The worst kind of suffering waits for me. Mari, though you don't want to hear this, and you don't yet understand it, do not forget that I have told you this."

His eyes searched hers. "Remember this."

Mari was not sure she understood, but she said. "Then let me give my life, such as it is to your work. Let me be set apart to serve you."

He nodded, "Then come."

Delighted, Mari gave a bounce of happiness. That day, she got up and went to tell her close and trusted friends, "The Rabbi has accepted my request to be his disciple! He has not excluded me for being a women from following him. He has accepted me to be taught by him and to serve him!"

Despite her apparent happiness, several people who she loved tried to dissuade her, thinking she was making a foolish decision but her course was already set.

When the time came, Mari entrusted the key to her business into Tabitha's capable hands. Mari was ready to leave Jerusalem behind. Susanna had closed up the apartment, refusing to be left behind, and Joanna had decided to go along for a set time, leaving her husband Chuza behind to run Antipas' household. He was jealous of her adventure, but he told her to bring back all her stories. The two women stood a short distance away, waiting for Mari.

The three women looked radically different in their ordinary clothing and comfortable shoes, with packs on their back. In Bethany, Martha made excuses while saying she wanted to go, but she couldn't leave her household responsibilities. She was sad to see Mari off again, not knowing when she might return.

Mari could hardly believe she was accepted as a disciple. No other rabbi would have considered such a thing. But she felt that with Yeshua the curse of being born a woman was being rolled away. The Lord was opening the way for women to enter into his New Covenant. His mission had become her mission.

When Yeshua told his men that Mari, Joanna, and Susanna were coming with them to Galilee, they were hardly thrilled or surprised. Mari had scarcely left Yeshua's side since he had saved her life. Yeshua chose whoever he wished, this time he had chose a woman. Some grumbled jealous of the women's presence, unwilling to share their Rabbi with them. The welcome was cool. Having been forewarned Mari stood her ground, unmoved by their suspicion and resentment. For Mari it was enough to know with certainty that she was accepted by Yeshua. He was the only one who mattered, he was the one she had come to serve.

~ 51 ~

MAKING ALL THINGS NEW

When the kindness and love of God our Savior appeared,
he saved us, not because of righteous things we had done,
but because of his mercy.
He saved us through the washing of rebirth
and renewal by the Holy Spirit.
Titus 3:4-5
Many were appalled at him—his appearance was so disfigured
beyond that of any human being
and his form marred beyond human likeness.
Isaiah 52:14

Jahleel was in his late thirties, a relatively handsome man with smooth olive colored complexion, a dashing smile and winsome personality. He labored with a group of men processing fish to sell at the markets. When he first developed the rash on the side of his nose, he thought little of it, hoping it would heal soon. But when the rash became red and inflamed, he found that his nose began to feel different...numb.

'That is strange.' He had thought.

When the rash began to spread toward his upper lip, he separated himself from his family just as Jewish law required for those with skin afflictions. His wife was secretly relieved, that she had not needed to make the suggestion. They both hoped it would heal quickly so their separation would only be temporary. Except the rash remained and grew angrier. It did not go away. He had been out of work for a few weeks, when he began to seriously worry for both his family and his health. It was the duty of a husband to provide for his family.

Jahleel sought a medical opinion. He was horrified to discover it was the dread of all who worked in such damp environments—leprosy.

He was told, "Do not even touch your own face."

He tried his best not to touch it for fear the fierce bacteria would find a crevice on his fingers and begin to eat away at his hands. Looking at his hands, he feared it might already be too late. He was filled with recriminations that he had been so slow to seek help, but he had never dreamed such a small spot could be something so bad. Even if he had sought help, there was no help to be had. Jahleel felt abominable. He was a young man, but his life had been stolen from him. Now, only his ghost remained to be tormented. He could never go home.

When his wife found out it was leprosy she was afraid to even approach him. Her fearful look was more than his heart could take. She examined her children over from head to toe. His family feared him, and one another as well because of the contagion.

He wondered, 'Is this how Job had felt?'

He sent a message to his brother asking for his help. But after a few weeks, his wife came and stood at a distance.

"Your brother says we are too great of a burden and we will not be able to stay. So, I am returning to my family. They don't want us either, but after undergoing examinations, they agreed to give us shelter. We must be purified and dressed in new clothes. Everything we have will be burnt and left behind. We will go to them with nothing."

Jahleel felt a deep shame. Because of him, his family had become paupers, forced to live on the charity of others.

"I am so sorry. I wish there was something I could do. All we can do now is pray for a miracle." He told her.

His wife eyed him bitterly, though she did not give voice to her cruel thoughts.

Jahleel was forced to wander aimlessly looking for a cave or a hovel in which to exist.

Finally, he had taken up residence in a cave with another leper away from the seaside. It helped to know someone who shared his misery, someone with whom to break the isolation, even though the man's bitterness was hard to endure.

They kept to their own side of the cave, as if their illness could somehow become even worse by nearness of the other. The disease advanced.

Jahleel's handsome face became swollen with large lumps of angry flesh as the creeping bacteria continued to grow larger and larger, eating away his smooth skin and leaving layer upon layer of scar tissue. His face was so swollen and distorted that he no-longer resembled his old self at all. His once charming smile was twisted into an eerily gaping wound.

Jahleel had been lucky enough to find a loaf of stale bread big enough to share. He invited his associate to join him. They sat down to share the meager meal. Each man sat on their side of the cave and turned away so they could lowered their veils to eat. They ate quickly, only to cover their faces again and engage in conversation.

Jahleel spoke first, his voice laced with a hope.

"Have you heard of the new healer in Galilee?"

"Yes, I heard something. What good will he do us?" The man said, through his muffled lips. "No holy man will see us. Not in this shape. We are the defiled, unclean. Besides, all the healers I know are just a bunch of useless charlatans. I tried to see a healer to find a cure, but they refused to even talk with me. They couldn't wait to point me away from their presence.

"You are right, of course, about the clinics. No one will even stand at distance to offer me advice concerning my disease. Still, I wonder. They say this man is different. He has been able to heal all kind of contagious diseases and even mental problems. He healed a man's shrunken hand. He has even raised a dead man to life! Who has ever heard of such a thing. And, he even healed the servant of a Roman! Without even entering his house! A Roman! I can't think of anyone who would do that? So maybe..."

"Jahleel, you will be humiliated by hoping a Holy Man would entertain your request, even at a distance. You are setting yourself up for a disappointment."

"Maybe not. If I remember the stories correctly, didn't Elisha heal a man with leprosy?"

His friend shrugged gruffly, "Mythical tall tales, he probably never had leprosy."

Jahleel thought of his family, of his old job, of the life he had once taken for granted and his former resentful attitude. His disease had changed him. He thought of synagogue. He had not been particularly faithful in attendance. He had made plenty of lame excuses. Now he wished he had kept the sabbath more devoutly. Was this a curse from God for co-mingling with the pagans and adopting their ways?

He thought, 'Once, I hated my work, all those stinking fish! Now I would give anything to be free to work again, even there. I would love to be free to kiss my wife, to carry my children on my shoulders, to celebrate life with my friends, and even go into the temple to make my required sacrifices to God. If I could go back. It all seemed a drudgery to me then, but now I see all my responsibilities had all been gifts of blessings to me.'

"I miss going to synagogue." He said plaintively to his friend.

"Why?" He asked. "Do you really think God cares about us? If so, where is he?"

"Maybe it would have been different, if I had not resented all of God's rules and the requirements of sacrifice."

His friend gave an angry snort. "How many cows and sheep does he need?"

"I long to hear the cantor singing the Scriptures in his strong clear tones. I would join my voice with his to sing the prayers, the psalms, the laments. I used to hate them, but now I understand the dirges of confession and lamentations. Now the words echo unbidden to me with the solemn tones of the lyre and flute. The words of lamentations have become sacred to me, resonating in the depths of my soul."

His friend begged, "Well, please don't sing them while I am around."

As Jahleel rewrapped his stale bread, he thought, 'What have I got to lose? Better to try than to die doing nothing. I will go to this healer.'

Recently, when he was hidden behind some bushes, he'd overheard two men talking about the healer Yeshua of Nazareth. He was due to arrive day after the next.

He had thought then, 'I will find a way to meet the man the people are calling the Savior of Israel. If he is the Savior, then surely he could save me from this body of living death. If Elisha once cleansed an unclean gentile of leprosy, then why couldn't the Messiah do the same for me? Why shouldn't I hope?'

Since that day, a glimmer of light shone in his eyes, half hidden in deformity.

'Yes. I am sure this man sent from God will be able to do it.'

When the day came, Jahleel crept cautiously along an uncharted path towards the valley where Yeshua was expected to travel. Pulling his face scarf close over his face, he remained at a watchful distance. Waiting, he avoided other people and the shameful experience of being rebuked like a rabid dog. Only another leper understood the shame and desolation of such encounters. He waited and watched for several hours, but his hope did not flag.

Finally, he saw a lone figure crest the rise of the steep road. His form seemed to glow with a bright purity even from so far away. The man was moving at a good pace. One by one, a large group of people appeared, following hard on his heels. From where Jahleel stood, the man looked just like a shepherd leading his flock of sheep. This had to be the Holy Man—the Healer.

Jahleel's heart hammered within him with anticipation. He made his move to stand out in the middle of the clearing.

'Oh, that he would see me, really see me!' Jahleel raised his desperate prayer.

"Do not pass me by!" His heart cried out his lament. "Look upon me, O Holy One from God! Look! See my desolation. My eyes have poured out tears night, after night, with no hope to keep me warm. Who will comfort me? Everyone has abandoned me. All my friends despise me. People throw rocks at me to drive me away like a wild animal. I am cast out. I live like a worm hidden in the tunnels of the underworld, I am no longer a man."

He raised his hands in supplication. "You LORD have dealt justly with me because of my many sins. I am an unclean man. I have no right to ask, but please have mercy upon me Lord. No one else can help me. Please! Don't turn away. You, O LORD, are my only hope! Cleanse me, if not for me, then... please for my children who are destitute... and my wife who is now like a widow."

Yeshua could feel the agony flowing up the rise to meet him as if it was coming in waves from the valley floor below. It drew him forward with even greater purpose. Someone was in desperate need. He scanned the valley below, searching for the source. He spotted a lone man, standing in a field, away from the road. His arms were lifted as if making a great appeal. He was dressed in tattered clothes; his face was veiled.

Yeshua picked up his step. He traveled swiftly toward the lost sheep bleating for help as if cast down and unable to help itself. Reaching the valley approach toward the town, Yeshua quickly veered off the road. He asked his disciples to stay where they were. He began walking toward the hooded figure.

Behind him Simon, James, Yohan and Magdalene followed at a tentative distance, while the others held the larger group at bay.

Jahleel saw the One they called "the Savior" coming approaching him, his eyes were fixed upon him! Jahleel began to move towards Yeshua with a halting step. 'Does he know? Should I meet him? Should I dare approach him? It is only right that I should warn him.'

"Unclean, unclean!" Jahleel called out, but he did not stop moving toward Yeshua. But silently his heart cried. 'Please don't turn away from me!'

Finally, Jahleel stopped to venture no further. He knelt pressing his face to the ground, his shoulders shook with great sobs. Two strong feet came to stand only a hands-breath before him. The Healer had come to him.

"I am unclean, Lord. I have no right to come to you as I am." He made his muffled request without even looking up. But...if you are willing you can make me clean." He felt a touch on his shoulder.

A deep, yet softly comforting voice answered, "I am willing."

Jahleel pulled his face cloth tight and looked up to scan Yeshua's face. Seeing the Healer's face, he drew back the cloth to reveal his horribly marred face. Yeshua did not flinch, but took a moment to take in Jahleel's affliction. His compassion palpable.

'He sees me.' Jahleel thought. 'But he doesn't turn away.'

Yeshua looked into the man's face, as if searching for signs of the image of his former creation. He willed the diseased skin to melt away like a waxed mask. He reached down and taking the man's swollen hand with its two missing fingers. He lifted him up to his feet. Reflected in the man's face was the depth of his sorrow and pain.

Yeshua spoke softly, "Be clean."

Instantly, the swelling, the bulges, the inflammation, and the damage melted away like a bad dream. Jahleel's face transformed as if it were being newly created.

Jahleel looked at his hand secured in Yeshua's strong grip, realizing he could feel Yeshua's warmth.

Wonder overwhelmed him. His hand appeared smooth and un-marred, his two missing fingers were restored. He touched his face then. His skin felt smooth and whole.

"You saw me!" He whispered in awe.

"Yes, I see you." Yeshua flashed him an compassionate smile.

"Jahleel, you are too handsome for your own good. It could get you in trouble." He gave his now smooth cheek a rough pat.

Jahleel beamed, feeling the playful sting of Yeshua's hand on his face. Yeshua reached out ran his fingers over Jahleel's face once again, examining his handiwork. Then he chucked his chin.

Jahleel watched him thinking, 'I can feel again. I am touchable.'

Yeshua became serious, meeting Jahleel eye to eye, "More, im-portantly your Father in Heaven has heard your cry. Your sins are forgiven."

Jahleel became serious too, "I am forever grateful. I have learned many valuable lessons. This changed me. How can I repay you for healing me? There must be something I can do. But I have nothing to give."

"What I am doing for you is free for the taking, but that does not mean it is not given you at a high price."

Jahleel tried to understand what he was saying.

Yeshua held his gaze. "It is right for you to show your appreci-ation to God now that you are healed. Here is what you are to do, go and show yourself to the priest. Offer the gift Moses commanded as a testimony to God's grace for your healing. Make a thank offering, and a fellowship offering for you are no longer an outcast to God. Then go and reunite with your family."

Jahleel nodded, joyous at the thought of regaining right standing and fellowship with God. He could not wait to see his family again. He felt as if he had just awakened from a terrible nightmare.

"Just one more thing, let's keep this healing between you and me. Tell no one." He said this for the man's own well-being as well as his own.

"You are getting a fresh start. Take it."

Jahleel understood and nodded. There was no need for the stigma to follow him. How could one be healed, if the stigma remained.

Jahleel sorrowfully thought of his friend who remained in the darkness with his disease, unwilling to humble himself or to take the risk of coming out into the light. How could he be healed if he was unwilling to seek God's help wherever it could be found? Naturally, Jahleel wanted to tell everyone, but he agreed. "I understand. Thank you for seeing me, for not passing me by, for coming to me, for touching me with your grace and giving me a second chance."

He wanted to hug Yeshua, but felt it was not appropriate under the circumstances. So, he bowed low, then Jahleel rose up to go do what Yeshua had told him.

After, he had traveled twenty yards, he looked back once more, hopeful that he would find Yeshua again.

Yeshua nodded his understanding to him and watched him go. He sighed with satisfaction to see the man stride into the newness of life. A Scripture stirred his mind, 'Just as there were many who were appalled at him—because his appearance was so disfigured beyond that of any human being—and his form marred beyond human likeness—in this way he will sprinkle many nations.'

Yeshua shuddered and pulled his cloak close around him for a momentary comfort. He tentatively touched his own face, knowing Jahleel's disfigurement would be nothing compared to his own mutilation when the time came. He would be so greatly marred he would be unrecognizable; but not by a disease or his own sin. No, his face would be utterly destroyed by those who hate him, so all of his creation could be made new.

Simon walked to Yeshua still standing in the field.

"Are you okay, Lord?"

Yeshua turned toward him sadly and nodded. He moved to rejoin his waiting students. He had no time to ponder this his disfigurement now, he had to make every moment count. He would worry about his suffering when that day came.

~ 52 ~

UNDENIABLE FAITH, UNMERITED FAVOR

Love your enemies, do good to them,
and lend to them without expecting to get anything back.
Then your reward will be great,
and you will be children of the Most High,
because he is kind to the ungrateful and wicked.
Be merciful, just as your Father is merciful.
Luke 6:35-36

Jairus watched as Miriam and her sons approached the synagogue. He struggled not to show his resentment towards them because of her son Yeshua. It was surprising how quickly her son had captured the hearts of many in Capernaum.

Whenever Yeshua was in Capernaum he attended synagogue and his followers came with him, a large number of men and women. On those Sabbath days, Yeshua never failed to perform some miraculous healing, which caused quite a stir of jealousy among the officials of the synagogue. They felt they were being upstaged. People clamored to hear Yeshua's words, while their teachings seemed to fall on deaf hears. The synagogue was over-run by outsiders and strangers looking for Yeshua. Regular attendees complained because they could no longer get a seat. What was worse, whenever the Nazarene was away, people made unflattering comparisons and complained that the officials did not teach with the same authority, nor could they heal like the Nazarene.

Other religious leaders from Jerusalem goaded Jairus. "How do you endure this upstart Rabbi in your town? Every time he comes to Jerusalem, he creates a scene. The High Priest has put a price on his head. He fears Roman repercussions because of the crowds this man draws. No self-respecting Jew should have anything to do with him. Caiaphas sends spies out to watch all his words and actions. We are looking for some fault in the man. At least, let us know if you find anything against him. We would be happy to come and put an end to him."

Jairus feared he would soon end up on the wrong side of the politics surrounding the man.

But before he could decide what to do, the Sanhedrin intervened commanding Jairus put a stop to Yeshua's breaking of the Sabbath law. Jairus did as he was instructed, confronting Yeshua about the miracles. But Yeshua ignored his rebuke and continued to heal people.

As the leader of the synagogue, Jairus felt pressured to take action against this unpleasant business. He remembered Yeshua's disapproving look when he asked him to leave, but he complied by moving to an outdoor venue.

Unfortunately, in his absence the synagogue suddenly felt empty and devoid of life even to Jairus. No matter what they did, the services blasé in comparison. Jairus was forced to make excuses to the complaints.

Yet even while the synagogue was left lifeless, he was being hardily congratulated by members of the Sanhedrin for confronting the man.

And, Jairus accepted their praise, saying, "Yes, the Nazarene tried to take over my synagogue. But I have made short work of that!"

"I guess your post of twelve years has taught you how to deal with people like him." They congratulated with a slap on his back.

Jairus tucked his head in false modesty.

"I guess I have learned a thing or two along the way. I could not allow him to take charge, you know."

"We are checking into his background, searching for ways to put him to the test. If you find anything, let us know, nothing has implicated him thus far. Caiaphas insists we must put an end to anyone that interferes with the rituals of our faith."

Now Jairus only hoped Yeshua would stay away so things could return to normal. He did not want the High Priest to think that he was in any way a supporter of this man as the Messiah. Or worse, that he should think him incapable of handling his own synagogue. He had worked too hard to gain his comfortable position. As the ruler of a larger synagogue, he enjoyed the respect of the community, his sizable income, and his nice home.

How can one man cause such threat? He decided to send whatever information he could scrape together to Caiaphas to insure his own innocence and good standing.

So when Miriam stepped through the portal, Jairus ignored her looking past her to her sons, fearful this widow might express some need from him. He had learned that unless widows were wealthy, they tended to be takers not givers. On if they were givers were they worth the time and effort.

'Let her sons provide for her.' He thought.

Miriam eyed Jairus briefly as if she could discern his thoughts.

To James he asked, "So, where is your infamous brother? Will he return to Capernaum soon?"

James shrugged as if anything Yeshua did was of little consequence to him, while under his tight smile he seethed. "I cannot speak for my brother. He keeps his own council, we are not informed of his itinerary."

Privately, he wondered, how long will Yeshua heap shame on the house of Yosef?

Months passed. Jairus, was feeling pretty good after Yeshua had been away for months traveling around the Sea of Galilee. For the most part, Capernaum had returned to its former a state. His troubles seemed to be cast behind him. That was until trouble found its way to Jairus' own door.

He had been busily occupied with meeting with the visiting Sanhedrin. At the end of a long day, Jairus arrived home a darkened house. No lamps lit his hearth, no dinner was waiting, neither was his wife or his daughter who welcomed him at the end of his busy days. The hearth held only dying embers. He felt an alarm, his house was far too quiet.

He called out to his wife. "Batsheva! I'm home. Are you here?"

Her muffled reply came from his daughter's room, just off of their own.

He found his wife apprehensively sitting by his daughter's bed. His daughters small face was barely visible under a wetted cloth.

Batsheva looked up with grave concern. "She hasn't been feeling well, but this morning she came home from Lilith's complaining of a really bad headache. She said she felt weak and was hurting all over. She has been shaking with chills. It's the fever, that has been going around. I am sure of it."

Jairus drew near to look more closely at his daughter.

Feebly, he tried to comfort his wife, "Let's not over react. Children get sick all the time and it passes. Our daughter is healthy and strong. She will be okay."

Batsheva shook her head. "I don't know. This illness seems different. She is burning up. And you know that the mysterious fever has been going around, I think we should take care. It has claimed a lot of lives. I couldn't stand it if anything were to happen to her. She is my only child." A frightened sob gave way.

"Let me sit with her." Jairus said. "Go and fix us some dinner. Put your mind at ease. I will go for the doctor in the morning."

Reluctantly Batsheva rose to prepare a simple dinner for her husband.

As though sensing her mother's absence, his daughter roused herself, "Abba.... where did Ima go?"

"She is fixing dinner, she will be right back. Rest now. I am here with you." She held out her slender hand to her father, he took it in both of his. He felt the scorching heat radiating into his own palm.

Her eyes drifted closed.

A helpless frown creased in his brow. He could see how weak she was. Jairus thought, 'Have faith. Adonai would not take my angel from me. Would you merciful One?'

Late into the night, Jairus retired for a bit of sleep leaving his wife keeping vigil over their daughter. All night the fever continued to burn, her herbs didn't seem to even touch it. Batsheva applied the cool plaster to her daughter's forehead.

Despite her efforts, as the late night progressed her daughter's breathing became shallow and ragged. By early morning her breaths became so diminished that Batsheva had to lean near to listen for each one.

She tried to awaken her daughter to drink some more cool water, but the girl was not responsive. Terror gripped her.

She ran to awaken Jairus, "Get up. Get up. You must do something before she is gone!"

When Jairus went out, the streets were still quiet. The sun had only begun its ascent. Jairus ran to get the doctor, who returned quickly with him.

Upon seeing the girl, the doctor spoke the harsh truth. "You have waited too long. There is nothing I can do about this."

He hesitated, seeing the grief in Batsheva's face; then the doctor pressed on. "However, there was a woman who had the fever here in Capernaum. They thought she was gone, but the Nazarene Rabbi supernaturally healed her straight away. And, he healed the servant of the Centurion Decimus—even from a considerable distance."

"But," Jairus grimaced, "the Nazarene is not in Capernaum. He is off teaching only God knows where."

"Yes, so I have heard." The doctor gave him an accusing look.

The rebuke was not lost on Jairus.

"Then, I suggest you use all your powers of prayer, that he will arrive this morning. I am afraid he is your daughter's only hope."

Pulling his hair in distress, Jairus set off into the street, desperately searching for the very man he had sent away. Ironically he had sent him away because he had healed people on the Sabbath day. He refused to consider what might happen if he couldn't find him, or if Yeshua refused his request.

Yeshua woke his men early that morning while quenching the last embers of the nights fire.

"Let's move quickly. We are returning to Capernaum this morning." He offered no explanation.

Leaning up on his elbow, Judas tried to focus in the misty morning light, then at Yeshua's purposeful face. "But Rabbi, we are expecting crowds today. Why are we leaving?"

Yeshua spoke low over his shoulder. "Let's go."

The men were still yawning when they stepped into the boat and set the course.

"Shouldn't we have eaten first?" James grumbled as the winds filled the sail and sent them moving toward Capernaum.

Yeshua patted James' slightly padded middle with a smile.

"I think you will make it to Capernaum with a little discipline, my friend. We will be there in no time."

"Yes," Simon said with surprise, "today the winds are surprisingly on our side."

The horizon of the heights behind them seemed to be brightened with the glory of God, and they skimmed almost effortlessly through the rising midst. A breeze pushed them swiftly towards their destination although Simon could not account for where it came from.

Making land fall, Yeshua did not pause for conversation. He stepped purposefully out of the boat. Wading ashore, he sat on a large rock to fasten his sandals into place. He heard a shout and glanced up to see a number of people headed his way. He stood and walked in their direction. Before he could reach the crowd, a small man dressed in official garments rushed forward to fall at Yeshua's feet. Yeshua recognized him to be Jairus, the same synagogue leader who had cast him out.

Jairus took hold of his feet as if taking hold of the horns of the altar itself. "Please! I know I have no right to ask you! Be merciful to me! My little daughter is sick and dying. No one can help her. But I have seen what you can do. Please, come to my house, lay your hands on her, so she will live!"

A throng pressed around Yeshua. Jairus was all but lost under the crush. With some effort and little help, he stumbled onto his feet with only a bruised finger to show for the trample. Yeshua began to move in the direction of Jairus' home.

A band of people swarmed around him. In mid-stride, a weakness overtook him so that his striding knees buckled. He reached out to grab hold of Yohan's arm momentarily wilting on his feet. He gasped, taking a few deep breaths, waiting until his strength returned. Power had gone out of him. He turned to scan the crowd, but he could not identify where his power had gone.

He called out in a loud voice, "Who touched my robe?"

Matthew said, "Master, everyone in this crush is touching you. How can you ask, who touched my robe?"

The crowd became quiet with expectation, drawing back a space to search for the culprit.

Who is it? How have they done this without my knowledge? Only by a powerful faith.

"Who touched me?" He called out again.

He waited searching the faces. "I know that someone touched me. I felt power going out from me."

His gaze fell upon Galenkah's meek and downcast face. He waited until she lifted her eyes. When she realized that he knew, she stepped forward guiltily; with fear and trembling she knelt before him.

"It was me." She said in a small voice. "I was desperate. I know I did the unthinkable." She paused, not wanting to explain her curse before all these people or confess that she an unclean and bleeding woman who had dared to reach out and touch this holy man.

Had she rendered him unclean by her touch?

She began to explain, "Twelve years ago I began to have a very heavy bleeding after I gave birth. It was obvious that something was very wrong with me. I asked for prayers for my affliction from the synagogue, but they cast me out. They said it was because of my sins that this illness had fallen upon me. I wanted to take my petitions before God so I could be healed, but the synagogue refused to let me in. It had been a difficult delivery and my husband said the baby was stillborn."

"Since then, I have gone to every doctor I could find. Some of the things the doctors did to me to stop the bleeding cannot even be mentioned. Over the years, the bleeding has only grown worse. My husband divorced me. I have been so tired, so depleted of life, that I have often wished to simply die in my sleep. I have given every penny I could scrape together trying to find a cure. For twelve years, my life has been stolen from me. There have been times when for lack of blood I can hardly breathe. When, I heard about you, I thought, if I could just touch your tassel, I could be healed and no one would take notice. Technically, I did not touch you, but the threads on your hem. I'm sorry, now that I say that out loud, I realize how it sounds. Is it possible that I have stolen a blessing, to remove my curse? Because the very moment I touched your tassel, my whole body was strengthened and healed. I didn't know what else to do."

It was true his power had entered her and she was healed.

Yeshua extended his hand to her to lift her to her feet.

She looked up somewhat self-consciously into his gentle gaze. "Daughter, rejoice and be glad, today your faith has healed you. I am not angry with you. Rest assured. Be at peace."

She began to weep with happiness, that this holy man had understood her suffering. He was actually happy for her healing. Such a burden of shame and guilt was lifted off of her. She lifted up her hands and laughed for joy. She had her life back.

She no idea that to heal her, Yeshua would one day lose so much blood he would hardly have the strength to stand. She did not know that his breathing too would become shallow for his lack of oxygen, or that he too would fight to take his next measured breath. Yeshua stored her rejoicing face to his memory so he could recall it later when his time came.

While he was still talking with the woman, a friend came from Jairus' household. "Jairus, it is too late, your daughter is dead. No need to trouble this rabbi anymore."

Jairus' hands dropped emptily to his sides in shock. 'Too late.'

It seemed to him that his whole world had just come to an end. His only daughter was gone. She was barely twelve. She had been a gift of joy left on their doorstep, when Bathsheva could not produce a child. He would never see her again.

Jairus was a Sadducee, so he held no hope of life after death or the possibility of the resurrection.

Yeshua turned, speaking to Jairus. "Listen to me, do not be downcast, only believe."

Jairus grabbed Yeshua's hand, a desperate high-pitched whimper escaped from a place within him where there were no words. Hope was resuscitated within him. Together they traveled on to his home.

Jairus' congregation was gathering to grieve with him. Mourners already stood crying in the courtyard to show respect due a religious leader in their community. The women wailed and keened, and the men groaned.

Yeshua paused as he moved through the mourners toward the door.

"Why do you weep? The girl is not dead. She is only sleeping."

Some who were against him taunted him.

"Ah! Here is the healer! Have you come with your bag of charlatan tricks. What can you do now? You are too late."

Yeshua looked at Jairus, tipping his head toward the door as if to say, 'Ignore them, let's go.'

Stepping inside the door, he told the interior mourners, "You should step out into the courtyard, you are disturbing the child's rest. Please go outside."

They were incensed, but Jairus urged them to comply, saying, "Yes, yes! Do as The Rabbi says." He shooed them all out, much to everyone's surprise. These were Jairus' closest allies.

Yeshua called to three of his disciples. "Rock, James, and Yohan, you three come with me." The three went in with Yeshua, Jairus, and his wife to the bedside of the young girl. She had just reached the age of betrothal, a whole life was left before her unlived. She was still small, making her look like a porcelain doll tucked in for a nap. Except, instead of a rosy hue, her skin was grayed with a bluish tinge. Her lips were cracked and white, slightly opened as if frozen in place from when she gasped for her last breath. Her mother had closed her eyes and lovingly combed her dark hair back from her delicate face. She had pulled the finely woven covers up to her daughters neck, with a neat fold. Her hands lay limp by her side.

Everyone in the room waited, looking to Yeshua. Solemnly he stepped forward to take the small cooled hand in his own strong one as if he were inviting her to dance.

"Little girl, arise." Immediately, color began to flow back into the features of her lifeless face. Her cheeks and lips pinkened. Her eyelashes fluttered, she opened her eyes. She turned her head sleepily towards his face. She smiled, then squeezed his hand that still held hers.

She pursed her lips and moved her jaw, licking her lips as one who was parched from thirst.

Seeing she was dehydrated, Yeshua ordered them, "Get this child some water and something to eat."

Jairus ran to do his bidding. Rushing back into the room with a cup of water and a piece of bread. The girl sat on the side of the bed eating and drinking as if she were ravenous. When the bread and water were gone, she laughed a delighted little laugh, tilting her face up to Yeshua's. Her mother touched her forehead, and laughed too. They were astonished that the girl was alive and now well. They all knew that without a doubt that she had been dead, her spirit had left her. They had all witnessed her spirits return.

"I dreamed I was in a beautiful garden. You were there talking to me and we were laughing." The girl said, "and now suddenly we are here." She touched his hand again as if she did not want to let him go.

"Do you remember what we spoke of?" She nodded, her eyes wide. Everyone was amazed wondering what they had discussed. But Yeshua touched his fingers to his lips, as if it were their secret. They smiled at one another.

When Jairus walked Yeshua to the door, he said, "I'm sorry, I didn't know, though I should have known. I was wrong. I should not have cast you out of the synagogue. Now, what can I do?"

Yeshua answered. "Jairus, it is easy to forget the pain and needs of others, when you have everything you need. But now that you know... the loss, the pain, the sorrow of being human. Do not forget who God is or confuse him with your man-made rules. Do for others, what you would want done for you." Jairus looked ashamed and sorrowful.

"It has all worked out for the best." Yeshua said. "It was never intended that I should remain within the walls of the synagogue. It is too small to contain me or my people."

"I feel so bad for what I said to you." Jairus said. "And yet you came at my request anyway."

"Yes. I did. I have room to accommodate as many as will come to me. I go freely where my Father sends me. Do not forget my Father's grace today or stop believing what you have seen with your own eyes. You are a religious man, you know what to do."

Jairus nodded. "Yes, I will give my thank offering to God. And Rabbi--Lord, I have heard a rumor that Jerusalem is seeking to entrap you and to find a way to put you to death. They have asked that we send back any information that can be used against you. Obviously, I will not implicate you. But others may."

"Yes." Yeshua said simply. "That too will work itself out according to the Father's will for my ministry among the people."

Jairus puzzled over his words. 'What exactly does he mean by that?'

But then his daughter stepped out before all the people to show herself healed to all of the mourners.

With repentance and gratitude, Jairus' heart ballooned in his chest filled with the Ruach of God's grace.

~ 53 ~

SECOND CHANCES

I revealed myself to those who did not ask for me;
I was found by those who did not seek me.
To a nation that did not call on my name,
I said, 'Here am I, here am I.'
All day long I have held out my hands to an obstinate people,
who walk in ways not good, pursuing their own imaginations.
Isaiah 65:1-2

The disciples gathered their packs for yet another journey. This destination had them all puzzled.

Andrew asked Yohan. "Why do you suppose he wants to go back to Nazareth? The last time he was there, they drove him out to the edge of the cliff to throw him down. For that very reason he, and even his family, eventually moved to Capernaum."

"Well do I remember!" Yohan shook his head. "But the Master does not give up easily. He grew up amongst these people. I think he believes in giving people second chances, and I don't see them coming to him."

Andrew looked up to search the distant rise, as if peering into the future. "Yes, but I don't see them ever changing their mind about him, do you?"

Simon overheard the conversation, "I wonder, what would be his limit? Does he ever give up?" Yeshua was generous with second chances, as they had all discovered as they journeyed with him.

Curious, he called out to Yeshua standing nearby, "I have a question, Lord. How many times should we forgive others who act against us? Seven times?"

Yeshua looked pained. Everyone stopped talking, waiting to hear his answer. He stepped nearer to the group. "Do you remember the scriptures which tell us that Cain was determined to avenge anyone who offended him seven times?"

They nodded, remembering the story.

"His offspring Lamech took revenge a step further. He declared that he would avenge the offense seventy times seven times. Essentially meaning, he would never forgive."

Simon stared at him, wondering where Yeshua was going with this.

He continued, "Of course, seven times of showing grace when your offender comes to you for forgiveness seems most generous, but sadly that will never be enough. I am telling you to show grace every time a person comes earnestly to you for forgiveness, seventy times seven times. Don't be like Cain or Lamech. This is how hatred grows and generational grudges begin that grow and never go away. It will perpetuate violence after violence."

"Instead, show grace to anyone who seeks to be reconciled to you, and wants to pursue a right relationship with you. Forgiveness brings healing to the world. Instead of revenge, leave room for God's wrath. His punishment will come at the appropriate time to the unrepentant. Only my Father knows the human heart, he will avenge and repay as he sees fit."

"But when?" the Zealot asked thinking of the Romans who killed his friend and so many others.

Yeshua chastened him with a glance. "I know your grief is still painful, but trust God Zel he will avenge at the right time."

"As for Nazareth, I am going there to extend my Father's grace to them once again. Whether they receive my message or not will be their choice. Repentance, admitting fault and aligning ones heart with the Father's heart is the key to receiving the grace he offers. Even when grace is offered, it does not mean grace will come easily."

Andrew said, "I don't see that happening. I saw how they hated you."

For only the barest second, everyone saw Yeshua's aggrieved expression.

"Let me tell you a story." Yeshua stared into space for a moment, before he began.

"The kingdom of heaven is like a king who wanted to settle accounts with his servants. He had a man who owed him ten thousand bags of gold. 'Bring the man to me to pay his debt in full,' he commanded his servants."

"But, the man was unable to pay him back. So, the master ordered, 'Take the man and his wife and children, and everything he has, sell them off as slaves to repay the debt.'"

Yeshua paused, eyeing his men. "Now, this would have been justice according to the Law."

He went on. "The man was distraught, knowing his life and freedom were forfeit. He fell on his knees before the King, begging him, 'Please. Be patient with me and I will pay back everything.' His master took great pity on him, canceled the debt and let him go free.

"But later on, the freed man remembered that one of his fellow servants owed him a hundred silver coins. He went and grabbed his fellow servant by the throat choking him. 'Pay back what you owe me!' he demanded.

"Just as the freed man had done earlier, this man fell to his knees and begged him, 'Please, be patient with me, and I will pay it back.'"

"But the man refused. Instead, he had his debtor thrown into prison until he could pay back his obligation. It was not long before, word of what the freed man had done to his brother reached the king. Furious, the king summoned the man he had freed. 'You wicked servant,' he said, 'I canceled your huge debt because you begged me for mercy. Having received mercy yourself, shouldn't you have had compassion on your fellow servant just as I had on you?' In anger, his master handed him over to the jailers to be tortured, until he could pay back all he owed."

He paused, leaning forward intently, "This is how my heavenly Father will treat each of you, unless you forgive your brother or sister from your heart. You have to let go. Forgive. Put it in God's hands and trust that God will take care of your situation."

"So, are you saying, you have forgiven them for having tried to kill you?" Andrew asked incredulous.

"Yes, I have. I give them a second chance. If today they will hear my words, seek to be reconciled, and show sorrow over their debts. I extend mercy to them, but they must accept the truth."

"What truth?"

"The truth that they cannot repay the debt they owe to God. Without God's mercy, they stand condemned. But, if they can accept the reality of their sinfulness and are willing to change their ways, then mercy will be theirs. This offer will remain as long as they have breath."

They arrived in Nazareth as the trumpet sounded, signaling the beginning of Sabbath. Yeshua and his men stayed with his Uncle Cleopas and Aunt Mary. They too were leaving Nazareth soon, moving to Emmaus to care for Mary's mother. Now that all of Yeshua's family had moved to Capernaum, there was little reason for them to remain in Nazareth.

The next morning, a hush fell when Yeshua entered the synagogue with his men. But soon, whispers began to swirl around them immediately.

"Look, it is the Rabbi from Galilee. They say he has done many, many miracles there."

"That is ridiculous! Look! He is only Miriam's son!" Another said.

"You remember Miriam's son of questionable birth?"

"Yosef married her, so he must have been his son. He was a good carpenter. He did some work for me. He was a devout man."

"Yeshua thought he was too good to marry my sister. He has always been a little strange."

"Who is this man, but the brother of James from Miriam's brood. They are not any better than us."

"But," Someone volunteered bravely, "he has raised people from the dead. He has healed people with all sorts of infirmities!"

Another said, "Don't you remember anything? Have you forgot the insulting way he spoke to us when he visited us the last time?"

"I must not have been here that Sabbath."

"Reuben, you should ask him to heal you of your affliction."

"Why should I humiliate myself to ask for his help?"

"Yes, who is he to tell us that we need to repent before God? He doesn't even know us."

Yeshua was aware of the low sound of grumbling, as if the beginning of an earth quake. Yet faithfully he delivered his appeal to them once again, just as he did wherever he went. The people of Nazareth recalled his previous offense and scoffed before he even began. Only a few sick people came to him to be cured. He was unable to do any real deeds of power among them. He was met with hardened faces and a staunch lack of belief. Even after the stories of all he had done had reached their ears, they wanted nothing to do with him. They would never admit they were wrong.

Later, when he left the village, Yeshua sat down to remove his sandals. He beat the dust of Nazareth off of them. His men watched him quietly, thinking he had picked up a stone.

He refastened his sandals, saying, "Whenever you are rejected by people to whom you have brought the good news of God's grace, I want you to shake the dust of their offense off of your sandals as you leave. Don't let their words and insults stick to you. Let it go. Let the dust from your sandals remain with them to testify to the truth that you came to offer them God's peace. If you gave it your best, let that be enough. If they reject your testimony, their guilt will remain upon them."

He stood then with a weary and disappointed sigh.

Andrew spoke hopefully, "After the last time, it did seem to go a little better. At least this time they didn't try to throw you off the cliff."

Yeshua reached out and ruffled Andrew's hair with a dismal chuckle. "Yes, but I had hoped for so much more. The saying has once again been proven true: A prophet is not received in his own home town. Others may honor you, but your own people will disown and refuse you."

He stood back to his feet, taking his staff in his hand. "Still, they can never say, that I did not give them second chance."

He looked out over the valley below, like a general marshalling his troops. "Let's get going now, for we have so many other villages yet to visit."

~ 54 ~

BETWEEN DARKNESS AND LIGHT

The way of the wicked is like deep darkness;
they do not know what makes them stumble.
Psalm 4:19

Antipas could not deny he was intrigued with Yohannan. He visited him frequently to banter against him and to hear what the man might say to him next. He wondered how long it would take for the Baptizer to bend, beg, or relent to gain his freedom?

Yohannan spoke earnestly to him, with such strength and conviction that occasionally Antipas actually tried to understand. But it was as if the prophet was speaking a foreign language, his words left Antipas mystified.

What am I missing? I am an intelligent and educated man. I don't understand the people's draw. He is a raving lunatic. Is it just emotionalism on their part? Myths? Delusions? Still, he amuses me.

The Baptizer's presence put Herodias in a spiteful mood. The household was feeling her fury. Antipas grew tired of her constant harping. It was as if she would not find rest until the man was dead. Antipas sought other diversions to avoid her ever accusing glare.

At one visit, Yohannan asked Antipas, "Has Herodias figured out your latest fascination?"

"What fascination?"

"The girl." Antipas' eyes narrowed.

"Who?"

"Will you feign innocence with me? You refuse to stop your incestuous ways."

"I don't know what you..." Antipas started.

"Salome. She is a child, your wife's daughter, already betrothed. She is forbidden to you."

Antipas' face registered his shock.

By what magic does this prophet know my thoughts?

It was true, his fascination with his step-daughter had grown with her coltish legs and lithe body. Since Salome had relocated from Rome, Antipas rather enjoyed the coquettish interest of the curious pubescent girl. She was a bud that promised a fresh and glorious bloom. Her coy flirtations continually occupied his imagination. When she was upset with her mother, he was glad to offer her his 'fatherly' concern and a listening ear.

She was intelligent and eager to ask him precocious questions about the running of his kingdom. She flattered him with her admiration of his position and power. She made him feel almost god-like. Emulating her mother, Salome already practiced skills meant to entice and control the lust of men, enjoying a great sense of power over them.

At Manchaerus, Salome particularly enjoyed the swimming pool. Antipas enjoyed watching from his private vantage point. Salome often mentioned her dance schedule. He would happen by to watch her through the curtains that enclosed the room. She danced all the more seductively when she knew Antipas was watching.

Salome learned early in life that money and power were much to be desired. Some girls dreamed of love; but Salome, dreamed of becoming powerful like her mother. She enjoyed opportunities to flex her feminine wiles. Especially when it held the attention of a powerful man like Antipas.

Herodias had recently betrothed Salome to Antipas' half-brother Philip who was the Tetrarch of Gaulanitis northeast of Antipas's borders. The brothers shared no familial affections, but Herodias devised the plan to unite the two kingdoms. Salome was pleased with her mother's long-term plan.

When Herodias learned of Antipas' fascination with her daughter, she realized, the prophet's words were true.

Once her anger reduced to a simmer, she saw it for the opportunity it was. She could use Antipas' lust to get her way.

Herodias posted her maid servant, to keep her husband from acting on his fantasies. Meanwhile, she began to weave a plan with a droll kind of pleasure. She had no compunction in using her daughter to get what she wanted.

I will become the queen of Israel at all cost. But first to silence that Baptizer's accusing voice! Better Antipas is seduced by Salome than by the Baptizer's guilting words. That man's influence will not rob me of what I have worked so hard to achieve. Let Salome leave Antipas weak in his knees, let him beg for her favors! Then I will whisk Salome off to Philip to consummate the marriage. Antipas' birthday celebration is just around the corner. He will assuredly drink too much and act rashly. When his desire gets the best of him, I will force his hand.

As his birthday approached, Herodias asked him, "What entertainment would please you most at your celebration my love? Would you like dancers?"

Antipas took her bait. "You could dance for me."

He moved in close to her, taking her in his arms.

"Yes, I could, but would that be appropriate for me in my position as Queen?" Herodias asked. "But you are right, we should have dancers for the kings birthday."

Seeing Herodias was in a generous and agreeable mood, he mentioned. "You have been training Salome, will you allow her to join the dancers?"

"Salome? She is still a bit young. Still, I think it would be most fitting to allow the princess to dance for the king's birthday. That would be very special indeed. But we can't upstage her with all the other dancers. I will have her dance solo."

"That would definitely be a fitting debut for her." He nuzzled her neck.

She turned toward him, "Of course, in honor of you. It would be perfect. I'm quite sure Salome would love to dance for you, darling."

She ran her hands down his chest admiringly, her eyes full of suggestion.

The birthday celebration ran late into the evening. With their cups in hand, the guests settled back on their cushions restless for the entertainment to begin. Under the influence, Antipas had already bragged to the men about the girl's attributes.

The dance began with a driving and energetic beat, that spun every head. Salome swept into the room swathed in a diaphanous fabric that both flowed and molded to her body, giving the appearance of nudity beneath it.

Every lecherous eye strained.

The tempo changed and the music slowed. Her body began to twist and rock in excruciatingly slow movements as mesmerizing as a cobra. Each movement highlighted her lengthened limbs and flexibility. She removed a layer of the sheer fabric to use seductively as part of her dance. Allowing an even more revealing view of her body. She was no longer a child, but not yet a woman.

The music sped up and the girl arched her neck as if she were offering herself up to the energy. The rhythmic beat began to build. Her body sped along with it, her hips gyrating as if she was controlled by something beyond herself.

Antipas sat forward, bewitched and aware of no one but the girl. His heart hammered as if he were dancing with her. The flush of lust was all too apparent on his face.

Seeing his desire for her, Salome was swept away by the heady power of her seduction. The eyes of every man were on her wanting her. Salome pushed all the acceptable limits. Her kohled eyes large and nymph-like simmered with heat and invitation.

When the music finally reached its apex and came to its end, Salome knelt submissively at Antipas' feet with her hands extended towards him, as if she were his offering. Her small bosom heaved to catch her breath. Once more she became the adoring pubescent girl, anxious for the praise of the King.

Herod Antipas caught his own breath while he clapped his hands in approval.

"Isn't she spectacular?" He asked the other men, who cheered and appraised her with lewd eyes.

Unbalanced, Antipas stood and stepped toward the girl to cup her face in his hands, "I will give you whatever you desire, my little one, in return for this great honor; even up to one-half of my kingdom."

Her eyes widened and she drew in a sharp breath of delight at such an outrageous offer.

Her mind raced. 'Does he naively think I will ask for some childish bobble? Up to half the kingdom? '

With sudden realization, dread and terror snaked up her spine. Had she gone too far? Was Antipas offering her the chance to usurp her mother. Fearing her mother's anger, the girl ran to kneel before her.

"Mother, what would you want me to ask for?" She asked meekly.

Herodias exhaled a low and mollified snarl, her eyes glistened dangerously she Leaned toward the girls ear.

She whispered, "Ask him for the Baptizer's head on a platter."

The girl paled. "You want the prophet's head?"

"Yes, on a platter." Herodias smiled, touching her daughters glowing cheek with encouragement.

"That prophet will only get in our way and cause trouble. Let's take care of this now."

Seeing her mother's anger and resolve, Salome stood to swiftly take her mother's request back to Antipas.

Bowing down to him, she raised her voice to make her request. "Give me the Baptizer's head on a platter."

Antipas was jarred from his revery back to reality. His eyes shot toward Herodias.

Herodias' chin shot up with an arrogant and triumphant dare.

Briefly, Antipas loathed himself for falling to his wife's demands. But when he looked around and realized all eyes were now on him with expectation, he called for his guard and gave the order.

Once the command was issued, the music began again. The other dancers took to the floor and the party resumed. Antipas took a long drink from his cup, still seething. He thought of his brother Philip in Rome. Now, he understood why he had offered no resistance when he had stolen his wife away from him.

Locked in the darks bowels of the palace, Yohannan heard the rhythmic sounds of the madding drums. He shivered with the premonition of evil. When the henchmen came with their torches to unlocked his prison door, Yohannan understood.

So this is how it will end! I will join the long succession of prophets before me in death. I should not be surprised.

He wondered briefly, 'Could I have spoken the truth differently or changed the course of these events? No. This is the price for speaking truth to power. I was compelled, I could not keep silent. God's words cried out from within me. The LORD appointed me to speak his truth here in this palace at this time.'

For months, Yohannan had prayed, hoped, and waited for his deliverance from the dark, dank, belly of Herod's prison. During that time, doubts and questions assailed him. Under duress the mind can play terrible tricks on a person. He had even began to doubt if Yeshua was indeed the Anointed One as he had proclaimed him to be.

Eventually, even though he was trapped in the darkness of his cell, the light of the words of Isaiah had shown through to reminded him of the signs and wonders of the Messiah and cleared away the clouds of his confusion. God's words restrengthened him. He revived from his stupor when he remembered the words spoken from the cloud on that day. And he remembered the vision of the dove alighting upon Yeshua. Yeshua was the Prince of Peace. He would bring peace with God to humanity.

Still, Yeshua was not the Messiah Yohannan or the others had imagined. He had not called together an army to rescue him or Israel. He was once again reminded, *'My thoughts are not your thoughts, neither are your ways my ways', declares the LORD.*

Still, he wondered, how would Yeshua become the savior and deliverer of his people? Finding no answers, Yohannan resolved to simply trust that somehow—Yeshua would do it. It was a matter of faith.

One of the guards came and jerked Yohannan roughly to his feet, and led him to a stark and stinking chamber with a large stone in the center. The guard got busy chaining Yohannan's hands to the brace below the stone. One guard yanked the chains roughly throwing Yohannan down upon the stone. While the other one held Yohannan down by placing a knee in the middle of his back while he wrangled the chains to secure him in place. Yohannan fought to gain a breath. His face, only inches from the rough-hewn stone that was caked with old blood.

To him it felt like a profaned altar. He felt nauseous.

'What of Yeshua?' He wondered. 'What will happen to him?'

Yeshua preached the same hard truths that had put him in this very predicament. Will God's Son also be killed for his witness of the truth? Will all God's words and the sacrifice of their lives all come to nothing?'

Yohannan recalled his own proclaimation. 'Behold, the Lamb of God, who takes away the sins of the world.'

The missing piece immediately clicked into place. Yohannan's eyes widen with excitement at this his final revelation from God. 'The sacrifice of the Lamb! It is by his death that Yeshua will do it!'

Yohannan's face became joyful. The dungeon took on a warm and glowing light and a lovely path opened beside a crystaline river. He looked up to see a vision of his cousin standing on the path before him as if he was waiting on him. He was smiling as if to congratulate him on his latest insight, like he had done so many times before when they had talked about the Scriptures together.

The guard hooked the last brace into place, then picked up his large and freshly sharpened sword giving it a quick practice swing.

But Yohannan was not watching him, his eyes were on Yeshua.

He felt a deep sense of satisfaction, 'It will be worth it after all!' Then with one swift strike, his mission as the forerunner was over.

Yohannan's severed head was carried into Antipas' banquet hall. The guards had arranged it on a golden platter used to serve the delicacies.

The music stopped. The whole room looked on with horror, as Yohannan's head was brought forth to be presented first to Antipas as proof the deed was accomplished. Antipas covered his mouth and drew back in stupefied horror at the sight. Yohannan's eyes stared back at him, as if seeing into his blackened soul. They seemed to be still full of accusation.

But then he noticed a strange and joyful smile frozen on the holy man's face. Antipas wondered at it. What does it mean? A smile in the face of death? Even so, the Baptizer's harsh words still seared his mind to condemn and curse him.

Antipas motioned the sight away. "Show it to every person in this room." He ordered.

Yohannan's head was solemnly carried from person to person, causing a myriad of reactions. Some drew back in fear, some cried out, some become ill, some pointed and laughed, some hid their face and refused to look upon the sight, but no one in the room sorrowed over the prophet's death. Their reactions revealed the depth of each person's depravity.

When the Baptizer's head was presented to Salome, she began to tremble with the feeling of doom. Until this moment, such power had seemed like a game. She felt sick, but knew better than to show it. She had made the request. This was at her doing.

She took the platter into her own hands surprised that the head weighed so much, a tangle of the Baptizer's hair fell over the back of her hand. She cringed at the touch of it. She took the head still oozing with blood to her mother, who had just ascended the dais to sit next to Antipas before all their guests. Salome lay Yohannan's head at her mother's feet.

Herodias offered an ugly smile of triumph to the girl. She reached out her finely sandaled foot, to give the head an indelicate shove.

"So! Baptizer! Who is laughing now?" She threw back her head in a raucous laughter. But when she leaned forward to looked into the face of the Baptizer, her smile quickly dissolved.

Yohannan appeared to be laughing at her.

For the barest moment she felt fear.

Then, she turned toward Antipas with triumph smile. "So much for your prophet!"

~ 55 ~

PRESSING FORWARD

He had compassion on them,
because they were like sheep without a shepherd.
Mark 6:34

Yeshua was praying when a great sadness settled over him.
Yohannan.

His candle was extinguished.

The impression of darkness closed in. His enemy was advancing.
Yeshua could feel death turning its gaze toward him in its determined pursuit. Foreknowledge of such things came to him from
within him when he prayed. Righteous indignation rose up from
within him. He released a low roar of sorrow. Bad news concerning
Yohannan had always been inevitable. How the rulers of the world
hated his Father's servants!

He recalled Jezebel's curse upon Elijah. In his day, Elijah had
been delivered from Jezebel, taken up in a chariot of fire. Now,
Satan's threat had found its fulfillment centuries later. He waited
in Capernaum for the arrival of Yohannan's men. They would need
comfort in their grief.

Yohannan's men knocked at the door, looking around fearfully.
They were surprised when Yeshua, himself, answered the door to
search their down cast faces. He motioned them in.

"Yohannan is gone?"

Hot tears appeared as Yohannan's disciples nodded, unable to speak the news for a moment.

Finally, one spoke with the anger of grief.

"Yes, he was beheaded by Antipas, that witch Herodias, and her minion child. He explained what he knew. How has God allowed this to happen to one so great? Where was God, when Yohannan needed him?"

Their harsh and accusing words shook Yeshua to the core. He turned away from the messengers, motioning to his men to take care of them. He walked to the other side of the room, his back to them all. He worked to regain control over his own emotions.

"His body?" He finally asked, over his shoulder.

"We have buried it. But the witch still has his head."

Yeshua closed his eyes shuttering to think of the gruesomeness of such an act. He didn't move for some time. Then he wiped his eyes and turned back to face the messengers.

"You must be tired, stay with us and be refreshed."

Mari moved quickly to prepare food and drink for the men. As she went a dreadful premonition seized her. And she remembered Yeshua's warning words. 'My passage here will be short.' Was Yohannan's death was an indication of what lie ahead for Yeshua, perhaps for them all? Hadn't he warned her, warned them all?

Mari had once visited Yohannan along with the masses in the wilderness. She had gone to hear the words of a real prophet. Yohannan's truth had been hard, inelegant, direct and powerful, but his words had been the first awakening of her conscious desire for more than a false religion. His words had persuaded her to enter the waters of repentance. Now, those words had brought him death.

Yeshua had assured them all, "It is no small thing to become a servant of God. There will always be danger." He had told her that Yohannan's message had to come first before his work could began.

Yohannan was his forerunner in the shared mission for the salvation of souls. Their work and destinies were twined together.

She realized, 'If this has happened to Yohannan, then wouldn't Yeshua be next?' But like the others, she had conveniently ignored his words. Even now, Yeshua's ministry surpassed Yohannan's ministry. Conflicts and threats followed him wherever he went. How long before they capture him, too?

Mari hurried to finish her preparation of the bread and wine for the messengers. She picked up the tray to scurry back to their guests. But as she entered the room, her toe caught an uneven stone in the floor. Her tray pitched forward, causing the pitcher of watered wine and the plate of bread to fall away. The men all jumped at the explosive sound of the shattering of pottery. Chunks and shards sprayed across the floor sending a crimson tide to spread across the floor. Everyone froze, taking in her clumsy mess.

Magdalene was paralyzed with mortification.

"I am so sorry!" She exclaimed, tears blurring her eyes. She stared at the wine and shards, sure it was an omen of the blood shed yet to come.

Yeshua lay a calming hand on Mari's arm to reassure her. "It's alright, Mari."

She shook her head, and quickly knelt down to pick up the sharp debris, as if she were able to pick it up quickly enough, then disaster would be forestalled.

She glanced across the floor; from her vantage point she saw red wine had drenched the hem of Yeshua's tunic. It was actually dripping from his hem, spatters covered his feet making him look like a warrior returning from a battle.

Isaiah's words came to mind.

'Who is this?...his garments-stained crimson? Who is this, robed in splendor, striding forward in the greatness of his strength? It is I, proclaiming victory, mighty to save. I have trodden the winepress alone.'

She was shaken by the vision and the words. She looked up to Yeshua. His eyes were on her. Her look beseeched him and she slowly shook her head at the sign before her. Yeshua offered a brief nod while still holding her gaze, saying all she needed to know. His eyebrows were raised, silently saying "Didn't I tell you?"

Her face collapsed into sobs.

To the onlookers, it seemed Mari was having an overly emotion moment over her accident. They cast her a critical eye for her feminine hysteria.

Mari bent her head to pick up the shards. Her tears falling as hard as they did the night she had knelt before the Lord in Bethany.

Seeing Mari's distress, Yeshua did what none of the others volunteered to do; he bent down to help her.

"Here let me get this." He took the sharp shards from her hands, placing them into his own hand. While reaching for another piece nearby, his hand tightened its grip to keep pieces from falling out. A sharp piece cut into his palm. He flinched, but continued at his task. He set those pieces aside, then reached to remove more shards Mari had gathered in her hand. A drop of his blood fell onto her fingers.

Seeing it, she said, "Look, you have pierced your hand. It is all my fault."

He looked mercifully into her eyes, giving her a sad smile.

"Magdalene, don't worry, it will all heal. Everything will be fine in the end."

That night a pall settled over them all. Almost of his disciples had been both baptized and taught by Yohannan before they had become his followers. Yohannan's words had greatly influenced their faith and actions. Tears flowed freely for their old teacher and friend. Andrew and Yohan remembered stories of 'the Baptizers' antics and exploits. They shared an exchange of sad chuckles, and thick throats. Together, they remembered Yohannan's convictions, his courage, and fire. They lingered around the fire, fighting off the night chill.

Light danced red around the dark shadows of their features. Under watchful lids, they covertly observed their grieving Rabbi.

They realized Yohannan and Yeshua had been far closer than they had known, they could see that Yeshua was very shaken by the news. They also realized Yeshua had far surpassed Yohannan's call to righteousness, taking the message of holiness to a whole other level. Tonight, all of his previously spoken warnings revisited them to warrant their attention.

Just before dawn, Yeshua woke his disciples, saying, "Come, let's get away to ourselves. We need some time to recover from this terrible blow." Yeshua didn't tell them that he felt the need to run as far and as fast as he could go, or that even then he felt death breathing its cold and putrid breath down his neck. To them, he appeared stoic in his grief. In reality, Yeshua longed for a moment to steady his determination for all that now loomed ahead, fearful he could not see it through.

The boat was quickly loaded and they were underway before first light. Yet, despite the early hour an incoming fishing crew spotted their departure. Not knowing about their intent to get away, the well-meaning messengers sent the word swiftly toward the villages. "The Messiah was once more on the move."

The sun was climbing when Rock steered their boat into a small and remote inlet. They pulled the boat ashore to prepare breakfast. Little did they suspect a crowd was already forming like a rapidly building cloud over the sea. By the time they had cooked, finished their meal, and began their trek to the space Yeshua had in mind. They found themselves traveling into waves of unexpectant people.

Looking into the distance, they appeared like scattered sheep searching for their shepherd. As each group made their way forward, the people began to converge like they were draw by a magnet toward Yeshua. Yeshua looked up to find a river of people coming from the direction they had just traveled. Some were running, some were hobbling, some leaned on the shoulder of a friend, all of them were determined to make it to him. Their hope was as palpable as was their need for a savior. Yeshua was overcome with compassion. He recognized at once what he had to do, even though his own heart was weighted with grief. He set aside his personal need for solace and his own feelings of brokenness; he pushed away his feelings of grief and gloom; and he allowed the needs of the people to sweep over him. As compassion overtook him he was infused with a renewed energy and purpose.

Turning to his men, he said, "Look at all of these lost souls. There is no time for sadness now. Today, it is still daylight. And, while there is daylight, we still have a mission to fulfill. Death and grief will have to wait."

Issuing instructions, Yeshua tightened his belt and walked into the very center of the gathering crowd of people. He began to speak, to touch and heal.

Even though the darkness pressed all around him, his light blazed all the brighter. Yohannan's death would not defeat him, his Father had called these people to him. There was still time left. He had best use this time wisely. He climbed up onto the large flat rock halfway up the mountain side. There, he looked westward to see people for as far as his eyes could see. His will was restrengthened.

He would press on to forge the soul saving way of the Lamb of God.

-

The End of Book One

EPILOGUE

Thank you for embarking on the first half of this imaginative journey in this novel, Way Of The Lamb.

Don't stop here, the best is yet to come and Yeshua has his most difficult and challenging moments ahead in the second novel, Victory Of The Lamb.

I hope this journey has provoked your imagination, touched your heart, offered gifts of fresh spiritual insights, and most of all inflamed your desire to study the Scriptures.

If you have enjoyed this novel, please tell your friends. Give it as a gift, suggest it to your book clubs, small groups, and group discussions. You did not come to this book by accident.

Continue to follow your calling. Faithfully seek the knowledge of the one true God who dreamed you, created you, and called you by the power of his name and the Lamb. Even from before the foundation of the world, God has planned for you a kingdom of eternal love, light, and life.

Please feel free to connect with me though my website lamb58.com.

K.S. McFarland

AFTERWORD

Jesus did many other things as well.
If every one of them were written down,
I suppose that even the whole world
would not have room for the books that would be written.
John 21:25

ACKNOWLEDGEMENT

It is wonderful to have people who believe in you and cheer you on in difficult endeavors. A very special thanks to my staunchest supporter, my husband, Len. You have never wavered in helping me complete any project I have ever undertaken. Your constant love and support mean the world to me. I love you.

Thank you to the following:

Chelsea S.

Anna M.

Scott M.

Debbie H.

Dorothy M.

Diane P.

Mae M.

Donna R.

Rhonda C.

Kay S.

All my friends who have encouraged me. Thank you all for taking time from your busy days to help me with the creation of this book, and for being prayer warriors and encouragers.

Also, to all my grandchildren and family, you inspire me. And to my comfort canine and writing companion, Ellie, I am glad you love 'working' in the office.

K. S. McFarland
by Len McFarland

ABOUT THE AUTHOR

K. S. McFarland is a retired pastor with credentials of Master of Divinity, and Certifications in Spiritual Direction, New Church Plant, and Worship Design, also Bachelor of Business Admin, and Master Certificate in Project Mgmt. Experienced with twenty-nine years in ministry, as Bible teacher, pastor, preacher, storyteller, retreat leader, and church administration. Specialized in congregational care, Christian education, elder care, small group and lay leadership development, and worship planning. This novel was written with a personal passion for the life, grace, and redemption offered by our Lord Jesus Christ.

Printed in the USA
CPSIA information can be obtained
at www.ICGtesting.com
JSHW082312180923
48389JS00004B/14